PRAISE FOR BARRY FRIEDMAN

"I haven't been able to get five pages in without having to catch my breath. You're a brave writer, my brother."

— CHARLES P. PIERCE, *ESQUIRE*

"Barry Friedman has written a raw, gut-wrenching book about the game-playing side of a marriage gone wrong. But this ain't a fairy tale. This is a brilliant look at a walk on the dark side of life."

— JERRY IZENBERG, RED SMITH AWARD-WINING AUTHOR OF *ONCE THERE WERE GIANTS* AND *AFTER THE FIRE: LOVE AND HATE IN THE ASHES OF 1967*

"This masterpiece would blow away the competition, if there were competition for such a masterpiece, which there is not."

— SHANE GERICKE, BESTSELLING AUTHOR OF *THE FURY*

"Seeing the broken yet still beautiful world through his eyes is cathartic."

— JENNIFER TAUB, AUTHOR OF *BIG DIRTY MONEY*

Jacob Fishman's Marriages

Barry Friedman

Jacob Fishman's Marriages

Print and eBook editions published by Balkan Press

paperback ISBN: 978-1-954871-32-8

eBook ISBN: 978-1-954871-33-5

hardcover ISBN: 978-1-954871-31-1

Cover design by Brian Roe

JACOB FISHMAN'S MARRIAGES

Barry Friedman

BALKAN PRESS

ACKNOWLEDGMENTS

Special thanks to Dr. Kenneth Lucey, chairman, Department of Philosophy, University of Nevada, Reno; Dr. Jacob Howland, chairman, Department of Philosophy and Religion, University of Tulsa; and Dr. Michael J. Futch, assistant professor, Department of Philosophy and Religion, University of Tulsa. Their collective patience, insight, and wisdom were invaluable. Further, I'd like to thank the students in The Great Conversation 1: Ancient and Medieval; Modern Philosophy; and Studies in Plato and Aristotle at the University of Tulsa for slipping me syllabi, and pointing me (sometimes literally) in the right direction, and Sheena outside the Philosophy Department at University of Nevada, Reno, who shared her notes and her fear of Cain Hall. My gratitude goes out to Nita, Bill, Ronnie, and Dave. A big damn thanks to Grant Jenkins, Associate Professor of English at the University of Tulsa, as well, and Tom Walsh, former editor at *Rolling Stone*, for giving this book more of their time and effort than it deserved. The book you have in front of you is not nearly as good without them. Thanks to my publishers, Bill and Lara, for without whom, the book you have in front of you doesn't exist at all. And Melissa for getting me the "big ass" white board, which hangs over my right shoulder in my office, so *I* could keep the characters and narrative straight. As this is a work of fiction, the characters depicted within are mostly not reflective of anyone I met at either the University of Tulsa or the University of Nevada, Reno or lived with or married or even knew. Having said that, any similarity to persons living or dead is not entirely unintended.

"My advice to you is to get married. If you find a good wife, you'll be happy; if not, you'll become a philosopher."—Socrates, Athens (married twice)

"How's my marriage going? . . . You know, about as well as these things can go."—Don Learned, Houston (married five times)

To all the wives

FUCK YOU...THANK YOU

"I want a fucking baby."

Cindi Fishman was grouchy.

Coming out of the shower, one blue terrycloth towel piled up high on her head, a brown one wrapped around her breasts, she accidentally knocked Gabriel, the fat ceramic archangel, to the hallway floor. It had been sitting on the small shelf between the bathroom and the bedroom, where her husband, Jacob, was lying diagonally across the couple's Tempur-Pedic.

"My body is drying up. Do you hear me?" she asked, coming into their bedroom.

"Yes," Jacob Fishman said from the bed, looking up.

"It was a rhetorical question."

"You can't scream a rhetorical question at someone and not expect an answer."

"Fuck you. You promised me a baby."

"'Fuck you'? Very nice. I didn't promise you a baby. Never did I promise you a baby."

"You said you'd think about it," she said, disappearing into her walk-in closet.

"I did. I am," he called after her.

"And? And?" Cindi came out, topless, grabbing her tits. "I want a baby to suck on these, to get milk, to give life. I'm drying up."

Jacob stared at his wife, as she and her breasts approached. She yanked a brown burka from under his feet and body on which he was inadvertently lying. Holding it to her chest, she slammed the walk-in closet door behind her with the back of her hand. Jacob then heard her kick the door once it was closed. And then kick it again.

"Goddamn it!" she said.

Jacob shook his head.

"Honey?" he yelled toward the closet, muttering to himself, "My wife's a fucking lunatic."

"I heard that."

"You're going to break the door if you keep kicking it."

She kicked it again.

"Honey?"

Another kick.

"What?"

The kicking stopped.

"You okay?"

"I hate my life. I want to die or just join the fucking circus."

Jacob heard hangers falling and shoes being thrown against the wall and the closed door. He picked up the stack of magazines and newspapers from his lap: *The New Yorker*, AAPG'S *Explorer*, a geology magazine for which he did some freelance, and the *The Reno Gazette*, in which he wrote a twice-weekly column.

He found his latest column.

Dawn was (is) in public relations. She was (is) good at it, but she doesn't know what tense she is anymore after getting laid off six months back. Nowadays, she sits at her desk in her apartment, looking at her résumé, her career, her life, searching for the confidence to hit SEND. This particular job opening wants a mission statement; she wants to smash the computer screen. She has a degree from UNLV. She's been out of school for 10 years. She's still $28,000 in debt.

"A lot of fucking good it did me," she says. "I want my money back."

Her narrative keeps changing. The past, the further away she gets, is a

distortion; the present, the longer it goes on, is suffocating; the future . . .
what future?

"I'm a loser," she says, the more she thinks about it.

She tries not to think about it.

It was from his piece about a single mother who had just applied for, and was now receiving, $76 per month in Supplemental Nutrition Assistance Program (SNAP) benefits. He liked reading his own stuff, except when he hated it, which was most of the time. It was an odd time to be thinking about Dorothy Parker, what with his wife screaming and tearing up the walk-in closet, and Parker's line about "hating writing but love having written," but it made him smile. He had gone through this particular piece numerous times before sending it in to his editor, a guy named Jezy who wore wide, black-framed glasses and was half his age. Jacob was astonished every time one of his columns actually made it to print, for he usually loathed every word of the finished work, regardless of what he wrote, including grocery lists and birthday cards. Cindi shouldn't see him reading, certainly not his own stuff, certainly not pondering over them, certainly not now, so he dropped the *Gazette* on the floor when he heard noise coming from the closet. She was having a nervous breakdown, and he wondered if his writing was ponderous. She bristled at his calm, his ability to block her out, his worldly and smug completeness and certitude. Jacob knew how his peace, sanity, happiness affected her, so lately in their marriage he acted more troubled, more uneasy and uncertain, especially at times like these, when his wife was melting down. All this acting uncomfortably made him actually feel uncomfortable. He started rubbing his neck, pretending it was sore, hoping she might take pity on him. He moaned.

He moaned louder.

She exited the closet, looked at him.

"What's with your neck?"

"Nothing."

"Why you rubbing it?"

"It's sore."

"From what?"

"I don't know."

She went back into the closet.

"What are you doing in there?"

"Fuck you!" she said again.

The door crashed open again and this time, the hinges shrieked. Cindi's face, damp, contorted, focused in wildness. She flung off the towel from her head and on to her side of the bed. She glared at him, then picked up a brush, full of hair, for she never cleaned them, and began violently stroking her head. Only forty, Cindi Fishman, while having the breasts of a teenage girl, was ten years older when she was angry.

"God, I look like shit," she said into the mirror. "It's all this negative energy. I have to get my own thing going on."

"What are you talking about? You're a tenured professor. It's going on. What more do you want, need? What else has to go on?"

He knew better than to ask.

"A fucking baby is what I need, what I need to go on. What do you know? You're just a writer," and with the statement, Cindi turned to face her husband and in an exaggerated motion swept her hand up from her waist in front of her head, as if she were a five-year-old drawing on a wall. "You don't know what it's like to research and read and figure anything out. You just write," and then she repeated the motion.

"You couldn't even give me a small script-like motion with your fingers with tight strokes and concentration? You needed to go that big like I was a child with a crayon?"

"You know what I meant."

"Jesus!"

This woman, Jacob thought, his wife, my wife, as he watched her hands and fingers punch and fly through the air around her, couldn't even give him that.

"When did you take that off?"

"What?"

"What? You know."

"What?"

"Really? What? The wedding ring—that's what?"

His wife was no longer wearing her wedding ring.

"I took it off. I don't like being branded."

"Branded? Are you cattle? You think a wedding band brands you? Where is it?"

Gabriel, a cherub with no distinguishing genitalia, the same one she had nearly knocked over, had been holding it, and had been ever since she deposited her $1,695 engagement/wedding combo on its wing eighteen days earlier. Jacob went to look. Getting out of bed, he saw the angel, with its Wayne Newton-like pompadour and Buddha-like paunch, holding it. He picked up the ceramic figure. With the ring perched on its outstretched wing, Gabriel appeared to be giving him the finger.

"Do you hear me?" she asked again, ignoring his moment with the angel.

"About what?" He glared at the angel. "Fuck you, too, Gabriel."

"What?"

"Not you, Cin, I'm not talking to you."

"Then who you talking to?"

"It doesn't matter."

"Who are you talking to? Are you on the phone?"

"Holy fuck, I'm not on the phone."

"Don't change the subject. I want a baby, do you hear me?"

"I'm not changing—I'm begging you, Cin, can we not talk about babies?"

"I don't care anymore."

"Of course you care."

"I don't," she said, coming out of the closet again, sitting on the floor in front of the mirror and violently brushing her hair again. So much hair, so much anger.

"Doesn't that hurt?" he asked, pointing to her head.

She brushed harder.

"So why aren't you wearing the ring? Honestly."

She stopped brushing.

"I told you."

"I know. You don't want to feel branded, but c'mon."

"C'mon? What do you mean, 'c'mon'?"

"What do I mean, 'C'mon'? You know what I mean: C'mon. Why are you not wearing the ring?"

"What do you mean?"

"Are we going to do this all day? You know what I mean. You're not wearing the wedding ring, which is bad enough, but why are you leaving it out so I'll be reminded that you're not wearing it?"

"I'm not doing that! I went swimming today at the Y. Let me get some coffee." She disappeared into the kitchen.

"It's not just today," he called out to her. "You know that. It's been off for a month."

"It hasn't been a month."

"Three weeks."

"Two weeks."

"Fine. Two weeks. But it's been longer."

"I forgot to put it on. Don't make a big deal about it. Besides, I bought it," she answered.

"You just forgot? For four weeks you forgot?" Jacob said, not addressing, for the moment, the business about who paid for it.

"It hasn't been four weeks, Christ, but, yes, I forgot," she said, coming back into view, holding a cup she put down on the vanity in front of the bed.

"You forget things. You forget I want a baby. Besides, you know, as I told you when we first got married, I might not wear it, that I don't like the symbolism of my belonging to you—your chattel, so to speak."

"My chattel? You're not wearing the ring because you're tired of being my property? I make you feel like . . . branded property?"

"It's not that. It's just I don't want to wear it right now. And don't be mad at me!"

"How long will 'right now' last? Days, weeks, months? By the way . . . chattel? Who says chattel anymore?"

"It just came to me."

"Amazing."

Cindi picked up her coffee and the wet towel, left the bedroom, and put the mug on the shelf next to Gabriel, on her way to the bathroom with the towel, but this time she did knock Gabriel and the ring to the floor. She quickly retrieved both. Gabriel, though ceramic, didn't break.

"Enough," Jacob said, hearing the crash, getting up. "Give me the ring!"

"No," she said, backing away.

"Why don't you just smash it with the fucking mug?"

"It's mine." She held out her hand like a Heisman Trophy winner to block him. Convinced he would stay put, as if her outstretched hand held some magical powers, she stood tall.

"I command you to stop."

Jacob started laughing. "You command me to stop?"

Cindi rushed by him with the ring and Gabriel and went into the bathroom, closing the door behind her. "You're not taking my ring. You didn't pay for it," she said from inside.

"We don't have a lock on the door," Jacob said, walking through it. "You're not preventing me from following you. Would you come out of the bathroom now?"

"No," she said, coming out of the bathroom.

"If I stopped wearing mine, it'd bother you, right?" Jacob asked, lying down on the bed again. "And if I unceremoniously threw coffee cups at it, you'd be a little pissed, yes?"

"I didn't throw a coffee cup at it. It was an accident. And why are you wearing jeans in bed?" she asked, standing over him. "Don't you realize how unsanitary that is?"

"You're changing the subject," Jacob asked, sliding up and down on the sheets.

"You're such a child."

"The ring . . . let's get back to the ring," he said, as he continued sliding up and down on the bed, rubbing the denim over the sheets.

"What are you, nine? And, no, let's not get back to the ring. Let's get back to the baby."

"Why are we having this discussion? I had a vasectomy. You knew that. You know that."

"My body wants a baby."

"My body can't give you one, so what do you want me to do?"

"Forget it. I have to go anyway. You never want to talk about it."

"Talk about what? I had a—"

"Forget it."

"Before you go, though, please, tell me, what is your problem with the ring—"

"For Chrissakes, not again. I'm not wearing it because I'm losing weight and the ring keeps turning on my finger. I don't want to argue about this. I'm going out now to buy your fucking birthday present, and then I'm taking your sweet, fat ass to dinner, so do me a favor and leave me alone. Portofini, right?"

"O! Portofin-o! It has an 'o,' not an 'i.' Yeah."

"Okay, but I still hate that place."

"I know."

"Can't you eat anything without tomato sauce or cheese?"

"It's my birthday."

"Fine. I can't afford it, but fine."

"You don't have to buy, then."

"Oh, yes, I do, because you'll keep a record of it." She blew him a kiss, waved, and walked through the kitchen.

"Where, may I ask, are you going, anyway?" Jacob asked, following her.

"'May I ask?'"

"I was being polite."

Cindi looked at him, rolled her eyes. "I just told you. And aside from everything else I have to do, I am going to school, which starts in a few days. It's some shitty orientation. I don't really know."

"You're going to meet students in this mood? Is your goal to scare them?"

"Always."

Thank God she was smiling.

"Will you be home the rest of the day?" she asked.

"Where else would I be?"

"Why can't you get a job like a normal human being?"

"I have a job."

"I know. You're a—"

"Don't do it again," Jacob told her, as she started to swoop with the hand. "I write from home. What's your problem?"

"Bye."

Cindi kissed her husband and walked out the back door. The female virtual voice on the alarm informed him: *Back door open.*

They lived on 1336 Codel Way in Reno, Nevada. Built in 1926, the house had been owned by two gay men when the Fishmans bought it a week before their marriage. When she and Jacob first came to see it, the gay men's Chihuahua tried to bite her, so immediately after buying the place and moving in, she burned incense in the upstairs bedrooms and then had her best friend, Sage, who taught pottery in the arts department at UNR—but who was not wholly qualified—do an exorcism on the home and property. Sage placed angels around the house, too, ceramic ones—she called them *objet d'arts,* including Gabriel, to ward off the evil spirits who'd come down periodically from the attic to turn off lights, slam doors, and change the settings on Cindi's printer—at least, that's how she explained it. When Jacob's first wife, Elena, came to offer them a Jewish housewarming gift—Elena wasn't Jewish—of bread, salt, and wine, Cindi threw them in the trash the minute Elena drove off.

"Why did you do that?" Jacob asked.

"Bad luck to accept a gift from an ex-wife."

"Where do you get this from?"

"Do you want a gift from your ex-wife?"

"It's fucking bread."

"I'll go get it out of the trash, then."

"Right. Because that's what I want. Bread that has been sitting in trash."

The Fishman marriage was a series of skirmishes before a war they never actually waged. They mistook this fighting, both did, the bickering, their increasing incompatibility for passion, as passion, as glue that held them together. Cindi didn't hate her husband as much as she hated being his wife, and Jacob hated that she hated it.

From the bedroom window, Jacob watched his wife's Toyota Scion back out of the driveway. Even when simply trying not to hit the fence and/or the house, Cindi rushed through life, always exhaling, trying not so much to function in the moment but to wrestle it to the ground and strangle it. As she drove away, Jacob walked into her closet and found Gabriel and the ring in a box containing a pair of Frye boots.

She had paid for it.

The ring sitting on the fat angel's wing replaced the origami-dollar ring he made for her at a Reno Silver Sox-Yuma Scorpions Pacific Coast League baseball game.

"What's this?" she asked at the stadium.

"It's a promise ring. I promise to marry you," he said, as he slipped the immaculately folded bill onto her finger.

"You better promise to get me a better one," she said with a laugh, as she held up her hand to see how it looked.

The real engagement ring, the one Gabriel guarded so jealously, was found at a pawn shop on Virginia Street, in Reno, near the Nugget Casino. The pawnbroker told them it had belonged to an heir to the Polish throne who was in Reno for a seminar in the early 1980s, but the princess—her name was Catherine—had to sell it to acquire enough money to get back to Łódź and reclaim her crown. Cindi loved the story, as insane as it was—Princess Catherine of Łódź stranded in Northern Nevada—so she gladly paid $1,695, a full $795 more than she and Jacob had agreed to spend, for the platinum and white-diamond ring.

"It's just something I want," she said to him as they walked out of the store. "I know we said we weren't going to spend much on these things. I'm not asking you to buy it for me. With your five hundred, you got me about thirty-five percent of it. You supplemented that with which you have betrothed me."

Cindi Fishman actually spoke like this.

Jacob always knew it would be a delicate topic, how he made his wife, the story would go someday—as the story went this morning—buy her own wedding ring. She could do what she wanted with it, then, she would tell him some day, like today, including not wear it.

Chattel? Weight loss?

Still, Jacob removed the ring from Gabriel's left wing, tried to slide it down his pinkie. He flexed his finger, slowly at first, then faster, repetitively, trying to crush it in the fleshy folds, until it dislodged and propelled off his finger, ricocheting off the wall, hitting the floor, bouncing twice, and rolling along the hardwood hallway toward the heating and air-conditioning grate.

He ran toward it.

Place *is* haunted, he thought.

Knowing he couldn't reach it in time, he extended his leg, trying to corral it with one of his toes; instead, he wound up kicking it into the office door, opposite the bedroom. It pinged when it hit the floor, but this time it lay motionless, as if dead.

The imagery didn't escape him.

He picked it up, checked for damages, and not finding any, he wiped it on his shirt, then returned it to Gabriel. Standing there, Jacob couldn't remember which wing had been holding it—neither one looked correct. Gabriel was once again mocking him. Jacob thought of murder mysteries and how the ring on the wrong wing would be the clue that broke the case, but he knew Cindi wouldn't remember either, much less start another argument, even if she did, by revisiting the topic.

He put Gabriel and the ring back in the Frye box.

During Jacob's first marriage, twenty years earlier to Elena, he didn't wear a ring at all, though he had bought one—a cheap band with an onyx stone from a soon-to-be-bankrupt Service Merchandise. That it was out of business, and had filed Chapter Eleven during the marriage, was something Cindi said cast a marital pall over that marriage. Elena told him that had always hurt her, his not being proud enough of her to wear one, so he had decided that in this marriage to Cindi he would wear his.

And he had.

Jacob stood on the bed, staring at himself in the floor-to-ceiling mirror. Not bad for fifty; not good for fifty.

He went back into her closet, pulled out Gabriel again, and, on the eve of his fiftieth birthday, Jacob Fishman slipped off his one hundred ninety-five dollar Israeli Diamond Supply wedding ring and placed it on the angel's other wing. Perfect, he thought of the symmetry—right before thinking how petty and infantile he was being.

He removed his ring from Gabriel, leaving hers with the angel, and went back to the bedroom and buried it in his dark-sock drawer, next to a Best Buy receipt and a plastic shoehorn.

And, maybe, if Cindi hadn't said in bed later that night after dinner (a dinner she didn't eat) that she didn't want to have sex with Jacob because she was gaseous, hadn't complained about her rheumatoid arthritis, which she assumed she had but had never been diagnosed with, hadn't given him a twenty-five dollar iTunes gift card for his birthday, along with a pair of SAS beige walking shoes that didn't fit, and, oddly, some blueberries she said he should plant, he would have let the matter drop, let this wife have the same freedom with her wedding ring that his last wife had given him . . . might even have put his back on. But as Jacob Fishman lay there, staring at a ceiling that was of little help, exaggerating his hand movements, hoping Cindi would notice his ring was gone too, he decided his dark socks could have his ring for the time being.

If only I had a new wife.

But that wasn't it, not entirely. He didn't want a new wife without gas, with greater tastes in birthday gifts—he wanted this one, Cindi, but a better Cindi.

A better Cindi.

He rubbed the curve of her back as she lay next to him. He was possibly the only married man in America, he told himself, celebrating a birthday and not having sex; the only married man, period, with an iTunes card he wouldn't use and a gaseous, self-diagnosed arthritic wife next to him.

The only man of any age being tormented by a fat ceramic angel.

After not having sex on his birthday, or the morning after, and after Cindi left for the university, Jacob once again entered Cindi's walk-in, found and then took Gabriel, still holding his wife's ring, up to his office and placed both in a file cabinet, behind a green Pendaflex hanging folder that contained the Fishmans' previous years' late-filed tax returns. It was about then, as he walked down the stairs from his office to his bedroom, that Jacob Fishman decided to write a novel about a writer in a bad marriage. He already had the names of his lead characters: Jacob and Cindi Fishman.

Go Through the Gateway

After walking around the campus at the University of Nevada, Reno, something he tried to do most mornings, Jacob got back to the house and, finding Cindi in bed, still sleeping, went to his office. He opened the Scrivener program, planning to start his novel about Jacob and Cindi Fishman, but could only think of Ampara, the Peruvian girl in the country illegally, whom he had dated before Cindi. If not for Ampara, he and Cindi might have had a child, a possibility that ended when he got a vasectomy. It was that decision, more than his behavior in his present marriage, that fueled Cindi's rage.

Fuck You

Thank You

One of those would be the title for chapter one.

At Flavors!, the buffet inside the Silver Legacy, he had once asked Ampara, "How many of these servers are here legally?"

"None," she said.

"None?"

"*Chancho*, they are all illegal."

"How is that possible?"

"I am illegal."

"Yes, I know that."

"That's how it is possible."

Ampara was at the moment pregnant for the third time. She was either unlucky, fertile, or manipulative, for the first time she got pregnant, she said she forgot to take the pill; the second time, she said she didn't know she had to take them every day and couldn't just double up when she was ovulating. This third pregnancy, this one, as it would turn out, ended when she went back to Peculpa in Peru and got an abortion. And even then, Jacob didn't break up with her, but got a vasectomy instead, such was the state of his passive-aggressiveness. Had he any balls, he told himself, as he created a file called JACOB FISHMAN'S MARRIAGE, Cindi could have been awash in live, motile sperm.

"Your soul is cold," Ampara said to him when he finally did break up with her. "My love is flying away. I will find a man who wants babies."

Two months later she did and was pregnant almost immediately.

Jacob would write a book about Ampara, *Peruvian Express,* the name coming from the coyotes who brought her and her family to America from Peru. He made $22,500 off the book because Sony Pictures had optioned it for three years. His agent, Lara Izenberg, had been after him for years to write something else.

Now he was.

"Would you ever consider having kids again?" Cindi asked on her and Jacob's second date, after she sucked his cock in her Toyota Land Cruiser down the block from where she lived.

"Absolutely," he lied.

He lied when she asked him in Fiji, on their honeymoon, the same question.

They had just taken a motorboat from the hotel to a small island, where they ate grapes and cheese and sausage and drank sparkling water.

"You have quite an appetite after sex," he told his new wife, who sat down in his lap and fed him a grape.

"Keep that in mind, buddy boy. I do want a baby, though. We should go through the Gateway."

"The what?"

"The Gateway, like Isaiah."

"What are you talking about?"

"In the Bible. 'Go through the gates; prepare the way for the people. And then we lift up a signal.' That's the signal to the people, our people. We should have a baby. The signal happens twice a day—at eleven a.m. and eleven p.m."

"What people are we signaling? We have people?"

"Fuck you. I'm serious. Don't make me laugh."

"I won't. Don't laugh."

"Think about it."

"I will."

"Jacob!"

"Really, I will."

"Lisa will love her brother or sister."

Lisa was his daughter from his marriage with Elena.

"You don't know her that well. She's very competitive."

"Do you always do this?"

"This?"

"Yeah, this. This thing you're doing in the conversation."

"What do you mean?"

"Taking a word from a conversation and making it about that?"

"I don't know what you're talking about."

"But you do. You deflect, and you're really bad at it. It's also weird and a little troubling. Anyway, we don't have to decide now, but my body wants one. I can feel it wanting one."

Even in Fiji on their honeymoon, when the moon and ocean and fresh lobster and fucking were glorious, Jacob was bothered by the lack of enormity and inexplicableness between them. She was beautiful, his new wife, on a beach in Fiji, post-orgasmic, eating fruit, but there was something completely explicable about her and about the two of them. The marriage, the reason for the marriage, were both decisions at which they arrived—rationally. It all made sense. It was the perfect marriage, she an associate professor of philosophy, he a writer. If plotted on graph paper, even on that Fijian island with his naked wife cutting up sausage with a plastic knife, he knew it wouldn't, feared it couldn't, last. So if they had children, if he had the vasectomy reversed, who would get custody of their daughter, which he knew they'd have? Of course she'd get custody. She was the associate professor; he was a local columnist with seven grand in the bank from an option on a book that was never made into a movie. They would name their girl Chloe—that would be the compromise. He would want Sylvia; she would want Pleione. Chloe would have curly black hair and green eyes and a dimple so pronounced it would look like someone had driven a tenpenny nail through her cheek. He'd get visitation on weekends after the divorce, and when he'd drive her back on Sunday nights to Cindi's new duplex, he'd stop first for pizza, a food he would teach his little girl to love. Cindi would soon be living with a guy named Ray—Jacob only thought it was strange that he didn't think it was strange he already knew the name of his wife's lover on his and Cindi's honeymoon—whom Jacob would ultimately like. Chloe would like Ray, too, and call him Daddy Ray, which Jacob would pretend didn't bother him.

Ray would have long, thick hair. Jacob would continue losing his.

"You like my tits?" Cindi asked, standing over Jacob.

"What?" Jacob said, closing one eye to block out the sun. "Your tits? I do. Why are you thinking about your tits?"

"Why aren't you? You're not even looking at them."

"I love your tits."

"No, you don't. They're little-girl tits."

"European."

"Little European girl tits, then. You have a really strange look on your face. What are you thinking about?"

"Ray."

"Who?"

"Your future lover."

"What are you talking about?"

"We should name our daughter Sylvia."

"We're having a daughter?"

"Yeah."

"I don't like the name Sylvia."

"I knew you wouldn't."

"Maybe Pleione "

"Wow, that's weird."

"What is?"

"I just thought—never mind."

"I so hate that fucking Ampara for ruining my life. Why did you get a vasectomy?"

"Because I didn't know I'd meet and marry you."

"How long have you been carrying that line around with you?" she asked, lying down next to him.

"Not long. Look, I didn't know I'd want kids, marry someone who wanted kids."

"I don't want to talk about it."

"Why are we fighting about it now? We're on our honeymoon."

"Sorry."

"I know it's important to you. I'm sorry."

"You don't want kids." She sat up.

He rubbed her lower back. "I didn't say that. I just . . . I don't know. I don't want to talk about it now."

"Promise me we will."

"I promise."

/

Jacob Fishman's Marriage

I want a fucking baby

The angel, Gabriel, a chubby, emotionless cherub, sat on a shelf outside the bedroom, its hand outstretched, but Jacob thought it was giving him the finger. Cindi Fishman's wedding ring, a $1,695 band that her husband, Jacob, bought her from Rogers Jewelry on Virginia, was on one of Gabriel's wings and had been for the past six months.

Cindi was in her walk-in closet, just out of the shower, half-naked, a towel on her head, sounding as if she was kicking something.

"You okay, sweetie?"

"I want a fucking baby."

"Huh?"

"I want a fucking baby."

"I thought that's what you said."

"So?"

"So. What do you mean, 'So?' You want me to decide right now?"

"Yesterday. I wanted you to decide yesterday."

Jacob couldn't remember the exact conversation he had with Cindi, but he did recall her being in the walk-in after a shower with a towel on her head and her distinctly saying, "I want a fucking baby."

It looked like a conversation you'd find in a novel, he concluded, after reading it over a few times. He decided, yes, to call it *Jacob Fishman's Marriage.* He and Cindi would be joined, a Craniopagus foursome of sorts, and lumber through the narratives together—of course nobody would be writing about him and Cindi, the real ones, so he would be the only real Fishman spending time with the fictional Fishmans. Jacob would cherry-pick his life's moments (Cindi's desire for a baby, certainly), re-plotting his actual marriage, and build a better Jacob and Cindi Fishman—that was the hope, anyway. He sat back in his chair in his office, then leaned forward and took an open palm to his computer screen. It shook back and forth. This fictionalized version of the Fishmans would be the penumbra and palimpsest of the real Fishmans, the verisimilitude, the indignities and corrosion, where he would not only be its author but its subject.

He reread what he'd written. He deleted it all.

✎

"What are you doing?" Cindi, the real one, said, standing at the office door in one of his long black V-neck T-shirts, looking the way he always wanted a wife of his to look in one of his black V-neck T-shirts.

"Nothing," Jacob said, "trying to write something."

"What are you writing?"

"Thinking about a novel."

"Autobiographical?"

"No other kind."

"Am I in it?" his wife asked.

"In it? It's your story. It's your liberation."

"Don't make me out to be a cunt, okay?"

Jacob Fishman's Marriage: A Novel

1. The Birthday

"Hey, hold it, birthday boy, don't come in yet!" Cindi Fishman called, running through the kitchen in her husband's gray boxer briefs and black T-shirt, toward the back door, holding a shoe box, just as Jacob, her husband, pushed it open from the outside, grazing her face with the side of it.

"Jesus, Jacob!" she cried, dropping the box. A shoe fell out. "Fuck!"

"Oh, sorry," he said. "I didn't see you."

"Ow! You broke my nose. I got you a fucking birthday present," she said, rubbing her nose and kicking the shoe by her foot toward him.

It was Jacob's fiftieth birthday.

"Here, let me see your nose."

"No, it's fine. Christ!"

"Did I even hit you? I could have sworn I missed."

"I'm making it up."

"No, I didn't say that. I'm just saying that I don't think your nose is broken. I mean . . . sorry. You got me something for my birth—"

"Fuck!" she cried, still holding her nose.

"—day. Oh, come on, stop acting like I punched you. It's not that bad."

"Fuck you. Here," she said, handing him an SAS Time-Out® shoe box, now with just one shoe in it, and moving back into the kitchen. "I didn't get a chance to wrap it." She came back toward him, bent down, and picked up the loose shoe, thrusting it into his chest. "Here's the other one. My septum is deviated."

"For the love of Christ, would you stop it? Shoes," he said, having removed the one from the box, moving them up and down, as if they were walking on air. "Thanks." He put his headphones, hat, and sunglasses on top of the refrigerator. He had just come back from a walk around the University of Nevada campus. "I mean, don't worry about not wrapping them."

"You don't have to be shitty."

"How am I being shitty? I'm serious. Don't worry about not wrapping them. I remember these shoes."

"You hate them."

"I don't hate them. SAS, I like the brand. I'd put them on, but, well . . . I'll wear them next time. I love them, really."

"You don't. I knew it."

He took his hat back from the refrigerator and inexplicably put it back on.

"What are you doing?" Cindi asked. "You going out again?"

"No, I'm just putting my hat back on," he said, walking through the kitchen.

"Why are you— okay, wow. Jesus! Anyway, these are the grandpa shoes? Remember?"

"The grandpa . . . ?"

"We called them grandpa shoes.'"

She followed him.

"Beige?" he asked, putting them on the counter in front of the pizza oven. "What made you decide on beige?"

"The company calls them bone," she said.

"Yeah, well, they're beige, don't you think?" he asked, picking up the shoe off the counter. "They look beige." He smiled at his wife and put it back down.

"You hate them and are not going to wear them—"

"I am going to wear them. Bone is good."

"You said they were the most comfortable shoes you've ever worn, and I know it's not romantic and . . . Goddamn it, I knew it. I'm such a loser. What did you want, Italian dress shoes?"

"Italian . . . what? Huh? I like them. I like these. Why would I want Italian dress shoes?"

"Because you have a pair."

"But . . . why? Anyway, I like them. These. I like them."

"That's the only color they fucking had, and I don't even know why I bother. So, you're not ever going to wear them, I can tell. Fuck me, fuck me, fuck me! I don't know what to buy. My family, we don't—"

"Honey, stop, I like them. They're just the wrong size."

"What do you mean?"

"Look." He picked up the shoe again and made her look inside. "I don't wear a nine."

"A fucking nine? Why did they give me a nine? Christ! Okay, I'll bring them back. And I don't know how I'm going to do that because I lost the receipt. This is why I hate birthdays. What if I just give you the money and you can buy what you want and we'll just, I don't know, do something with the shoes? Throw them out!"

"Cin, I don't want the money. I like the shoes. We'll take them back. They'll exchange them without a receipt, and I'll get a bigger size. Don't worry. Thanks, really."

Jacob went to kiss his wife, but she held her hand to her mouth.

"Don't kiss me."

He kissed the back of her hand, tasting her knuckles, as she gently rapped his face.

"You are so tough to buy for."

"Why would you say that? A pair of shoes, size thirteen. That doesn't seem that difficult. Thank you for these. I would like to kiss you now, so move your fucking hand," and with that, he grabbed her face and kissed her on the lips. He tried sliding his tongue into her mouth. Cindi pulled away.

"No, no, my breath."

"Your breath is fine."

"No, it's not. It's very interesting."

"Your breath is interesting?"

"It's putrid, okay?"

Beige walking shoes? She got me beige walking shoes for my fiftieth birthday? Jacob repeated to himself, hours later, as he left their house on Codel Way on this, the eighteenth day of August, and headed toward Manzanita Lake at the University of Nevada, Reno, for his second walk of the day, something he almost never did. He had been walking every morning for the past few years, ever since suffering what he thought was a heart attack at a Sacramento Denny's, which landed him at Mercy General Hospital, which turned into a $1,879 tab for the emergency-room visit, which indicated mild hypertension (but no heart attack) and severe indigestion, which annoyed and scared him enough to start an exercise regimen (this exercise regimen). Even though the walks did little for his weight or his blood pressure, he found them, usually taken before noon, to be relaxing enough, even when he was followed by the ducks that would leave the lake and inexplicably join him, often shitting along-side him.

Crossing South Virginia Street, he thought about the seven thousand dollars he had left from the sale of *Peruvian Express,* a novelized version of the book he wrote about his ex-girlfriend Ampara and her family's struggles with coyotes to get into this country. With that money and Cindi's salary from the University of Nevada, where she was an assistant philosophy professor on a tenure track, the Fishmans managed. Jacob got along on freelance work, mostly writing for a geology magazine, *Explorer,* put out by the American Association of Petroleum Geologists, even though he knew very little about the oil-and-gas sector and repeated the same joke to anyone who inquired about such work: that he could hurt himself pumping his own gas. Mostly, he filled his days with trips to the casinos in Reno, playing nickel keno, or walking. When the weather was bad, which it often was in Reno, Jacob would go to the Silver Legacy and walk through the corridors between it and the adjoining Circus Circus and Eldorado casinos, dodging senior citizens in motorized carts and conventioneers with name tags. He always loved walking, even as a child back in New York, when he used to walk the Flatbush section of Brooklyn with his grandfather, along the Brooklyn-Queens Expressway, back when the Verrazano-Narrows Bridge was being built. He and Grandpa Nat would then walk over to the department store Korvettes and buy snacks and little glass bottles of Coca-Cola and sit on the bench and look out toward Staten Island.

"Jacob," his grandfather would tell him, "Staten Island is a dump. I don't even know why it's part of New York City."

"You know, Cindi," Jacob told Cindi on a walk through the campus, "Reno is now behind Henderson as Nevada's largest city. Las Vegas, of course, is first."

"You do know I work at the university, right, that I'm an assistant professor of philosophy, so I do know some of this?" Cindi told him.

"What would a philosopher know about the population density of Nevada's major cities?"

"I read other shit, you know. You don't have much of a life, do you?"

"You have to ask?"

For months after the "heart attack," as Jacob kept referring to it, Cindi in fact did join him on these daily walks, even though she hated the university's predilection of naming buildings after senators and silver barons, a complaint she never failed to mention as she passed those buildings.

"White men blowing other white men," she said outside Paul Laxalt Mineral Engineering Building, striking a defiant pose with one hand raised high, beating her chest. The university had for the past year been in the midst of a beautification campaign, which entailed the uprooting of many old trees to make way for new ones, which looked remarkably similar to the ones they were replacing.

"*Alto, alto,*" she had yelled to the Spanish illegal workers cutting down a large sycamore in front of the library the last time they walked, three weeks earlier. "*Alto el árbol!*"

"Why do you always scream at them? They can't understand you. Besides, I think you just said, 'Tall the tree.'"

"They know, they know. And by the way, fuck the government, too. I don't want to pay my taxes."

"May I remind you where you are. You work here. Quiet down."

"I don't care what they think."

"I don't, either, but since your tenure is coming up and the tenure police—"

"Committee. Not police."

"I know, I was joking. You might want to stop acting like you're about to call in a bomb threat. With your luck, the grand high exalted Grand Poobah of Tenure will be out for a morning stroll when he starts hearing about your desire to overthrow the government and burn down the Laxalt Building. And what do you mean, you don't want to pay your taxes?"

"I never had to pay taxes before."

Their pace picked up.

"You do now. And I need the tax stuff the university sent you and your W-2. And wait a minute. You're blaming me that you have to pay taxes?"

"I'm just saying that I never had to before and I think we should just not pay them."

"Yeah, okay. Let's get that cabin in Ketchup—"

"You know it's Ketchum. Stop!"

"Fine. Wherever. Let's go to some secluded part of Idaho, too, while we're at it and wait for the Rapture and the return of Jesus and/or Hemingway. Meanwhile, I have to file by, like, tomorrow, so you want to help me or what?"

"Slow down," she said, out of breath, putting her hand on his arm. "Your heart, don't forget. Just tell me what I owe."

"I'm not your accountant. Half. You owe me half. You always owe half. Of everything. Probably about $2,300."

"Why is it half?"

"Why shouldn't it be half?"

"You make more than I do."

"I don't make anything, remember?"

"Just put it on my tab."

"I'm not your bartender."

She didn't walk with him the next day. And he didn't ask her to.

The ducks were waiting for him.

It was his birthday. As exhausting as she could be on these trips, he found himself missing his wife's rants about government interference, the gamma rays coming from computers and cellphones and satellite dishes that control thought processes and cause glioblastoma. There was also her latest conspiracy theories involving the Saudis and those "pulling the strings," who were not, inexplicably, the Saudis but someone who controlled the Saudis. As Jacob completed his second lap around the lake, he became increasingly bothered by the unimaginative scope of Cindi's present.

An unwrapped box of beige walking shoes?

He headed toward the quad, walking by the Mackay School of Mines Building, the Science Hall, yes, the Laxalt Mineral Engineering Center, Morrell Hall Alumni Center, and Silas E. Ross Hall, all the buildings and all the names Cindi hated. He headed north to the Lawlor Events Center and then Mackay Stadium, before walking back to the Frandsen Humanities Building, Thompson Hall, the Nobel Getchell Library, and Jot Travis Student Center, where he finished.

"Hey, Annie," he said to the Asian girl, as he paid for his twenty-ounce Diet Dr Pepper, package of Dentyne Ice gum, and bag of pretzels.

"You eat bad, Jacob. And you old now. Your colon."

"Sweet of you to worry about my colon, but not today, it's my birthday."

He handed her a five. She gave him back change, held his wrist.

"What?" he asked, as she rubbed her hand over his. She flipped his hand over to trace her forefinger through his palm.

She studied it.

"What?" he asked again, thinking she would tell him he was going to live a long, productive life.

She smiled, kept rubbing.

"You no work hard."

Jacob laughed. "What do you mean?"

"Look at hand. Smooth, no callouses. You no work hard."

Still smiling, outside the student center, he turned on his iPhone and sat at a cement table across from a girl with auburn hair and a yellow highlighter who was reading *Critical Perspectives in Sociology.*

Beautiful.

He tried not to stare.

He stared.

She mouthed, "Hi."

He turned off his iPhone.

She smiled. "Hi again." She spoke.

"Hi."

"What are you listening to?"

"Van Morrison."

"Who?"

"Never mind. Before your time."

"A lot is."

"What are you reading?"

She lifted up the book.

"For the summer?" he asked.

"I took it this spring, but I didn't go to class and, apparently, the professor took it the wrong way and failed me. Have to retake it."

"My, uh—never mind. Why didn't you go to class?"

"I may have slept with him."

"What could go wrong there, huh?"

"Then I stopped. That he really took the wrong way."

"Unreasonable bastard."

"Exactly."

Jacob wanted desperately for the conversation to continue.

"I don't mean to bother you," he said, "but I have to tell you, your teeth are astonishingly white. I was going to offer you some gum, some Dentyne, which is good for whiter teeth, but it would be redundant."

"You often comment on a girl's teeth?" she asked, looking up, flashing a wide smile.

"Unless she's missing some teeth, then I don't mention it. I usually go to a part of her body that's, you know, intact."

"Your teeth aren't bad, either."

"Mine? Nobody's ever mentioned my teeth before. Eyes, calves, sure, but never my teeth."

"Calves?"

"Yeah. What do you think?" he asked, sticking out his leg.

She gave him a thumbs-up.

"Good thighs. Firm, yet not intimidating."

Christ, she's perfect. And she's flirting back.

His and Cindi's anniversary, if they made it, was in September, and while he watched this girl highlight what looked to be an entire page (was nothing unimportant?), he couldn't remember if Cindi had ever been this perfect. He couldn't remember, and why he was thinking this he didn't know, if he and Cindi had ever had a month, thirty consecutive days, in their five years together with no anger or histrionics or threats or thrown cookware?

That wasn't right. They had been married six years.

How could I forget a year of my marriage?

He looked at the girl again—he figured she was in her early twenties —but she was working and he didn't want to disturb her. He took a breath and, when exhaling, felt his chest tingle. He took another. Another tingle, almost a chill. It started to rumble. Indigestion. He couldn't belch. He couldn't catch his breath.

The hell is this?

Jacob put his head on the cement tabletop. He felt cramps, gas, something. His mouth was dry. The pain he felt at Denny's felt like indigestion. This felt like a four-foot marble slab was sitting on his chest.

I'm going to have a heart attack on my fiftieth birthday? How is this allowed to happen?

He opened the Diet Dr Pepper, took a swig, and immediately belched, quietly, hoping the girl with the perfect teeth and overactive yellow highlighter wouldn't notice. He felt his heart thump, groan, and then a pain shot down his right arm.

Here it comes. Fuck! This is what a heart attack feels like.

He put his hand to his chest to see if his heart was beating. It was then he felt his forehead to see if he was sweating. He was.

"You okay?" the girl asked, looking up with the yellow highlighter now in her mouth like a cigar.

She noticed me. She cares. Wonderful! I'll be dead soon.

"Think I'm having a heart attack."

"Really?" she said, getting up.

"No, no, no, I'm okay. I'll be fine, thanks. Sit, sit, sit."

"You sure?"

"Yeah." He wasn't.

She sat.

She sat. *Fuck! Why wasn't she more concerned?*

"My dad had one. He died."

Jacob thought this was a strange way to calm him down.

"Mine, too," he said, which wasn't true. His father was very much alive.

"Look, I have to go, but I can call someone, if you want." She took a step toward him.

"Oh, it's okay. Really, thanks. Sorry you have to go." His chest, he was certain, was about to cave in on itself, but he thought, considering he would probably be dead within a few minutes, he was handling the moment well and she would be impressed by that.

She got up, waved a little, and bounded away. Jacob watched her and thought about that moment Lillian Hellman wrote about in *Pentimento* when she describes the time in a woman's life where she would never be more beautiful.

To be thinking of Lillian Hellman moments before death. Who does that?

He wondered if he was foaming at the mouth.

The pain subsided. Jacob took a breath. He looked at the girl, now farther away, her perfect ass and gait, and wondered if this girl knew this was her moment in life. How her body, teeth, the quality of sex, the taste of peaches would never be better, never sweeter. Of course she doesn't know.

He then remembered it was the left arm that was the danger arm, not the right.

The pain left as quickly as it came. Nothing.

He sat, drinking diet soda and eating gum and pretzels, exhaling deeply, as if his respiratory and circulatory systems were new toys he was playing with. He wondered what it would be like to sleep with this girl in her dorm and then take her to lunch and then be shown off to her sociology friends a few months before she would break up with him because he had failed to maintain an erection on successive occasions or because she just got tired of dating someone older than her father, who died of a heart attack.

He belched again.

He checked his pulse, thought about death, more specifically dying and how Tennessee Williams, alone, choked on a medicine cap in a hotel room and how suffocation was the one way Williams feared death would come.

First Hellman and now Williams. He would have preferred, if he was going to die and going to have two twentieth-century writers on his mind at the end of life, Philip Roth and Joan Didion—or maybe Faulkner without all that Southern incestuousness. What if he had an actual heart attack, near the ducks, which would surely come and corral the pretzels and gum around his dying body, before anyone would notice—what then?

He had no identification on him.

Cindi said something in the kitchen about going out after she gave him the beige shoes, but he hadn't listened. Did she say she was going out? To her parents', errands, school? Maybe she'd walk by him on her way to her office on campus in a few days and see him dead, if nobody came across him earlier, or incapacitated or lying in duck shit as the ducks ate his snacks.

How best to be seen dead. How best to be found?

He started home and thought about the vacation they were not on.

"I am not staying in a cabin," he told Cindi a week before his birthday, when she handed him some brochures of cabins in Idaho.

"Why?"

"Because they're cabins in Idaho. I'm a Jew."

"Stop being a baby and stop doing Woody Allen. My treat. It'll be part of your birthday present."

"A birthday present is supposed to be something the person celebrating the birthday wants."

"I'll just go myself, then. I have some work I have to do anyway."

"You're going to take yourself away on my birthday?"

Tenure. Cindi, in her sixth year at UNR, was up for it, and while there was no reason to think she wouldn't get it, Jacob knew she wouldn't. Her yearly evaluations were solid, if not spectacular, and, in parlance only understandable in the world of universities, she was considered to be on trajectory, but something was not right. UNR required six scholarly articles and/or a book to be published, and while her book was years away, she did have the six articles published, even if two had appeared in less-than-stellar publications.

"Are you worried?" he asked a few weeks earlier.

"You think I should be?"

"No," he lied. "It's in the bag."

"In the bag? That's a dollar."

They charged each other for using clichés.

"Why would you go to Idaho by yourself? The tenure stuff is out of your hands, right? It's in committee and . . . departments and stuff?"

"And departments and stuff? Glad you're so concerned about my life."

"I am. The philosophy department."

"Yeah. Wow. Okay, it's not important. You don't get it—or don't want to get it. The process starts in, actually, it already started, and everybody knows things you don't, your status, so you walk down the hallways and Howland, let's say—"

"The chairman?"

"Yeah, let's say he smiles, but not as big as he used to. What does that mean? And then you get shitty sections, survey courses, which I'll probably get in the fall. What does that mean? It's just one awful year, and I'm probably going to be even crankier and bitchier than ever, if that's possible, so let me apologize now for everything I'm going to do. For now, though, I just want to go away. By myself."

"To Idaho?"

"Stop it. We're not going to Idaho. It was an idea."

Unwrapped beige walking shoes in the wrong size.

I should have taken the Idaho trip, he thought, still sitting outside the student center, now certain he wasn't going to die. But now there was something else bothering him. It was an argument three nights earlier about babies and vasectomies and how she wanted the first and how he had the second.

Chewing on three pieces of gum now and washing it down with his diet soda, he couldn't remember exactly why Cindi called his daughter, Lisa, a skanky little whore weeks earlier, or why she threw a cast-iron skillet, depending on whether you believed Cindi or Jake, at the wall or his head.

"I didn't say she was a 'skanky little whore.' I said if she kept dressing in torn hose and short skirts and acting like one, people would think she was a skanky little whore, but I did not call her that!" Cindi said, following him into the kitchen that night.

"'Your daughter is a skanky little whore.' I remember those words."

"I did not say that!" Cindi said, stomping her foot.

"I know you want children. And I know my having a daughter is difficult—"

"It's not difficult. That's got nothing to do with it. I love Lisa."

"Then why did you call her a skanky—"

"I did not call her—" and then Cindi picked up the skillet that was on the stove and hurled it in his direction. He ducked. It hit the wall and broke at the handle.

"Why don't you leave?" he asked as calmly as he could, as anyone could, he thought, after having a skillet hurled at one's head.

She did, rushing by him, slamming the back door with such force that it knocked magnets off the refrigerator, sending a yoga schedule, a drawing from Cindi's niece, Elise, and two tickets to a road show of *Spamalot* onto the floor.

Jacob stood with his back to the kitchen sink, arms behind him, trying to push the countertop through the floor. He didn't know if she was coming back, didn't know if he wanted her to, but did know he wasn't picking up the broken skillet from the floor.

The back door opened.

"What?" he asked.

"I wasn't trying to hit you."

And then she slammed the door again.

Later that night, after Jacob watched *The Late Show with David*

Letterman and two episodes of *The West Wing* from Season 2 on DVD, Cindi returned with a half-gallon of Häagen-Dazs® Strawberry, an ice cream he didn't like, to make up. This was how Cindi apologized when the arguments were her fault, as most lately, even she would agree, were. She'd bring home a snack or agree to eat at Nu Yawk Pizza, another restaurant, like Mario's Portofino, she hated but he loved.

The day after the Skillet Incident, as they agreed it would be known, Jacob went out and bought her another one, which Cindi dropped on the kitchen floor to see if it could take her wrath. After it landed, she jumped up and down on it and rocked back and forth, one leg on the pan, one on the handle.

"What are you doing?" Jacob asked, laughing.

"You just can't get a good skillet anymore," she said. "They should be able to take a little PMS rage."

"Is that what that was? Most people don't have problems with skillets. Sure, the coating comes off and people die from eating asbestos or mercury shavings that wind up in their omelets, but handles falling off from being hurled at walls, not really a problem for most. By the way, you should have seen the expression on the guy's face at Bed Bath & Beyond when I told him that the other one had broken."

"What did he say?"

"He said, 'But they're cast-iron.' And then he asked me to keep you away from the store."

She laughed, which was good.

"I told my father I broke the old one by throwing it against the wall," she said.

"What'd he say?"

"He was impressed and scared."

"Smart man."

This was fine, Jacob thought, this exchange.

Not fine, necessarily, but better, for Cindi's tirades were becoming vile, irrational, and tougher for him to forgive, but then, as the Fishmans sometimes did, they called a truce and they sat together in bed, eating Häagen-Dazs® Strawberry Ice Cream. His wife had called his daughter a skanky little whore and had thrown a skillet at him, but he found himself joking with her and scraping the spoon up her chin as ice cream dripped out of her mouth.

"A skillet, honey, really," he continued. "Most women, plates, an occasional lamp, but breaking off the handle on a cast-iron skillet?"

"I have a bit of a temper. I did mention that when we got married, didn't I?"

"No."

"I didn't?"

"No."

"Sorry," she said in a singsong little-girl voice he found both endearing and infuriating.

"It's a good thing, honey," she continued, "that we can talk about this."

"Maybe."

"Don't you think so?"

"I don't know." He could feel her getting angry again.

"You don't, do you?" she asked again.

"No, I do, I just . . ."

"What?"

"Communication, like loyalty, is overrated."

"What?"

"Eichmann and Himmler were all loyal," he said. "As for communication, it's good we're talking about flying skillets. Better, I think, if they're not flying at all."

Jacob waited.

Cindi laughed. "You're referencing Nazis? Quite the relationship-builder."

Jacob headed home. He saw Argenta Hall, a dorm on the north side of Artemesia Way, something he saw every day on these walks, but he stopped in front of it and scanned as many windows as he could, as if the girl with the perfect teeth and yellow highlighter would be standing in her room, looking out, ruminating about the man she met with the good calves who had suffered a heart attack. He thought about the last time he and Cindi had made love, two months earlier, in the guest bedroom with Cindi on top of him.

Sex would be nice. An affair would be nice. Sex on my birthday would be nice. Sex with the yellow-highlighter girl was what he wanted.

His mood darkened, looking at the building. There was the sex the Fishmans weren't having, sure, but there was also the $1,695 wedding ring he had bought Cindi from a pawn shop and that she had stopped wearing and had placed on a ceramic angel with an extended belly in the hallway. The angel appeared to be flipping him off, so he took it and hid it, along with his own ring, in a sock drawer. There was now the matter of the skillet and the "skanky little whore" comment, which he could no longer bring up now that they had joked about it, ostensibly putting that breach behind them. There was the business about the blueberry bushes he had inadvertently mowed down a few weeks back and the three packages of seeds he bought to replace them, which, upon seeing them, Cindi said, "Thanks, but I'm not planting anything anymore, ever. Things die."

And there was the Idaho trip, which was bound to come up again.

Now the beige shoes.

By the time Jacob got to the bottom of Codel, he was furious and promised himself the next time she threw a tantrum, he would throw her out of the house for good. He'd tell her to come get her stuff the next day. He'd change the locks, move the furniture around. He'd file for the divorce. He'd find the girl with the perfect teeth and yellow highlighter and thank her for saving his life and ask her out. And he wouldn't accept Cindi's calls or ice cream when she begged to be forgiven.

He'd show her.

He opened the front door.

Cindi, who had spent most of the afternoon on the chaise, covered in an afghan, had forgotten she had an appointment with Howland, her chairman, so she'd gone to the university after his office called. She left a note on the kitchen counter: "B back" with a heart and the letter C. Jacob went into the living room, sat on the sofa, and noticed the afghan on the floor. He picked it up and put it back on the chaise. He noticed something under the chaise cushion. It was her diary. She must have been writing. He knew she kept one, knew she kept a stack of them under the bed, but he'd never looked at them. It was her privacy, her business. But it was right here. He pulled it out, remembering its exact placement under the cushion for when he had to return it.

3 May 2011

I can't fucking win. I thought I was doing the right thing by getting J these SAS shoes for his birthday. It's the most unromantic present ever. J bought me a tennis racket one time, but this is worse than that. I knew it when I bought them and I didn't care. I'm getting worse about the baby. He's not going to give me one, but I can't let it go. Men and their fucking sperm control everything and yet—YET—women are still expected to be nice, to buy presents. I don't know what he wants from me. I don't know what I want from him. I have to get my own thing going on. Finally, he's gone . . . to the university to walk. Maybe he's having an affair, I don't know, but he sure walks a lot. I don't care if he is. I mean, of course, I care.

We had a really tough couple of days, which, as usual, was my fault, but I am getting tired of apologizing for myself all the time. I should have done more for his birthday, but I didn't have time. I also didn't want to.

I wish I were dead.

It's Jacob's birthday and I'm ruining it for him, and I don't care about that, either. My tenure review has started and, yes, you guessed it, I don't care about that, either. They can take their tenure and shove it up their collective university ass. Anyway, Jacob and I had this enormous fight where I threw a skillet against the wall and broke it. Jacob thinks I threw it at him, which I didn't, and thinks I called Lisa a 'skanky something or other,' which I didn't.

Or maybe I did.

Still, I have been an absolute bitch lately, a monster, and someone should just shoot me.

I don't want to be married; I love my husband, but I DON'T WANT TO BE MARRIED. He hid my ring, which I'm sure he doesn't think I'd notice, but I don't know how to ask because I don't want to wear it and then he's going to make a big deal about "Well, why did you want it back, if you're not going to wear it?"

IT'S MY FUCKING RING, THOUGH. I PAID FOR IT, EVEN THOUGH HE NOW TAKES CREDIT FOR IT.

I hate this FUCKING marriage, this FUCKING house. I'm a prisoner here. I love my husband . . . I LOVE MY HUSBAND, a lot more earlier in the marriage than I do now but I still love him, but I can't stand this thing we're doing. His daughter, who's been acting like a slut, and his ex-wife are all part of my life. I wanted to break up with him after our first date, I wrote that five years ago—exactly that. Why didn't I? I checked. I really did. "I do not want to go out with him anymore." And then this, '. . . met a guy, nice, but I'm not going out with him. He had his life'—my exact words. I should have. I should go live in a cave. I need a vacation, too, and maybe that will help, but it's not that.

I WANT A BABY!!!!!!

And I'm not going to have one with Jacob because he had to have the vasectomy. I could shoot that Louisa or Blanca whatever her name is—oh, yeah, Ampara (what kind of stupid name is that?). She doesn't take her pill, she gets pregnant, and so Jacob decides to get a vasectomy after she miscarries so it won't happen again. HOW ABOUT BREAKING UP WITH THE CUNT INSTEAD? But I'm angry at myself for marrying him when I knew he had a vasectomy and a family. I really didn't think it was going to bother me this much, but I'm forty now, and I've got to do something. I WANT A BABY! I tried to talk to him about a reversal, but he talks about the money and the insurance and being fifty, but I don't think he believes I'd be a good mother—and maybe I wouldn't be. But fuck him, he's not such a great father. Oh, he thinks he is, but it's all pomp and circumstance when he does something— 'look at me be a good dad.'

I have to stop. I have to get in a better mood because it's his birthday— his fucking birthday, something he keeps reminding me of. It's all I've been hearing about for a month. I bought him the shoes—like I need to spend $139 so he can walk. What does he do? Opens the box, picks them up, studies them like they're the key to the Grail and puts them back in? Why do I bother?

He is everywhere. He's suffocating me, sucking the oxygen out of the room. I can't go anywhere without him being around. His presence is huge, *like a storm that's always approaching. Even though it's not raining, you know it will and it's all you think about. Well, when he's in a room, he's the only thing that matters—like a cat on stage, like an owl sitting above everyone and everything watching, commenting. It's all anyone looks at. I can't work. His presence is everywhere. And everybody loves him.*

STOP, Cynthia. (Thought I'd call myself what my mom calls me.) ☺

Saw Sage the other day, she looked great. I think she's divorcing Dave, had an affair on him. She's got six kids! How can she not be happy? I don't know anything anymore. I don't.

And now I have to go to some awful Italian place tonight, which sucks. Between the shoes and dinner, this day is going to cost me over $200.

Sometimes I think I should just die, for all the good I've accomplished in my life. What a waste I have been. I have no progeny, I am useless. And this world hates women who are not mothers. Women are the niggers of the world!! Of course when I tell Jacob that, when I try to get some sympathy, he always says, "You enjoying yourself?" or tells me to stop stealing a title from a bad John Lennon song. My husband can be such a smug, sanctimonious bastard sometimes.

I'm not sleeping with him anymore. And I don't mean that as a declaration—just a fact. I have no sex drive, nothing. And to be truthful, the sex hasn't been great—not since we were dating. It's all a performance with him. I think he fantasizes about other women. But I have no libido, no interest, and nobody to fantasize about.

Someone has got to give me a baby.

I hate needing him so much. I can't decide which credit card offer to take without asking him or which laptop to buy. He makes me coffee, even though he doesn't drink any. I told him to stop, and he said, "You're just telling me to stop so you won't have to feel guilty for not doing anything for me"—which may be true. I don't cook, I don't clean, I'm a bad wife. I know it. I care, but I'm not. Maybe if I had eight kids to look after, having to wipe their noses, their asses, it would be different. This marriage is an albatross, my work sucks (I'm not getting tenure, I can feel it, even though I should).

I WANT A BABY!!!!
I WANT A BABY!!!!
I WANT A BABY!!!!

. . .

He heard her car pull up and stopped reading and returned the diary under the cushion.

He knew all this, except the part about Sage. He actually was relieved she wasn't having an affair—or maybe she just wasn't thinking about it today. He walked into the bedroom, feeling less ashamed than he thought he might.

Cindi came in the back door.

Back door open.

"Babe?"

"In here," he said, looking at himself in the bedroom mirror to see if he looked like a man who had just read his wife's diary.

"What are you doing?"

"Just changing," he said, deciding to actually do that. "We're going to dinner, right?"

"Yep."

Cindi went into the living room, sat down. She picked up an old issue of *Reason* and turned to an article titled "Will Climate Change Ruin Your Sex Life?"

"Hi," he said, coming out of the bedroom with a new shirt on.

"You changing your pants?" she said.

"Yeah, but I couldn't wait to see you."

"How one person can be so full of shit is beyond me."

"Why can't I be happy to see you? You're in a bad mood, aren't you? How is that possible? You just got home."

"I'm just reading. Can you not see that? I'm tired. I work."

"Oh, okay. I thought you were in a bad mood."

"I'm not always in a bad fucking mood. Jesus!"

"Sorry."

"You know, I don't belong in this world. I want to die," she said, throwing down the magazine.

"You were fine when I left. Something happen at school?"

"I was not fucking fine when you left."

"Honey?"

She shook her head.

"Honey?" he asked again.

"What?"

"I like the shoes."

"No, you don't. Take them back. I don't care," she said crossing her arms.

"No, I really like them."

"Whatever."

"Why are you in a bad mood?"

"I'm not."

"Did the meeting with Howland go badly?"

"No."

"You sure?"

"I'm fucking sure. It was fine."

"Just wanted to see what's wrong."

"My life, my work, us, this fucking house. I hate everything. Somebody should just shoot me."

"Something happen between the time I left and you—"

"Nothing happened. Stop asking me that. I went to school. I came back."

"I was there too."

"I know, but you walk, I drive. We're on different parts of a campus that holds almost twenty thousand people, so it's not so weird we wouldn't bump into each other. Sorry, I'm just a little grouchy."

Jacob didn't say anything.

"I know what you're thinking," Cindi said. "'You're always grouchy.' "

"I wasn't thinking that," said Jacob, who was thinking that.

"I'm sorry I'm such a lousy wife."

"Oh, stop, you are not," he replied.

"Do we have to do this today?"

"'Somebody should just shoot me.' You said that."

"So? So what if I said it? Somebody should."

"Could you stop? Please, today, stop."

"Why?"

Because it might not kill you to think about me and my birthday, he wanted to say.

"Because you just might."

"Because it's your birthday?" Cindi had a way of spitting out her words like a corner man in boxing, and "birthday" was spat.

"Not because it's my birthday. I don't want to start with you," Jacob said, knowing he was, "but it might not kill you to think about me and my birthday."

There, he said it.

"Grow up."

"You're right, it's childish, but you know what, it is my birthday, and a relatively important one at that, so you could humor me a little and think about taking your head out of your ass."

"I'm sorry," she said.

Her agreeing surprised him.

"Forget it," he said.

"Do you know how many times we say 'Forget it' in this marriage?" she asked. "Is it okay if I don't go eat with you tonight?"

"I knew it."

"I hate the food there, you know that. I'll give you money. You go."

"You'll give me money? You want me to go to dinner by myself and you'll give me money?"

"Fine, I'll go. I hate fucking wherever we're going, though."

"Take this the right way, Cin. It's not really important whether you like it. I like it! See, that's the way birthdays work. The one celebrating gets to eat what he or she wants and the one accompanying the birthday boy or girl finds something on the menu to eat and shuts up about how he or she would rather be somewhere else. It's a simple concept, really."

"I hate when you use that tone."

"Then stop making me. Let's go somewhere else, then. We can go anywhere else."

"No, fine, we'll go to fucking wherever it is—where is it?"

"Portofino's."

"I'm not going to eat, though."

"For the love of fuck."

"No, it's your birthday, we'll go, but I don't want to. See, this is why I hate birthdays."

"You hate birthdays because . . . why? Someone wants to eat food you don't like, or because you're asked to make an effort?"

"You hate me, don't you?"

"Cindi, why is every moment about you? Your not liking this restaurant is not important."

"I want to kill myself."

"Is it too much to ask that you don't talk about killing yourself every five minutes, especially today? Could you give it a rest?"

He stood up, but had nowhere to go, so he sat back down.

"Never mind," he said. "The day is officially gone. And you barely got off the chaise to do it. Nice work."

Cindi thought about what she had just written in her diary, now sitting under her, about her loneliness, her wanting a baby, her anger at the marriage and her boredom, but she knew he was right, knew she had hurt him, and knew that even if she had sex with him tonight, something she was considering, he would only remember this moment, this argument from his fiftieth birthday—the moment where his wife said "I want to kill myself" over and over.

She apologized enough that they did go to Mario's Portofino, where their good friend Tim, an astrologer, was the bartender. Called Nomad by everyone who knew him, Tim had given them an astrological chart a few months earlier, because, as he said, he saw something "cosmically certain" in their marriage. He had taken the twenty-three-page evaluation to FedEx Kinko and had it bound. Cindi kept a copy by her bed. Jacob had left his in the back seat of his Honda.

"Can I buy you a drink?" Nomad asked.

"Let me check the chart first, see if my moon is in the right position," Jacob said.

"Shut up," said Cindi. "He's so jaded."

"Actually, he's got a point."

"See," Jacob said to her, "I'm in tune with my planets."

Ciara, the small dark-haired waitress with some kind of matching tattoos above her breast and on her lower back, was their waitress.

"Hey, big boy, happy birthday. What are you, like, sixty now?" she asked, as she bent down to give him a kiss on the cheek.

"Careful," said Cindi, "you'll make me jealous."

"Yeah, sure. I'm going to make you jealous. You're hot, Cindi."

"Thanks."

"No, I mean it."

After Ciara took the drink orders and walked away, Jacob found himself smiling.

"What?" asked Cindi.

"Nothing, just nothing."

"Ciara," Cindi leaned forward, "has a crush on you."

"She does not," Jacob said, but hoped, in fact, she did. "She has a crush on you."

"She's cute. It's okay," Cindi said, looking at the menu. "God, I hate the food here. But I take my husband out for his birthday here anyway, and some waitress with a black bra and a white shirt has the hots for him. What . . . she get dressed in the dark?"

So that's all it takes? One cute brunette in black stretch pants and an exposed waist smiles at me and now I've got my wife's attention.

Jacob smiled at that thought, but then realized he had no chance of fucking either one of them tonight.

Ciara returned with a chardonnay for Cindi and a Diet Coke, both in a glass and a full carafe, for Jacob.

"I brought you a carafe, baby," Ciara said.

Cindi smiled and repeated the words when Ciara left. "'I brought you a carafe, baby.'"

"Would you knock it off?" Jacob said, laughing. "I deserve a carafe."

"How well do you know her?"

"I know her as well as you do."

"Would you sleep with her?"

Jacob smiled.

"Wouldn't you?"

"She's got a cute ass."

"That's my point," said Cindi. "And nice breasts."

"I'm not a breast guy, you know that."

"Never understood that about you. You're really weird. I love boobies."

"Boobies? See, right there, that ruins it. You can't have rough, nasty sex if you insist on calling them boobies."

"You like 'tits' better?"

"Yeah."

Jacob was self-conscious whenever Ciara came by to refill the carafe or talk about her latest DUI or her boyfriend, who, she told Jacob and Cindi, had just been fitted with an ankle-bracelet monitor by the Washoe County Sheriff's Office. Cindi was watching him, something he knew she was doing. She was expecting him to act like he wasn't interested in Ciara. Sensing this, Jacob acted interested in Ciara to prove to his wife he wasn't actually interested.

This marriage was exhausting.

Jacob noticed Ciara was missing a molar. When she bent down to pick up a napkin, he saw vine tattoos on her lower back. To live with her, he thought, he'd have to learn to live with a girl who occasionally abused Xanax, had bad credit, was late on her utilities, and had no relationship with her mother or father.

But an incredible fuck.

"She so wants you!" Cindi said, as the manager brought tiramisu for them.

"You think?"

"Pretty obvious."

"Anything else, stud?" It was Ciara, stopping by with the check.

"You two want me to leave?" Cindi asked.

"Forgive my wife," Jacob said, "she's very jealous."

"All right, break it up, you two," Cindi said, looking at the check.

Ciara smiled at Jacob and left.

"I don't have money for this. We don't celebrate birthdays in my house. This is crazy." He grabbed for the check. She said, "No, no, I'm sorry. I'm still ruining your birthday, aren't I?" And with that, she pulled it out of his hand and went to the bar to pay it.

When she returned, she asked, "Ready?"

On the drive home, Jacob suggested stopping at the Silver Legacy to listen to a cheesy lounge band, maybe talk to his bartender friend Ken, play penny slots, and then go for one of the sundaes that were discounted after midnight.

"I don't feel like it," Cindi said, "but drop me off and go back by yourself if you want. It's okay."

"Are you doing this on purpose?"

"I'm sorry. I'm just having a shitty day and I want it to be over."

In bed, before falling asleep, but after Cindi's less-than-inspired birthday blow job he got at the kitchen table, Jacob opened his night-stand drawer, and under a pair of socks and some shoelaces he found where he had placed Gabriel, the chubby angel, with Cindi's ring still on its wing, the three packages of blueberry seeds, and his own wedding band. He never told Cindi he took the angel.

She never asked, either.

As Jacob Fishman, on the first day of his sixth decade, lay in his bed, alone, for Cindi had moved to the chaise to write in her diary, he thought about girls with yellow highlighters and perfect teeth and girls with tattoos and missing molars.

You're Thinking Too Loudly

About 20 years after its inception, seismic coherence volumes have been routinely used to delineate structural and stratigraphic discontinuities such as channels, faults and fractures, to highlight incoherent zones such as karst collapse and mass transport complexes, and to identify subtle tectonic and sedimentary features that might otherwise be overlooked on conventional amplitude volumes.

Jacob was finishing another piece for The American Association of Petroleum Geologist's *Explorer,* this one on the exploration in the Middle Pennsylvania Red Fork Sandstone of Oklahoma and, as near as he could understand, the problems with identifying the best places to drill.

Tong Du, a Chinese geoscientist from Texas Christian University, told him that on the phone—at least he thought that's what she told him. Jacob rarely knew what any of the scientists he interviewed were talking about, which is why he always sent the scientists, authors, and explorers questions via email, so he could just cut and paste their answers. He was paid $600 for an 800-word story (more if he found art or photography) and wrote two or three stories per month. They took nothing out of him, except the palpable notion he was a fraud passing himself off as someone who could write about such things and, worse, was an unconscionable shill for the extraction industry. Once, in a piece on offshore drilling in California, he added a Joan Didion line: *"California is a place in which a boom mentality and a sense of Chekhovian loss meet in uneasy suspension; in which the mind is troubled by some buried but ineradicable suspicion that things better work here, because here, beneath the immense bleached sky, is where we run out of continent,"* which he rather liked, especially the end about running out of continent, especially because, he figured, Joan Didion had never been quoted in a geology trade publication.

It would have been, too, but the editor took it out.

"Her grandfather was a geologist, but it's such a fabulous quote," Jacob told his editor.

"Yeah, I know," the editor replied, "it is, but I don't know who she is."

He couldn't concentrate on the Anadarko Basin and the fifty-million-year-old gap between something or other, so he closed the file and opened the "Thank You . . . Fuck You" chapter. He opened the chapter to the discussion when his fictional wife, Cindi, called his fictional Jacob's daughter a "skanky little whore," which Cindi, the real one, had, and had also disputed. He thought it best to give the Fishmans that story unsullied. He had forgotten to give the girl with the yellow marker a name, but perhaps it was better this way, for he couldn't see her being a major character in the novel, nor could he find a plausible scenario where she would fuck Jacob. She shouldn't be completely real, anyway, certainly not as real as Jacob and Cindi were—and they, as he kept telling himself, weren't. There was no girl with the yellow marker, but the Asian girl who sold him the pretzels and gum and diet soda at the student bookstore was based on a real Annie. Real Annie was the manager at the Buffet at the Eldorado Hotel and once did overturn Jacob's palm and told him, "You no work hard!" There was an actual Ciara, too, a waitress who did work at Mario's Portofino and did flirt with him, so it was easy to embellish and fictionalize that relationship, if you could even call it that. Jacob hadn't thought about making his character Jacob a geology writer, for he didn't technically know enough about the industry to pull it off. As to the matter of fictional Cindi's tenure, his real wife, Cindi, got tenure, but just the year before, after initially being rejected, from which she still hadn't recovered or forgiven those who put her through the academic ringer. She received it upon appeal, but it was no longer the victory she wanted. In *Jacob Fishman's Marriage*, Jacob decided that Cindi would go through a similar battle but hadn't yet decided if he'd let her get it.

"It depends how she behaves," he muttered to himself, looking at the chapter.

All of this paled in comparison and bothered him less than the matter of his real wife's diary, which he gave to fictional Cindi, word for word. Jacob had, on at least three occasions, found himself prostrate by Cindi's side of the bed reading her diaries, which she had stacked under a comforter and old magazines.

"Hon, what do you think of the title *Jacob Fishman's Marriage*?" Jacob asked Cindi as he came into the kitchen.

"I hate it," she said, eating a bowl of strawberries. "I hate the book."

"That you haven't read, and I have barely written?"

"Yes."

He looked at his wife, wondering if she knew of the thousands of small hiccups and indignities and disappointments in their lives together and the toll each one of them took on the Fishmans.

He returned to his office and vowed to deny Cindi tenure.

There was an alternate version of the "Thank You . . . Fuck You" chapter he found.

Dinner was better than expected, and something happened to Cindi. Maybe it was the wine or the guilt or her own horniness, but somewhere between the eggplant and the tiramisu, she wanted to fuck her husband. She found his calf under the table at Mario's and began rubbing her toes down the back of it.

"Can I help you?" Jacob asked, smiling.

"I want to fuck you when we get home," she whispered.

"You do? Me?"

She pointed at him and nodded her head.

When they got home, she quickly went down on him. He asked her to swing her legs around, a position she hated, but agreed to nonetheless. She felt him grow in her mouth and then slid down and mounted him, facing away, so they could both fantasize about others. He came before she did, and while she was satisfied, she wasn't happy.

"I love you," she said. "Happy birthday."

"Beats a pair of shoes, I'll tell you that."

"You should have seen the shoes I was going to buy you, though."

Jacob reread the scene and realized it was not only poorly written—her own horniness?—it wasn't the Jacob and Cindi he had wanted to lead off the book. Who would believe that the same woman who, hours earlier, was on a couch with a blanket up to her eyes and talked of suicide and wrote in her diary, a diary her husband would read, "I hate this FUCKING marriage" would suddenly want to fuck her husband because she had an epiphany in a restaurant—and in a restaurant she hated.

Jacob was making notes on the women Jacob could possibly sleep with—and at the moment, he could only come up with Ciara—when he heard Cindi coming up the stairs.

She appeared.

"Can I come in?"

"Sure."

Jacob quickly saved the file and stared at the desktop.

"What are you doing?"

"About to delete my novel. You?"

"I didn't mean to be negative about it."

"That's all right. I shouldn't have asked. I was just fishing for a compliment."

"It's just that I don't want to be fodder for you. I told you that when we were still dating."

"Cin, the book . . . I don't even know what I'm going to do with it yet."

"I know, it's fiction," she said, rolling her eyes. "You told me. I'm serious about this. I don't want to be a character in your book, especially a book about us."

"I'm writing a book about marriage. It's not necessarily our marriage."

"Not necessarily?"

"Yes and no. The Cindi in the book doesn't do what you do, the Jacob in the book doesn't do what I do," he said, making air quotes when he mentioned their names. "Well, not entirely. He's a bit of a prick, and she's a bit of a cunt. I don't really like them right now, and I just started writing them."

"A cunt? Great," she said, laughing. "And I don't know why I'm laughing. I guess it's because we can be those things, too. I can be a cunt, you can be a prick. More than a prick, too, buddy boy."

"I don't know why it is, but I like when you call me that."

"I do love you. Not all the time, mind you. I don't even like you that much."

"You trying to get me in bed?"

"Rarely. Can I read it?"

"No, you cannot read it. In fact, nobody we know can read it, because everyone we know is going to wonder how much of it is about us. And that's not the point."

"I'm going to hate this, you know that, and then I'm going to hate you."

"Be nice or I won't give Cindi tenure."

"Leave my tenure out of this. I'm serious."

"I will," he said, lying.

"I mean it. The appeal, all of it, was just embarrassing."

"Okay."

"Jacob, I'm serious."

"I won't. But remember, that Cindi is not real."

"You prick."

"What?"

"Just give her the fucking tenure."

"No."

"Don't be a brat." Cindi laughed. "Give her tenure!"

"I don't have to if I don't want to."

"What are you, five? I am so going to hate this book."

"Why do you keep saying that?"

"'Cause I hate it already. I don't want to be in it. Take me out. Jacob's not married."

"You're not in it, and he is married. I'm God here. Remember, it's fiction. I read this book recently where the main character cuts off this Asian girl's tits and buried the tits in the sand. Do I care if that actually happened?"

"What are you talking about?"

"It'd be nice to know if it's true."

"It would be nice to know if the author really cut off the tits of a young Chinese girl and buried them in the sand?"

"Asian."

"The reality of that act is important to you—not the mind of the person who wrote it?"

"Yeah."

"You don't even need me in this marriage, do you? I have no children, no life, I'm a prop to you, fodder. I should be dead."

"Fodder. I guess that's the word of the day. Wait! You wish you were dead? You enjoying yourself?"

"Fuck Lipner."

Dr. Morris Lipner was a Brooklyn psychiatrist who Jacob's mother, Ria, saw for ten years with limited success. According to Ria, the only thing she could remember Lipner saying to her was, "You enjoying yourself?" every time she started feeling sorry for herself.

"How many times am I going to hear what some therapist told your mother forty years ago?"

"This is not just some therapist. This guy had an office filled with African masks and spears and played jazz in the background and who, my mother told me, saw her after a twenty-five-year absence—she went as a little girl and then in her forties—and met her by saying, 'Okay, let's continue.' Back then, Cin, these guys were the shit."

"I wish I were dead."

"I think I'll have the Cindi in the book say she wants to be dead. A lot."

"I will kill you if you make me, her, say that."

"I'm not. But why aren't you happy, other than the baby?"

"Other than the baby? Isn't this when Mrs. Lincoln says she loved *Our American Cousin*?"

"I'm not following you."

"It was the play they were watching when Lincoln was assassinated."

"I didn't know that."

"I know something you don't? Write it down."

"I'm serious, though, Cin. You have a pretty good life. You have a beautiful house—Okay, you hate it—"

"I don't hate it."

"My point is, why do you think your life is so bad? You know how many people would change places with you?"

"That's not the point."

"But it is—or should be."

"Hold on there, you sanctimonious fuck. You're writing a fucking book to get out of your life. Don't talk to me about acceptance and perspective and how I choose to get out of mine."

"I'm not doing that."

"Yeah, you are. My husband is creating a life where his wife is palatable."

"You never refer to me as your husband. And why do you think I'm making her anything other than what you are?"

"I think of you that way. I married you, didn't I? I fucking converted to Judaism for you, for Chrissakes!"

"That's funny."

"You win."

"I don't want to win."

"Yes, you do. Anyway, the book. I'm glad you're writing again. I just don't want to be in it. And I wish I was doing something as important."

"You do. A hundred and fifty students a year would be philosophically fucked without you."

"You're sweet."

"The book is fiction and, yes, you're going to be able to pick out you in it and some of our conversations, but the plot isn't ours, the people they meet are not our friends. It's not about us, even though one of the characters is a philosophy professor."

"You gave me a promotion to full professor?"

"No, sorry, I misspoke. She's just an assistant professor."

"Make her an associate professor, at least."

"No."

"Bastard! And what are you in the book?"

"A writer."

"Of course. So, you're really not going to let me read this thing of yours?"

"No, I'm not going to let you read this thing of mine."

"Why not?"

"Because you'll divorce me. I mean, you may do that anyway. I'll let you read it when I'm done. I just hope at that point you will have engaged in some horrible moral backsliding for which I would have magnanimously forgiven you, and then we'll be even."

"You're scaring me. These people—us, them, whatever—sound despicable."

"I think so."

"You're writing about people you don't like? What does that say about the two of us?"

"I don't know if it says anything."

"You're going to include this conversation in the book, aren't you?"

"Probably."

"So we're all—the four of us—the same pathetic people."

"Jesus, I hope not."

"Can't you make them better?" she asked.

"I'm trying, but I have to get rid of us—or maybe dive deeper into us."

"Let me read it, c'mon!"

"No."

"Why not?"

"I told you why not. Besides, I only have one chapter."

"That's it? What so far?"

"Jacob has a heart attack."

"What?"

"Sort of. And there's a girl with a yellow highlighter who's kind of cute and there's a waitress with tattoos."

"Who?"

"You don't know her."

"Do you, him, fuck her?"

"No."

"But you, him, wanted to."

"Oh, my God!"

"C'mon. Somebody wanted to fuck her."

"Cindi wanted to fuck her."

"Good. I'm liking this story now."

"No," Jacob said with a laugh. "Okay, I'll give you something. She, the waitress, flirted with Jacob and you got upset."

"So she did want to fuck you?"

"No. Cindi thought she did. It's fiction. There's no fucking in the chapter. Wait—no, there is. We do. They do. Cindi and Jacob."

"Fascinating distinction. And who's the chick with the yellow—"

"She doesn't exist."

"I have to put up with this, put up with you writing a book that will expose our marriage to ridicule and all these fantasies of yours just so you can call yourself a real writer because we can say, '*Oooh*, look at him channel.' And, most importantly, you think you'll be able to sell this?"

"Lara thinks so."

"She does?"

"You're going to have to trust me on this. I'm writing about two people. They look like us, argue like us, live like us, but they're not us. Things will happen to them that won't to us."

"Like what?"

"I don't know yet."

But he did.

He had started a chapter, one in which Jacob was talking with his psychiatrist, Dr. Jovanovic, about Cindi and how disappointed he was in their marriage and how much he longed for the days where girls with scrunchies in their hair and glitter in their eyes smiled at him. Jacob, himself, was not seeing a therapist, but Cindi was, and Jacob was certain she told Aurora, her counselor, how unhappy and sexually deprived she was. Aurora was too good a name, he thought, to change in the novel. While Cindi was talking to him, he tried to remember that he needed to remind himself about writing a scene for Aurora and Cindi.

"Jacob? Jacob!"

"What?"

"Hello, I'm here."

"I know."

"What are you thinking about?"

"Nothing."

"You're thinking about the book, aren't you? I'm talking to you and I'm not even here."

"Yeah, you are. Here and . . . here," he said, pointing to the computer, which held *Jacob Fishman's Marriage.* "Keep in mind, sweetie, please keep in mind: It's all fiction. None of it is real."

"And yet, I think, all of it is."

Jacob was silent.

"You really don't care about this marriage, do you?" Cindi asked.

"Of course I do. This is just a book."

"Jake, if you humiliate me, we're done."

She almost never called him Jake.

"You—you—can be a parasite, let's face it. Don't take that the wrong way, buddy boy, but you think nothing of betraying confidences and secrets if you think someone will admire your honesty in doing so."

"I so like it when you call me 'buddy boy.'"

"Why do you keep saying that? It's not like I say it with love—well, not always."

"No, you don't."

"You suck the life out of people."

"Glad you came upstairs, because I almost felt okay about myself."

"Enjoying yourself?"

Jacob laughed.

"Fuck you."

"Fuck you, too."

"I'm going downstairs now."

"Wait, wait, we need something more dramatic to end this conversation, you know, in case it somehow makes its way into the book."

"What do you have in mind?"

"Blow job?"

"Ask the other Cindi," she said from the top of the stairs.

Cindi was asleep when Jacob got into bed, so he lay on his back, crossed his legs, sat up, stared at the ceiling, and wondered how he was going to do this. Cindi was not his wife, Cindi was, but then again Cindi didn't call her husband a parasite. Cindi did, and she wasn't even being nasty when she did.

What kind of wife says that to her husband . . . and what kind of husband would put it in a book and attribute it to someone with his wife's name?

Cindi was right: If he was going to reveal this marriage, he'd have to betray it.

Cindi and Cindi were the same woman. Their words and thoughts should be interchangeable. Maybe Cindi could breathe life into Cindi. Jacob suddenly had an urge to finger one of his wives. Would Cindi hate having sex with Jacob as much as Cindi hated having it with him? Jacob knew that before his next birthday, either he or Cindi would have an affair—or maybe Jacob or Cindi would.

Or both.

If his marriage didn't survive, and he didn't see how it would, would Jacob and Cindi split up, too? How could they not, Jacob thought, as Cindi turned to face him in bed. He reached down between her legs and parted her thighs with his forefinger (she was not wet). She said something he couldn't understand, flipped over, and turned her back to him. She was asleep. This was their sex life: an approach, a consideration, ultimately a refusal. As Jacob stroked his wife's back softly enough so as to not wake her, he thought about the prospects of going through two divorces with the same woman. Wouldn't it be something, he thought, if Jacob and Cindi found a way to live together while he and his real wife couldn't? And what if all four of them lived happily ever after?

Cindi stirred. "Jesus! Stop."

"Huh?" Jacob asked. "This?" he asked, removing his hand from her back.

"No. That's fine."

"Then what?"

"Your thinking."

"My what?

"You're thinking too loudly. "

Jacob Fishman's Marriage: A Novel

2. Anyone's Baby

"What is it?" Jacob asked, four days after his birthday dinner, as he and Cindi stood in the kitchen, both slightly bent over, both staring into the refrigerator. Cindi had a piece of cheese in her mouth.

"Nothing."

"Anything good in here?"

"I'm not hungry. This sucks."

"What sucks?"

"Nothing."

"C'mon, what? We go through this all the time. I ask what's wrong, you say nothing, and then it *is* something, and then you get upset I didn't ask about that thing, which I already asked you to tell me about but you didn't want to talk about. But, for the moment, what are you going to do with that?" he asked, pointing to the cheese in her mouth, specifically the piece still hanging out.

"I haven't had a meal in days," she answered through the cheese.

"That's not even remotely true, but if it were—let's say it was—bite down on the cheese in your mouth."

"You don't get it," she said, ripping the cheese out of her mouth, turning away from him, and throwing it into the sink.

"'Don't get it'? You're hungry. What is there to get? Eat. And what did the cheese do to you?"

"I don't feel like eating."

"Then don't eat."

"If you had blood gushing between your legs, you'd understand."

Cindi was on the first day of her August period.

"That's how you describe being on your period? Jesus!"

"I think I scared my father when I told him, too."

"You told your father you had blood gushing between your legs?"

"I do and I did."

"You don't, and what is wrong with you? You're on your period and he's eighty-seven. There's not this river of blood coming out of you, spewing in all directions, closing malls and neighborhood pools and parks."

"Closing malls?"

"Bit of a reach, agreed. But who tells her father that?" Jacob asked.

"There is nothing wrong with me," Cindi replied, laughing. "You're right. Maybe that was a bit much. It's just the thousands of years of neglect and humiliation that women have suffered at the hands of men. It's just God fucking with women again—and he does it every month."

"What did he say?"

"God doesn't care about women."

"Your father."

"He wanted to come over and take me to the hospital. Did you know," Cindi asked him, rejoining him at the refrigerator and getting another piece of cheese and putting that one in her mouth, "that the ancient Romans thought women on their periods were witches and that in Nepal, women on their periods are sent to menstrual huts? Don't you dare make a joke."

"I'm not."

"Men should have periods, just once, to have blood spewing from their weenies."

"Weenies?" Jacob asked. "You finish a tirade like that with a word like weenies? Honey, it needs cock or prick to make your point."

"Go ahead and laugh, but I hate boys."

"Boys? What are you, nine? Besides, you hate girls, too."

"I'm a misanthrope, I know. I'm a mess."

The days following Jacob's birthday and the birthday dinner were calm, as calm as days for the Fishmans went, meaning Cindi did not talk much of suicide or joining the circus. But with the onset of Cindi's period, their earth shifted, as it usually did. Jacob looked at the toaster, where the SAS Time-Outs had sat for days, and smiled. There wasn't a "bone" in size 13, as it turned out, so Cindi just got her money back.

"I'll get you something else, I promise," she told him.

"That's fine," he said. "Don't worry about it. Let's never celebrate another birthday again."

"I really ruined it, didn't I?"

"Forget it."

"Don't be mad at me."

It was as if Cindi thought the sheer exhalation of those words really would end whatever current argument she and Jacob were in. It was an absurd, arrogant belief, all the more impossible to explain because such logic usually worked.

"You know your periods are like those South American insurgents who get stronger and stronger and then they charge, knocking down communication towers and ransacking towns."

"They're not that bad," Cindi said, smiling.

Thank God she was smiling.

"In any case, I'm going upstairs."

"In Italy there are two mountain belts, Alps and Apennines, but they are so different. The Alps are higher, involve deep-seated metamorphic rocks, thick-skinned tectonics is dominant, they have two shallow fore-deeps, a

thick crust and lithosphere, no back-arc basin and a shallow subduction zone. The Apennines are exactly the contrary, having low topography, one single deep fore-deep, the accretionary prism is mostly composed by sedimentary rocks, i.e., dominant thin-skinned tectonics, a widespread back-arc basin and a steep westerly directed subduction zone."

Seems this Italian geologist was winning some award for his work in Italy, which is what most of these geology associations, in practice, were all about: giving old white guys awards. Jacob Fishman, who knew little about geology, knew enough to pull off this writing. The work paid his share of the bills. Cindi's salary from UNR paid hers. Jacob rarely knew what happened to the stories once he sent them to the AAPG home office in Tulsa, Oklahoma. The editor there, an uber-religious climate-change denier, threw Jacob three to four stories per month, so Jacob, even though he was no fan of either the extraction industry or uber-religious climate-change deniers, was grateful. He had checked the spelling on Doglioni, the geologist, for the third time, when he heard Cindi ascend the stairs. He could tell by the sound, the purposefulness and arrogance and sound of her shoes against the wood, her hand tapping the wall above the guard rail, that her mood had worsened.

"Hide the porn!" he heard her yell. "Hide the porn!"

"Walk slower."

She appeared.

"You're not doing well, honey, are you?"

"How would you feel if you had a wad of paper up your weenie?"

"Again with the weenie?"

This was Day One. Her mood, he had to admit to himself, was no worse than usual for the first twenty-four hours of her period.

"Hi," she said, entering his office, her voice devoid of any emotion or energy.

"Hi, what's up?"

"What are you doing?"

"Looking at porn, told you."

"Let me see," she said, quickly coming around to his side of the desk. "Geology? Fuck. I'm going back downstairs.'

"No, sit," Jacob said.

She did.

"How can you write for these people?" she asked, staring at him. "Don't you understand? They rape the fucking earth."

"I know."

"So tell them."

"You want me to call AAPG and tell my editor he rapes the earth."

"Ask him why."

"You want me to ask him why he rapes the earth?"

"Don't mock me."

"But you're mockable at the moment. What do you want me to do here?"

"I hate this world."

"Oh, Jesus!"

"I do."

"I know. You want to talk?"

"I want a baby."

This was a marriage in a loop.

"I know."

"So?"

"So."

"You had a vasectomy."

"I had a vasectomy."

"Reverse it."

"It's not that simple."

"Why not?"

"Because, again, it's fifteen thousand dollars just for the reversal, which your insurance doesn't cover. No insurance does—and thank you again for putting me on it—and the baby would be another ten thousand, which your insurance may not cover, and we don't have the extra money for that, and I just turned fifty, and . . . I don't know."

"So why did you say you'd think about it when we got married?"

"Because I did, I do. I have thought about it, I still do. I just don't know what to tell you. I know that every month your period reminds you how disappointing this all is for you."

"Don't patronize me," she said, as she picked up some magazines, papers, and envelopes on his desk. "I know you're sorry, but I'm dying and you really don't care." She threw the mail on the chair. "So I'm going to have to do something, okay?"

"Do something?"

"I need a sperm donor."

"A sperm donor?" Jacob laughed. "You're not a bee."

"Go ahead, make fun. I'm serious. I want a fucking baby!"

"You know, you keep modifying 'baby' with 'fucking.' Is that good, you putting that out into the universe?"

"I can't be articulate when my body is screaming. I can't always find the right word, okay with you, Mr. Geology Writer?"

"Nicely done, Cin—geology writer?"

"Just don't placate me, and don't think I'm a nutjob, because if you do, I will throw your computer out the window. I am dying, I am literally dying here, do you understand? And I have to do something."

"What about adoption?"

"You're not listening to me. My body wants a baby! My body!" she said again, pushing her palms into her breasts three times.

He motioned for her to come sit on his lap.

"No."

She went back to the chair but sat sideways, so that she looked out the window onto Codel.

"What do you want to do?" he asked. "I'm listening."

"I've been thinking," she said, suddenly smiling, leaning forward, "what if someone else fathered the baby and we raised it?"

Jacob Fishman looked at his wife like the crazy person she was.

"Jacob?"

"I heard."

"Well?"

"Well?"

"Huh?"

"What?

"What do you think?"

"It's tough to know if you're serious or if the insurgents are talking."

"Stop with that!"

"Okay. What do you want me to say? I don't want you to take this the wrong way, but did you hit your head today? You want someone else to father the child? Are you insane?"

"Why is it crazy?"

"Because, for starters—and I'm kind of thinking out loud here—you can't just sleep with another guy, get pregnant, and then come back and live with me."

"Why won't you be open-minded about this?"

"This is not open-minded. This is fucked in the head. You want me to be open-minded about you sleeping with some other guy?"

"Just for the sperm."

"Have you actually thought about this?"

"Yes. I mean, not a lot, but yeah."

Jacob looked at his wife, who was still looking out the window, and he tried to imagine what he would think of her if he didn't know her. And then he imagined what it would be like to grab her by the arm, lead her downstairs, and usher her out the back door, and then watch her stand in the back yard in the rain. The fact that it wasn't raining but he imagined it that way was an odd thought, even for him, to be having at this moment.

"What is wrong with you?" he asked.

"What? It's just sperm. And we could raise it."

"You want to fuck someone else, get pregnant, and then raise the child that came from that sperm—it, as you delicately call it—with me?"

"Bad choice of words. A baby. It's a fucking baby—not an it. Do you have a better idea?"

What bothered Jacob at the moment, more than the realization that he was married to a woman who could actually suggest such a thing—more even than he was married to a woman who would go through with such a thing—was that, no, he did not have a better idea.

"I love you, so don't take this the wrong way, but no. No. No. No. And you are seriously out of your mind if you think that could ever happen. Again, tough to know if you're serious."

"Then I guess I'll just die or go to Idaho."

"Those are the only three choices you can come up with: fuck a strange man, get pregnant, and have the baby and raise it with your husband; die; or go to Idaho?"

"Here's the fourth one, buddy boy. Get a reversal. We should take the financial hit. I'll make more money soon. You keep writing for this organization that rapes the earth. Maybe they'll give you a raise too."

"I really do think about the reversal. I know you don't think I do, but I do."

"While you do, I am dying, so if you want to speed up the process, anytime now."

"But a strange guy? Why would you think that would be an option?"

"He wouldn't have to be strange. We could agree on someone."

"I should really write a book, because nobody's going to believe this conversation. What if I brought you the same proposal?"

"You can't get a girl pregnant, remember? Besides, it's not like I'd enjoy it."

Jacob looked at his wife, hoping to see a smile, a wink, something to let him know that she was in on the joke.

Nothing.

"If you come home pregnant, I will be hurt, I'll be devastated, but, and this may surprise you, I will understand how important it was for you to have a baby. I won't be angry—at least I don't think I will. I won't even ask who the father is. Listen to me. I will understand why you did it. But this is important too. You, his sperm, and I will not be together."

Cindi stopped talking. Jacob was not known for declarative statements, and he could tell his resolve scared her—and this counted as resolve for Jacob Fishman. He continued. He was empowered that she was back on her heels. "And another thing: I can't believe we're talking about this. I can't believe there is any other conversation we can ever have after this."

"Don't be so dramatic. It was just an idea. I'm trying to come up with a solution and you're dismissing it."

"You think this is a solution?"

"Yes. What about Dave?"

"Dave?"

"You know."

"Sage's Dave? What about—that's the Dave you want sperm from? The guy who already has six kids?"

"Does that matter?"

"Perhaps to Sage."

"I've talked to her."

"What?"

"I asked her what she thought about me having a baby and the two of us, you and I, raising it—the baby, I mean—and she said it was a great idea."

"Did you mention the part about wanting to fuck her husband and that your husband, me, might take it badly?"

"I don't want to fuck her husband—gross!—but I would. They're very spiritual people. I think they'd do this for us."

"This is like a bad takeoff on *The Big Chill,* which was already pretty bad, where the Mary Kay Place character fucks what's-her-name's husband."

"I know this one. Glenn Close."

"Yes. And what do you mean . . . us? I don't want this done for me. Have you even considered how humiliating this could be?"

"Who would have to know?"

"I'm not talking about announcing the baby's father to the world. I am talking about you fucking Dave."

"Stop saying that! I don't want to fuck anyone else. It's just for his sperm."

"Is there any part of you, right now, at this moment, any inner voice saying, 'Cindi, stop talking about fucking another man to Jacob and wanting him to agree and getting angry that he won't'?"

"I don't want to fuck someone else, for the hundredth time. You have a daughter and I . . . want . . . a . . . baby!" and with that, she slammed Jacob's door and went downstairs, back to her chaise, her comforter, and her diary.

"How else are you going to get his sperm if you don't fuck him? With a turkey baster?" he called after her.

"I can't win. I can't fucking win," Jacob overheard her say to herself, as she made her way completely down the stairs.

When she got to the chaise, she opened her diary, pulled up the comforter, and started writing.

14 May 2011

Goddamn it, I have to do something. And have to do it before school starts. He won't even discuss this. I tell him I'm unhappy and he asks if I'm fucked in the head? Christ!!!!! Why do I want one with him anyway?

THE CALM

After writing "Anyone's Baby" three times, a chapter in which he decide to, in fact, make the fictional Jacob a geology writer, Jacob Fishman came downstairs, still not certain whether it was plausible for the Cindi, even the fictional wife, to suggest to the Jacob, even the fictional husband, a) She get pregnant with another man's sperm, b) Have that sperm belong to Dave, and c) Suggest that her husband would be okay with this. Dave and Sage actually existed. Former Mormons, parents of six, they had left the LDS Church after finding it too liberal, an exit they celebrated by putting an ax through their 55-inch Sony, saying it was a repository of filth and porn. The idea for the borrowed sperm came from Cindi herself, the real one, who had once made a similar request about another man fathering her child. She hadn't specifically suggested it be Dave—or anyone, for that matter— but Jacob was never certain how serious she was about the idea. Certainly, the fictional Cindi had given this much more thought than his real wife had, but that Jacob would allow her to relentlessly articulate it was an early indication that he would allow the fictional Fishmans, especially the fictional Cindi, to embrace all the fears, insecurities, and insanity of their doppelgängers. That Jacob decided she would be serious about such a proxy was simply one of those tweaks one made for literature, Jacob decided, as he bounded down the stairs—either that or he was, as his fictional wife had uttered, just a prick, a realization that slowed down his gait before he got to the bottom of the stairs.

He was angry. Cindi—this Cindi, the real one, the one on the chaise —put him in this mood, for she made him write such a scene. What wife, even joking, suggests carrying another man's baby?

His wife.

"Am I doing something wrong?" she asked, looking up, seeing his expression.

"No, you're fine. By all means, sit."

"What's up your ass?" she asked, pointing the channel changer at the television and the show *Alaskan Bush People,* muting it.

"What do you hear from Dave?"

"Dave?"

"Dave."

"Why would I hear from Dave?"

"I don't know."

"You're weird sometimes. Hey, how about these people?" asked Cindi, pointing to the screen. "Some have never used phones, some have pierced eyebrows, some don't have teeth, and some are brilliant. They build shit and burrow holes in the ground."

"So, nothing from Dave?"

"What is with you? No, I haven't heard from Dave. I mean, they're getting divorced. I think she's cheating on him—or wants to."

"Aha!"

"'Aha'? What is 'Aha'? What is with you?"

"They are getting divorced, definitely?"

"Yeah, I think."

"That's interesting."

"Why is that interesting? You don't even know them very well."

"What happened?"

"She got restless."

"She has, like, twelve kids."

"What do you want from me? I don't know why."

"You're right. Just, you know, divorce is sad. It's a shame."

"What the fuck are you talking about? They will be fine. Or they won't be. We're fine. Everybody's fine. Can I watch about the bush people now?"

"Yeah, like you need my permission."

"What is with you?"

"Nothing. I told you, nothing."

He sat on the sofa, watching his wife watch television.

You'd fuck Dave, but you won't fuck me?

"What . . . do you want?" she asked, looking at him again. "Go write. Leave me alone."

He did as he was told.

"Enjoy your aborigines."

"Bush people!"

Heading back up the stairs, Jacob wasn't sure how he liked being in two marriages. The fictional wife seemed further along in her alienation from the marriage than the real one did, certainly less in love with Jacob than the real Cindi was with him. That was a good thing, he reminded himself. Cindi did want a baby, did feel some ambivalence about being a stepmom to a teenage girl, so to that extent, both Cindis were one, but he didn't have to have the fictional Cindi call Lisa a skanky little whore or toss a skillet at a wall—the real one did that.

It was better for *Jacob Fishman's Marriage*, he told himself, to make Cindi more shrill, more desperate, and to give her all of the real Cindi's peccadilloes. His fictional marriage should be both mirror and distorted mirror to his marriage. Perhaps someone reading the "Anyone's Baby" chapter—perhaps even Sage, with whom Cindi smoked pot on Sunday mornings in the upstairs bedroom, across from his office—wouldn't be horrified to see Cindi characterized in this light. As far as anyone else, the fictional Cindi would just be an unhappy woman in a bad marriage. There would only be a number of people, including Sage (and, yes, Dave) who would know both marriages. *Jacob Fishman's Marriage* would be untethered from the real Jacob and Cindi Fishman and their marriage, but both marriages would be held together by something resembling an invisible magnet.

Ever since her last period, Cindi was nothing like fictional Cindi—nothing like herself, either, inexplicably enjoying, as she described it, her "nest," this house on Codel. She'd started planting coreopsis and black-eyed Susans and other perennials in the back yard.

"Were you singing out there?" Jacob asked the first time she came in from the back yard.

"Yeah, why?"

"You're a philosopher. Wasn't it Voltaire who said, 'That which is too stupid to be said is sung'?"

"Is that the only quote you know from Voltaire?"

"It's a good one, don't you think?"

"That's not even the quote. It's 'Anything too stupid to be said is sung.'"

"I like mine better."

"Of course you do. Look, don't ruin this day for me. I'm baking bread for you."

"Baking . . . for me? What have you done with my wife?"

"Stop it. I'm trying to be fucking nice here."

"Sorry."

Cindi also spent time writing in her diary about the Greek Isles and the oneness of God—she wrote, "HE is not he, SHE is not she, IT is not it."

She was as momentarily content as any woman in a marriage where neither the man nor the wife was wearing a wedding ring and in which the husband was writing a book about how bad their marriage was.

Upstairs, Jacob, after adding that Sage and Dave were getting divorced in the "Anyone's Baby" chapter, wondered if he would stop writing the book if he could be guaranteed a happy marriage, if he could guarantee this Cindi, this happy one, would always be his wife. He didn't know how to answer his own question.

That night, the Fishmans went to play craps at the Eldorado, and while she leaned over the table to scream, "C'mon, baby needs a new pair of shoes!" as he instructed her to, he found himself staring at his wife's ass and wondering what it would be like to fuck this woman with the bandanna wrapped around her brown hair, who was smiling at the croupier, a name she loved—"Hey, croupi-ay, show Mama some love," which was a line she made up.

He liked thinking of his wife in the third person. He liked this ass in the third person.

When life was good for the Fishmans, such as this night, they'd pretend, upon seeing each other at a Chinese buffet or a Starbucks or a mall, that they had never met. The first time they played this game of pretending they were just meeting, they had been married a year or so, and they were at a Sunday brunch at the Hilton, when Cindi returned to the table and said, "Jesus, I looked up and saw this guy and I thought, 'Wow.'"

"Who was he?"

"You."

"Me?"

"Yeah."

"Let me tell you what's weird. I didn't know what to call it, but I had a similar moment when you were picking up cheese squares with that toothpick."

"C'mon!"

"Hand to God. I wanted to fuck you by the omelet station."

"Guess what I just had?" he said to Cindi, returning to the present, as she rolled a seven.

"You did?" Cindi asked.

"Yeah."

"Oh, c'mon, I look old and haggard, and I can't believe how fat I'm getting."

"I was staring at your ass as if I had never seen it."

"Thank you."

They were first introduced to each other at UNR. Jacob had been invited to speak at a conference on nonfiction after the book about Ampara came out. Cindi, who hated what she called writer-types, came to the event with Sage. Jacob saw them as he was signing books.

"You want to have dinner with me some night?" he asked Cindi, as she brought her book to the table.

"Did you write this book just to hit on women at the merch table?"

"Seemed like as good a reason as any."

"Okay."

He signed the book "Put me on a shelf next to someone good."

"Cute," Cindi said, reading it.

As she and Sage walked away, Jacob, thinking of Ampara and the book in front of him, wondered, "Why can't I ever get something like that?"

That first night, she went online and read excerpts of the book and called him to say she would not go out with him.

"Why?"

"You're terrible with women, you know that?"

"Yeah, I'm coming to that conclusion, but c'mon, one date."

"No."

"Think about it. What's the worst that could happen? A few laughs, some moderate to heavy petting, and then if you want, that's it. And then you can tell people how you dumped me."

"Okay, one date, but that's it. I mean it."

The date went well—they went to Mario's Portofino—as did the petting afterward in the car, and while she knew it wasn't a good idea, she agreed to another date and then another, and then, when his lease was up on his condo, she agreed to have him move in till he found a new place, a place he never found.

She fell in love quickly, but not completely, and after six years of marriage, she was tired of sex, probably generally, but certainly with him. They didn't talk about it much, sparing each other that humiliation of this lack of passion and desired technique between them, but once, after making love, when neither of them came and they both just sort of called it off, Jacob said, "That was a chore for you, wasn't it?"

"Yeah."

Cindi was the one who had read and traveled, received a doctorate, knew French and Arabic fluently, and had studied abroad; still, she had convinced herself Jacob was smarter, a quicker wit, and he did have a way of articulating his arguments, seamlessly, with enough anecdotes to intimidate and overshadow her. But she was no longer impressed when he'd quote Joan Didion about living in a place with a moat, or what Burt Lancaster said about the ocean in *Atlantic City,* or what Carl Sandburg said about babies, or what Michael Corleone said about anything.

"Someday I wish," she said to him, "you would tell me something you never told anybody else."

Now, with *Jacob Fishman's Marriage* being written, she feared she would soon be not just a character but a caricature, a thought that made her want to take a sledgehammer to his desktop.

Though she hated *Jacob Fishman's Marriage,* she desperately wanted to read it.

On the drive home from the casino, she started thinking of the days when she would travel through Europe with unemployed Mediterranean poets, take long rides on old, noisy trains, and the one time she had unprotected sex with a heroin addict in Paris. She longed to be bent over a table or taken in the kitchen or in a hotel room, but then she remembered Jacob had done that with Ampara—she didn't want him looking at her ass and thinking of Ampara's.

"Do you want to make love?" he asked her that night in bed.

"I do and I don't."

"I wish I could follow that."

She rolled over and pointed to the spot on his chest where she used to lay her head when they were first married.

He extended his arm and let her in.

"This feels good," she said.

"Been a long time, too."

"Yeah, sorry," she said.

"Don't apologize. So, you want to make love, or do you just want to skip all that and stay with the cuddling?"

"Is it okay if we just do this?"

"What happened to our libido?"

"I guess I don't have one anymore."

But she was lying.

Jacob Fishman's Marriage: A Novel

3. Cindi Picks on the Paraplegic

"So who can tell me about Bacon?" Cindi asked, after shutting the door of her class inside the Jones Center on the Monday of the third week of the fall semester.

Silence.

"Come on, anyone?"

Silence.

"Apparently, students in Nevada know three philosophers and it's my job to find out which three. Francis . . . Bacon?" she asked slowly.

She looked at the names of the students enrolled in this PHIL 102 Critical Thinking and Reasoning section, now meeting for the fifth time, and was already bored and wished she had gone to that cabin in Idaho and stayed there and started a garden, or, better, as she watched a large student, a football player, in the back of class yawn without covering his mouth, whilst in Ketchum, shot herself in the head like Hemingway. Had she done so, had she put the shotgun to her temple after breakfast, the way Papa had—she actually mouthed the word "Papa" to herself—she could have spared herself the indignity of a course like Critical Thinking with its sixteen different euphemistic names, Intro to Philosophy, Great Conversations, and From Socrates to Sartre, to name three, and the further embarrassment of being civil to her chairman, Hal Howland, his alliterative name a daily annoyance to her. Her friend, her colleague, her Friday-afternoon pot-smoking buddy, Mitch Aloisio, reminded her during the faculty meeting a week before the semester: "This is a big year for you—you know, with the tenure—so try not to annoy Hal, try to control the unkemptness of your attitude, for he, and he alone, will ultimately decide if you wind up here or at Truckee."

Truckee Meadows was the community college in town.

"Easy for you to say, you sanctimonious little whore, you don't have to teach this bullshit course."

"See," said Mitch, "that's exactly the attitude I'm talking about."

She had taken his advice, at least since the beginning of the semester, and accepted the survey courses and the early-morning classes, but now, as the big, yawning jock rested his head on his desk, she was furious with herself for not holding out for at least one upper-level course, like Global Ethics and Justice, or Aesthetics.

"Going once, going twice, Bacon . . . anyone?" she asked again.

There was a young woman, Casey, a paraplegic, in the front row in a special desk to Cindi's right, who was suffering from numerous maladies, including but not limited to multiple sclerosis, Asperger's, and, something at which Cindi could not stop staring but much less severe, bad teeth. Cindi had had Casey in class before and was never fond of the girl or the department's leniency when it came to the work she did or, in most cases, didn't do.

Cindi decided to try. "Casey?"

"What?"

"Bacon!" Cindi repeated.

"Bay . . . Bay . . . Bacon?" the girl tried saying.

"Yes, Francis . . . Bacon," Cindi replied, exhaling.

"What?"

"Bacon," Cindi repeated.

"What . . . was the . . . question?"

"Christ!" Cindi muttered to herself, then out loud, "Who was Bacon?"

Cindi felt the beginning of a migraine over her left eye. That's where they started.

Cindi remembered what Howland had told the faculty at the start of the semester, at the start of every semester since Casey had arrived. "Do not press the girl for answers or stay on her about work, and do not, under any circumstances, fail her. Give her an Incomplete, if you have to. I'll work it out later."

"Hal, that's bullshit," Cindi said at the time.

Mitch, shaking his head at the self-destructive stupidity of his friend, covered his eyes with his hand. He glared at Cindi and mouthed "Shut up."

"Just do it," Howland replied.

"Bay . . . ca . . . con?" Casey tried saying again. Cindi did not remember the girl having a speech impediment.

"Today, Casey, okay?"

The pain, now over Cindi's right eye as well, was throbbing.

"Yes," Casey said again. "Bay . . . con . . . like bacon? I don't know," she said, slowly, maddeningly.

Cindi bit her lower lip, tried to smile. She felt like tearing the young girl's hair out and force-feeding it to her.

"Wasn't he, like, a chef or something?" Casey asked, her stutter suddenly gone.

"A chef?" someone repeated in the back as laughter engulfed the class. "A fucking chef?"

"I . . . I don't know," Casey said, haltingly, the impediment now back. "Probably not a chef. I'm not . . . not . . . not giving you a coherent answer. But he sounds like a chef a little because ba . . . ca . . . con."

And the impediment was back.

Cindi took a step toward Casey. The laughter continued.

Cindi stepped back.

Trying to compose herself, Cindi looked again at Casey and held out her hands, palms up, almost in prayer. Cindi squinted. The pain of her migraine shot to her teeth. "Is that it? A chef? That's your answer?"

The girl shook her head.

"Does anyone else," Cindi asked, looking up at the rest of the class, "have a coherent, or even sane, answer and could articulate that answer in less time than that took or, at least, someone who doesn't have an intermittent and selective speech impediment? Because what just happened there is time we will never recover, and, more to the point, short of that answer, any fucking answer to any question I have today, because if not, I'm going to blow my brains out and then some of you are going to have to clean up brain matter and then waste your entire afternoon filling out forms except, except," she stammered, "well, ya, ya, ya, you know."

The class was silent. Cindi immediately knew she had blown it, all of it. Mocking Casey, mocking a stuttering paraplegic, and threatening suicide. The trifecta.

Then the laughter was back.

"That's some cold shit, Professor," said a student in the second row, holding his mouth. "You kill yourself, can we go early?"

The class erupted once again.

Cindi tried to salvage the situation.

"No," she said, "you cannot. Not unless you clean up really good and fast—and, Casey," she said, forcing her attention to the girl who now had her head on the desk, "I was just joking."

Holy shit, I'm still making blown-out-brain-matter jokes.

Cindi didn't take the time to correct the student that she wasn't, in fact, a full professor, but just an assistant professor, saw students sitting up, straining to see Casey, straining to piece together what just happened.

"He stole from Shakespeare, right, along with that other guy," said another student, Michael S.

"Who stole . . ." asked Cindi, momentarily forgetting what Michael was referring to.

"Bacon and . . . uh, Sherman Johnson," he said.

"Samuel."

"Whatever," said Michael S.

She looked at her three Michaels in the class: Michael L., Michael D., and Michael S., the LDS, whom she called the Michaels of Latter-Day Saints. This usually made her smile.

She wanted to get back to Casey.

"I, uh, hold on—" Cindi started to say. She sat on the edge of the desk. She needed water. She needed pot.

"Casey."

Casey still had her head down.

C'mon! Don't pout, you little shit!

"Casey, I'm sorry. I lost my temper. I was joking, but it was a bad joke. Really. I'm sorry."

But Casey wasn't moving, and Cindi didn't know how long she should pursue this apology. "Anyway, I'm sorry," she said again.

"Shakespeare, Marlowe, Bacon, whoever wrote them, together wrote only about six good plays, anyway. The rest were horseshit and if anybody had the balls to admit it, it would be fucking fantastic. I mean, *Coriolanus.* What the hell is that about?" asked Nina, who sat directly behind Casey.

Cindi wanted to mute the class, so she could try again with Casey, tell her she didn't mean anything, didn't mean to offend her, give the girl a chance to laugh it off and explain that she had provoked it, but the class was unraveling. She had threatened suicide. It was a joke. Everyone knew it was a joke. Surely, they knew that. Cindi could not form words. She could not catch her breath. She felt like vomiting.

"Six plays?" another girl, the German, Siggy, with the short black hair, repeated. "You're saying Shakespeare wrote only six great plays? Maybe if you read something other than *Jane Eyre* and *The Handmaid's Tale,* you'd know how stupid you sound."

"Fuck off," said Nina.

"The question," Siggy continued, "was: Did Bacon write Shakespeare's plays? Let me ask this: Does it matter? They exist, so it's not important six hundred years later. And there are more than just six, just so you know. You Americans are the most arrogant, ignorant people. It's all personality and fame and your connection with the artist, whether there's a happy, understandable ending, a throughline, a narrative. It's the work, the work, the work! You're missing an entire world. No wonder everyone hates you."

"The fuck are you talking about?" asked Nina. "You're two generations away from throwing Jews and gypsies in ovens and practicing skeet-shooting with their babies, Frau Siggy, so don't lecture us about behavior and sophistication and national intelligence. You fucking murdered people."

Siggy stood up, grabbed her bag, and walked toward the door, but before she exited, Nina started singing, "*Deutschland, Deutschland über alles, über alles in der Welt.*" Siggy stopped, glared at Nina.

"Bring it, bitch," Nina replied, standing. "I'm here."

Siggy kicked the door, opened it, and said, "Fuck all the way off, whore" in an exaggerated German accent before leaving. Nina started to follow.

"Sit down, Nina," Cindi said, catching enough breath to form words again.

"Just trying to help."

"Thanks, I think."

This was not supposed to be about Bacon's supposed ghosting of Shakespeare, nor the problems with American students and their approach to literature, nor the international incident happening before her eyes, but rather Bacon's advocacy of Aristotle and an empirical, inductive approach to scientific and philosophical discovery. That's what Cindi wanted to talk about, what she had prepared to talk about.

"This is—" Cindi started to say

"Fucking dead rich white guys anyway. Why are we studying them, Mrs. Fishman?" asked Derek, another UNR football player in the class.

Mrs.? Jesus!

"Why are these the masters?"

"This is . . . not what I want to talk about," said Cindi, standing up and throwing the chalk she held toward the back of the class. It pinged off a window.

"For the love of absolute fuck, Derek, those dead rich white guys— and I don't like them any more than you—while making a lot of money in their day, weren't as well off as students at public universities, okay? They didn't get free tuition, for starters, for playing a game."

The class was silent, shocked.

"What's up her ass today?" a student in the back asked.

Cindi knew this was untenable.

"Here's the thing," Cindi said, trying to recover. She remembered a joke Jacob had told her. "As Woody Allen once said, 'Whether Shake-

speare wrote all his own plays or Bacon did or Marlowe, I wouldn't
write any of their checks.'"

The joke fell flat.

She had gotten the punchline wrong. It was supposed to be "cash"
any of their checks, not "write," not that it would have mattered. Even
her Michaels of Latter-Day Saints were frowning. Nina was suddenly
disinterested. Derek was glowering. Other students were giggling.

The class was gone. The moment was gone. Her career was probably
gone.

Casey looked up.

Don't tell me she's crying.

"Bacon talked about idols," Cindi said, because she didn't know
what else to say. "Remember what we were talking about last week,
what seems like a lifetime ago, and how Bacon said"—she picked up *The
Masculine Birth of Time*—"'On waxen tablets you cannot write
anything new until you rub out the old. With the mind it is not so; there
you cannot rub out the old till you have written in the new.' So what's
he saying there?"

Silence.

"Let's talk about the importance of the palimpsest."

Nothing.

"Let's try this." Cindi turned to face the board, wishing someone
would shoot her in the back, or that the board would come unmoored
from the wall and knock her unconscious, at least, and, if there was a
God, mortally wound her. She could feel herself starting to hyperventilate. She wanted to cry. She must not cry.

She bit her lip, hoping to draw blood, and wrote "Idols" on the
board and underneath:

1) The state of nature

2) The state of the human mind

3) The deplorable limits of man's dominion over the universe to
their promised bounds

4) The solution: to find a new method for "quiet entry into mind so
choked and overgrown"

"Remember," she said, though she knew no one was listening, as she turned around, "Bacon eventually called Aristotle the 'worst of sophists, stupefied by his own unprofitable subtlety.'"

The class stared at her. Those who weren't scared of her had lost interest in her.

"You mean like religion?" Casey asked.

Cindi had no idea what she was talking about, asking about, but saw an opening.

"Yes, but more specifically than just religion," Cindi asked.

"I don't know, like, organized religion?" Casey asked. "Religion that's, you . . . you know . . . oh, I don't know," she said, dropping her head to her desk again. "Like religion," she said, popping up her head.

Watching Casey's head pop up and down, Cindi thought of the game Whack-a-mole and her sudden, explicable desire to play it.

JACOB FISHMAN'S MARRIAGE: A NOVEL

4. Plato's Guide to Schwarzenegger

It had been eighteen months since Hal Howland replaced Bill Belsky (and what was it about the alliteration in the names of department heads at UNR?) as chairman of the department of philosophy at at the school, and in that time, he had called Cindi at home only once, and that was to alert her to a new time for a group faculty photo. With Belsky, with whom she got along, officially gone, the university wanted a new photo of those in the department. When she asked Howland what to wear, he said, "Business casual."

"I don't have business casual. I don't wear business casual. I don't even know what that is, frankly," she told him.

She came in a cotton brown abaya, a bowler, and black Frye Boots with buckles on the side. The photo was taken on the UNR quad with Cindi in the back, smiling, with her bowler pulled down almost over her eyes.

"Cindi, today if you get a minute, stop by," her chairman said on the phone.

"Sure."

"Thanks. Make it around two."

She knew.

Casey Morgan.

"You worried?" Jacob asked, as she left the house.

"Yes. No. I don't know. I screwed up."

"You get fired, I'll support you. I don't know how, but I'll support you. There's a world of geology out there, a lot of rocks, a lot of extraction companies anxious and eager to rape the earth, and I will write about every one if I have to."

"Thanks, babe. Maybe the sweetest thing you ever said to me."

Edmund J. Cain Hall was, by all accounts, the ugliest building on the UNR campus, with its long hallways, dim lighting, and off-white walls. A two-story building, it housed the military-science department (which could be used as a bomb shelter), the Latino Research Center, KUNR, the public radio station, the computer repair services center for the university, and, almost as an afterthought, the philosophy department, though not all the classes were held there, which explained Cindi's section in the Jones Center. From the outside, Cain Hall, with the bowed and raised white exterior on the back of the building, looked like it could be the university's physical plant. For reasons not entirely clear—the child-care center was not housed there—blue and yellow and red playground equipment sat alongside the building. The joke was that it was insurance for when all the philosophy majors had nervous breakdowns and reverted to their childhoods. Cindi used to sit on the teeter-totter by herself, at times, between classes, and eat lunch or read or review her current professional predicament.

The philosophy department had three full-time professors, of which Mitch was one, along with Howland and a man named Milt, with whom Cindi was not on speaking terms for reasons she could no longer recall, one associate professor, four assistant professors, including Cindi, and one lecturer, Beene Olde. Like many philosophy departments across the country, the program at UNR was in a disciplinary civil war between the Analytic and Continental Divisions. Analytic philosophers delineate philosophical problems by reducing them to their parts and to the relations in which these parts stand and which can be conveyed adequately in language, whereas Continental philosophers address the large questions synthetically and consider particular issues to be parts of the more expansive unities and think reality is ultimately beyond under-standing because of the limits of language. Analytic philosophers would include people like Bertrand Russell, Ludwig Wittgenstein (even if Continentals claimed him, too), G.E. Moore, and Gottlob Frege, while the continental philosophers included Kierkegaard, Nietzsche, Hegel, Heidegger, and Bergson.

The Analytics were at the moment ruling UNR. Cindi, of course, was Continental.

"Cindi, sit."

When he was angry, Howland spoke to her as he would a dog. It was not the time, Cindi deduced, to call him on his tone.

Stop thinking about the alliteration of Hal Howland, Hal Howland, she told herself when she felt herself about to giggle.

Howland, a New Yorker, a graduate of Columbia, was behind his metal desk, trying to figure out his new twenty-inch iMac, which the university had given to most, but not all, faculty members.

"This isn't good, is it?" Cindi asked, walking to the chair in front of her desk to do what he commanded. She was thinking about the Dell laptop she was still working on and the iMac the university had not gotten her.

"Why don't you tell me?"

"Why don't I tell you what?"

"Cindi."

"Let me guess. Casey."

"Casey," he repeated. He picked up a piece of paper from his desk, started reading to himself and then aloud, " . . . time we will never recover, by the way—and, short of that, any answer at all, because if not, I'm going to blow my brains out and . . . brain matter . . . and there's going to be a lot of forms to fill out after I do." He put the paper down. "You working on a club act?"

Cindi reminded herself to breathe. She inhaled. She had forgotten to brush her teeth.

Don't curse, don't curse, don't curse.

"Oh, fuck, Hal, you should have been there. She was playing with me. And who told you all that? Was someone transcribing the class without my knowledge? I don't approve."

Howland looked at her, expressionless.

"Maybe that doesn't matter," she said, "but that was bullshit, what she pulled." Cindi took another breath. She could taste Nutri-Grain Strawberry, Coca-Cola, and a banana from the last twelve hours, but not toothpaste.

"You made fun of her speech, her stuttering . . . her intelligence?"

"She doesn't always stutter, that's the thing. She was playing with me. She was playing me."

This was not how she had rehearsed it. She continued.

"She kept saying, 'Ba . . . Ba . . . Ba . . . con. She can say 'Bacon.' I've heard her say 'Bacon.' She called him a chef. A fucking chef. That should prove she was playing with me."

Howland spread his hands in front of him.

"That's it? That's your explanation?"

"She said she couldn't give me a coherent answer to some question," Cindi said slowly, "so I repeated it, which, okay, was kind of stupid, but she was smiling when she said it and then she put her head down on the desk. She was mocking me. I was smiling when I said it. The kids around her knew I was. And if that little shit Casey were honest, she'd tell you the same thing."

"Didn't I tell you to leave her alone? Didn't I say—Mitch was there, too, everyone was—if there were any problems to let me know first?"

"But, Hal—"

"Let me finish!"

"Sorry."

"I didn't think I had to say 'And if she has her head down in class and doesn't want to answer, don't mock her speech or throw a chalk at her—'"

"I didn't throw it at her—"

"And I didn't think I had to say, 'Cindi, do not threaten to blow your brains out and then remind your class it had to clean up the mess.'"

"I didn't throw anything at her. I threw chalk at the back window, not at her, and my suicide threat wasn't really a threat. But, okay, stupid."

"I didn't think I had to say that, either, because I figured you, even you, would be smarter than that, kinder than that. I thought, considering Casey's condition and the fact that many eighteen-, nineteen-, and twenty-year-old kids might be horrified by the professor blowing her brains out, you were smarter and kinder than that."

The "kinder" hit Cindi like a punch.

"She is now walking, rolling, around campus bitching about her treatment in the—and listen to what I'm telling you—philosophy department. Not in Cindi Fishman's class, not in a philosophy class, but her treatment in the whole, to use a word you would understand, fucking department. Am I making myself clear? She came to see me and wondered why you were allowing the whole class to laugh at her."

"What? I—"

"And wondering," he continued, his voice rising, as he pointed at Cindi to stop talking, "a: If she should go to the provost with this, b: If I would go to the provost for her, and c: Why you hate the disabled."

"I don't hate the disabled."

Hal Howland. Hal Howland.

Howland took off his glasses and tossed them on his brand-new computer keyboard. They fell to the floor. He made no effort to retrieve them.

"Sorry, Hal. Can I say something here?" She continued without getting an answer. "Who answers essentially a yes-or-no question with 'This isn't going to be a coherent answer'?"

"You're missing the point," Howland said in almost a whisper.

"The point," Cindi said, "is I don't want to be doing this class to begin with. The point is Beene should be teaching it because he's the graduate assistant."

It may not have been the worst response she could have given, but it was close.

Exasperated, Hal smiled, shaking his head, and then cupped his head in his hand.

"Sorry," she said quickly. "Should I apologize?"

"If you can do it without making it worse."

"Hal, I—"

"Cindi—"

"I didn't pick on—"

"Goddamn it, Cindi! Just listen to me."

"Sorry. Sorry," she said again.

"She'll probably let it go," said Hal, already calmed down, "which will be good for all of us."

Us? Oh, me. Tenure. Fuck.

"Hal, I didn't fucking do anything."

"That's it." Howland raised his hand and turned his back. "You can go."

Cindi Fishman had been dismissed.

She walked down the hall to Mitch's office, passing Fitzermann's office and Fitzermann, who happened to be in.

She waved. He didn't wave back.

She stopped at Mitch's door. He was wearing a Reno Aces baseball hat, wrapped in a crocheted afghan, black and red with stars and three Lucky 7's in the design of a slot machine. Mitch had a Ph.D. from Penn State, and taught primarily in the honors program at UNR, though also lectured on Plato, Aristotle, Xenophon, and Kierkegaard, as well as the Hebrew Scriptures and the Talmud. He was the smartest man Cindi knew. Bright, bold with a welcoming smile and a mop of salt-and-pepper hair, he was the light in every room, the hand everyone wanted to shake, the shoulder everyone wanted to touch, the mind into which everyone wanted to peer.

He was who Cindi wanted to be.

With the dartboard and the preposterous afghan and the beginning of the last verse of Van Morrison's "Saint Dominic's Preview"—she loved and hated the part about determining the state you're in—coming from the coral-red Bose Bluetooth speaker on his desk, Cindi was overwhelmed and intimidated by Mitch's calm and identity, which was simultaneously self-conscious and genuine.

Cindi could feel the chill as she walked in.

"My nipples are hard."

"My work is done."

"Why is it so cold in here?"

"I work better," he said, as she walked to the front of his desk and sat down. He was still facing the board.

Mitch threw his last dart.

"I saw Howland."

"I heard. Everyone heard. You got him to scream?" He turned to face her. Mitch was eating Wiley Wallaby Red Licorice.

"You could hear him scream? Oh, Jesus."

"Loud and clear, pal."

"God, how can you eat that stuff? It's all wrong. You eat Twizzlers or you eat nothing at all."

"Hey, who's got tenure?"

"Blow me," said Cindi. "Oh, I said hi to little pig man. Thought it was time to bury the hatchet, but not in his head."

"Why do you call Milt 'little pig man'? He's actually a good-looking man."

"I don't know. Because I'm a terrible person and he did something sometime somewhere that pissed me off."

"What?"

"I don't remember."

"Perfect. Hey, Hal didn't bring up the tenure, right?"

"Why would he?"

"He shouldn't have, but I was curious. You're no longer A.B.D., so it's not like he can throw that at you, if he wanted to deny you."

"Tell me what that means again."

"All but dissertation."

"Ah, right. Oh, yeah, it's done. I am no longer an unrelenting rabid procrastinator."

"Nobody can say you're not overly dramatic. Good God!"

"Guilty."

"Excellent. You're done. Now, you wait."

"Not really excellent. You think 'Life as Literature: Self-Invention in Nietzsche and Beyond' is an excellent dissertation?"

Mitch was expressionless.

"I knew it," said Cindi. "I knew. It sucks."

"It doesn't suck. It beats another paper on the Novel Savage in us all, or something about Queequeg, Daggoo, and Tashtego. You want to kill the whale or just talk about it for six hundred pages?"

"I'm not fighting with you about Melville again. Besides, after today, Casey has a better chance of getting tenure. By the way, nice computer," she added, pointing to his Mac.

"What?"

"Nothing. It's just a bad day."

"Casey works the system. She works you."

"Hey, do you . . . I mean, you don't think . . ."

"No, this thing with Casey is not going to affect your tenure. It didn't help the chitchat around you, but, no, if that's what you're worried about."

Cindi nodded.

"The tenure committee doesn't mark off for bad comebacks or errant tosses of erasers and chalk," Mitch continued.

"I didn't fucking throw anything at anybody!"

"Relax, I'm joking. Of course, in your case, mocking the only disabled student in the department who's trying to make a better life for herself is not something I'd recommend to others. Want some licorice?"

"Got any heroin?"

"I'm out."

"I guess I can't blame her. I don't know how she does it. I have a hard time getting off my chaise most days, so having to do what she does, damn, it's impressive. It's a shame she's such a cunt."

"You were almost home."

"I know. It was *soooo* close."

Cindi sat on the corner of his desk, picked up a dart and threw it at the board. Its trajectory barely made it to the other side of the desk before crashing to the floor.

"I'm so fucked."

"Nice throw."

"She can't get me fired, can she?"

"I don't think so."

"Damn it!"

"She won't get you fired."

Cindi exhaled, picked up another dart, leaned back, and threw it at the ceiling. It stuck in the Cortega lay-in tile.

"Look at that. Do I win something?"

"A bag of licorice," Mitch said, tossing her the bag of Wiley Wallaby.

"We on for this Friday?" she asked, opening the bag and putting two in her mouth.

Late on Friday afternoons, since Nevada's passage of legalized adult-use cannabis, Mitch and Cindi would sit in his office and smoke pot from the six growing cannabis plants Mitch was allowed by law. Since UNR was a state school, funded by taxpayers, and pot was technically a controlled substance, at least as far as the feds were concerned pot was still illegal, he hid the plants behind an autographed 2009 UNR Wolfpack football also on the windowsill.

"Then next week, Vegas, right?" He reminded her of the Wittgenstein and Heidegger Conference they were both attending.

"I hate Vegas," Cindi said.

"Most beautiful city in the world," said Mitch, "if you start from the premise that a city, by its nature, is man-made, and since there was nothing in Southern Nevada but desert and Las Vegas is nothing but man-made, no nature to help define it, it is actually more magnificent than Rome."

"Unless you don't start from that premise. How about starting from the one where it's filled with sewers and pasties and sweat and desperation."

"You say that like it's a bad thing."

"And you think Rome is magnificent?"

"How does Jacob live with you?"

"Tell me about it. He asks himself that all the time. But last week was good, somehow."

"Really?"

"For me, anyway. Jacob didn't stare off into space every time I talked to him."

"Oh, shit, I have class. Plato. Wanna come?" he asked, grabbing some papers.

"It's the one I should be teaching."

"Maybe you can teach it at Truckee—you know, after you get fired."

"Blow me." Cindi laughed. "Or did I already tell you to do that? Those military guys make me nervous," Cindi said, as they passed the military-science department and KUNR on the way to his classroom.

"Those NPR guys make me nervous," said Mitch. "Behave," he said, as he opened the door and walked into class in front of her, which still had PHIL 610: PLATO on a piece of paper on the bottom-right section of the window.

"Welcome me!" he bellowed, his hand sweeping down in front of him, as the class stood and bowed in unison. He headed to the front of the class, as Cindi stood at the door, astounded at what she had just witnessed.

"Guys, some of you may know Professor Fishman. She's going to be joining us today and has, she assures me, promised to behave."

Cindi smiled at Mitch and motioned to him that she would be sitting in the back. The room was set in a semicircle. There were a dozen students, half the number she had—one of the Michaels, too, who smiled at her. She smiled back. She took a seat in the corner, near the window, next to the open blinds. Two students sat in front of her, six to her side.

Mitch started with some small talk, handing back some papers. Cindi started sweating almost immediately. It was January, but in the seventies, inconceivable for Northern Nevada. She was not near the rod to close the blinds, so instead of moving, instead of asking to have them closed, for she didn't dare interrupt, she sat. And began to sweat.

Mitch sat at a desk in front, facing the class, eschewing the portable lectern that was on a desk behind him. He was still wearing the Reno Aces hat and, along with his books and papers, had taken the bag of Australian licorice, which he, before putting one in his mouth like a cigar, placed on the lectern.

He already knew the students by name, even the one who wasn't supposed to be there.

"Jesse," he said, "before we start, are you officially in the class, auditing, or just stealing knowledge from a master?"

"I'm auditing," Jesse said. "Is that okay?"

"You missed an easy opportunity for cheap praise. Don't let it happen again. Still, you may stay."

Mitch began reading from some notes on a ledger pad.

"All right, we'll review what Ethan started last week, the Nicias and Laches debate over this business of courage and confidence, but I want to bring something up. And since we're early in the semester, and a little off the subject, what do the rest of you think of the statement by Socrates that no one under thirty should even engage in philosophy?"

Four started talking at once. Mitch let them all speak, in turn, cajoling, praising, making them expand on their answers.

Cindi sat mesmerized, feeling the perspiration run down the small of her back. He was a maestro. She smiled at Mitch, who smiled back and winked, while he introduced the discussion concerning Socrates, Nicias, and Laches about the best way to raise young men.

"Socrates talks about, essentially, being 'decent by nature' and what that means in terms of children and how they would relate to their adopted parents, if they were to have them, and their biological parents, who they may not know.

"Should there," he continued, "be a distinction between the two sets of parents? Can what you know about yourself, say if you were Baptist, change once you find out about Baptists? If you are raised a Baptist and come later to reject it and then you say, 'Well, that's not me,' you, as the adopted child, are saying to the adopted parents, your adopted parents, I am not from you.' At that point does the adopted parent have a right to say, essentially, 'Listen, you little shit, we made you who you are. We raised you.'"

Cindi smiled at "little shit."

"A child, if decent by nature, as Socrates says, would have to see that those adopted parents deserve something. You, in essence, have one foot in that cave, one outside."

The heat from the window was making Cindi dizzy, but she was mesmerized at the ease and love Mitch had for his world at the moment. She thought of her caves, UNR and Jacob, and what she owed both. She felt like crying.

"Courage is not," Mitch said, "at least in the context of the discussion with Nicias and Laches, only about strength. There must be something to overcome, some fear. If an NFL team plays a team consisting of junior high school students, there is nothing courageous about them. Confidence, yes, but where's the fear? Without overcoming fear, and let me say it again, there can be no courage. Cindi!" she heard Mitch say.

"Yes?" she answered, stunned.

"Are you hot?"

She heard laughter.

Mitch was smiling and blowing from the front of the class as if to cool her down.

The class was laughing.

She felt embarrassed. How badly was she sweating?

"Yes, I'm going to move or I'll pass out, which will ruin the show if you have to revive me before the paramedics get here."

The class laughed. Mitch laughed.

She got a laugh.

I got a laugh.

"No, no, stay there. Lacy," Mitch said to the girl in front of Cindi, "will you close the blinds, please, as our guest is about to pass out, which will necessitate many, many forms having to be filled out when the authorities arrive."

"I'd be happy to."

The class looked at Cindi, as Lacy got up and swiveled the rod closed on a window that Cindi felt like jumping through.

"Better?" asked Mitch.

"Much," Cindi said, though she felt no cooler, as she already felt her shirt and pants sticking to the linoleum seat.

Mitch turned his attention back to the class.

"Now, let's talk about this statement: 'Fighting in armor is like a drug for the eyes.' Is that, in fact, true, as Socrates points out? If you are in armor, and essentially Laches says that Nicias looks ridiculous when wearing his, what does that say about the notion of confidence and courage? Where is the courage if you are covered head to toe in armor? Now, remember in *Terminator Three*," Mitch said, perpetuating a favorite pedagogical stunt of philosophy professors, throwing in popular culture to illustrate antiquity and to prove their hipness, "Ahnold doesn't kill anyone. This fierce warrior who destroys everyone in the first two movies doesn't here. What does that tell us about what Socrates calls 'prudent steadfastness,' other than not sleeping with your maid, impregnating her, if you eventually become the governor of California?"

The class erupted.

He barely took a breath and then went on to talk about the Athenians and the Spartans, whom he referred to without pretension as the Lacedaemonians, and then went to the board and wrote "KLEOS."

"Glory," he said. "Nicias is about his own glory, not about the souls of these young men. So much so that he later loses an entire naval battalion because he's afraid to retreat, which would have been the smart thing to do in this fight with the Syracusans, because he was afraid to go back to Athens because of what it would mean to his"—Mitch tapped his chest—"honor, his glory."

Mitch wrote "MOROS" on the board.

He was just playing darts, Cindi thought.

"Moros. The god of Doom. This is your friend nobody likes."

The class laughed again.

Those were the only two words Mitch wrote on the board all day— "MOROS" and "KLEOS." When not at the lectern, he sat at the table in front of the class, crossing and uncrossing his legs, removing and putting back on his glasses, reading from the text quickly, but authoritatively and clearly. No missteps, strategic open-mic comedy moments, no stupid comments in the direction of a paraplegic girl.

She would never invite Mitch to one of her classes.

As Mitch was making a reference to the power of Bill Gates, the power of secularism, one of the students, a thin girl from Bangladesh, asked about God and whether Socrates ever talked of heaven.

"Ask two Jews that question," said Mitch, "you'll get three answers."

Mitch winked at Cindi.

"What about mind and body?" the girl asked. "Is Socrates saying that one was more important than the other?"

Mitch smiled. "I have a friend who's brilliant and worked on his mind at the expense of his body, so he grew fat and old and developed diabetes and eventually died. Socrates is saying that both, mind and body, need attention. In other words, even philosophers need Zumba."

And Cindi got Casey.

The class was over.

Cindi waited in her chair by the closed blinds and watched the students, all twelve of them, stop to ask Mitch something, to get an assignment, to make sure they got a quote right, to flirt. She heard laughs and saw smiles.

When they all left, Cindi got up.

"I want to quit teaching now and sell cellphone face plates at a mall kiosk. You're amazing."

"Thanks. What did you think of my joke?"

"You mean about the Jews?"

"Yeah."

"It was all right. Personally, I like to threaten suicide to lighten things up."

That night, with Jacob asleep and Cindi on the chaise, she pulled out her diary from under the seat, which she had to remind herself not to leave there anymore, and started writing.

"I cannot begin to talk about today. I fucked with Hal . . . again. I wouldn't give me tenure at this point, even though I deserve it. I don't know, maybe I don't. Hal Howland . . . Hal Howland. Mitch was a maestro, and I don't know whether it's his intellect or temperament, but he wasn't just respected, he was loved. They fucking loved him. I FUCKING LOVED HIM!!!! He turned me on (and I was also burning up). He winked at me. I lost my breath for a second. They were in awe of him, but he was approachable. He was their friend. I can't do that. Even if I wasn't so angry all the time, wasn't so angry at Jacob and my life and at not having a baby, I can't do it . . . can't do that. Something in me is not right. There's a gap in my—I don't know—my maturity, my growth, my soul, my being. I was watching Mitch and thought, 'Quit.' Everybody should just quit and get out of the classroom. Let Mitch teach everything. The cliche can choke me, but there was a light today, there was heat today. He had LIGHT AND HEAT! I bring none of those things to class. On my best fucking days, I bring none of that. I should fuck my husband tonight."

THE BOTCHED
COLONOSCOPY

"What am I doing to my wife?"

As the Midazolam and Propofol coursed through his body, the colonoscopy literally moments away, Jacob wasn't sure this, any of this, was going to work—and he might also have colon cancer. He was rethinking his first three chapters, their names and their content: "Anyone's Baby," even with another draft that he liked only slightly better than the earlier ones, for it still had the fictional Cindi anxious to sleep with Dave to get pregnant; "Cindi Picks on the Paraplegic," with its depiction of the fictional Cindi as cruel, petulant, and suicidal; and "Plato's Guide to Schwarzenegger," specifically her jealousy of Mitch and her functionality, or lack of it, around adults. He wasn't convinced he had made the case that Cindi was a university professor, even though the real Cindi, in fact, was, and was good at it. The last thing he remembered thinking before the drugs took their total effect, though, was not about either Cindi or Jacob, but Michael Jackson, who had died from an overdose of Propofol—or maybe it was the Midazolam that killed him in bed. He remembered reading about Jackson's room, the dirty socks in the closet. He had also met Joe Jackson, Michael's father, in Vegas once and found him the most disagreeable man he had ever experienced. His mind wandered from the evil of Jackson's father to the incompetence of Jackson's doctor to the weirdness of Jackson's keeping all those monkeys and began to feel sympathetic to the pop star.

I could die, so why are my last thoughts about Michael Jackson's lot in life?

Maybe not his last thoughts—not entirely, for he was also thinking about how much of the inner workings of the UNR philosophy department he should include in the novel. He knew about its dynamic from what Cindi told him, knew about Mitch and Howland, and Belsky, as well as a little about the discipline itself—and by that, he knew about Socrates, Plato, and Aristotle—but his eyes invariably glazed over when she began talking, say, of Kierkegaard, who was Danish and one of the early, if not the earliest, existential philosophers, or Wittgenstein, who was Austrian, a classmate of Hitler's (but even that was in dispute), who some believe initiated Hitler's hatred of the Jews by being mean to him in class. He also knew John Locke was important, but no matter how many times Cindi told him, he couldn't recall why. He would need to have at least a working knowledge of the major philosophers for *Jacob Fishman's Marriage* to have any authenticity. His wife could be of some help, but she was not inclined to elucidate these figures just so his trashing of her, adding to the fodder, as it were, in a novel would seem more real. How much did he need to include in *Jacob Fishman's Marriage,* anyway? Getting Francis Bacon in the story seemed right, as Bacon would be covered in a Critical Thinking and Reasoning class, so he did the research on Bacon's connection to Plato. The fictional Mitch's lecture on the Moros, Kleos, and Lacedaemonians sounded, to Jacob, at least, authentic, if a bit of a mash-up. As part of his research for *Jacob Fishman's Marriage,* Jacob sat in on a Critical Thinking and Reasoning class at Truckee Meadows Community College and found the instructor dynamic and funny and instructive. Jacob made notes about how his students adored him, hung on every word, so when it came to creating the fictional Mitch, Jacob gave Mitch these qualities. Jacob thought of asking Mitch, himself if he could sit in on a class, but decided it was a peculiar betrayal (and literary device) to use the real

Mitch for the underpinnings of the fake one who would probably wind up fucking Jacob's fictional wife.

But first he needed to find out if the blood in his stool was from colon cancer. He could feel the cocktail about to complete its rounds.

As Cindi sat in the waiting room at St. Mary's Regional Medical Center, waiting for her husband to come out of recovery, she knew that someone might find it funny that a day starting with her husband's colonoscopy would end with her watching Carrot Top at the Luxor in Las Vegas.

She, however, was not one of them.

The nurse walked in.

"He's awake," she said. "You can go see him."

In his hospital cubicle, enclosed on three sides by a blue curtain, Jacob was awakened by the sound of a doctor and a woman patient in the next partitioned cubicle.

"Well," the woman said, "how am I?"

"Fine. No polyps."

"None?"

"None."

"Thank you, Jesus."

"You can call me Dr. Milsten."

Jacob awoke to a punchline. He was alive.

"This is good," he thought. Michael Jackson is dead.

Why am I still thinking about Michael Jackson?

He wanted to go back to sleep.

"Hey," Cindi said, walking into the recovery room.

Jacob sat up. "Hey. How am I?"

"You're the biggest man he's ever seen."

"Huh?" he asked.

"The doctor. He said you were the largest man he had ever seen."

"What?"

"Something about your colon? I don't know. A big colon, a big anus, a big rectum, a big prostate. I stopped listening at rectum."

"Smart woman. What else?"

"Here he is," said Cindi, noticing the doctor behind the doctor, "ask him yourself."

"Can I come in?" said Dr. Milsten.

"Sure," Jacob said. "All those years of meatball parmesan sandwiches destroyed my colon, yes?"

"No," he said. "Three polyps, small. Took them out. Not cancerous —I mean, pretty sure they're not. But we didn't get to see it all."

"I'm not following you."

"As I told your wife," said Milsten, "we had to do a barium enema."

"What does that mean?"

"You weren't cleaned out all the way."

"Cleaned out. That's a medical term, right?"

"And you woke up in the middle of the procedure."

"Lovely."

"You're fine, really. We'll redo the test in five years."

"Five? Why not ten? Because of the polyps?"

"Five because the doctors need to make money," interrupted Cindi.

"Wow. Never mind her," said Jacob.

"You're fine," Milsten said, ignoring Cindi. "You can go home whenever you feel like getting up."

"Thank you, Jesus."

Milsten smiled and left.

"I think they botched the colonoscopy," Cindi said.

"Why would you say that?"

"What do you want to bet?"

"I don't want to bet."

"Mark my words."

"You're a strange girl. You want to help me get dressed? You have to go soon, right? Your conference."

Cindi helped Jacob up and to put on his shirt and pants.

"Be gentle. I've been massively probed."

"You big baby. I need to get you home."

"When do you have to go?"

"It's not that—I mean, it is that. Unless you want me to stay home?"

"You want to go, you can go."

"Can I?"

"Go. Go. Do. Do."

"I so want to hit you now. You have to rest anyway, and Lisa said she'll check on you."

"I thought I was cleaned out."

"Jacob, I don't know. You heard him."

Cindi guided him in putting on his shoes and then held his arm and led him into the wheelchair and wheeled him out. She tried not to appear that she was rushing as she wheeled him through the lobby, but she was. Her plane to Vegas left in three hours. She and Mitch, the real ones, were, in fact, actually going to a conference on "Philosophy of Language" and "Early Analytic Philosophy," in which the schedule looked like a fight card, including a symposium on "Realistic Analysis Versus Pragmatist Explication," Leonard Linsky on "Russell and Meinong, Predicativism and Referentialism about Proper Names," and Wittgenstein on "Logicism."

"You know," said Cindi, wheeling him past the front desk, "you could have done this any other day but the day I was leaving."

"This is the first day he had, and I was a little concerned, you know, with the blood and all, so I took today. It couldn't be helped. Sorry."

"I don't mind. I'm your wife. I'm just saying. I'm still pissed you didn't tell me you saw some blood."

"It's not something you talk about."

"You shouldn't have kept this from me."

"Kept it from you? I'm not having an affair. I didn't tell you about blood in my stool. That's different, no? I figured if I had colon cancer or whatever, I would tell you when I knew for sure. What husband says to his wife, 'Honey, I think I have colon cancer' because he comes out of the bathroom and sees blood? 'Come look, why don't you?' Where did you park the car, Salt Lake City?"

"As close as I could. Stop busting my balls, Jake. And you should have told me, is all I'm saying. And you drink too much Diet Coke. That shit causes cancer."

"What? It does not."

"Don't be a moron. Of course it does."

"Slow down a little. I'm getting dizzy."

"I'm your wife, for Chrissakes! If you're not going to tell me, what's the point of even being married?"

Jacob thought this a strange time to construct the sentence quite that way, an odd time to call him a moron, but maybe, he thought, it was the drugs and he heard it wrong, even though he knew, even if the barium dye overstayed its welcome in his bloodstream, he had not. His head wasn't pounding as much as he felt underwater.

"Are we having a fight?" he asked.

"No."

"You sure? 'Cause it sounds like one."

"You're on drugs, you're hallucinating. We're not fighting. I'm a sweet fucking wife."

"If you say so, but I don't know, it sounds like we are," he replied, the words not wanting to come out.

"We will if you don't stop talking about having one."

Cindi got Jacob in the car, put his seat belt on for him, and pulled onto South Virginia Street for the short drive home.

"I'm sorry," he said, "I should have told you, and, promise, next time there's some unusual activity around my ass, blood, for instance, I'll let you know. I wonder what the blood was, though, if I'm generally okay."

"He told me while you were in recovery you probably just had trouble squeezing one out."

Jacob started laughing.

"Yeah, that's what he said."

"Squeezing one out? Twelve years of medical school and that's his expert diagnosis: squeezing one out? I want to be the insurance adjuster who reads that. Did he say why the gunk I drank didn't clean me out?"

"Apparently you didn't drink enough of it."

"I followed the directions."

"Apparently not."

"I did what it told me to do."

"Don't yell at me. You were supposed to drink the whole bottle."

"I drank the whole bottle."

"Why are you arguing with me?"

"Who else am I going to argue with?"

"Not me," Cindi said, putting on the radio.

"That's Van Morrison, right? 'Saint Dominic's Parish'?"

"*Preview*—not *Parish*. And I'm the one who was with you all morning and I hate hospitals, remember?"

"I think, as the kids like to say, this isn't about you."

"Was I not a good wife?"

"Yes, you were great."

"Who's been there for you?"

It was a game they played.

"You were, dear."

"Who gets wifely duty points?"

"You. Now," Jacob continued, "did he say anything else?"

"Stop! I don't know. Call him. You're fine. Your ass is fine. You had three polyps, you drink too much diet soda."

"He didn't say that."

"He should have."

Cindi was darting in and out of traffic, running yellow lights. Jacob smiled as she maneuvered.

"Mario, slow down. My colon."

"Mario?"

"Andretti. Jesus! What kind of life did you lead that you get no popular references?"

"Blow me."

"Nice."

"I'm in a hurry. I have to get you home, in bed."

"Take me to bed or lose me forever."

"One more *Top Gun* reference and I'm throwing your ass out of the car, sore colon or no sore colon."

"Good. You got one."

"Now. Do you want me to get you some ginger ale or something?" she asked as they drove by the university. "Not that I have the time."

"I'm fine. I'm going to bed. I appreciate you doing this."

"What do you mean . . . appreciate? I'm your wife. I'm not doing you a favor. Jesus, don't make me feel bad."

"I'm not trying to make you feel bad."

"I feel that way."

The medication was, as best he could calculate it, forty percent out of his body, so Jacob was still dizzy. His marriage was making him dizzy. Cindi was making him dizzy.

"You sure you don't want anything?" Cindi asked again.

"No."

When they got home, Cindi helped him inside, straightened up the sheets, made the bed, and then unmade it, so Jacob could get in.

"You're not going to take your pants off?" she asked as he climbed in. "I mean, don't you think you should?"

"I think you think I should."

"It's really unsanitary to sleep in a bed with your pants on."

"We've had this conversation before, haven't we?"

"It's your fictional couple."

"It is not."

Jacob really couldn't remember which Fishman couple had said it.

"Okay, we've had it. Take your pants off."

Her attention to detail, both quirky and cold, made him smile. Maybe this was all he would get out of life, out of marriage, out of this marriage. But if that was the case—and it was—why, now thinking about "Anyone's Baby," "Cindi Picks on the Paraplegic," and "Plato's Guide to Schwarzenegger," did he not, could he not, make Jacob and Cindi happier?

"I'll take them off."

"Do what you want, but I think you should."

"I am. I am going to take my pants off."

They both were incapable of letting the other have the last word.

"Let me help you," Cindi said, getting on her knees.

"Now this is working out," he said, putting his hands behind his head.

"Oh, stop it. You're not getting a blow job. God knows what's going on down there. Just sleep, okay, sleep."

"Yes, sleep. I will sleep and rest my weary anus."

He felt Cindi kiss him gently on the lips. He closed his eyes, expecting another kiss.

He didn't get one.

"I'm leaving," Cindi said, gently pushing on his shoulder. "Sorry, but I have to get to the airport, check in, meet Mitch. Do you need anything, though, before I go?"

"Go. I'm fine."

"Am I losing points for going?"

"No."

"You're going to put this in the book, aren't you, how your/his wife leaves you/him after a colonoscopy to go to Vegas, aren't you?"

"I am not."

The fictional Jacob Fishman was probably going to get a colonoscopy.

She touched his forehead and walked out the back door. Jacob heard the automated voice of the alarm—*Back door open*—which was the last thing he heard until the phone rang.

"Father?" said the voice as he picked up the phone, which Cindi must have moved to the mattress. It was Lisa, his daughter.

"It is the daughter," she said.

"You make me laugh when you do that."

"Hi, Daddio," she called him, another of her nicknames for him.

He looked at his phone. He had slept for three hours. It was 5:30. He felt rested or exhausted, he couldn't tell which.

"Why didn't you tell me?"

"Tell you? Oh—that. Cindi tell you?"

"Yeah."

"Sweetie, it's not something fathers talk with their daughters about."

"It's not something daughters want to hear from their fathers, or that their fathers even have asses, but it's part of the job when you're the daughter. You need anything?"

"Ginger ale would be great."

As he hung up, he reached behind his head and searched on one of the three shelves of the headboard, a red shelving unit Cindi and Jacob had purchased from a local carpenter, who had killed himself before finishing the paint job, and found a pad and a pen and a pair of +1.5 readers. He wrote down, diagonally, "Jacob, barium enema, 3 polyps . . . Cindi . . . Willie Cicci . . . Cindi and Mitch fucking in Vegas . . . ginger ale . . . Michael Jackson . . . Saint Dominic's Preview/Parish."

The fictional Jacob was definitely getting massively probed.

Jacob Fishman's Marriage: A Novel

5. Willi Cicci and Martin Heidegger

Jacob Fishman woke from his post-colonoscopy nap, ecstatic he didn't have colon cancer, but still concerned three pre-cancerous polyps were removed, even though he was told by a nurse that to an oncologist, every part of the body is pre-cancerous.

"It's how they think," she told him. "You'll be fine, you will. Stop worrying."

Cindi, who had brought him home after the surgery, was in a rush to get to the airport to go to Las Vegas for her conference. Lying in bed, still dazed, Jacob remembered a weird conversation on the way back from the hospital about Cindi's fear of flying, which was the case for as long as he had known her, was always prevalent, but was now made worse as it was rooted, and he didn't know why it was now rooted, in physics and engineering.

"Steel tubes that weigh thousands of pounds should not be in the air," she said recently "and if they are in the air, they shouldn't be able to stay there for very long."

"But you used to fly to France to study in Plum Village with Thick Nhat Hanh. How did you do that?"

"Don't make fun."

"I'm not making fun."

"He is a Zen master."

"He's a Zen master, but what does that have to do with your fear of flying? That's my point."

"That wasn't your point. You were hoping to catch me in an inconsistency, while making fun of Eastern belief systems, because you think you're so above it all, so you could lord your maturity and sarcasm and Western and patriarchal hegemony over me."

"Christ Almighty, where do you come up with these things? I'm not out to get you and I wasn't trying to Lord, my Jesus, what was that again: Western and patriarchal hegemony over you"? Jacob responded, though he, in fact, was doing exactly that.

After Cindi dropped him off at home, got him to bed, and kissed him ever so briefly, she left for the airport. She parked in short-term, as she couldn't find the long-term lot, and ran to the Southwest check-in gate with her rollaway, cursing every step of the way.

She saw Mitch waiting at Gate 5.

"I got a B," she said, referring to Southwest Airlines' cattle-call boarding procedures.

"You?"

"A," he said, flashing the boarding pass.

"Why doesn't that surprise me?"

"I'll wait and board with you."

"That's friendship," Cindi said.

"You can buy me a drink on the plane."

"Everything has a fucking cost with you guys."

"What?"

"Nothing. Sorry. I'll buy you a fucking drink."

The flight from Reno to Vegas was seventy-five minutes, and though she hated flying and Las Vegas with equal passion and felt guilty about leaving Jacob, prick though he often was, she was looking forward to three days away. Her friend Virginia Butler, a creative-writing professor at UNR, who also read Tarot cards and collected stray cats, had given her half a Valium before she left, which Cindi took with some white wine midflight.

As Southwest 1615 made its final descent into McCarran Airport, the thin desert air caused the plane to buck back and forth.

"Hey, hey, hey," said Mitch, as Cindi dug her fingers into his upper wrist, causing him to spill the remainder of the scotch Cindi had bought him and that the flight attendant had failed to retrieve on his pants.

"Oh, shit, sorry. I hate this," said Cindi. "This is just not right. Metal tubes filled with gas and weighing God knows how many tons should not be in the air—oh, God!" she exclaimed as she heard the landing-gear doors open. "What the fuck was that, now?"

"The plane just landed, Cin, relax."

As it taxied to the gate, Cindi left her hand on top of his.

"Thank you," she said.

He patted her arm.

The conference wasn't starting until the next morning, so after checking in at the Luxor and taking the Inclinators—elevators that moved more horizontally than vertically, another piece of modernity that confounded and annoyed her—to their rooms, they agreed to meet at the Aurora Bar, where they agreed to not see Carrot Top on purely sociological terms.

"I hear his eye makeup is tattooed on and he's pumping iron, so he's a bit of a cartoon figure anyway," said Mitch.

"He's actually lying about who he is. It's a facade, a cultural dodge with props—with a drink minimum."

"We can't encourage such depravity. It's pure debauchery," said Mitch. "I won't be a part of it. So we drink, right?"

"All night long. The way I see it, Mitchey—"

"Do not call—"

"Oh, calm down. I'm joking," she said, whispering "Mitchey" to herself, which he heard and for which he pulled her hair.

"You're such a child," she said, smoothing it out, before punching him in the arm.

"Bitch!"

"You're the bitch. Grow up. This is important. It's seven o'clock. This place has five bars," and with that Cindi picked up a pamphlet and read the names: "High, Flight, Aurora, LAX, and Playbar. We have to be at that first seminar at nine tomorrow morning. Figure we need seven hours of sleep, so by my calculations, one drink per hour per bar puts us at one in the morning. You in?"

"Good thing we're not wasting time with actual dinner and a show because that would be stupid, not to mention mature. But let's increase the degree of difficulty: new drinks at each bar, no repeats."

And that's what they did, though by their last stop, LAX, after a woman named Margot with a lazy eye tried to pick them both up, they were drinking club soda and cranberry juice, as the combined total of their Jaeger shots, rum punch, scotch and sodas, Manhattans, and Coronas, had taken its toll.

"Let's go to Lo-Lo's and get chicken and waffles," said Mitch.

They took a cab and did.

By the time Cindi got to her room, her head and the strangely designed room spun in clunky unison, even though, surprisingly, she thought, the chicken and waffles were resting comfortably inside her and not being splattered on the bathroom floor and walls from the expected projectile vomiting. Her last thought, before passing out, was to remind herself to take her boots off and call Jacob, neither of which she managed to do.

The next morning, she woke late, showered quickly, and met Mitch at the Starbucks inside Mandalay Bay, downstairs near the convention hall.

"I think I know what the problem was last night," Mitch told her, nursing a black coffee and a piece of pound cake.

"You having second thoughts about Margot?"

"Don't judge my onanism, first of all, and, no, the problem is we shouldn't have had the scotch after the rum. That's what screwed everything up."

"You think it was the order of our drinks last night and not the sheer volume of them?"

"Yes. It's all about the order. Everyone knows that."

The morning session included seminars on "Ghettos, Prisons and Racial Backlash" and "Social Identity: The Ethics of Punishment," as well as a series of classes on "Philosophical Origins of Early German Romanticism" and one called "Can a Philosopher Be a Nazi? The Heidegger Case," a seminar both Cindi and Mitch were looking forward to, as such titles always promised, and delivered, the most fireworks—in academia, Heidegger always brought out the best in moral relativists, Holocaust deniers, and neo-Nazis.

Part of Cindi's tenure track, part of everyone's, was participation in these kinds of seminars. The American Philosophical Association sponsored three major symposia each year, with dozens of smaller ones, and, as part of the forty-percent research requirement at UNR, Cindi had spoken at two or three of them. Her specialty, even though her dissertation was on Nietzsche, was Montesquieu, who was often derided, as Howland told her more than once, as "a political philosopher not unlike America's Founding Fathers who, while impressive, could not, with the possible exception of Jefferson, be considered among history's 'great thinkers.'" Her speech, given in Portland a few years back, on the importance of Montesquieu in the drafting of the Separation of Powers, specifically, and the U.S. Constitution, generally, attracted two dozen, but Cindi noticed immediately this Heidegger seminar had attracted, as close as she could estimate, close to a hundred.

"Germans," she muttered.

"What?" asked Mitch.

"Nothing."

Having read the schedule wrong, Cindi and Mitch walked in during the Heidegger seminar and stepped quietly over four people in a row in the back, as Jonas Bremer, the chair of classical German philosophy at Humboldt-Universität in Berlin, was speaking on Heidegger and his imprimatur on the national socialist revolution.

"We owe it to ourselves," said Bremer, "to discuss the potential ramifications of aspects of the Holocaust having been embellished for political and financial purposes."

"For the love of absolute fuck," Mitch didn't quite whisper.

"Shhh," said Cindi, grabbing his thigh.

"What are we listening to?"

"Mitch, quiet!"

There was a crackle from the microphone.

"*Entschuldigen sie, bitte.*" It was Bremer.

"Nothing," said Mitch.

"Was *ist dein* problem?"

"*Nichts,*" replied Mitch.

"*Lass uns von unserem amerikanischen Bruder hören,*" said Bremer, closing his notes and opening his arms.

Many in the crowd looked back toward Cindi and Mitch.

"*Und du bist?*" Bremer continued.

Mitch winked at Cindi and stood up.

"I'm Mitch Aloisio, University of Nevada, Reno."

"*Schön, dich zu treffen Mitch Aloisio von der Universität von Nevada, Reno—*"

"You suddenly forgot you know English?" Mitch asked.

Cindi was petrified. She looked down, not wanting to make eye contact with anyone, but kept sneaking looks. She was full of piss and fear. Literally, she had to urinate and was scared.

"You have a problem?" said Bremer in almost perfect English.

"I've been sitting here, barely just sitting here," Mitch said, "and the problem is everywhere . . . and with everything. The problem with you new Germans," Mitch said, elongating the "new," "is you're just like the old Germans without the goose-stepping and straight-arm salute."

"Mitch," Cindi whispered.

Mitch continued. "You learned the art of self-deprecation and equivocation, but you do it badly, so, while you don't deny all the Holocaust, you don't let the enormity of it ruin your day—"

"I fully," said Bremer, "stipulate to the horrors of most Germans during that period."

"You fully stipulate to the horrors of most Germans? You're a prince. Thanks. As one of our famous philosophers, Chris Rock, would ask, 'Want a cookie?' Here's the problem, in a Nazi nutshell. Yes, you fully stipulate to the horrors of the Holocaust, but then four milliseconds later explain how the Jews deserved it or, at best, how they're embellishing its horror for political and economic gain, sympathy, and to cover their positions and actions and political stances, for instance, vis-á-vis the Palestinians. More to the point, Heidegger was too smart to be that stupid. He knew he would be used, and he let himself be. The Holocaust is, let's say this again, as if we need to, the single most-studied event of the twentieth century. We have eyewitness accounts, the physical evidence of the camps themselves, the Nazis' own immaculate record-keeping. On this there is no philosophical wiggle room. To stand here, or anywhere, and, I'll say again, mitigate the cancer of National-sozialistische Deutsche Arbeiterpartei," Mitch said, proud of his German, "is to embrace it. Do you know what the difference is between a Nazi and one who contextualizes Nazism?"

Bremer smiled.

"What is that, my American *freund*?"

"Nothing."

Some of the crowd applauded; some squirmed in their seats.

Mitch stood and said to no one in particular, "*Cicc', a porta,*" offered Cindi a hand, which she took, and they made their way out the door, just as organizers from the event and hotel staff security were heading in their direction.

"That was fun," Cindi said, sitting at the Starbucks a few minutes later. "I've never actually left a seminar moments before being thrown out of one."

"Nazi bastards. I got pissed the minute we walked in."

"Really?"

"Didn't embarrass you?"

"No. Not at all. As I said, it was fun, but we did miss the group *über alles* at the end. I have to ask you, though. The German I kind of followed, but what was that Cicci . . . what?"

Mitch laughed. "It's a *Godfather Part Two* reference. Frankie 'Five Angels' Pentangeli, after being rebuked by Michael about the Rosato brothers, says to Willie Cicci, his bodyguard, '*Cicc', a porta*!' It means 'the door!'"

"I sometimes think the whole world is losing its mind."

"Sometimes it is. You want to get high?" Mitch asked.

"We're not going back to the conference."

"We're good. I'll tell Howland it sucked."

"Good. I'll tell him you made me leave."

"We weren't there long enough for people to know we left."

"Wait. High? You brought some with you?"

"You never know."

"Why'd you get two beds?" Cindi asked, as she walked into his room and lay down on the one closest to the door.

Mitch shrugged.

"Look at this," Cindi said, spotting the mirror above her head. "You could make love with someone, and it would just be the four of you."

Mitch, who went to get the pot he was keeping in a Seagram's pouch he brought from his office, either didn't hear or wasn't listening.

"What?" he said, turning around and seeing Cindi lying down. "Make love with four people. I have it on good authority that's bad math."

"Who said that? Skinner? Lewis?"

"No, I think it was Johnson."

"Johnson? Samuel?"

"Magic."

"Oh. I don't know . . . Who's that?"

"Basket—Never mind. After this, want to go eat?" Mitch asked, as he rolled two joints. "Let's go over to the Gold Coast. There's a great place called Ping Pang Pong."

"You're kidding."

"Nope. That's the name of it. I guess they want you to know it's Chinese. Kind of like on *The Honeymooners* when Gleason wanted his viewers to know he had an Italian neighbor downstairs, he called her Mrs. Manicotti."

"I have no idea what you're talking about. I don't know any of these references," Cindi said, replaying in her mind the conversation from Frank Pentangeli to Magic Johnson to Ping Pang Pong to Mrs. Manicotti. Then, studying a piece of loose spackle on the border of the ceiling while watching herself in the mirror, and the childless mother looking back at her, the one with an empty screaming womb, and then thinking about the woman in the reflection who was probably not going to get tenure, and her husband, whom she still hadn't called, she closed her eyes tight, tried to will herself to sleep. She wanted to wake up as another person—and not still be the forty-one-year-old woman who longed for a baby. She wanted to scream. She wanted to call in a bomb threat. She wanted to sleep. She had neither the desire nor the interest to speak. If the last thing she would ever say was "Is everyone nuts?" and if the last thing she would ever hear was "Mrs. Manicotti," it would be more than okay. She was out of words, humor, humanity. With Thich Nhat Hanh, she was taught the Fourteen Precepts—she had the seventh one memorized.

Do not lose yourself in dispersion and in your surroundings. Practice mindful breathing to come back to what is happening in the present moment. Be in touch with what is wondrous, refreshing, and healing both inside and around you. Plant seeds of joy, peace, and understanding in yourself in order to facilitate the work of transformation in the depths of your consciousness.

She was in a Las Vegas hotel, in a room with a mirror on the ceiling, and she wanted to fuck the person sitting at the desk—she had just decided that—who was rolling joints, who was not her husband, yet she also wanted to call the man who was, to tell him she was all right. It was all shit.

"What are you thinking about?" Mitch said, bringing her a joint.

"Shit and husbands."

"Sometimes I really feel for Jacob."

"Me too."

"Seriously, what are you thinking of? You look like you want to suffocate yourself."

She lit the joint, wondering after exhaling whether she could actually suffocate herself with a hotel pillow or if, reflexively, the body, even her body, would not allow it. "Nothing," she said, picking up the pillow and trying to balance it on her forehead. "Nothing," she repeated, handing him the joint.

"Defenestration, maybe."

They watched *Dr. Phil,* and then took a cab to Ping Pang Pong and ate dumplings.

She opened her fortune cookie and thought of Jacob and how he always said the same thing, always repeated the Alan King joke—she thought it was Alan King—after opening it. "Help! I'm being held hostage in a Chinese-cookie factory."

"What does it say?" Mitch asked.

"Shit!" she screamed.

"It does not. It says 'Shit,' really?"

"What?"

"What are you talking about?"

"I forgot to call Jacob."

When they got back to the hotel, Cindi went to her room and called her husband, while staring at the Patrick Nagel print on the wall. "Shannon," 1989. The girl, Cindi assumed, Shannon, it had to be, was in a pink dress and black pumps, looking over her shoulder. She imagined what it must be like for a man to lift up Shannon's dress, to fuck Shannon like this, to hold on to Shannon's hips, to look down once in a while, to see Shannon's pumps. But for Shannon, too, there were advantages, for any woman, Cindi thought, to be able to look ahead, close one's eyes, think of whomever, to fantasize, to endow the breathing and grunts coming from behind with metaphor . . . to not have to see the man, the specific man, behind you.

Cindi was wet.

The call went to his voicemail.

"It's Jacob. You probably know that. I had a really funny joke on this last week. Leave a message."

"I'm here, everything's fine. Hope you slept well. Call me when you can. Sorry about last night, but I got back late and didn't want to wake you. Hope your ass is better. Love you, honey. I'm going to take a nap but call me later." She said it quickly and hung up, in case he was on another call and clicked over.

She did fall asleep and dreamed about a conversation with a dog, a smart dog, that was giving her advice about men and sex. The dog was small, like Mr. Peabody on the old *Rocky and Bullwinkle* cartoon, a reference she actually knew, and at first it sounded like Thich Nhat Hanh, but then it sounded like James Mason, then like James Lipton, the host of that *Actors Studio* show, then like the guy leading the Heidegger lecture. It was an articulate, rational, calm, and wonderful dog.

She woke up laughing and wrote down the dream on the Luxor stationery by the phone.

Mr. Peabody, me, advice and something about sex. James Mason? Actors Studio. A dog!

After taking a shower and finding a long teal cotton abaya and her brown dress boots, she walked down to the lobby and waited for Mitch. When he saw her, he said, "Well, you look rested."

"What did you think of *Rocky and Bullwinkle*?" she asked, as they walked out to get a taxi to the Paris Hotel.

"'You forget about moose and squirrel . . .' That one?"

"Yeah."

"The best ever."

"Was Sherman the dog or was that Mr. Peabody?"

"Now this is seminar material. The dog was definitely Mr. Peabody, a genius. Sherman was the boy, a little troubled, if I had to guess. Why?"

"I had a dream, and I was the Sherman character."

"What do you think it means?" Mitch asked, in an exaggerated German accent.

"I'm getting good advice from dogs. That can't be good."

"Oh. I think it's very good."

They ate at Le Provençal before heading back to the conference and an insufferable speech by a representative from the APA, who talked of job opportunities in the profession.

"I picked the wrong time to stop doing heroin," Mitch said.

"In the past, we used to have three or four pages of openings," the rep said. "Now, there's more than forty in our latest magazine." Mild applause. "And with many of you retiring and dying, those openings are sure to increase."

"What a pleasant thought," Mitch said, leaning over to Cindi. "Die faster, would you? The kids need jobs."

After dinner, Mitch took her to the Peppermill, a diner-nightclub next to the Riviera at the north end of the Strip, across from Westward Ho. To the right of the front door was the diner; to the left a room with couches, fireplaces, secluded alcoves, dim lighting, and aging waitresses in floor-length black gowns.

"This is so tacky," said Cindi, walking in ahead of Mitch. "I love it."

"Isn't it great?"

"You've been here before, obviously," she said.

"Yeah, old man Roth, he'd never come here, but Johnny Ola, he knows these places like the back of his hand."

"What?"

"Nothing."

"Why do I know only, like, forty percent of what you're saying?"

"Don't flatter yourself. You don't know that much."

They sat in a corner booth, which was lined with mirrors and a sectional sofa, a table with an ashtray, a drink list, and a carafe of stale honey-roasted peanuts. The waitress, a girl with a name tag saying "Freedom," came by.

"You know what you want?"

Cindi laughed. "How philosophical of you."

Freedom looked confused.

"Don't pay attention to her. Two Blue Hurricanes," said Mitch, looking at the drink list.

"Good," said Cindi, "because after the crepes and the shrimp, not to mention these honey-roasted peanuts and having to breathe in this air in here, what we need is blue alcohol."

Of course her name is Freedom, she thought.

Cindi noticed a woman in another booth stroking a man's crotch while sitting in his lap.

"Pretty weird, huh?" asked Mitch, seeing the same event.

"He's getting a hand job over his pants in a public place. I can see why you come here, but it will take more than blue drinks and these"— she pointed to the peanuts—"to get me to jerk you off on a strange sofa." Cindi surprised herself at how easily that had come out. "Sorry."

"It's okay."

"Whew. No, it's not."

"What is it?"

"Nothing, I'm sorry. I just . . . just." She exhaled. "Nothing."

"Here you go," Freedom said, standing over them with a fresh carafe of stale peanuts. Cindi remembered she still hadn't spoken to Jacob.

Well, fuck, he could have called me.

"What time is it?" she asked.

The light was terrible, but Mitch finally deciphered his watch.

"One thirty."

"One thirty? Can't be."

"This I wouldn't lie about."

"Oh, fuck, I gotta go. On the other hand, how much more trouble can I get into?"

"So let's sit."

"Will Natasha be worried?"

"Rouslana."

"Sorry, I was thinking about *Rocky and Bullwinkle,* and it's none of my business, but . . . really—Rouslana?"

"Well, as Tennessee Williams once told Dorothy Parker—I think it was Dorothy Parker—about all those young, strapping twenty-some-things who used to accompany him to the Algonquin Hotel in New York and about one of them in particular: 'I need him.'"

"That is, as the kids like to say, some heavy shit."

"And Jacob? Will he really be upset?"

"He'll probably be upset, but it will be mostly an act. He'll say that I'm the one disrespecting the marriage."

"He'll say you're doing that or you're saying you're doing that?"

"Yes. To both. We're not getting along."

"Really?"

"Shut up. Is it that noticeable?" she asked, laughing.

"Yeah. Anything you want to talk about?"

"I want a baby, I want a baby, I want a baby. That's all. I want a baby. I don't care about tenure—I mean, not really. I'm almost forty-one. I have got, by my estimation, about seven more months to get pregnant."

"How do you figure?"

"I have to have a baby before I'm forty-three. Have to."

"Why?"

"Because she, and I know it's going to be a girl, will graduate high school early—that, too, I know—and I want her to start college before I'm sixty."

"Doesn't make a lot of sense. Some. Not a lot."

"Really?"

"No. And Jacob?"

"Been snipped." Cindi stood up, or tried to, but then lost her balance and sat back down onto the sofa and into Mitch's lap.

"Hi, there."

She tried getting up again, but he held her.

"Just sit, relax. You'll be okay."

Cindi put her head in her hands, leaned forward, and felt Mitch's hand on her back.

"I'm not jerking you off."

"Tell me again."

When Mitch walked her back to her room, she hesitated. "I had a . . ."

"Yeah, me too," Mitch said.

"If I invite you in," Cindi said, "you'll come, won't you?"

"Yeah."

"I'm not going to invite you in."

"Tease."

She was hoping, as she moved closer, as she saw his hand over her head, resting on the door, that he would do something so boorish, so inappropriate that she wouldn't want to invite him.

"Been thinking," Mitch said, "about this moment since you bought me that first scotch on the plane yesterday and then I kind of forgot about it after I spilled it on my pants. That was yesterday, wasn't it? So I was thinking, Cindi, we might be standing in this very hallway, just like this. In my choreography of this moment, I kiss you about now."

And with that he moved his hand around to the back of her neck.

"Is this okay?" he whispered.

"I can't ask you to come in," she said, putting her finger over his lips. "I can't—"

"Shhh, I'm putting the big moves on you."

"You're going to kiss me, I'm going to kiss you, and then we're never going to talk about it, right?"

"Right."

As unhappy as Cindi was with marriage in general and hers in particular, she hadn't kissed any man other than Jacob since marrying him, nor had she wanted to. Six years of the same above-average kissing with Jacob was enough—not end-of-the-road enough, but okay enough.

Mitch grabbed her face with both hands and lightly kissed her, leaving his lips on top of hers, so she could make whatever move she wanted next. Cindi grabbed the back of his neck and let her tongue brush over his lips. She pulled his hair, slightly, stood on her toes, and kissed him hard.

He reached between her legs, slowly moving his hand up the length of her abaya. She could feel the material rubbing against her skin, acting like a sheath against his fingers, which had found her pussy, for she hadn't worn and didn't wear underwear.

"Please stop."

"Sure?"

"Yes. No. I'm going to go now," she said, pulling away from him.

"Me, too, because . . . because . . ." and then Mitch smiled, blew her a kiss and walked backward toward his room.

"Sorry."

"Don't be."

Cindi let herself in, took off her boots this time, washed her face, and, standing in the bathroom, looking at herself in the mirror, masturbated.

She then sat on the edge of the bed and checked her voicemail.

No messages.

BITE ME

Though she didn't think it was a good idea to clog her father's recently cleansed colon, Lisa Fishman brought her father what he wanted: A two-liter ginger ale, Vienna Fingers, seedless green grapes, French bread, and provolone cheese, which Jacob ate from a cutting board in bed.

"La-la-la," she said, putting fingers in her ears. "I can't hear you. I can't hear you," as he began telling her about his barium enema and his polyps.

He loved his daughter.

After she left, he retrieved his laptop from his office, brought it downstairs, and transferred the notes that he had written to the file named JFM, brushing breadcrumbs from the keyboard as he typed. He also reviewed Willie Cicci and Martin Heidegger in *Jacob Fishman's Marriage*. While he researched Montesquieu, Heidegger, philosophy degrees at German universities, seminar offerings at philosophy conferences, and just how many bars were at the Luxor in Vegas, and felt it important to include it all, he suspected the chapter was too long and the philosophy details either too much or too obviously a result of an evening's Google search, which, in large measure, it was. Still, there were moments, passages, where, immodesty aside, he thought his literary conceit was rather impressive, borderline brilliant, and found the moment where Mitch, sporting his German, stormed out of the seminar hilarious and Hollywood-worthy. Jacob, as was his hope, was tackling the deconstruction of the manipulation, the examination of the examination, and revealing his own long and short con in the work.

There was also having the fictional Cindi masturbate after cheating on him.

Around three a.m., he took a Lorazepam, a Tylenol PM, and melatonin, and turned on *Dateline*. He didn't remember falling asleep, didn't remember talking to Cindi, if she had even called, and then woke at 11:37 a.m., feeling something sticking to his side. It turned out to be a piece of provolone and a smashed grape. *Dateline*, owing to whatever network he'd been watching running a marathon of them, was still on, and he found it perfectly serendipitous when Keith Morrison said, "It seemed like a perfectly normal morning . . . but was it?"

Jacob felt for his phone, just missing the knife that was still on the cutting board.

He tapped the screen.

Drank Blue Hawaiians or something. Been sick. See you tomorrow. Won't call. You're probably sleeping. Love-C

Cindi, the real Cindi, had texted him. But she hadn't called. It's where he got the idea that the fictional Cindi hadn't called the fictional Jacob. Still, his wife had made contact.

He won life. He beat fiction.

His wife, his real wife, called. His imaginary one had masturbated to another man.

He sent a text.

OK, be careful. Elvis did an album called Blue Hawaii.

I don't get it, she texted back.

Never mind. See you tonight.

His mood soured quickly. Why didn't she cancel her trip, the real one? Fact is, he could have postponed the colonoscopy, but he'd wanted to see what she would do if he didn't. Would she cancel the Vegas trip? Would she make him a priority? The fictional Cindi couldn't because of the tenure business, but the real Cindi could have, for she had tenure. In his mind, she wanted to get away. She was not the Cindi who wanted to fuck Mitch—or was she? Keith Morrison was now doing commentary on his life.

Cindi grabbed the back of his neck and let her tongue brush over his lips. She pulled his hair, slightly, stood on her toes, and kissed him hard.

Cindi, his Cindi, never kissed him like that. He was turned on by her, this wife he created, this wife in the laptop, the wife masturbating to a man based on the man with whom his real wife was at a real convention, even amid all his spelling and syntax errors in the draft. The wife in the book was unfinished, unrefined; yet not evanescent. Cindi was already sexier, more mysterious, and intelligent than Cindi—no, not more intelligent. His real wife was funnier, too, her humor darker, less whiny, even if not—and why he hadn't made her so, he wondered— appreciably nicer. This fictional Cindi masturbated standing up in the bathroom; the real one didn't masturbate at all. The fictional Cindi let Mitch almost finger her. He wanted to finger her. He thought of making this Cindi thinner, too, than his real wife, though Cindi was not heavy. He imagined the tits and pussy of this Cindi were those of a younger woman, what he imagined his wife was in her twenties, when she traveled through Europe and had sex with dangerous men. This was the Cindi who, in fact, spent time in Plum Village (he would give the fictional Cindi the same history) and yelled at Thich Nhat Hanh when the Buddhist master overcharged her for her stay.

Where had that Cindi gone—not the fictional one, but the forgotten one, the real one?

(That he would use this story in a chapter in *Jacob Fishman's Marriage* was a certainty.)

. . . sitting at the desk, who was rolling joints, who was not her husband, yet also wanted to call the man who was.

Fuck both of them. Neither was happy with him.

Still dazed from the Tylenol, the Lorazepam, and the melatonin, his first day with a clean colon, Jacob decided to go for a walk around UNR. He did not want to think about *Jacob Fishman's Marriage* today, Cindi or Jacob—or for that matter Cindi or himself.

The phone chirped. Another text.

Will call you later but going to spend another night. Hope that's okay. The conference is going well. Love-C

Why wouldn't she call with news like that? But good, he thought. He wanted the day to himself.

Fine. Great. Let's talk later. J

They never used initials, yet they were using them. Who were the real Jacob and Cindi becoming? Was there now a third couple?

He walked, went all the way to Mackay Stadium, where he walked inside the stadium, before heading home.

He fell asleep on Cindi's chaise.

There was another message waiting when he woke up.

Tried calling. Why is your ringer off?

He responded.

Napping. Sorry.

Talk later?

Yep. How's Mitch?

How's Mitch??!!

Yeah, how's Mitch?

He's fine. I'm fine, too.

Me, too. I'm fine.

Good.

Yeah, good. We're all fine.

You're weird, Jake.

Why you love me.

This is not why.

But no initials this time. They were they again.

He made a note on his phone: Ciara for me? Ciara for Jacob.

At Mario's Portofino, Ciara was near the cash register, cleaning wine glasses, wearing black tights and a blue V-neck T-shirt, burgundy bra, looking strikingly similar to how he described her in *Jacob Fishman's Marriage*. Nomad, also real, also in that chapter, was, as usual, behind the bar. He was standing with one foot up on the sink, watching television and talking with two overweight men in their fifties who were sharing a plate of calamari.

"Nomad," one of them said, "let me try the martini with the Grey Goose now."

Nomad set down a Diet Coke in front of Jacob.

"These things are going to kill you," Nomad said.

"So I've been told."

"Where is Cindi tonight?"

"Vegas, fucking a philosophy guy she works with."

"Oh, stop it," said Nomad. "She is not."

"Right. The other Cindi is."

"What the hell are you talking about?"

"Do I know? Okay, Cindi is in Vegas at a conference with a co-worker, and I don't think they're fucking. I mean, nah, they're not fucking. Okay, maybe they're fucking."

"Hey, stud," Ciara said, looking up from the end of the bar. She came around to hug him.

Her tights turned him on.

"How was the surgery?"

"You heard?"

"You said something last time you were in."

"I did or did Jac—never mind. Sorry. We shouldn't have shared that."

"Be careful with her," Nomad said. "Don't let that harmless flirting fool you. She's wicked and dangerous and not harmless."

"And the problem . . .?" asked Ciara.

"And the problem . . .?" Jacob repeated.

He noticed she was wearing a small silver nose ring, which hooped around one nostril.

"You want something to eat?" Ciara asked.

"Yeah."

"Chicken parm? You want to eat outside?"

"If it's not a problem."

"You're never a problem, baby."

"Damn, I want to be a problem."

"Go sit. I'll be out in a minute."

"I would like my own personal waitress."

"You want me to feed you, too?"

"I'm not ready for a serious relationship."

"Cute."

He sat out there, drinking his Diet Coke, munching bread and salad that he didn't really want (he had come just for Ciara), breathing in the late-January air and suddenly felt very good that he wouldn't be fitted for a colostomy bag or lose his hair from chemo, or need a walker, things about which, when he first saw the blood in his stool, he was sure would happen.

I'm not going to die.

"What's that, baby?" Ciara asked, startling him.

"Nothing. Hi. That was quick."

Jacob looked inside and saw the rich guys were gone and an elderly couple was watching *Anderson Cooper 360* and drinking wine.

"Where's Nomad?"

"In the kitchen checking inventory, I think."

"Sit?"

Jacob had taken a table as far from the restaurant as there was, closest to the parking lot, which looked over a residential housing addition. The restaurant was located on a lot previously used by an industrial air-quality-equipment plant that was cited numerous times by the EPA, and while it had since been pronounced safe by every national and state environment regulatory agency, Jacob knew that he and everyone who ever ate here, especially out on the patio, would eventually come down with lupus or leukemia from the seepage of toxins and asbestos into the well and groundwater and then develop, he told himself, colon cancer.

His phone rang. It was Cindi. He didn't pick up.

"You want to get that?"

"Later," he said, motioning to the empty chair with his hand.

She put the sandwich and another Diet Coke on the table and moved one of the four chairs closer to him.

"Unless you have to do something inside."

"I'm done. Mind if I smoke?"

"No." He did.

Ciara put one leg under the other.

"So, how's your legal problems?" he asked.

"My DUI? You know about that?"

"Yeah, you mentioned that before I mentioned this," he said, pointing to his ass.

"Settled. Had to pay my lawyer about four grand and got my license suspended."

"Next time you want to drink and drive, look in your purse. If you don't see a spare five thousand dollars, you can't afford it."

"Yes, Dad," Ciara said and saluted. "How are you? How's your life, marriage?" She leaned in and stole a french fry from his plate.

"My marriage. Got a half hour, I'll tell you the whole story."

"I don't."

"Why do you ask?" Jacob asked, picking up two fries, offering them to her, which she ate out of his hand.

"Why do I ask?" Ciara said, stretching out, dropping one of her legs to the ground and keeping one underneath her. "Let's see. We're sitting out here and Cindi is wherever, and you're not taking her calls and you're feeding me—and I'm trying to rub your leg under the table."

He moved closer so she could.

"This is . . ."

"Yeah."

"So?"

"What? A man can't eat a chicken parmesan sandwich outside by himself? Keep rubbing, by the way."

She did.

"You know that's not it, because chicken parmesan," she said, "isn't always chicken parmesan."

"That's some poetry right there, Ciara. Really good."

"Yeah, it's Rimbaud."

"You know Rimbaud?"

"A while back, if I remember right, 'my life was one long party where all hearts were open wide, where all wines kept flowing.'"

"You do know him. Very, very impressive. 'A Season in Hell.' Only you got a DUI after all that wine kept flowing."

She moved her leg so he could stroke inside her thigh.

"I don't even know why I know that poem."

She put her hand over his. Her fingertips scraped the back of his hand.

"I don't want to talk about Rimbaud."

She continued scraping.

"I want to kiss you," she said.

"Then kiss me. And thank God I didn't say that, because that would have been really embarrassing if you said no."

Her tongue immediately found his. He reached his hand around her neck, scraped it, and pulled her close. He kept one eye open on the restaurant door and removed his hand from her thigh and cupped her breast, finding her nipple through her shirt.

"You want my nipple?"

"Yeah."

She, too, glanced back at the restaurant and slid her left hand into her burgundy bra and took out her breast, leaving her shirt below it. Jacob ran his thumb over her breast and forefinger over her nipple.

Cindi let herself in, took off her boots this time, washed her face, and, standing in the bathroom, looking at herself in the mirror, masturbated.

"Let me ask you something," Ciara said, pulling away, exhaling, but leaving her shirt down and one breast exposed. "None of my business, okay, none, but I look at you and Cindi and I gotta tell you—I don't know what you're getting out of it. So what are you getting out of your marriage?"

"Who can answer a question like that?"

"Maybe someone who gets something out of his marriage."

"Good point." He smiled at her. "What am I getting out of it? You know, you're more impressive than one might think."

She smiled and kicked him under the table. "You have a strange way of complimenting a girl."

"I've been told. Sorry. I mean—"

"I know what you mean. Rimbaud, the tats, I'm a regular Renaissance girl. You okay with this?

"Yes. No. I don't know."

"You want me to go?"

"Not at all. I'm just . . . never mind. Happened easier than I—"

"Planned?"

"I thought about it. It's why I came. Stay, though."

He picked up his sandwich. He put it back down. Ciara stole another fry off his plate.

"What am I getting out of it?" he repeated. "I . . . I don't know. Let me ask you—why are you doing this to yourself, you know, the DUI and stuff? What do you get out of it . . . what you do?" Jacob asked, putting his hand on her thigh, gently cupping and squeezing it.

Ciara uncrossed her legs. "I like to drink and I like to party and I don't know when to stop."

She licked her lips.

"You want me to stop doing this?"

She put her fingers on his and pushed down, grabbing his wrist and pulling it up her leg. "What do you think?"

"Spread your legs a little."

She did as she was told. His index finger moved up slowly between her legs. He found her clitoris through her tights and tapped it with the edge of his thumb.

"Can you come like this?"

"Uh-huh."

She moved his plate, put her elbow on the table, and leaned in. He found her neck with his mouth, licking it, gently biting it, while continuing to finger her clitoris over her tights. He could still see into the restaurant. He turned her head toward him, kissed her, first running his tongue over her lips and teeth and then into her mouth. He tasted her breath, her cigarette smoke.

"What, baby?" Ciara said, sitting up straight, then standing, between him and the table, then pushing the plate away and sitting on the table, then pulling down the right side of her blouse, exposing both breasts. "Is this what you want?"

Jacob couldn't remember the last time he was asked that . . . the last time he was this turned on. A girl with a DUI and a suspended license in polyester tights and a blouse pulled below her breasts who could quote a nineteenth-century French poet was now feeling his cock with her foot.

Ciara pushed in closer.

"Bite me. Bite me."

He did, his teeth coming down on the nipple he had been rubbing.

"Ouch!"

"Sorry."

"It's okay." She pulled away. "Bite it again, softer, though."

He did.

"I want to fuck you, Jake—"

A glass broke inside, then another, then a third. The noise came from the bar.

"Shit," Jacob said, seeing a man at the bar.

"Shit," they both heard the man say.

"Ciara?" It was Nomad, quickly coming out from the kitchen. "Ciara!"

"Yeah. Out here," she said, stating the obvious. "Be right in."

"Gotta go," she whispered, and ran her fingers over Jacob's cheek, then into his mouth.

"Suck them."

He did, quickly.

She stepped to his side, still facing away from the restaurant, pulled up her bra and her blouse, turned, and made her way back inside.

He drove home. Jacob/Jacob and Cindi/Cindi were one now—or two. Or four. One cheats, one wants to cheat, they both fantasized about it. They would be parasitical. *Jacob Fishman's Marriage* would be a familia/fictional stew. Jacob had gone to Mario's Portofino because his fictional wife had masturbated to another man—the wife he created was fantasizing about someone else.

That could not stand.

Jacob got home and opened his manuscript.

He reached between her legs, slowing moving his hand up the length of her abaya. She could feel the material rubbing against her skin, acting like a sheath against his fingers, which had found her pussy, for she hadn't worn and didn't wear underwear.

Why didn't he stop himself and write something else? He was God. He could have. Aside from how furious his real wife would be if she ever read the above—and how could he stop her?—was he really now going to use his fictional wife's almost act of infidelity as cover for his own real act? In the hands of a good writer, Jacob imagined, the very dynamic of an author getting back at his fictional wife was convoluted but also delicious. This was an R-rated funhouse mirror. But there was no such author watching him write *Jacob Fishman's Marriage*. It was just Jacob Fishman typing in his upstairs office and trapped, willingly, between two worlds of his own making. Yes, this was his plan: to meld, to blend it all so the narratives would intersect like a literary double helix. He made a note on his whiteboard, "Rewrite Willie Cicci and Martin Heidegger so Cindi invites Mitch into her room and have them fuck in the shower, standing up."

He should have been disgusted by what he had just written.

He wasn't. He thought of Ciara and masturbated.

JACOB AND
CINDI SHOW

J acob didn't move.

He remained lying in bed, arms folded, fingers interlocked across his chest—he had assumed this position, practiced it. Cindi was back from her Las Vegas trip and Jacob could hear her walk through the kitchen.

"Honey," she called out.

Jacob told himself not to answer. He didn't.

"Honey."

"In here."

Fuck. Why did I say anything?

"You don't greet me anymore," Cindi asked, appearing at the door to the bedroom after dropping her bag in the living room. "You used to jump up. And you used to want to pick me up at the airport."

"Your car was at the airport, for one thing, and for another, you never hop up—I mean never—when I come in. Why is that?"

It came out the way Jacob had hoped—the "Why is that?" delivered with the appropriate pacing and snark, just as he had rehearsed it in the mirror the hour before she arrived.

"Oh, God! We're going to start right away, huh? No 'Hey, Cin, how was your trip?' No kiss, no nothing like that? Just going to go right to the Jacob and Cindi Show?"

"I know how your trip was—"

"What? You know how my trip was?" she asked, disappearing in the walk-in closet, where she kicked off her shoes before returning to the bed. She stood by the edge, looking at her husband. She squeezed his big toe.

"I'm just saying," he said, "I can imagine, and, hey, how about 'How's your ass after surgery, Jake?'"

"Can I go to the bathroom first before you yell at me?"

Jacob didn't say anything.

"I'm not yelling at you," he called after she left.

Cindi walked into the bathroom, shut the door, and stood facing the mirror, which she would have put her face through if not for the sink being in her way. She quickly peed, washed her hands, then, looking at the mirror again, lightly smacked it with an open palm.

"What are you doing in there?" Jacob called out.

"I'm peeing. Is that all right?"

She watched herself exhale, before returning to her husband.

Sitting on the edge of the bed facing him, this time pushing his feet, which he grudgingly moved to give her more room to sit, she asked, "Okay, what did I do wrong now?"

"You didn't do anything wrong, and I'm not your father."

"Hey, what did you mean, by the way, that you knew how my trip was?"

"I'm just saying, we didn't talk, you didn't call, so I assume . . ."

"What do you mean?"

"I assume, you know . . ."

"What? What are you assuming?"

Jacob patted his chest three times.

"I imagine you and Mitch, uh—"

"Me and Mitch . . . what?"

"How I know how your trip went."

"You're not making sense. What does Mitch . . . I'm really not following you."

"What did you and Mitch do?"

"Do? We went to the conference. What do you mean . . . do?"

"You know."

"What?"

"You and Mitch—simple question."

"What did we do?" Cindi asked. "Oh, really? Are you fucking kidding me?" She stood up. "You think I, what, fucked Mitch? And that's why you think I stayed? And that's why you're acting so fucking strange?"

"I'm not acting strange."

"No, you are. This is strange," she said, pointing two index fingers at him.

"I just wonder why you stayed."

"I told you why I stayed. There was an extra day to the conference. We called Howland, who told us we could stay on the university's dime, and that's why we stayed. I didn't fuck Mitch, if that's what this is about. Mitch! Why would you think . . . That's why you didn't get up and greet me at the door? That's why you're in here pouting? Wow! Okay, let's . . . what about what you did while I was gone, not fucking Mitch."

"I wasn't pouting, first of all. And I stayed here. Lisa came over and then I went to dinner."

"Dinner? And where did you go?"

"Does it matter?"

"I bet you went to the Italian place I hate."

"Yeah . . . yes, I went to the Italian place you hate."

"Did you see your girlfriend?"

"What are you talking about?"

"You play dumb really badly. You know—what's her name? The little cunt."

"Nice. Why do you call her a cunt?"

"Sorry I hurt your feelings. I won't call the cunt a cunt."

"She's not a cunt, and you're not hurting my feelings."

"Why are you defending her?"

"Why are you changing the subject?"

"From what?"

"Mitch."

"What about Mitch? I didn't fuck him. I didn't fuck Mitch! That was your question, right?"

"I didn't fuck Ciara."

"I didn't say you fucked Ciara. Why would I think that?"

"That's what you were implying."

"I'm implying you fucked a waitress? I was not implying you fucked a waitress. I'm implying you make a fool of yourself when you're around her—that was my point. She's never going to fuck you, Jacob, you do know that, right?"

"I never said she wanted to fuck me."

"What are we talking about?"

"I just worry that you—"

"—that I am fucking Mitch, or fucked Mitch, or will start fucking Mitch."

"No, I'm not. I mean . . . Okay, yeah. But you know."

"Can I sit down again?"

"Yes. You didn't have to stand up before. You look ridiculous standing there."

Cindi sat.

"Okay," Cindi said, "are we good? I didn't fuck Mitch and you didn't fuck the cunt."

"Do you have to?"

"Kylie."

"Ciara."

"Ciara, got it. Whatever. Now, can I tell you," Cindi said, standing again and walking back into her closet, "what bothers me?"

"What bothers you? This is supposed to be about what bothers me. The baby bothers you," Jacob said. "I know that."

"I'm not talking about the baby," she said, coming out of the closet. "You accuse me of shit I didn't do and then get angry when I notice."

"I'm not accusing you of anything."

"You think I fucked Mitch but are denying that's what you think, because even to you, it's kind of absurd and you're too much of a pussy to own it."

"That's nice."

"Well, you do. And then you do this."

"Do what?"

"This."

"What this?"

"This this."

"I wonder if you fucked Mitch—I'm not accusing you."

"Interesting distinction."

"Fine, you win. I'll be less passive. Did you fuck him?"

"No! And what about you and—the fuck is her name? Candace?"

"Ciara."

"Stupid-ass name. Whatever it is. Did you fuck her?"

"Yeah, I went to the restaurant, she was working, and fucked her at the restaurant."

"Maybe you fucked her after you went to the restaurant. Brought her back here, or she took you home."

"And maybe I fingered her outside on the patio and, I don't know, bit her nipples. Who would notice?"

He had done this. The fictional Jacob Fishman had not. He thought, perhaps, though, Jacob might, as well.

"'Bit her nipples'? Who imagines that? Who comes up with that scenario? Jesus, you're weird. But you wanted to, right?"

"I want to fuck ninety percent of the women I meet, but I don't."

"That's a shitty thing to say to your wife. And you're proud of that?"

"The important thing is I don't fuck those women. And most importantly, I didn't fuck Ciara."

"I'm not saying you did. I'm just saying me fucking Mitch last night is as crazy as you fucking . . . uh—"

"Ciara."

"—last night."

"Okay, sorry," Jacob said. "I'm just—I don't know."

The Fishmans looked at each other, each waiting for the other to show some kindness, some smile, some sign, which is when Cindi pointed to the bed and to him.

"Can I?"

"Yeah, I wanted you to since you came home."

"No, you didn't."

"We're trying to make up, don't argue with me."

"Move over, Chubs," she said, patting his stomach. "You're getting a little heavy."

"But my colon is good."

"I'm beyond happy. Nothing is more important in a successful relationship than a clean, un-cancered ass."

"You're not going to get me in bed if you keep talking about my cancer-free colon."

"I probably will. Now, move over."

He did as he was told.

"Jesus, we gotta do this better," she said, curling up in him.

"You're right. I know you're right."

"I mean it, Jacob. We have enough problems without this. I don't even know what this is, but we're not going to make it if we keep doing it. It drains everything between us."

"You think we will anyway?"

"Make it?"

"Yeah."

"At this moment, yeah. I like you."

"That works out well."

She put her head on his chest. He stroked her head, wrapping a strand of hair around his finger.

"Stop," she said.

"Sorry."

"No, no, just gently," she said. "I don't want you to stop. Like this," taking her finger over his and stroking her own hair.

"Am I doing it right?" he asked, extricating his finger from hers.

"Better."

Soon, Cindi Fishman was asleep in her husband's arms.

JACOB FISHMAN'S MARRIAGE: A NOVEL

6. Peaches

Cindi had been in northern Nevada ever since she returned from France, where she taught English in Clermont-Ferrand in the Auvergne-Rhône-Alpes region, and from McGill University, where she received a master's and a Ph.D. In her summers, before she met and married Jacob, she'd return to Europe, especially France, but also Greece and Portugal, often inviting friends from America to join her on the trains and steamships and motorbikes on which she loved traveling. It was while in the South of France she studied at Plum Village with Thich Nhat Hanh, spending weeks in silent meditation, meaning no phones or television, obviously, but also no books, no notepads, and no talking. Thich, a Vietnamese Buddhist, was once nominated for the Nobel Peace Prize by Martin Luther King Jr., but he was also a savvy businessman. The last time she attended the retreat, and she participated in three, while waiting to pay, Cindi discovered that the Vietnamese girl in front of her was charged a third less for the same length of stay.

Cindi tried arguing with him in Vietnamese: *"nhảm nhí!"* ["Bullshit!"]

Thich responded, "ngôn ngữ của kẻ yếu" ["the language of the weak"]

"For a solid week?" Jacob once asked her about the lack of talking.

"Honey, you wouldn't make it ten minutes."

She had also converted to Judaism before marrying Jacob, even though he was not the reason.

Before being hired by UNR, she worked at a Great Basin Community Food Co-op in Reno, then at Reno Massage and Wellness, for a brief time, quitting when a man flipped over and asked her how much extra she would charge to "do my privates."

She was hired as an assistant professor in UNR's philosophy department and had come through her second-, third-, and fourth-year reviews with solid if not spectacular recommendations, so tenure, while never a sure thing, was not supposed to be a problem.

The university, being so close to where she and Jacob lived, was the best thing about the house on Codel, a house she hated for reasons that had to do with the identity of being a wife, a neighbor, a homeowner, when all she wanted to do most was to sit, nude, out back of a place without a mortgage, smoke dope, and write in her journal. She also longed to return to Clermont-Ferrand, with a baby on her back.

"Why don't you just do that, then?" Jacob would ask her about returning to Europe, on those days when her unhappiness was the only thing defining their marriage.

"You don't understand," she said.

He didn't, and when she didn't leave, he assumed she was not as unhappy as she said, or believed, she was.

Cindi fancied herself a rebel, one who could and would, in fact, strap a baby on her back and camp or hop those trains in Europe and not someone who had to wait for a plumber on a Monday morning because the toilet was backing up into the tub. She didn't have a baby, she didn't have a husband who would camp, and she didn't have the Pyrenees.

She had a house on Codel and a sick feeling she wasn't getting tenure.

"When I was a freshman at McGill," she told her students during her first year back in the classroom, "I was taking an Introduction to Philosophy course, but since it was McGill, they made a point of saying it wasn't a course to introduce students to philosophy but to introduce them to a philosophical way of thinking," and then she mimed a hand job.

Which was not the first time she mimed a hand job in class.

The class laughed.

"I was so annoyed at the instructor's attitude, like he came down from his bell tower to grace us with his presence, I stood up and walked out. Before I got to the door, though, the man in the bell tower asked, 'Where are you going, mademoiselle?'"

"I turned around," she told her class, "and said, 'This class sucks. This course sucks. This discipline sucks. The people in it suck. And you, I'm afraid, as the embodiment of it all, suck. I'm leaving.'"

"'Mademoiselle,'" he said, 'please sit.' And I did.

"I'm telling you this," she said to the class, "to remind you that if you want to get on my good side, speak to me in French."

Her students, if the evaluations were any judge, loved her, the day with Casey notwithstanding, especially in those early years, even if the administration frowned on her unapproved field trips to places like Lake Tahoe and the three-hour tour of the lake on the *Tahoe Gal*, a tourist boat, where she went one year. A drunk student fell overboard and was kept at a hospital in Tahoe overnight for evaluations.

"Everybody bitches," she told Belsky, who was chairman at the time, "about the one who didn't come back, but nothing about the nine I brought back safely."

"You think that's funny?" he asked.

"Kind of, but I can see your point."

There was also the affair, albeit a brief one, before she was married, with Sanjay, an Indian exchange student who played percussion instruments. She got pregnant, had an abortion, and never told him, or anyone, including Jacob. Sanjay left school after that and returned to Delhi. She met Jacob less than a month after the procedure.

That was my baby, that was my chance, Cindi thought, riding her bike to school on a day she didn't have class. *Fuck!*

"I want to teach that Maimonides seminar," Cindi said, walking into Mitch's office, a week after they returned from Vegas.

"Let it go already. Besides, it's too late. Why is it so important, anyway?" Mitch asked. "By the way, you still okay about Vegas?"

"Fine. It happened. It almost happened. Nothing happened. How do you want to view it?"

"Second. Almost happened. You wanna get high?"

"I didn't come here to talk about almost fucking you in Vegas," Cindi said. "I love the fact the Jewish prophets are such putzes, even Moses, who was the shittiest fucking husband."

"Why are we talking about the Jews?"

"Moses even makes his wife wait while he talks to his father-in-law— his fucking father-in-law! Oh, the Christians, the Buddhists, all their prophets are perfect, and in the case of the Buddhists, chubby, but the Jews, what a bunch of imperfect fuckheads."

"Why are we talking about this?"

"I don't know. They're all fuckheads. Every last one of them."

"Fuckheads? I don't know why Howland won't let you teach the good stuff."

"Thing is, the way they treat women. Jesus! I mean, I'm a Jew, I can say that. On the other hand, for all the patriarchal hierarchy, at least the Jews, especially reformed Judaism, are making an effort . . . Changing the male names of God and including the matriarchy as well. All religions, all through history, it's like one big circle jerk. Boys sucking boys' cocks."

"'Boys sucking boys' cocks. All through history.' That should have been your dissertation."

Jacob didn't smoke dope, and he always made Cindi feel like a child when she wanted to, so it was nice to have someone who enjoyed getting high as much as she. Mitch kept his stash on a windowsill beside some planters, a plastic baseball helmet he once got a sundae in, and a purple Seagram's pouch.

She didn't hide her smoking from Jacob, who more than once asked, "How good can the pot be? What do you get out of it? Is there really universal elucidation watching a roach scurry across the hardwood?"

"'Universal elucidation'? You know, my darling husband, nobody actually talks like this."

Mitch handed Cindi the pipe.

"This is the only setting," Cindi said to Mitch, inhaling deeply, "where I like Van Morrison."

"He's very shy onstage," Mitch said, taking the pipe from Cindi.

"But there's some debate as to whether he's shy or just a prick," she said, putting her feet on her side of the desk. "When I saw him in France, he only performed for forty-five minutes. It was a fabulous forty-five minutes, but the French were not happy."

"Are they ever?"

"I have something for you," said Cindi, and pulled out a package, neatly wrapped, from her knapsack. "I missed your birthday."

"You did. Not that I noticed."

Mitch opened the package and discovered Van Morrison's *Magic Time.* "I love it. This is that Canadian set that's kind of tough to find."

"I assumed you had it, but you've never played it. And I'm afraid we might have to start recycling the old music without some new tunes. And there's just so many times a girl can hear 'Moondance' without wanting to stab herself repeatedly in the lower abdomen."

"No, I don't have it," he said, ignoring her comment about stabbing herself, and placed the compilation on his desk. "It looks good. I thank you. My desk thanks you." He leaned it against the lamp base.

"You're welcome."

"Thanks, Cindi. I mean it." He came around and hugged her and kissed her on the cheek.

"You want to go to the door and put your hands over your head? We do good work there."

"Would you stop it?" he said, returning to his desk.

"I just hate my life sometimes. And it is amazing to me that here in the office, it all goes away."

"Nice transition."

"Sorry," she said, taking another hit from the pipe. "How about you?"

"Me?"

"How do you stay so sane?"

"I don't know that I'm sane, but you remember Kurt Vonnegut's son Mark?" he asked.

"No."

"Mark Vonnegut. There was a time he was out of his mind, so he wrote a book, *The Eden Express*, and in it he said that knowing he was crazy helped. A little, but it helped. Well, for me, too. Knowing about the proverbial spit and bailing wire that holds me together does stop the really destructive stuff around the edges from coming to fruition. So if I'm sane, it just means I can see where the ledge is, which is why we're smoking dope and not shooting heroin."

"Right, because that would be wrong."

"Criminal."

"Dangerous."

"Expensive."

"What's amazing about this," Cindi said, "is you're not even high yet, so there's no excuse for you not knowing what drivel that all was. Knowing you're crazy stops the crazy stuff from happening? Does that get anyone in bed? And I'm teaching the survey courses?"

"Don't be so cynical. And it does get women in bed. We have a problem, you know, you and I. Everyone in this building; everyone in philosophy. We have a really healthy self-image with an equally unhealthy self-loathing. No matter how smart we are, I am, you are, there are fifteen, twenty guys out there five times smarter, still figuring out the problems of man, but not being able to figure out how to email on a cellphone."

"Oh, Professor Aloisio, you're so brilliant. Help me off with my pants."

"Give me back my pot," he said, grabbing the pipe. "How's Jacob?"

"Please."

"Not good?"

"It's exhausting. He's exhausting. You?"

"You mean with my girlfriend."

"What's her name again? Natasha?"

"You're not going to stop, are you?"

"Irina? Tatiana?"

"Rouslana. She's from Russia."

"I know, I know," she said rocking back and forth on a chair not meant for rocking.

"It is, but, you know, nobody can keep anybody happy all the time. I mean, we don't do a lot of talking about Kierkegaard over Froot Loops, but I'm not sure that's wise anyway."

"No! She eats Froot—"

"Yup. And Cap'n Crunch and Chocolate Frosted Flakes."

"No shit!" Cindi said, pushing back on the desk with her foot, causing the chair to move out from under her. She hit the floor mid-laugh.

"Stuck the landing," Mitch said.

"Does she smoke?" Cindi asked, getting up from the floor and sitting in the chair. "I think I bruised my ass."

"Coke."

"You've got a Russian girlfriend who drinks Coke and eats Froot Loops? Is it just the pot or is that just really fucking funny?"

"It is what it is. And Jacob?"

"Diet Coke."

"And you're making fun of me?"

"You think this is strange, you know, us, reasonably mature people, in our forties, smoking dope and talking about Natasha and Jacob?"

"Rouslana."

"Right, sorry. You forget about moose."

"That joke just doesn't get old."

"I'm sorry. You're lucky. Jacob drops Kierkegaard references and Michael Corleone references and Ria Fishman references and Randy Newman references and even ex-girlfriend references, and I wish I could just have a normal conversation for once, without the allusions and morals, without feeling like he's trying out his intelligence on me, without feeling like it's a conversation he had before or he's rehearsing to have again. I would like him to sit at the kitchen table and eat cereal,

even Froot Loops, and not talk about the fat content or the dextrose
or—"

"Who's Ria Fishman?" Mitch asked.

"His mom."

"Sure, who else would Jacob Fishman quote?"

"Let me ask you," said Cindi, "have you ever regretted every decision
you've ever made and found yourself hating everyone and everything in
your life?"

"No more pot for you."

"I bruised my ass for you."

"You're right," he said, "and to answer your question, not a lot, but
yeah."

"I do. Not right now, with you, but yeah. I'm insufferable to everyone, including myself."

"You bought me a Morrison CD. You're not insufferable."

"You know what I mean. Jacob is beyond description sometimes,
but it's not him. Well, it is, but . . . but I am . . . I mean, I don't know
why, how he puts up with me."

"I'm sure people don't know how you put up with him."

"You're nice to say that, but I'm on good behavior with you. I can
be awful, a cunt, actually. So why are you so nice to me, Mitch?"

"Before, it was to get you in bed."

"Not anymore?"

"Not until your ass heals."

"Stop it."

"I like your hair. Do you straighten it or something?"

"What did you say?"

"Your hair. I like it. No good? Did I say something wrong?"

"No, no. It's just, you don't know how funny that is."

"We're not so different, the two of us. You and me."

"It's 'I,' isn't it?"

"Did I correct your 'It's not him' earlier when you should have said,
'It's not he'? I'm stoned. Gimme a break."

"What do you mean, though, we're not so different? We really are.
You're sleeping with Boris' wife from *Bullwinkle* and I'm . . . not. Never
mind."

"I'm sorry," Mitch said, putting away the plastic bag of marijuana in the Seagram's pouch. "I mean, there is something about—"

"Don't you know that's the first place immigration and the narcs look?" she asked, pointing to the bag.

"Am I in trouble with immigration or narcs? Now, what were you saying?"

"No, you were saying."

"Pretty sure you were saying."

"No, I'm sorry," Cindi said, laughing, "I'm confused. Who was talking?"

"Go. You," Mitch said.

"I shouldn't be talking about this."

"What are we talking about?" he asked, laughing.

"Sex. I shouldn't be talking—"

"We were talking about sex?"

"Yeah, I was. You, by contrast, are actually having some. I'll shut up now."

"It's okay. What is said here stays between you, me, and Van."

"I'm fucked up," Cindi said, leaning back, putting her feet up on the desk.

"Don't fall again. Remember this, my friend," Mitch said, pointing a finger at her, "there are three truths in life."

"Oh, God. You're so sexy, Professor."

"You are a cunt sometimes!"

"Established."

"Let me finish."

"Go. I love when you're all rabbinical and shit."

"I'm not rabbinical and shit. Okay, the peach, the baby's smile, and the orgasm: the three truths."

"That's beautiful."

Mitch closed his eyes briefly, shook his head. "Do you have to mock everything I say?"

"No, I mean it. That is beautiful. You're going to make me cry."

"Cindi, please."

"I'm serious. Maybe it's the pot, but I'm serious."

"You want a baby, is that it?"

"It's a long story. Yes. No. I don't know. Jacob and I . . . he has a daughter. He said . . . well, he said that he would, but then he wouldn't, couldn't, never said he wanted . . . I am so fucked up, forget it."

"No. Tell me."

"I have a peach story."

"What do you mean, you have a peach story?"

"God, this is weird. I have a peach story. I had a peach at a farmer's market about a year ago, and there's a story."

"I'm not following you."

"Jacob and I stopped at one of these fruit stands, I don't know, near Carson City. And the farmer had in this bushel, basket, whatever they keep the peaches in, one of the biggest peaches I had ever seen. But he said that the smaller ones he had in another basket were the better-tasting ones."

"Okay."

"But I didn't buy those. I didn't believe him. We bought the big ones."

"Peaches in Nevada? I didn't know we had any."

"Me neither. That's what makes the story even better."

"Go ahead."

"Well, we drive down the road and I start eating these peaches and they were good, really good, but, fuck, it bothered me I didn't believe the guy, so—"

"Are you crying?"

"Let me finish. So I told Jacob we have to go back. So he agrees, surprisingly."

"Cindi, everybody knows the small peaches are better. You didn't know that?"

"What do I know about peaches? Anyway, we're about twenty minutes away and go back and try to find the guy."

"Did you?"

"I've never tasted anything so wonderful in my life, so there you go."

"How's your ass?"

"Fuck off."

When she got home that night, Jacob was in bed. She wanted to wake him up, remind him about the peaches, wanted to cup his face in her hands and kiss him and apologize and promise . . . what? She didn't know.

"I promise, I promise," she whispered. She watched him sleep. He was on his side, in a fetal position. He looked cold, so she pulled the blanket over him and then went into the bathroom and vomited.

Princess Charlize-Louise de Secondat, Baron de La Brede Cougar Mellencamp

Jacob was working on fictional Cindi's big-peach/small-peach story in *Jacob Fishman's Marriage* and hoping the burgeoning romance between Cindi and Mitch was plausible when he heard his real wife, what sounded like Sage, and what definitely sounded like a barking dog come in the back door.

He heard his name and then more barking.

"Jacob?" Cindi called out.

"In a minute."

"Come down."

"Coming."

"Jake, please!"

"In a second. I'm writing."

"For Chrissakes! I would come down for you."

"I'm coming."

"I want to show you something."

"I think I can hear it."

"He was there. I say, 'You probably don't remember me, but we bought the big peaches instead of the small ones and the big ones are good, but I have to have a small peach. You told me the small ones are

better . . . please. So he gives me one of the small peaches. And, I . . . uh . . . uh . . .

He left it on the screen because he had to rework it. For one thing, the quote wasn't exact and the whole scene was probably too long. It wasn't terrible, but it wasn't right either. He went downstairs. The Jacob he wanted to be—maybe the Jacob he was creating—would have taken the steps two at a time. He didn't.

"What? What?" he asked, as something white with black spots and no bigger than a cat headed for him.

"This is," Cindi started to say, "well, I don't have a name yet, but I'm thinking of naming her Princess Charlize-Louis de Secondat, Baron de La Brede—"

"Cougar Mellencamp?" Jacob added.

Cindi laughed. "A reference I get. What a day for me! Isn't she adorable?"

"It's a small dog."

"It's a puppy. I wanted to surprise you."

"It's a dog."

"I know. She's so cute."

"It's a dog."

"Would you please stop saying that?"

"Why did you get a dog?"

"'Cause I don't have a baby."

"Let's start again. Why—"

"No, no. I'm in a good mood."

"Hi, Sage. You're looking . . . I don't know. Wild. I mean that in a good way. Is your hair something?"

"Teased, streaked."

"Good look. Almost intimidating. And, again, I mean that in a good way."

"Let's assume I'm here, too, okay?" Cindi asked.

"Anyway, the dog—you were in on this?" Jacob asked Sage.

She waved her hands in front of her and pointed to Cindi. "I just drove."

Turning his attention back to Cindi and the new dog with the long name, Jacob asked, "Do you have time to take care of a dog?" as Cindi cradled it in her arms and played with its underbelly.

"I have time and stop being passive-aggressive."

"I'm not being passive-aggressive."

"Yes, you are. Instead of saying you hate the dog, you're worried, well, you say you're worried—you really don't care—that I'm not going to have time to take care of it."

"Did you rehearse this argument on the way here without me? I don't hate the dog. Sage, tell her I don't hate the dog."

"Jacob, you hate the dog."

"Cougar Mellancamp," he said to the dog, "I don't hate you."

"*Her* name is not—"

"I'm joking. I don't hate the dog. I don't like dogs. I don't get them. And I don't get people who get them, and I wasn't expecting one today."

"Didn't you have a dog growing up?" asked Sage.

"I don't remember. I think my mom or sister had one. But, no, I didn't have a dog that was mine."

"How sad it is to be you," said Cindi.

"What's to get?" Sage asked, "You love them, they love you back."

"That's setting the bar pretty low."

Sage, who had joined and left the Mormon church, knew about the Ephemerides, read palms, did Tarot readings, and baked bread, put her hands over her eyes and shook her head. "Unconditional love, Jake."

"You should try it," Cindi added.

"I understand that," he replied to both of them, "but dogs also drink from bowls in the garage and run out of the house the minute you leave the door open. What kind of love is that? And, anyway, again, don't we want to raise the bar somewhat on the level and sophistication of our interpersonal relationships?"

"You like the bar metaphor, don't you, honey?" asked his wife.

"Jacob, your wife, my best friend, wants a puppy or a baby. Since the second is not going to happen, I would suggest you drop your opposition to the first."

"But the big thing is this dog? She's really keeping it?"

"Again, I'm fucking right here and can hear you both. Tell you what, while you two figure this out, I'm taking Princess Charlize-Louis de Secondat, Baron de La Brede out for a walk," Cindi said. She headed for the front door.

"You going to use the full name every time you refer to it?"

"Blow me," Cindi said, closing the door behind her.

"Is she really a dog person?" he asked Sage. "Don't you have to love animals to do it right? And what happens the first time the little beast pees on her *Being and Nothingness*?"

"You're funny, Jacob, and you're cynical, neither of which are particularly welcome at the moment. But you raise an interesting question. No, she's not, but yes, she wants to be."

Cindi came through the door.

"That was quick."

"She already peed, so there."

"'So there'? I can pee that fast. Where did you find this dog, anyway? Did you buy her?"

"No. We were driving around Tahoe, near Incline Village, and we bonded."

"I'm not following."

"Sage and I were walking up by Steve Wynn's place—"

"Walking by Steve Wynn's place? You can do that? There's not security around?"

"Jacob, goddamn it!"

"Sorry."

"We were walking by Wynn's place, and we ran into this strange little man with a big head and a roving eye who was carrying this precious dog."

"I'm not laughing. Sage, you're a witness. I'm not laughing."

"Anyway," Cindi continued, "he asked if we could find her a good home, because he had rescued her from some circus people who had panthers who were going to be fed my dog."

"Come on!"

"It's true," Sage said.

"Go on," Jacob said.

"So we said yeah, sure, we'll take her. I was going to call you, but I was afraid if I didn't say yes right away, the little man—"

"With the big head?"

"Right . . . would take her back to the panthers—"

"—that the circus people owned."

"I'm going to fucking kill you, I swear to Christ, if you don't stop it!" Cindi screamed.

Jacob stopped.

"I love her. We belong together," Cindi said, starting to cry. "And besides, it'll be great, because you can give Cindi a dog."

"Cindi?"

"Cindi."

"Cindi from the book? You're worried about Cindi in the book?"

"Yes, she needs a dog. You need to make her more lovable."

Jacob looked at his wife, cuddling with the dog on the chaise, a chaise usually host to an unhappy woman, and thought at that moment he could stay married to this woman for the rest of his life.

"Okay."

"Okay?"

"Okay."

"Thank you," his wife said, though he knew she hated herself immediately for saying it, as if she needed his okay. "Here," she said, getting up, bringing Princess Charlize-Louis de Secondat, Baron de La Brede to him. "You want to hold her? She is so sweet, so sweet."

"Cindi," Sage said, seeing Jacob recoil, "it may take Jake a few months to warm up to the princess."

"Years," Jacob started to say, when the front door opened. It was Lyla, Cindi's friend from the English department, with beer and pizza and a PetsMart bag.

"Hey," Jacob said. "Where'd you come from?"

"Look, Princess Charlize," said Cindi, "it's Aunt Lyla."

"Aunt Lyla?" Jacob said to Lyla. "You were there?"

"Feel the love." Lyla kissed the dog, still in Cindi's arms.

"Look at that face! Look at that face!" Cindi said to everyone.

"You should have seen your wife's face," said Lyla, "when she picked up Princess Charlize-Louis de Secondat, Baron de La Brede from the man with the big head."

"*The Man With the Big Head* is now the name of the novel. I heard. He really had a big head?"

"Huge. Circus-like."

"Nobody will ever believe this."

"He had this goodness, though," said Sage, "you could just tell, but there was an evil there, too."

"The evil man with the big head—nah, title doesn't work."

"Yes, he did!" Cindi said to Sage. "You're right. He was dark but light, good but evil."

Princess Charlize-Louis de Secondat, Baron de La Brede barked when Lyla emptied the bag of toys, treats, scarves, and stuffed animals.

"Everything in the house," Lyla continued, "was miniature, too, even the big-head man's wife."

"She had a small head?" Jacob asked, about to pee in his pants.

"Yes," Sage said, now also laughing. "They had, like, rodents and wild boar out back and these panthers, big, black panthers, that we heard were fed little dogs."

Cindi started crying.

"You went to the house?" Jacob asked. "You didn't tell me that!"

"They were going to eat lit . . . lit . . . little Jackie," Cindi said. "But the man with the big head said he had to make sure it was okay, because it wasn't really his dog."

"Girls, really, stop. There are no circus people and men with big heads and wives with small heads in Tahoe. But it's a great story nonetheless."

"There's a world out there," Sage said.

"I don't know what that means. There's a what out there?" Jacob asked, sitting on the sofa and watching the three of them on the chaise, as they all hugged the dog and each other.

He caught the dog's eye.

"Eaten by panthers?" he asked.

The dog continued staring.

"Yes," said Cindi, and she burst into tears again. "Don't ruin this for me, okay? Please, not this."

"I won't. I'm just nonplussed."

Sage laughed. "Nonplussed? Very good, Jacob."

"Where's the dog going to sleep?" Jacob asked, trying not to ruin his wife's happiness, but an important question nonetheless, especially to a couple not having sex in a bed he was now fearing he would be sharing.

"In bed?"

"With us?" Jacob asked, smiling, pointing at Cindi and himself. "Not with me."

"I know you'll love the princess. C'mon, hold her."

"No."

"Why?"

"I don't want to."

"Cin," said Sage, "maybe no dog in the bed for a while."

"Listen to Sage, my favorite friend of yours, except when I like Lyla more," said Jacob.

"We'll see," Cindi said.

Cindi, Lyla, and Sage took Princess Charlize to the front porch, leaving Jacob on the sofa, surrounded by dog toys and treats. He peeked out through the blinds and saw the dog in his wife's lap. Cindi was stroking the dog's underbelly and neck and kissing its nose.

"Mommy loves you," he heard her say.

Mommy?

"Jacob, I heard that!" Cindi screamed from the porch, rapping on the window. "Stop smacking."

"He smacked," he heard her tell her friends.

"Jacob," Sage said, "don't smack your lips."

Jacob went back upstairs and gave Cindi a dog.

Dr. Jovanovic and the Girl with the Scrunchy in Her Hair

The office of Dr. Oliver Jovanovic, Jacob's psychiatrist, was in a converted three-story house, across from a Wells Fargo Bank and a Starbucks. Parking was in front, which Jacob assumed was part of the therapy, not being ashamed to admit you needed help and for people to see you weren't embarrassed to walk in the front door, rather than slink around back like you were entering an adult-movie theater—though he still would have preferred not having everyone outside Starbucks, drinking Arabian Mocha Sananis and Caramel Macchiatos, to see him and his orange 2004 Honda Element pull into the parking lot. The building, Positive Behavioral Strategies, a name that both confounded and annoyed him, housed psychiatrists, psychologists, marriage counselors, and, inexplicably, a chiropractor. Cindi's psychologist, Aurora Sims, had an office here as well, which was where the similarity ended. Aurora—she insisted Cindi call her by her first name—was a family counselor, who had a bachelor's from Cal-State Northridge in psychology, whereas German-born Dr. Jovanovic had an M.D. from the University of California-San Francisco department of psychiatry and the Langley Porter Psychiatric Institute, where he worked on traumatic-memory research. Jacob thought Jovanovic was overqualified to treat his garden-variety neurosis and displacement issues, which the Germans call *verschiebung*, but Jacob loved the doctor's ability and willingness to call him on his rationalizations and general bullshit and do so in German. Jovanovic, too, told Jacob to call him by his first name—Jovanovic said everyone called him Ollie—but Jacob did not want to call his psychiatrist Ollie, especially his German psychiatrist Ollie, especially a German psychiatrist named Ollie who charged him $145 per hour. Jacob was competitive enough to take pleasure in the fact that he had the real doctor, one who had actually been born and raised in Germany and, hence, sounded like psychiatrists are supposed to sound, part Freud, part Einstein, part Kissinger, part Arte Johnson. Aurora, by contrast, was born in Sacramento and sounded like Swoosie Kurtz.

Dr. Jovanovic didn't hug his patients, as Aurora did, nor did he burn candles, lower or turn off the lights, give writing assignments, or sit around an oval table drinking herbal tea. In Jovanovic's office, there was still the sofa, but most patients, including Jacob, opted for the over-stuffed red leather recliner, purposefully placed—or Jacob liked to think so—under Edvard Munch's *Scream*, which Jacob found both perfect and clichéd.

"So?" Jovanovic asked without pleasantries, as Jacob came in and sat down. Jovanovic sat, as he always did, legs crossed, with a timer and notepad in his lap, at his desk chair.

"Could you change the sign out front?"

Jacob said something similar at the beginning of every session, even though Jovanovic never took the bait.

"Okay," Jacob said, responding to the silence and thinking he'd bring out the *verschiebung* first thing, "she got a dog."

"Good!"

"Why does everyone think that's good?"

"Not good?" Jovanovic asked.

Was that a smile?

"Problems?" Jovanovic asked again, taking out his pen.

"Not with the dog," said Jacob. "She loves the dog. The dog loves her. Probably had it six weeks. Cindi is in an incredibly good mood."

"Is that bad?"

"She accused me of trying to kill it."

"Did you?"

Jacob looked at Jovanovic, waiting for him to smile.

"No, I didn't try to kill it. I put out some Tomcat pellets that kill mice—and I can't believe I remember the name—these little green square things, which mice eat and then go somewhere to die, and Cindi is under the impression that if her dog with the extra-long name ate some of it, which she didn't, she would also die, which Cindi thinks I did on purpose because apparently I'm the type of person who kills dogs with mouse pellets."

"You're upset by that?"

"Shouldn't I be? She thinks I would poison the dog she got from the gypsies and the guy with the big head in Tahoe outside Steve Wynn's place."

"Am I supposed to know—"

"No."

"Go on."

"Go on?"

"Go on."

Dr. Jovanovic crossed his legs and started scribbling something on his pad, which was the kind of pad used for graphs. He wrote in short, precise strokes, using only capital letters.

"Let me guess," Jack said, pointing to the pad. "'Jacob Fishman is jealous of the dog.'"

"Is that what you think I'm writing?"

"Isn't it?"

"Want to see?"

"Yeah."

Jovanovic handed Jacob the pad.

Jacob Fishman DOB 5/3/57.

Lorazepam 1 mg

Omeprazole 20 mg

Aspirin 81 mg

Tadal 7 mg

Jovanovic had been writing down the date.

"Oh," Jacob said, handing the pad back. "I'm not taking the Tadal anymore. That's Cialis."

"I know what it is."

"Of course, because you're a psychiatrist. A psychologist—"

"Jacob."

"Sorry. But you can cross it out because I don't take it. I mean, once in a while. Okay, don't cross it out. Whatever."

"Are we done with your medication?"

"Yeah. So, okay, I am jealous of the dog."

"Go on."

"I have nothing to do with my wife's happiness—I mean nothing. And for a man with a pretty big ego, that's a little tough to take."

"What do you think of the dog?"

"It's a dog. I mean, it's a . . . dog. I don't know. I don't get the whole thing with pets."

"You're smart enough to know this isn't about pets."

"Is that a compliment?"

Jovanovic started writing again.

"Dozen eggs, Diet Sprite, Frosted Mini Wheats, get Didion documentary from Red Box," Jacob said, smiling.

Jovanovic looked up but didn't stop writing and wasn't smiling.

"I'd be bored with me too," Jacob said, motioning again to the pad. "Sometimes I just want to stop talking. Go sit in a cave in my underwear in the South of France with a Vietnamese master and eat berries. I mean, every week it's the same: I pick up the same rock, turn it around, flip it upside down, and then put it down and think how wonderful it is that I have a new insight into the same rock."

Jovanovic stopped writing. "You enjoying yourself?"

"Ah, you remember. Very flattering."

"Your mom, right?"

"Yeah. Cindi's still not wearing the ring, there's still no sex, and now I have to hear her kvell over this fucking dog nineteen hours a day."

"Kvell?"

"It's a Yiddish word, means 'gush.' You're German. I'm surprised you don't know."

Jovanovic was now smiling.

"What?" asked Jacob. "What?"

"How long did you rehearse that opening, about the rock?" Jovanovic asked. He closed the pen and put both on the desk.

"I don't know." Jacob smiled back. "Maybe twenty minutes."

"How long?"

"An hour."

"Why?"

"Why did I rehearse the opening or why did I rehearse it for an hour? Because," Jacob said, not waiting for an answer, "I am trying to articulate . . . I don't know. I guess I wanted to be . . . um, intelligent, articulate . . . I just said that, didn't I? I would like to think I can articulate my own happiness or the reasons that I'm not. I want you to respect me."

"Why is that important to you?"

"People I respect, well, it would be nice if they felt the same."

"But it's not that."

"Maybe so that when the marriage ends, I'll be able to sum it up for people who want to know what happened?"

"Why is that important?"

Jacob exhaled.

"Because they're going to ask, and maybe I shouldn't sound like a sniveling dolt when they do."

"Do you know what people are going to ask?"

"Pretty much."

The office was filled with old records in frames and *Playbill*s and some pictures of the doctor's family, his graduation, on a boat holding a marlin, and, strangely, one of Debbie Reynolds, which was autographed. Dr. Jovanovic did not have a computer in the office, which Jacob admired, and the phone, if there was one, never rang.

"I'm lost," Jacob said. "I don't mean philosophically—or maybe that, too—I mean, really. I don't know what I'm missing that you want."

"You know."

"I do? All right . . . um . . . look, I keep waiting for her to leave me, keep expecting to find out she's having an affair, keep planning how I'm going to act when it happens. I'm rehearsing the humiliation and hurt and the stoicism."

"Do you want her to leave you? Have an affair?"

Jacob smacked his lips, bobbed his head, smiled.

"Yeah. No. Maybe. I can see life pretty clearly on both sides: staying married and getting divorced. I mean, I don't know about the affair, but—"

"So you're impatient she hasn't left you yet?"

"Pretty stupid, huh?"

As if Jovanovic was going to answer that.

"I told you about the book I'm writing, yes?"

"Yes."

"I didn't know that I did."

"You did."

"Maybe I should have that Jacob kill the dog. You know, when I got married, I thought, I mean, I don't know what I thought, but it was supposed to be better than this. Cindi wasn't too young, she wasn't too old. She wasn't so negative. Well, I didn't think, anyway. I thought, 'Jesus, a mature woman, never married, no kids. Perfect.'"

"And?"

"And I sometimes think . . . no, I know, I was happier before I got married, although before, I was thinking how great it would be to have someone like Cindi."

Jovanovic leaned forward.

"I married someone for everything she wasn't," Jacob said, "namely everyone else I ever dated, or like my first wife. I ever tell you the time that I was in a bar in Chicago with an old girlfriend with some of her friends?"

Jacob waited for a response.

"Anyway, so we were standing around—another couple and this girl I was dating—at the bar, and one of the women started talking about a relationship of hers that just ended. She said it ended because her boyfriend couldn't take her independence, the fact that she didn't need his money and, here's the part that got me, that he couldn't take how together she was."

"And you said something."

"I told her that in all the relationships I ever had that ended, I never thought it was because I was too wonderful. I always blame myself."

"Why tell me that story, which, you know, you've told me before? Why make it sound like you were the only one at the bar that night that had any perspective on this? The only one to see the woman's interpretation was flawed?"

"Oh . . . because while she was talking, the hostess walked by, the cutest girl, with one of those scrunchy things in her hair. She was tanned, gorgeous, and for some reason she tapped me on the shoulder and smiled at me, and said, 'Having fun?'"

"What did that tell you, mean to you? Was she supposed to save you? And you didn't answer my question but go ahead."

"Just that . . . here I was with women my own age, mature, successful women, talking about relationships and real life and then this girl walks by with the scrunchy and I could see the metaphor—she was the metaphor, had to be fifteen or twenty years younger than I, and for the life of me, I wanted her, even though she had this scrunchy in her hair and probably didn't know or care who Paul Mazursky is."

"Who's Paul Mazursky?"

"You don't know who Paul Mazursky is?"

"No."

"A director. Contemporary of Woody Allen. Did a number of movies. I think my favorite is *Blume in Love*—"

"Jacob."

"Sorry."

"Go on."

"Go on?"

"Did you . . . have her?"

"Have her? Oh, oh . . . that." Jacob laughed. "Well, I gave her my number."

"Did she call?"

"No."

"So why did you tell me that story . . . again?"

"I don't know, really, but I have to come up with new material. It's been dawning on me lately that the happiest times in my life have always been with women who made no sense for me to be with. I mean, Cindi and I, on paper, are perfect together. And yet we're miserable. I had a colonoscopy thing, and she didn't stay with me afterward—"

"You told me already."

"Is there anything I haven't told you?"

Now Jovanovic smiled.

"How's it been since?"

"My ass?"

"Jacob."

"Up until the dog thing, I don't know. I mean, I don't know. The same. She's not happy in bed. I don't know whether she doesn't come because I don't turn her on or because she doesn't see any upside to having an orgasm."

"Do you," Dr. Jovanovic asked, leaning forward, "realize how much of yourself that you present as an essay? How much you spin and hide and manipulate the telling? How often you speak in italics?"

"I do."

"I don't think you do. You plan the planning. You present your life in vignettes and you're smart enough to present yourself just a little quirky, a little vulnerable, a little more deserving and intelligent than other people in the story, but always with enough self-deprecation to inoculate yourself from claims that you're self-aggrandizing."

"Doesn't everyone?"

"You know the answer to that, and that answer motivates you. When it works best for you, people respond and give you a line worthy of your script—and when they do, you think it's Kismet, rather than just coincidence, rather than your choreography of the moment."

"What do I do about that? Of course, you're not going to answer."

"What do you want to happen?"

"Can I tell you about the trailer first?"

"No, you cannot. Cindi wants a trailer. I know that. You're quite accomplished at deflection. Why don't you tell Cindi the truth?"

"The truth?"

"Yeah."

"I don't know. Which truth?"

"The only truth. The one you dance around, the one Cindi knows you dance around."

"My ambivalence at being married? That's not it, is it?"

Jovanovic looked through him.

"My inadequacies?"

Jovanovic put his forefinger between his lips.

"Jacob, when you're ready to deal with it, you'll deal with it."

"I swear to you, I don't know what you're talking about. What truth?"

"And I swear, you do. But for now, if you want to tell me about the trailer, tell me about the trailer."

"Okay, Cindi wants to buy a trailer. She found one, too. It needs plumbing, electricity, carpentry. It's terrible. She is going to move it to some friend's property. Thirty-five hundred bucks, but it's not the money. And it's not my money, anyway. But here's the thing: She's excited about this trailer, living there, getting away, et cetera, et cetera."

"You're unhappy about that?"

"She's going to fix it up, so she'll have a place to go when she decides to move out, even though the place is half hers. I mean, that is what it's for—the trailer."

"Once again you're upset that she's apparently planning on leaving you and yet relieved that she's actually planning on leaving you?"

"I think so. This reminds me of a time when my first wife and I were splitting up. She had gotten a job at a department store, I think, and I remember thinking, 'At least she'll have a job when she leaves.'"

"I want you to do me a favor. From now on, try not rehearsing before you come here. Don't learn your lines. Try to remember what you have already told me. You are working on your act, and it's a good one, but it's an old one and it's dusty and, most important, it's not nearly as germane, certainly not as helpful or dispositive to your life, as you think. Your greatest hits, as it were, are not that great—and you should see that. And even if it were, it's not the point here."

"That truth that I don't know is, right?"

Nothing.

"I don't know," Jacob continued, "whether my marriage is bad because I won't give her a baby, or I won't give her a baby because my marriage is bad."

Jovanovic cocked his head slightly. Jacob thought he saw a smile.

"I'm doing it again, aren't I? Working on the act? Worse, I think I stole that last line."

Another smile.

"What do you want, Jacob?" Jovanovic asked.

"I want to know what I want. I want some girl with a scrunchy to smile at me and I don't want to work at things that shouldn't need work. I want my wife to not only fuck me, but want to fuck me, which is never going to happen again. I'm in a bad marriage and I'm defining myself by it. I'd like that to stop."

"You enjoying yourself?"

"I'm afraid so."

Jacob Fishman's Marriage: A Novel

7. Comet

For a woman who would not handle a salt shaker in a restaurant unless she had first wrapped it in a paper napkin, preferably three or four, to prevent germs, Cindi displayed calm and understanding when cleaning up her dog's shit that was, Jacob concluded, positively Zen. She got Princess Charlize-Louis de Secondat, Baron de La Brede, half miniature pinscher, half rat terrier, in Lake Tahoe, or so she said, telling Jacob a preposterous story about a circus family that was feeding small animals to their collection of panthers and how this dog, whom she called Princess when she had neither the time nor energy for a full recital of the name she gave it, was given to her outside Steve Wynn's house in Incline Village by a small man with a big head. There were arguments for which Jacob could simply not summon the energy, and the dog's backstory was one of them. He told Cindi he was not cleaning up dog shit under any circumstances, a condition Cindi accepted, so when the dog defecated, she would calmly grab two or three napkins, pick up the offending sadness, and flush it down the toilet. As time went on, though, and they had Princess for only a few months, Cindi took

Jacob's reluctance to make an effort with Princess as personally as he took her getting Princess Charlize-Louis de Secondat, Baron de La Brede in the first place, even if she begrudgingly accepted his unwillingness to police their home for dog feces as not entirely unreasonable.

From her diary:

My husband won't pick up dog shit. The least he can do for not giving me a baby.

"Sorry you have to do this, but, damn, your dog shits a lot," Jacob told her, as he stood over her and watched her spray the carpet with Resolve.

"It's not your job. It's not your job. Don't worry. I, and I alone, am raising Princess Charlize-Louis de Secondat, Baron de La Brede."

"You're raising the dog alone? That's how you're going to spin this?" Jacob replied. Nothing grated on him more these days than her using the dog's full name in casual conversation.

"If you gave me a baby, we could raise it together," she said.

"The 'it' is a problem. You should use the third-person singular —'he' or 'she.' It's more humane."

"I've said this before, Jacob, but I mean it now. Fuck off."

Cindi wanted Jacob to love her dog, and Jacob knew that, but there was something about the Fishmans and an inability to extend small favors and kindnesses to one another that made this impossible. Cindi wanted Jacob's love for Princess to be organic, Jacob-to-dog, not just to placate her, even though Cindi wondered what it would be like to have a husband who did such small favors like love a wife's pet. And it was because she expected that, because she expected Jacob to love her dog willingly—and because she loved Princess so much, even more, Jacob suspected, than she loved him—that he refused.

"You're going to love Princess Charlize-Louise someday," Jacob remembered Cindi saying a few days after she brought her home.

"Keep telling me that," Jacob said, "and I can guarantee that's not going to happen."

"How can you not love this face?" Cindi would ask, as she'd pick up Princess and bring her to Jacob. Often when Jacob would go for his morning walks, Cindi would be sitting on the porch with the dog in her lap. Cindi would then walk to the top of the driveway with her and hold out the dog's paw and together they would wave goodbye.

"See, she's saying goodbye to you."

"You're moving her paw back and forth."

"Why can't you give me this, you prick?"

Jacob smiled.

"We love you," Cindi would call after him.

"I don't want *we* to love me."

This notion of love and expectation and the small graces was something Jacob had been thinking about in bed, a few days later, when he felt another sharp pain in the center of his chest. It was months after his first "attack" at the university, when he met the girl with the perfect teeth and the yellow highlighter. This episode was stronger, longer, and included pain that shot down his left arm, burning as it went, and traveling to the center of his palm, where it stopped and moved in a small, tight circle. He got up and sat on the edge of the bed. He put on one shoe, but the other one proved too difficult, so he lay back down. He tried again. He stopped midmotion, paralyzed—or he thought he was. Cindi was sleeping with Princess on her chaise in the living room.

I can't wake her. She'll panic or try to talk me out of it. This is crazy. It's indigestion.

Then another pain.

He moaned, hoping Cindi would hear him.

"Cindi," he called, but so low there was no way she could hear. He wanted her to wake telepathically.

His willingness to choreograph even this moment didn't surprise him.

Cindi would take him to St. Mary's, he was sure of that, though there would be an argument. She would yell about his diet.

He couldn't catch his breath.

The thought occurred to him it was neither a heart attack nor indigestion. Maybe it was psychosomatic or, worse, a need for attention? How pathetic can a man be, he thought, feigning a heart attack so his wife would give him more attention than she was giving a dog with whom she was presently sleeping. Better to die half-dressed in his bed with one shoe than to be disappointed by his wife again.

The pain subsided.

"What are you doing?" Cindi asked, appearing at the bedroom door, holding Princess in her arms. "Why do you have one shoe on?"

"Nothing. I thought I was having a heart attack." He sat up. "You?"

"What?"

"I had some chest pain, but it passed."

"You sure?"

"Indigestion, I think."

"You want to go to the hospital? I'll take you, honey."

"Good to know."

"'Good to know'? Did you think I wouldn't?"

"No, I knew you would. Sorry, I don't know why I said that. You're the person I wanted at that moment."

She sat on the edge of the bed. "I'd be lost without you. Don't die, okay?"

"Okay."

Honey.

When Cindi would leave the house, she'd put Princess in a carrying case designed for a cat, for the dog was not much bigger than one, something the neighbor's nasty cream-colored feline took advantage of, first by eating Princess' food when Cindi set it outside and next by hissing and mocking Princess from under her owner's car. Princess Charlize-Louise de Secondat, Baron de La Brede might have scared off two panthers in Tahoe, but she was no match for a stray cat named Boxo under a Ford Taurus.

Cindi was going to a departmental meeting with Howland and was putting Princess Charlize-Louise in the cat cage when Jacob, sitting at the kitchen counter, said, "All right, leave her out. I'll watch her."

"You will?"

"You won't be long, promise?"

"Promise. I love you." Cindi came over and kissed him.

"Sure you do," Jacob replied, accepting the kiss. "I love you, too."

"Daddy is going to watch you, Freckle Butt," she said to the dog, apparently adding yet another tag to Princess Charlize-Louise de Secondat, Baron de La Brede's name. "You can let her out. She'll stay by the house. She doesn't even go in the street."

"You sure?"

"She was traumatized as a baby. She's afraid to."

"How do you know this? You're anthropomorphizing again."

"I am not. I know."

At the door, Cindi and Princess rubbed noses.

"Would you stop that, please?" Jacob asked.

"How can you not love her? How can you not love her?" Cindi said. She walked out.

Instead of going upstairs to his office, Jacob sat on the sofa. Princess came to him and lifted herself up on two legs and started barking.

"What?" Jacob asked, looking at the dog. She dropped to the floor and started scratching an ear with a back leg, which Jacob assumed was one of the hind ones.

"She loves you more than she loves me, you know that, don't you?"

The dog stopped scratching. She stood on all fours, tail erect.

Jacob had heard an erect tail was a bad sign.

"Just relax."

Princess picked up a stuffed white monkey and started chewing and wrestling with it. She brought it to Jacob.

"Put it down and I'll throw it to you. I'm not taking it out of your mouth."

The dog did as she was told.

Jacob threw it into the dining room. Princess ran after it. Jacob heard feet scamper across the wood floor.

He repeated this three, four times until Princess stopped bringing it back.

"We're done playing? C'mon, I was liking this . . . liking you."

The dog barked.

"Out? You want to go out?"

Nothing.

The dog barked again.

"Out?"

Nothing.

Jacob went to the front door and opened it. Princess ran out. He returned to the couch and turned on *Judge Joe Brown*.

The judge was listening to the impassioned pleas of a man who insisted he didn't know he was married and shouldn't be held liable for his wife's bills.

"You mean," said Judge Brown, "you didn't know?"

"No, sir. 'The bitch,' as Marion Barry once said, 'set me up.'"

"Don't," the judge warned, "come into my courtroom and talk like that. And another thing: How can you not know you're married, son? I have heard just about everything, and I have—"

The sounds of a horn and a car screeching to a halt came from outside.

Jacob knew.

When he got outside, the driver was already out of his car and looking at Princess Charlize-Louis de Secondat, Baron de La Brede, who was already dead, as best Jacob could tell, lying half under the driver's front left tire and half in the open.

"Oh, fuck," said Jacob as he approached his wife's dead dog.

"Man, I tried to stop," said the man. "I did, man. It just ran out."

"Oh, fuck, fuck, fuck. Fuck!" Jacob said as he reached Princess.

"What do we do?" asked the man.

"I don't know. Shit! Didn't you see her?"

"No, man, I'm sorry."

Jacob didn't know what he was supposed to do.

"Pull your car off my dog," Jacob said. "I'll be right back."

As Jacob ran to his back yard, something told him to get the shovel that was leaning against the shed. He was going to move the dog. When he returned to the street, the man had driven off. There was some blood, but mostly Princess just looked deflated. Her eyes were closed and her hind leg, the one she had just scratched herself with minutes earlier, was crushed. Jacob quickly slid the shovel underneath Princess and brought her to the back of the house.

What to do, what to do?

He knew of two friends who had buried their pets in the back yard. There was land on the other side of the shed, away from the house. He thought the city, the county, someone would have a protocol for this. No! He'd just bury her, or maybe just wrap her up in . . . what, exactly? . . . and put her in the ninety-six-gallon trash container provided by the city. If he could find an old blan-

ket, he could wrap her up and put her at the bottom of the
trash.

What was he thinking? He couldn't just throw her out. You don't
throw dead animals into the trash.

He had to bury her. He would tell Cindi when she came home and
then his marriage would be over. But he had to bury her. He could not
let Cindi see Princess Charlize-Louise de Secondat, Baron de La Brede
Cougar Mellencamp Freckle Butt lying deflated on a shovel. He gently
carried the dead dog on the shovel to behind the shed and then allowed
her to slide off. She landed face down, paws out. He started digging next
to her. It was thirty-five degrees, but the ground was soft enough for
Jacob to make progress with the hole; nevertheless, he started sweating.
His chest tightened.

I'm going to die digging a hole for a dead dog I didn't want but for
whose death I'm responsible.

The more he dug, the more his shoulders tightened.

He kept digging, furiously, relentlessly.

The hole was now big enough for two dogs. His sweat dripped into
the hole.

He scooped up Princess with the shovel and slid her into the grave.
She landed on her side, in the same position in which she had died. He
knew, or thought he knew, that he had to put down something like lye
in the hole to kill the smell or repel the rodents that would soon be
coming.

Lye? Who has lye?

He went in the house and looked for something, some kind of disin-
fectant, something to . . . he didn't know what it was supposed to do,
didn't know what he was supposed to get. Under the kitchen counter,
he saw Windex, steel wool, Comet, Formula 409, sponges, an old coffee
maker.

Comet!

He brought the container outside and headed for the grave. He
shook the can. White flakes came snowing down on Princess' face and
body, making her look like she had gotten into flour. He emptied the
can. The dog was still visible. It would have to do. He then started
refilling the hole, just as furiously, but inexplicably the dirt he had dug

up was less than what was needed to fill it back up. He started digging another hole and transferred that dirt to the hole with the dog. When the dirt in the hole was as close to level with the ground as it was going to get, Jacob got down on his knees, patted the dirt to smooth it out, and then found a stick and placed it on top of the grave of Princess Charlize-Louise de Secondat, Baron de La Brede Cougar Mellencamp Freckle Butt.

"I'm sorry," he said.

Jacob went back into the house.

Judge Joe Brown was now on to another case.

LARA ON LIFE AND DEATH

The email from Lara Izenberg arrived: "You're not killing that fucking dog!" —LI

  P.S. If not for me, do it for your marriage.

THE DOG IS ALIVE

Princess Charlize-Louise de Secondat, Baron de La Brede Cougar Mellencamp Freckle Butt would not be hit by a car or disfigured and buried out back in a big hole under half a container's worth of Comet, which meant Jacob Fishman would not have to write a chapter about how the fictional Cindi took the news about her fictional dog being killed by her fictional husband's willful neglect, which is how he would write the scene and how she would take it. Jacob also knew, seeing, at the moment, how the real dog was sitting on the lap of his real wife, that Cindi, the real one, would view the death the same way; so, yes, he thought, he would discard the chapter and spare the dog.

Jacob found himself smiling.

I brought you back to life.

The dog growled.

He had written to Lara.

Lara,

Was just a draft. Fine. The dog lives. I decree it.

JF

"You can't decide these things!" Jacob remembered Martha

screaming at George when he kills their imaginary son in *Who's Afraid of Virginia Woolf?* as he hit "send."

He wouldn't. But he had written it. He thought of it.

My soul is a prick.

JACOB FISHMAN'S MARRIAGE: A NOVEL

8. Swinging Balls

After being discharged from the Lassen Indian Health Center in Susanville, California, after his second botched suicide attempt, this one having come about as a result of a potent combination of Smirnoff, Dilaudid, cocaine, Percocet, and unwanted anal sex with a bipolar transient who wouldn't leave his home, Kenny Hann, Cindi's closest male friend, was moved to Sparks, Nevada, a town just east of Reno, by his wealthy parents, who bought him a home with a two-acre backyard. There, he raised chickens and goats and grew tomatoes, endives, squash, and marijuana. In Reno, he had co-owned the restaurant La Poule Française, but he sold his share to his partner after his first botched suicide attempt, when he slashed his wrists in a bathtub while drinking a bottle of 19 Crimes Shiraz. That landed him at Rosewood Rehabilitation Center. When Cindi and Jacob went to visit him at Rosewood, they overheard a nurse say to Kenny, who also suffered from Graves' disease, "You keep fighting everyone who's trying to help you, you're going to die here, you know that?"

Kenny pointed two fingers to his protruding right eye—along with being a drug addict, he had an overactive thyroid—turned around, and pulled down his hospital-issued pajamas.

"Kenneth, pull up your pants and sit down," the nurse said. "Surely you don't think your little pimply ass is the first one I've seen."

He did as he was told.

"I have pimples on my ass?" he asked, flashing a smile that would save him on many occasions. "Kill me now."

"Oh, honey," the nurse said, sweetly, "you don't want to die. I want to kill you sometimes, but you don't want to die."

He did, but he was no longer actively trying to kill himself, mostly because he was so inept at carrying it out. As a result of the first attempt, his Graves' got worse and he was no longer able to blink. Irrespective of the Graves', but maybe not the abundance of Smirnoff, Dilaudid, cocaine, Percocet, and moderately priced red wine, he had also lost his sense of smell and taste, which was not good for a chef. After leaving Lassen, he spent most of his time naked at the house his parents bought him, save for occasionally putting on overalls, high-top black Converse sneakers, and a ratty dark-blue French beret. He was, visually, an acquired taste. Cindi, who had known him since graduate school, was going out to Sparks two or three days a week to see him and to help feed chickens, prepare and dig up the garden, paint the barn, and play with his dog, an obnoxious little Chihuahua named Josh, whose yelp, even to Cindi, was insufferable. Kenny's parents, indefatigable and guilt-ridden, thought it would be therapeutic if their son got into the restaurant business again, so they loaned him money to open another restaurant—this time, a food truck in downtown Reno, Queso and Quiche, which specialized in both French and Mexican food. He hired a chef from the fancy La Poule Française, Luis Roman Garcia Rico Jefferson, known as Jeffy to everyone, to run the truck (and because they were fucking), and until Jeffy got thrown out of the country for selling meth and having a Social Security number belonging to one Vicky Schwartz, a retired Jewish dental assistant living in Las Vegas, business (and the relationship) was good. Kenny couldn't keep up the business himself, nor did he want to. One night, after he forgot to lock it, the truck was ransacked, stripped of its tires, its windows smashed, and knocked on its side for good measure. The words "Speak American" were sprayed over Queso and Quiche. The truck, wounded and defeated, sat for weeks, ticketed daily, before it was towed.

Kenny never went to retrieve it.

"I liked the truck," he told Cindi on one of her visits. "I just hated the customers."

Kenny had been openly gay for almost two years, having come out of the closet shortly before the first suicide attempt, neither of which surprised anyone but his parents.

"Cindi," he said to her after his first weekend of uncloseted homosexual fucking, "you should try gay sex."

"I'm not half the girl you are," she said. "Besides, I could never take it in the ass."

"Me neither. I've already decided. I'm strictly a top."

Cindi enjoyed being out in Sparks, even despite the snakes that were everywhere and the chicken coop, though it shouldn't have surprised her, smelled like chicken shit, exacerbated by the worst heat wave to strike the region in twenty years. The shit smell, relentless, lingered in Kenny's backyard like a weighted blanket. She used to bring Princess Charlize-Louise de Secondat, Baron de La Brede Cougar Mellencamp Freckle Butt with her to play with Josh, and while they did, Kenny and Cindi sat on cheap lawn chairs on the back porch and drank pre-made vodka cocktails kept in an old cooler.

"I can see your balls," Cindi said, "through those overalls. They swing. It's disconcerting. Your balls are huge."

Kenny, despite being in a coma for four of the previous twenty-four months, having lost half the vision in that drooping right eye, and the ability, strangely enough, to even do the simplest math problems in his head, was still a joy to be around for Cindi.

"You want one of these?" he asked, pulling out a Cutwater Fugu Cucumber Vodka Soda twelve-ounce can.

"The hell is this?" Cindi asked, taking it and reading the label. "Sure." Cindi watched Josh mount Princess Charlize-Louise.

"No! No!" screamed Cindi.

Josh dismounted.

"God, Jacob would hate this."

"Where is Jacob today?"

"Therapy."

"Christ, you two are so fucked up."

"Coming from you, that's quite troubling."

Kenny reached into the blue ice chest, which was filled with Bud Lights, Bacardi Breezes, Cokes, and assorted specialty drinks, pulled out the large plastic bottle of vodka, and poured some into the quarter-drunk plastic Ocean Spray bottle at his side.

"Ahhh, now that's better."

"Your balls are killing me. Oh, God, I love this," she said, as Josh jumped up on her lap.

"No, get off, you little shit," said Kenny, and he smacked Josh in the back of the head.

"Don't hit him. He's sweet. Aren't you, Josh?" said Cindi as she leaned down. "Go find Princess Charlize-Louise, Josh."

"Go, get, boy," Kenny said, pointing to the barn. "Mangy-ass dog!"

Josh ran behind the barn.

"He's sweet."

"But no fucking!" Kenny screamed toward the barn. "You can let her blow you, though."

"Stop it!" said Cindi, hitting him. "My dog is not like that."

"Like dog, like mother. What does Jacob think of your dog?"

"He doesn't like dogs, doesn't like nature."

"As long as he likes you."

"I'm not even sure about that."

"Then neither one of you likes the other."

"I like him," she said quickly. "What are you talking about it? I love him."

"Whatever," he said in an exaggeratedly gay voice, waving his hand dismissively and repeating, "Whatever."

"You little gay shit. I do love him."

"Okay."

"I do."

"Fine."

Cindi put the beer can of cucumber vodka soda to her lips and sucked off the condensation.

"Oh, that feels good. I don't want to move. And I fucking love him."

Cindi couldn't stay angry with Kenny, even though she was tired of his suicide attempts and the opportunities he pissed away and his habit of calling his father a cocksucker and his mother a cunt, especially after all they had done and were doing for him.

"So don't move. How's the tenure thing?"

"The tenure thing is fine, I think. Nobody's told me I'm not getting it, so I guess that's a good sign. It's complicated, but there's, like, fourteen different committees it has to go through. I know I'm going to be okay with the people in my department, I should be okay with Howland, my boss, but after that, I don't know. Howland has to make a recommendation to a tenure committee, which then makes a recommendation to the dean, who makes one to the provost, but I seemingly piss Howland off every time I'm near him—"

"Cindi, stop, you're hurting my brain. How many people have to approve you?"

"I don't know. Seems like I have to please half of Reno. Anyway, I think my department approved me."

"So you got it, then, right?

"Yeah, well, except, no. And you weren't listening. Thing is, I have a feeling I wasn't unanimously approved from within my department, which means Howland may decide to be a prick—well, he is anyway— and that may affect things, because it's really him that they listen to."

"This is exhausting. Who listens to him? I can't even follow this."

"Yeah, and I don't even care. I want a baby, I want out of this town, and . . . I care, I do. I've been here six years. I don't want to be fired."

Josh came out of the barn with a dead chick in his mouth.

"You motherfucker!" Kenny screamed, and threw the now-empty Ocean Spray bottle at his dog, who ran away.

"I think this is Jacob's problem with nature," said Cindi. "All the random death."

"I like your husband, but, Cindi, I got to tell you, he intimidates me."

"Me too. He's so lofty, so inside his own head."

"But you're not going to divorce him over that. You're saving up for something else, right?"

Cindi loved this Kenny, the one who could stop the conversation cold and remind everyone in one sentence what they were really talking about.

"I don't know. Thing is, he's fine. I'm the crazy one. I want a baby and I'm not going to have one with him. So what do I do with that?"

"Have another vodka with cucumber, I think."

Cindi laughed, but she took one anyway. "My life is shit."

"Your life?" Kenny asked, rearranging his right testicle through his overalls. "You're not sitting around in overalls with your balls hanging out and being supported by parents you hate but need. My mom is a cunt, I hope she dies."

"Kenny!"

"Fine. I don't hope she dies. But she's still a cunt."

"I've been using that word too much, too. Jacob says I should be more judicious with it."

"What if I called my mom a judicious cunt?"

"That should do it. It really is beautiful out here, Kenny. You know what I want to do, and I wanted to ask you about this: You know the guy who sold you the food truck? He has others, right?"

"Yeah. His name is—"

"I don't care what his name is. Why would I care what his name is?"

"Don't you want to call him?"

"I want you to call him."

"Sure. You want to buy a truck?"

"A trailer. An RV. And if I do it, can I put it out there?" she asked, pointing to a place near the coop.

"What do I care?"

"I love you."

"What would Jacob say when he finds out you bought a trailer?"

"It's my money, and I told him I might buy one."

"But you're buying it to, you know, get away from him. He has to know that."

"That's not why I'm getting it. I'm getting it to have a place of my own."

"That's why you're getting it?" Kenny laughed.

"Fuck you! It is."

"Whatever you say, Virginia Woolf. Get the trailer. Put it out there."

Cindi's phone rang. She looked down, saw it was Jacob, and let it ring. "It's Jacob."

The phone continued to ring, and Cindi continued looking at the screen.

"Aren't you going to answer that?"

"No."

"Why not?"

"Long story, but I was in Vegas a few weeks back and my husband never called me. Not once."

"Was he supposed to?"

Cindi laughed. "Was he supposed to?" she repeated. "Yeah. No. I don't know. Yeah, he should have."

Kenny started rocking in his chair, though it wasn't designed for that. Cindi thought he might flip over.

"I was never good at, uh . . . I don't know," he said.

"What do you mean?"

"Math, planning."

"What are you talking about?"

"Cunt, cunt, cunt, cunt."

His left eye wide, scary, unblinking, but his right drooping, expressionless, he stopped rocking. "Never good at math, never good . . . cunt." He stopped and began pounding his forehead, first softly and then increasingly hard. He was sobbing.

Cindi grabbed his hand, pulled him close.

"It's okay, honey, I love you, you know that. I love you."

Kenny started singing. "There was a time you let me know, what's really going on below, but now you never show it to me, do you?"

"Why are you singing 'Hallelujah'? And why that verse? That's about a girl who won't fuck Cohen anymore. That's what the below means."

"I thought it was about wisdom."

"Most of Cohen's songs are about cocaine and anal sex, so I guess there's wisdom or direction in that. I don't know."

Kenny started rocking again.

CINDI'S DIARIES

Jacob, the real one, wasn't at therapy. He was lying on the floor, face down, by Cindi's side of the bed, reading her diary—the real Cindi's diary—which he had retrieved. He found it where he always did, because she never moved it, underneath a blanket and next to a stack of old diaries, for Cindi Fishman was a hoarder of such things—old newspaper clippings from Paris and Montreal, and Thich Nhat Hạnh's *The Path of Mindfulness in Everyday Life.* Cindi's other diaries, completed ones that were bulging with pictures and drawings and watercolors, were bound together by a thick ribbon. She wrote in big swooping letters in multicolored inks of mauve and teal and burgundy, yet her narrative unfolded gracefully. As her unhappiness grew, though, the narrative stalled and then raced, flying off in various emotional directions, her use of caps and double underlining more prevalent and prominent. Cindi wrote three pages most mornings.

"How do you write, Jacob?" she once asked him.

"I just wait till I have a deadline or a thought. And the geology stuff just doesn't take anything out of me."

"I need order."

"When you're not desiring chaos."

"Right. There's that, too."

Having found the latest diary, the one with the two-inch-by-three-inch photo of Princess Charlize-Louise de Secondat, Baron de La Brede Cougar Mellencamp Freckle Butt on the cover, Jacob slid it out from under the bed and propped himself up on his elbows, opened the binder, and saw the nude Cindi had drawn on the inside front cover. The woman had wide hips, small breasts covered by waist-length hair, and was scowling. The word "Muse" was written in the bottom right corner. His wife was more beautiful than this. It was, clearly, a self-portrait—she had drawn the mole over her left breast—and Jacob vowed to tell her someday that he saw her more beautifully than she saw herself.

He turned the page.

4 November 2010

Mitch, sweet, sweet Mitch, bought a Pez dispenser for PCL. And, of course, Jacob shit all over it. Oh, he made a big deal about keeping P-C-L, as if I needed his permission, as if the house isn't half fucking mine. I need to get out of this marriage, talk to Ethan about that trailer, I really do, and just live like a hermit, a gypsy. I should never have married this man or anyone. MEN ARE SUCH FUCKING PIGS! BUT I HATE WOMEN TOO!!!

12 December 2010

My ass is getting not bigger as much as it's getting lower. But I hate the patriarchy of this fucking country that says women have to shave their underarms and pussies. In France—well, fuck, it's not any better— but women can be angrier without self-consciousness. I'm offended by everything. I actually feel sorry for my husband—and I HATE THAT FUCKING TERM—for having to put up with me. He's not a bad guy, not really. I could do worse, have done worse, but he doesn't know what to do with me. I don't know what to do with me. I'm awful. I don't know why I'm thinking about this now, but he's still making me feel guilty about the colonoscopy he had. I had a conference in Vegas so couldn't stay with him. I don't know. It was no big deal, except it's all a big deal, and maybe he's not making me feel bad. Maybe I'm feeling bad because I didn't want to be there, I didn't want to be a nurse, I didn't want to wait on him and make him feel better. I mean, I love him but I hate him. But he's the only person I know who can put up with me. I WANT A BABY!!! I WANT A BABY!!!!!

22 January 2011

First day of the spring semester and I rode my bike today to school. Was good to see Howland and, of course, Mitch, and I didn't even mind the students. I saw Casey in her wheelchair in the hallway. God is she a cunt, but it's not like I would have ever crossed her in class, though sometimes I think, if I could reach out of myself, I would say something about her using her infirmity, but I won't. It would be suicidal. The classes are fine. Who cares anymore? I actually decided to change my attitude this semester. On the way to school, I promised myself I was not going to get upset anymore over every little thing, but that lasted until we had this ridiculous meeting in Howland's office. He was saying to think of students like customers. He wasn't looking at me when he said it, but I knew he was talking about me. Mitch looked at me, pointed his finger, and mouthed the word "B-A-C-O-N," which made me laugh—it had to do with a time that Casey kept saying 'Bacon' in class, like being able to pronounce the word was an achievement—which of course pissed off Howland, who said, "Cindi, is there a problem?" And I said—I actually fucking said, "Mitch started it," which made Mitch laugh, which, of course made me cackle and sound like a third grader.

Good thing I already have tenure.

19 February 2011

Ethan tried to kill himself last night, again. He's fine, but he's really the lucky one. He wants out and he's not afraid to try to find a way. How much longer, I keep asking myself, does this life go on? Jacob tells me I'm not nearly as depressed as I keep saying, nor as bohemian, because I know good wine from bad and spend money on expensive boots. He's right when he says it, so I should probably stop talking about suicide, but fuck him. I often wake up and the darkness isn't the worst of it. I mean, I don't talk about this black hole I feel like I'm in, but I guess any talk is more than enough, and I hate that I scare and hurt people, including my husband.

Ethan is such a sweet fuck-up. I should go out there soon. His parents bought him a place out in the country. One of these days he's going to kill himself. You ever know for a fact something terrible is going to happen? And I'm going to be the one who finds him dead, I know. I just hope Jacob is with me.

Jacob closed the diary, stacked the newspapers and blankets, the Hanh book, and the pictures that had fallen out of the other diaries, and slid them under the bed, before getting up and walking around to his side of the bed and lying down.

How many different ways could she say "Fuck Jacob"?

He must have fallen asleep, for he was jarred awake by *back door open.* He heard Cindi come in.

"Honey?" he called.

Nothing.

"Honey?"

He wanted his wife to lie down next to him, to point, as she used to do, to that part of his shoulder where she wanted to rest her head, wanted to then lift up his arm so she could slide her head to exactly where she wanted it, wanted to stroke her hair, wanted to say nothing at all, but wanted to hold her, however much of her was left, and tell her she got the drawing in the diary all wrong. Maybe they would make love. Maybe they would just lie there. Maybe they would become different people.

"Honey, I'm in bed, just lying here. Want to come lie next to me?"

She appeared.

"I have to pee."

SAGE AND THE WET WOODY

"She pierced her *what*, again?" Jacob asked, as he and Cindi drove on Interstate 80 to Lake Tahoe to meet Sage.

"Her clitoris."

"Her clitoris?"

"Yes. Her clitoris. Do you just like hearing the word?"

"There are worse words."

"Now, don't say anything when we see her. I don't know if she wants you to know."

"I won't."

"Jacob, I swear to Christ, do not embarrass her."

"I'm not. That's got to hurt, though."

"I shouldn't have told you."

"I'm not going to say anything."

"Let's talk about something else. Please."

"Okay, tell me, again, what did Howland say when you met him?"

"You just don't listen to me, about anything, do you? Again: Essentially, he called me tenacious, which kind of sucks."

"Why do you say that?" Jacob asked, turning down the Ani DiFranco CD. "I kind of like it."

"Tenacious is what you think of when you think about a dog.

Princess Charlize-Louise de Secondat, Baron de La Brede Freckle Butt is tenacious. I am not tenacious."

Jacob looked at his wife, raised his eyebrows, and smiled.

"What?" she asked.

"How do you remember all that?"

"It's my child, it's her name. I don't really have one, so that's how."

"One conversation, is all I ask. Just one time we talk without a mention of a baby. Anyway, did the thing with Howland bother you, the tenacious business?"

"Why would it bother me?"

"Just because, you know, everything going on in your life."

"My life? What's going on in my life?"

"What's going on in your life?"

"You mean the baby?"

"Yeah, I guess."

"Maybe I'll just quit teaching and become a sheepherder in the Golan Heights."

"Always good to have a backup plan, Cin. Sheepherder. God, you make me laugh sometimes."

Sage Daniel, Cindi's best friend, mother of six, unfulfilled Mormon, who, along with her husband, Dave, had once put a sledgehammer through her television because she thought it was a delivery system of what she deemed "debauchery and coldness," had, in fact, moved out of her house and was now living . . . well, Cindi didn't know where. Sage had called Cindi a week earlier and asked if she and Jacob—and he was surprised he was invited—would like to meet her at Gar Woods, on the lake's north side. She was already at a table out on the deck, drinking her second Wet Woody, a strange mix of three one-hundred-proof-plus liquors and fruit juice, when Cindi and Jacob walked in. The last time Cindi had seen Sage was at the house on Codel, and they were both topless. They did this occasionally, going topless at the house, and usually wrote poetry together, but that day, they were in the bedroom, painting, trying to portray each other's breasts with watercolors on 8x10 tablets. Sage had already dyed her hair blond and red with a streak of purple, and, though she hadn't yet left Dave, had contacted an ex-boyfriend, Scott Peterson, a mass murderer on California's death row, who used to fuck her in public places.

"Jesus," Cindi had said, "you've been in touch with Scott Peterson?"

"Yeah, I was flipping through a magazine and saw a picture of him on trial for killing Lacey and thought, 'Scotty?'"

"Why did you contact him? Weren't you scared?"

"Fuck, yeah, I was scared, but kind of excited. I knew Lacey Peterson. He left me for her."

"Wow!"

"You don't know, Cin. You don't know how a strange cock can make you feel. It reminds me of when I ran marathons."

"Wait, wait, you fucked him?"

"No, no, not him. Someone else. I wouldn't fuck Scott again—that would be too weird."

"Wait. Okay, so much going on right now. How is strange cock like running in a marathon?" Cindi asked, adding brown pigment to the areola.

"I can't explain it, but it's like doing something you never thought you could do and then doing it and realizing you can do it and should have been doing it. And then . . . there's the actual fucking. The friction, dude. It's righteous in its wrongness."

At the deck table, Sage stood up as Cindi and Jacob approached. Jacob noticed Sage had lost weight and had pierced her nostril.

"You pierced your nose?" Jacob said.

Cindi pinched a fleshy part of his arm.

"Ow! What?"

"Nothing," she said, whispering in his ear. "Don't."

"You two okay?" Sage asked.

"Yeah, we're fine, probably better than you've seen us. But are you okay?" Cindi asked, hugging her friend. "You look fantastic."

"Totally. Dude. I have, like, never, ever been better. Really, Jacob, you like my nose ring?"

"I kinda do, but maybe only because it's only one nostril and you don't have a loop connecting both of them."

"I also pierced my clitoris."

"You can hardly tell," he said, laughing, and then said to Cindi, "Apologize."

"For what?"

"You know for fucking what."

"What is going on with you two? You sure you're okay?"

"Yeah. Jacob is just being Jacob and . . . never mind."

"You're doing okay, really?" he asked, pointing to the stud in her nostril and to the rest of her body, "because I never imagined you for piercing so many areas."

Cindi picked up a knife, smiled, and waved it at her husband.

"Oh, that's fine," Sage said to Cindi. "Jacob's fine. But tell me, what's going on with you two? You guys don't look all that terrific."

"Thanks," they said in unison.

"We're the same as ever," Jacob said.

"My husband, ladies and gentlemen, on the status of our marriage." Cindi shook her head. Jacob exhaled.

"You two have the strangest marriage of any two people I know. It's like you're not even here and are in some other novel or something."

Jacob smiled.

"Why are you smiling?" Sage asked.

"I'm not."

"Why is he smiling?" Sage asked Cindi.

"He's writing a book about us."

"A what? Of you two?" Sage asked, pointing to both of them.

"Yep."

"No, I'm not," Jacob said, "but it's based on the two of us."

"I don't follow," said Sage.

"Me neither," Cindi put in. "Forget that. Tell me what happened with you!" She grabbed Sage's hands.

"Let me start at the beginning," Sage said. "I love Dave, you know that, but he's so . . . I don't know. He's Dave. I have been having these feelings about me and him and . . . I don't know, it's just so weird."

The waitress came by. Jacob pointed to Sage's drink and signaled for three more.

"You, Jacob, drinking?" asked Sage.

"Why not? It isn't every day a born-again Mormon with six kids gets divorced and gets her clit pierced—"

"Jacob—" said Cindi.

"Dude, right on," Sage said, who lifted her hand to high-five Jacob. He responded in kind.

"Dude-ette," he said clumsily.

"So?" asked Cindi. "Dave?"

"A few weeks ago, Dave and I are driving, you know, somewhere and, I don't know. I just told him I was unhappy and asked what did he think about me having an affair?"

"You asked him that?" said Cindi. "Good for you."

"Good for you?" Jacob asked Cindi. "Like I could say that, and you'd be happy."

"Shut up," Cindi said, smiling. "You know what I mean."

"I don't know what you mean."

"Nothing. I didn't mean anything. Sage, go on."

"And what did Dave say when you shared that with him?" Jacob asked.

"Let her tell the story," Cindi told her husband.

"Well," Sage said, finishing her drink with a big slurp, "he kind of pulled over, stopped the car, told me to get out."

"He did?" asked Cindi.

"Can hardly blame him, really," said Jacob.

"Oh, dude, I know," said Sage. "I mean, what a shitty thing to say, so I started walking. I'm really peripatetic these days."

"Peripatetic?" said Jacob.

"It means—"

"I know what it means, Cin."

"Anyway, anyway, we were not that far from home," Sage said, "so it wasn't that bad. I walked back to the house and am sitting on the front-porch swing, and when he comes home, just a few minutes later, he tells me, and he was so sweet, that he just doesn't think he can live like that, you know, if I want to take a lover. He wasn't even judgmental, and I totally respect that."

"I love Dave," said Cindi. "He's such a pure soul. "

Jacob smacked his lips disapprovingly.

"Jacob, stop smacking your fucking lips!"

"I'm not doing anything," Jacob said, smacking again. "But maybe if you think Dave's such a pure soul, Cin, you shouldn't have given him *The Last Temptation of Christ*—the Kazantzakis version, not Scorsese's —for Christmas last year, knowing how he felt about the Gospel."

"I miscalculated," Cindi conceded. "He didn't like it, did he, Sage?"

"He cried."

"What?"

"He cried and said that he was sorry you were so lost, and so without any understanding of God that you would think that book is great literature. He couldn't take it. But, yeah, he cried. He burned it."

"Burned it?" Cindi asked.

Jacob started laughing. "Hon, you do a lot of things well. Your gift-giving skills, perhaps, need a little work. I guess re-gifting is out of the question, huh?"

"Fuck off," Cindi said, thinking about the SAS shoes and the blueberries and how they were not bad presents and how her husband was a prick for bringing up her gift-giving skills. "So does Dave know about the guys you've slept with?"

"'Fuck off'?" Jacob repeated.

"Let me go back," Sage said. "First, I had met this guy, Mel, who, you know, I always knew wanted me, but I never did anything, because I was, like, married."

"Who?" said Cindi excitedly.

"The drummer from Dead Trousers."

"A drummer? How humiliating!" said Jacob.

"Are you going to do commentary throughout?" Cindi asked.

"We hung out a little and everything was fine," Sage said. "We didn't do anything, a little kissing maybe, and then I sort of went down on him once when I was drunk, but it was, like, whatever." She waved her hand.

"You can 'whatever' a blow job?" said Jacob. "Please go on."

Cindi glared at her husband.

"What?" he asked. "You can't."

Cindi bit her lip, trying to draw blood.

"But I just knew that I was unhappy. Dave's wonderful, but I just don't get into him anymore. I just don't, though there was a time I really loved his cock. Just a great, great cock. God, I loved it. So, I think that was a problem, and then one night I go out and it starts snowing and I'm drinking and then Demko, he's also in the band . . . anyway, he happens to be at the same bar. He lives close by and invites me over and, I'm telling you, man, he wanted to, and I said okay, and we did."

"You had sex with him?" Cindi asked.

"No, dude, I totally fucked him."

"And?"

"It was fucking fantastic. It was, like, the best sex I ever had."

The waitress came by with three Wet Woodys.

Sage extended her palm for Cindi to high-five, which she did.

"Then what?" Jacob said.

"I had to go home and tell Dave."

Jacob did a perfect spit take. "You what?"

"I told Dave. I had to be honest."

"Wait, wait, wait," Jacob said, wiping his hand on his shirt. "You felt the need to be honest after you fucked a drummer? What would possess you to do that?"

"I wanted to be honest. I told him about the blow job, too."

"You don't think you get points for that, do you?"

"You don't?" she said, laughing.

"No, you don't."

"Why doesn't she?" Cindi asked.

"Because it's hurtful."

"She does get points, Jacob, because she was honest. She didn't hide it from Dave—like in a book."

"This is not the same thing as the book."

"What book?" Sage asked.

"Jacob is writing a book about our marriage, remember?"

"Oh, right."

"Anyway, he's putting all sorts of shit in there about me and him, but mostly me."

"What?"

"It's too complicated. And I get furious when I think about it—never mind."

"And that's not the book, anyway," said Jacob.

"The fuck it isn't the book."

"It's not the book."

"Sorry I brought it up," said Cindi. "How did Dave take the news about Demko?"

"He was still sweet about it. He said, 'Well, if that's what you did, that's what you did. I can't live with you anymore.'"

"That's amazing," Jacob said. "Implausible, but amazing."

"Why is that implausible?" Cindi asked.

"Because it's something that happens in literature, not life. People aren't that calm when it comes to infidelity, or even the fear of infidelity. I mean, if you were cheating on me and you told me about it, I'm not sure you telling me about it would mitigate the pain and hurt and betrayal I felt. In fact, I'm sure it wouldn't."

"I'm sure you'd put it in a book."

"What are you talking about?"

"She just told you it happened in real fucking life. It's not literature, and Dave was fine about it. She was being honest with her spouse. I know that's a foreign concept to you."

"When am I not honest with you?"

Sage looked at them. "Guys, wait, wait. Dave said we should gently split up. And he meant it this time. He used the word 'gently.'"

"Gently—I love that," said Cindi. "That's so Zen. So how do you feel now? Have you seen Demko since?"

"Yeah, but that's not going anywhere. But it's such a trip, man."

"You have, like, a million kids, honey," Cindi said.

"They're fine," she said. "Thankfully, they're too young to know much."

"So how's the sex since?" asked Cindi.

"Like I said, it's fucking awesome, and maybe because he kind of disgusts me."

Jacob looked up from his glass. "Huh?"

"He's, like, ten years younger than I am, and he does heroin—not a lot, but, you know?" she asked Cindi. "Like with Bilal."

The waitress returned with some artichoke dip, which Jacob couldn't remember anyone ordering.

"Ah, yes, Bilal," said Jacob. "It's tough competing with a ghost."

Cindi had met Bilal in Marrakech, while she was backpacking around Morocco. He was from Algeria and was selling sunglasses and trinkets to tourists when he offered Cindi a ride to Casablanca on a beat-up motorcycle. Their relationship, Cindi had told Jacob when talk of past loves didn't highlight how happy each of them had been before their marriage, was a volatile mix of sex and drugs and lies. Bilal died after crashing his Honda XL250 into a Greek Orthodox church, or after contracting hepatitis C from a prostitute in Hamburg with a gargoyle tattoo (Jacob couldn't remember which; maybe both). It was at his funeral that Cindi met both of Bilal's wives, neither of whom knew about each other, or Cindi. After the ceremony, the three women went out and toasted their dead lover and husband with Moroccan beer.

"You're not competing with Bilal," Cindi said. "And I don't long for him. He's dead. And I don't think about him. It's just, you know, when you . . ."

"What?" asked Jacob.

"Well, you know, sometimes sex with someone you shouldn't be with is fabulous. I mean, Jesus, it was so good!"

She and Sage high-fived again.

"And better sometimes than the people you're supposed to be with, too, right?" Jacob asked, thinking about Ciara and Mitch, the real and the imagined, and the sex, real and imagined, that they might be having in real life and were definitely having or going to have in fiction.

"Not better, just different. It's great with you," she said for Sage's benefit. "The sex with Bilal was nasty and relentless and I hated him. He was also disgusting."

"That seems to be the operative word tonight."

"The sex was awesome, though, right?" asked Sage. "And Jacob, I think that's what Cindi's talking about. It's the otherworldliness of it."

"That's it!" cried Cindi.

"I'm wondering," said Jacob, "if I were sitting here right now telling you about how great the sex was between me and, say, some cabin girl in the Bahamas, a cabin girl named Alison, who was nasty and tattooed and possibly diseased, or what's-her-name . . . Ciara—how would you take the explanation of its otherworldliness?"

"Yeah, like you didn't remember Ciara's name? You fucked her, didn't you?"

"I didn't."

"Okay, anyway, my point," said Cindi, "is everyone has a past, even you, my perfect husband, who thinks everyone else's is fodder but his are off-limits, so don't judge me because I have memories of a dead lover. A cabin girl? Bahamas? How conventional."

"You fuck a bigamist through half of northern Africa and into Europe and I'm supposed to find the poetry in that, but you can't see the excitement of fucking a cabin girl named Alison on the upper deck of her employer's boat? You even criticize my fantasy. Who does that? Would it be better if I named her Inga? I thought I'd at least get a high-five out of it." Jacob extended his open palm upward.

Cindi hated her husband at this moment more than she ever had. Sage patted her friend's leg under the table, squeezing her thigh.

Cindi took a breath. "Never mind. Let's just not talk about Bilal. Sage, what happened next?"

"I'm like a teenager," Sage said. "I fucked Demko and then Ace and then actually fucked Mel."

"You fucked the whole band?" Cindi asked.

"Jacob, don't tease me," Sage said, "but, yeah, the whole band."

"I won't say a word, but Ace, Demko, and Mel. Fucking Mel? This is hilarious. Tawdry as hell, but hilarious."

"But then . . . I've been fucking . . . everything. I have been experimenting with . . . you know, others."

"Others?" Jacob and Cindi asked as one, smiling. They looked at each other and stopped smiling.

"You know, two at a time. And then once even three."

"You're shitting me!" said Cindi, her mouth literally open.

"Down, girl!" said Jacob.

"Tell!" Cindi demanded.

"Just one time with a girl and a guy, one time with a guy and a guy, one time three guys. I'm not really into girls, though. And have you ever looked at a cock, Cin, really looked?"

"All hail the cock," said Jacob, standing.

"Sit down, Jacob."

He did.

"They're beautiful," said Sage. "It took me some time to, you know, get into them, but they're gorgeous. I'm so into cocks."

"Three guys?" Cindi asked, holding her drink, transfixed, in front of her.

"Yeah, you know the joke: three holes, no waiting."

Cindi spilled her drink. "Anal?" she whispered.

"Yeah."

"My God! Who came first?" Cindi asked.

"That's what you want to know?" Jacob asked his wife.

"Yeah, it's a perfectly legitimate question."

"Who can remember?" Sage said with a laugh.

"Wow! That's fucking torrid," said Cindi, putting the Wet Woody to her forehead.

"You going to come right here?" Jacob whispered. "It's embarrassing and, okay, a little hot."

"I'm not excited," Cindi said, shooting him a disgusted glance.

"What, then? Or is that, please God, it?" Jacob asked.

"I moved out to my mom's here in Tahoe, but now I'm thinking of moving to Oregon with the kids."

"Dave will let you do that?" Jacob asked.

"He's coming."

"What?" Cindi and Jacob both asked.

"He's coming. We're all going."

"I think that's great, don't you, honey?" Cindi asked Jacob.

Honey?

"On what planet are you two living? No, it's not great."

"Why not?" asked Sage, slurping down the second Wet Woody.

"How's this?" Jacob asked. "Dave decides, eventually, that you fucking everything and everyone is kind of humiliating. I mean, Sage, we love you, no judgment. But let's say he gets a little pissed at the turn of events. You know, his former Christian wife, now a band groupie, having unprotected anal sex in threesomes."

"I didn't say it was unprotected," Sage said, smiling.

"Noted. Anyway, so he then decides, in his pissed-off-ness, he's not giving up his business here to live in a big house in Seattle with his ex-wife, who is, again, fucking, albeit responsibly, everyone, just to babysit your/his children. Again, I'm not saying that, but he might come to that conclusion that you have been cheating on him and those six children, your six children that he's now babysitting, and may decide, 'I'm not doing this anymore.' And then, he may very well decide he has better things to do with his life than follow this woman who ruined his life and ripped out his heart to, again, watch her fuck her way through the great Northwest."

"Jacob, could you stop already with the 'fucking' business?" Cindi said. "And stop lecturing us."

"I'm not lecturing you. What are you talking about? I'm just telling you—"

"This is what I'm talking about."

"No, I guess I can see that," said Sage.

"But he wouldn't think what Jacob is thinking," said Cindi.

"I'm telling you," Jacob said back to his wife without irony, or at least any conscious irony, "we love Sage, but if we heard this story from someone else, if you told me this story, if you told me you were planning on doing this . . ."

"What?"

"What?"

"Yeah, what? I wouldn't tell you this story."

"Of course not, because . . . you dream of me and my great love."

"What the fuck does that mean?" Cindi asked, throwing down her napkin.

"Anyway, Sage, did you get a lawyer?" asked Jacob.

"No, we're going to do it without one."

"With six kids? I don't think that's smart."

"Why does she need one?" Cindi asked.

"These things get complicated when there are no kids involved, but when there are six of them and when one of the two participants feels wronged, and Dave, believe me, will soon feel that way, if he doesn't already . . . well, you're going to need an attorney."

"But I don't want one."

"It's not for you, but your kids."

"What do you mean?"

"There is this thing called no-fault, where it wouldn't have mattered if you fucked Demko, Ace, and Mel in front of Dave—it's just Dave who gets hurt—and the courts don't care. Maybe they should, but they don't. They'll have you split everything anyway. Thing is, even if you do that, he is still responsible for childcare for the kids, which means he'll owe you money, even if you fucked Demko, Ace, and Mel in front of him and the kids. And then there's just the guilt of, you know, of the family unfaithfulness."

"That's heavy, dude."

"Well, we don't have to worry about that, do we?" Cindi asked. "A family?"

"And we're off. What was that, three minutes without mention of a baby?"

"Ja—"

"Hold on," Sage said. "You mean, it doesn't matter what I do to Dave? He still has to pay me?"

"Yeah, it's not fair, but it's right—or I don't think it's fair. Maybe it is, who knows?"

"How much can she get?" asked Cindi.

Jacob smiled. "Well, with six kids and what I think Dave makes, probably fifteen to eighteen hundred a month for them. At least."

"Really?" asked Sage.

"Hold it, there's more. How long have you been married?"

"Fifteen years."

"Figure at least another five years of alimony, especially if you stopped working to have kids."

"I did. Cindi knows I did."

"She did, yes," said Cindi.

Jacob noticed his wife's excitement.

"I don't have that kind of money, honey. Relax. Now, I don't know for sure, but I'd say at least two thousand a month, total, for at least five years. Then a part of his pension."

"Dude, you're kidding?"

"Nope, that's an estimate, obviously, so believe me, he's going to want to get a lawyer when he finds that out, and you're going to want to get one when he finds that out."

"Jacob went through a divorce once and now, apparently, he's an expert in divorce law."

"I'm just giving what I know, Cin, I'm not saying this as legal advice, but I do know, babe, you'll be happy to know, when it comes to divorce, husbands can get as fucked over as wives."

"Babe?"

"Forget it."

"Why do you think Dave is getting fucked over?" asked Cindi.

"I'm sure his thinking will be, 'I didn't want this divorce, didn't want to be humiliated, don't want to raise kids while my wife is making up for all the sex she's missed with me, and enjoying it, and now, my thanks for all this is I get to pay her two thousand a month.' I would, were I him, think I was getting fucked."

"Dude, that is really some heavy shit," Sage said.

"Dave's not like that, though," said Cindi.

"You think when a man has an affair," Jacob told his wife, "that he's just fucking and it's just sex and meaningless, but when a woman has one, it's because she's unhappy and frustrated and out of options and needs the human contact, and if only the man had shown her more love and affection, she wouldn't have been forced into this position. It's a nice spin, but it's got holes in it."

"So you couldn't forgive me, if I had one?"

"Could you forgive me?"

"I don't know."

"I don't know either, with you. It would depend, I think, on the state of the rest of our marriage."

"So do you think Dave could have forgiven me if we weren't getting along at all?" Sage asked. "Because we really weren't fighting and arguing that much."

"Sometimes people understand infidelity when the marriage is really awful," Cindi said, staring at the lake. "I don't know, obviously, but it doesn't matter, because you didn't want to be forgiven, right? You're not going back with him, are you, under any circumstances, so it doesn't matter in any real sense what he thinks of you, does it?"

"Right. Except I'd like him to like me."

"Yeah, but . . . never mind," Jacob said.

"What?"

"The friends thing afterward—I never understood."

"Why not?" asked Cindi, looking at her husband.

"Because it's usually . . . listen, I'm talking too much."

"And that's ever stopped you?" asked Cindi.

"I don't know what I want from him, really," Sage said.

"My guess is, as you say, you want him not to hate you," Jacob said. "You want him to forgive you, see if you can maintain a friendship, because that way, you'll feel okay about yourself. Nothing wrong with that. Nobody wants to be an asshole, even when they are an asshole, which I'm not saying you are or were."

"Yeah, I guess. So it's not going to go smoothly?"

"It might, but . . . well, it's quite a position to be in if you're Dave," he said, finishing his drink, "having to make someone feel better for breaking your heart."

"David doesn't hate her," said Cindi.

"He probably doesn't, but he might."

"But what about now?" asked Sage. "We're getting along better than ever."

"Don't let this adrenaline rush you're on fool you into thinking all is going to be well. It's probably not."

"How do you know so fucking much?" asked Cindi, despising her husband again.

"What are you getting mad at me for? All I'm saying is don't expect the men in your life that you fuck around on, no matter how well you think you hide it, to applaud and appreciate your sexual reawakening and growth and your new appreciation of strange cock, no matter how touchingly you write about it or your unhappiness in your diary."

Shit, Jacob thought, *don't mention the diary.*

"Sage, he's just being Jacob. The smartest guy in the room."

"Don't do that. Sage is being a little unrealistic to think this is all going to be one big, happy ex-family. There are people's emotions here."

"You mean like your book."

"Again? Let it go, please!"

"What," Sage asked, "is with this book?"

"I hate it," Cindi said.

"You haven't read it."

"You won't let me, and I hate it anyway. Sage, just because Jacob would behave that way doesn't mean Dave will. Dave's different."

"Am I in the book?" Sage asked.

"You will be now. Three holes, no waiting," he said, high-fiving her.

On the drive back to Reno, Jacob decided to take 435 over Mount Rose back to Reno rather than Interstate 80. Usually 435 made him sick and dizzy with its winding roads and signs announcing the feet over sea level.

"Why are you going this way?" Cindi asked.

"Sage sleeps with three members of the same band, so I thought I should do something different too."

"What does that mean?"

"Fuck, I shouldn't say anything."

"Say it."

"I'm trying here, I really am."

"Say it!"

The argument was starting.

"Just didn't realize how much you liked change."

"What are you talking about?"

"Nothing."

"Tell me."

"The most excited I've seen you in months is when Sage was talking about being with three guys and having anal sex. That excites you, but I look at porn on my computer and that disgusts you."

"You think I want that kind of life?"

"I don't know. I mean, I don't. Most days, Cin, what you want is tougher to understand than what you don't."

"I want my life. This one—with you."

Jacob looked at her, smiled. "You do?" he said, exaggerating both words.

"Yes, I love you."

She was lying, but she could see the hurt in her husband's eyes and how much the hurt would be if she told him the truth, that she didn't, which almost made her cry. She hated herself more than she hated him most days.

"I love you, too, and I do want to know if you don't want this life . . . with me. Tell me, even though I'm convinced honesty is overrated."

"Overrated?"

"Usually people are just honest in a marriage when they don't care about hurting the other's feelings anymore, so, that's why I don't think it's always such a wonderful dynamic, but I do want to know if you're happy, or unhappy, or somewhere in between. Tell me."

"I mean, six kids, it was the perfect marriage. I'm just surprised, is all," Cindi said, "but I don't want to be her. Jesus, what do you take me for?" She pounded the dashboard.

"I don't want to do this anymore with you, fight like this. Remember, we promised each other? But, what, you're getting your feelings hurt that I noticed how excited you were and how unhappy you might be?"

"I was not excited and I'm not fucking unhappy!"

"Did you hear what I just said—about honesty and love and if you want to be with someone else? I am trying to be better than I have been."

"Sorry. I just don't want you to think I want to be Sage. I don't."

"All right," Jacob conceded, "forget it. I'll just say, though, that Sage is out of her mind if she thinks this is all going to wind up like *Big Love*."

"What's that?"

"It's a show on HBO about Mormons and polygamy."

"Why do I never, ever get the fucking references?"

"That's my fault."

"You and Mitch."

"Mitch? What do you mean?"

"He does it, too."

"That's terrific you're bringing him up."

"I'm just saying he also has *Godfather* and weird-ass references."

"*Godfather* is not a weird-ass reference, let's get that straight right away, and I don't want you sharing Michael and Fredo moments with any other man."

"They're the brothers in the movie, right? Michael is the head of the family and Fredo is kind of—"

"—the slow one."

"Yay. Yay! I got one right."

"Yes! Very good. Speaking of other men in your life, how's Ethan?"

"What do you mean, other men in my life? Ethan? You know, he came out."

"He's gay."

"Yeah, full-bore gay."

"Is he happy?"

"No. He's worse. He's doing drugs and not doing well and he's not happy and hates his mother and father and he's sleeping with some addict."

"What is with the attraction to addicts?"

"Wait, you're jealous of Ethan? Of Mitch? Is this a new thing for you? It's really not a good look. And, please, don't write about him. It's none of your business. It's none of mine."

"Fair enough. Back to Sage, then."

"Ping, ping, ping," said Cindi. "Let's talk about everyone's life but our own. This marriage is like Whac-a-Mole."

"There's no pinging in Whac-a-Mole."

For all the decay and unhappiness between them, Jacob and Cindi could, almost chemically, still have a moment like this, arguing at once about fidelity and suicide and the children they were never going to have and then, without transition, talk about anal sex, Mormons on cable television, the Corleones, and games with toy mallets.

"Cin. Cin?"

"What? Sorry."

"Nothing."

"This marriage is like a roller-coaster ride," she said, "isn't it?"

And with that Jacob made brief clicking sounds, indicating a roller coaster ascending.

"It's not funny. Sage had it all, though, a husband, kids. Wish I had that."

"You do."

"I have kids, where?"

"You have a life, I mean."

"Jacob, let's not talk about that. It pisses me off."

Jacob saluted in her direction.

Cindi stared at him and thought about bolting from the car. Jacob stared back. He wanted to kiss her. He wanted to punch her.

"Maybe, I don't know," Jacob said, "maybe it wasn't so great with Sage. And you would think their religion, their faith, would have helped. I don't get it, but people with religion are usually happier than people without it, don't you think?"

"Patriarchal bullshit!"

"Huh?"

"I became a Jew, and it's the same shit. Boys sucking boys' cocks. It's a man's club."

"Boys sucking boys' cocks? Where is that from again—Leviticus?"

"Don't make fun of me," Cindi said, laughing, "but it pisses me off. So you remember when I did the talk on Rousseau for that philosopher series for the temple?"

"No."

"Yeah, you do."

"What was it called?"

"It's not the part of the story I want to tell you, but it was about 'Reveries of a Solitary Walker.'"

"Those French were hilarious."

"Cute. Rousseau hated France. You done now?"

"Yes, sorry."

"I didn't expect to get paid, and I didn't, but then I find out the men doing the other lectures got paid."

"Who?"

"Doesn't matter who. They got paid, I didn't. I'm a Jew. And that's how the little pig rabbi treated me! And I converted, for Chrissakes!"

"Oh, that's hilarious," Jacob said, laughing. "I mean, that's funny. I don't care how many times you tell me that story."

"What is?"

"'I converted to Judaism, for Chrissakes' is what's funny."

"Anyway, it's a fucking man's world. If we didn't adore you, if we didn't stroke your egos for the past four thousand years, if we had spent more time on what we want, we would be in better shape right now, but no, woman is the nigger of the world. And that's why we sleep with drummers sometimes. You guys can sleep with whomever you want."

"Woman is the nigger— you're quoting Lennon? John Lennon? And extra points for using 'whomever.'"

"What's the use? Why don't we just shoot all the girls? Just line them up and shoot them all. The world kills and maims us anyway."

"Kills and maims all the girls? The world does what to them?"

"Yeah, just today a girl was dragged into the woods. How come boys never get dragged into the woods and raped? They're going to find that girl dead."

"What girl? What woods?"

"Just so you guys can jerk each other off." Cindi put both hands a foot apart, spread her fingers, and started masturbating an imaginary large penis with both hands and her tongue out of the side of her mouth.

"Who do you know with a cock that big? And, really, two hands?"

"You don't get it."

"I know. Hey, I've been thinking because I've been thinking about not getting it—all the times I don't get it. I think, I really think . . . we have to stop this."

"What are you talking about? This? This marriage?"

Jacob heard panic in Cindi's voice.

"No. No! I mean, is that what you want?"

"No. I want a fucking baby."

"I want to talk about something else . . . okay?"

"Okay."

"We . . . we can't keep doing this to each other."

"Doing what?"

"This! Look, I love you. You're a pain in my cock most of the time—"

"Nice."

"Sorry. Fuck, that's what I mean. It's like we play—I play—for the laughs, the . . . the . . . I don't know. But we can't just be about cynicism and the argument and the winning of the argument and . . . I'm not making any sense, am I?"

"Not as much as you think, but I hear you. I know what you mean."

"So, could we—Jesus!—could we just be nicer to each other? I do love you."

"You act surprised?"

"Cindi, I mean it. I don't want to do what we did with Sage before. I don't want to just win the moment anymore, look for the opening, the weakness in each other. I don't want to attack you with shitty sarcasm just because I can. We put ourselves on display and we feel like someone is going to appreciate our tension or honesty. Can we just act more . . . normal? We said we would try, and today wasn't a good day. But can we please behave like people in a marriage, in love, because we are, or think we are, or should be."

Cindi put her hand on his thigh and squeezed it.

He exhaled. "Did any of that come out right?"

She loved this Jacob. She squeezed his thigh again, shifted her body so he wouldn't see her cry, looked out her window, and whispered, "I'm such a cunt."

"No, you're not."

"You weren't supposed to hear that."

A fire, caused by a single-engine recreational aircraft, raged near Mount Rose Ski Tahoe, and Jacob imagined it spreading and torching all the homes, including theirs, and imagined, too, he and Cindi walking, after the conflagration, aimlessly with blankets and baskets and some clothes, through Washoe County. It would be Armageddon. He looked over and saw his wife, leaning against the window. He put his hand on her shoulder. He could tell she was sleeping. He stroked her hair. End Times was up ahead, and here she was blissfully unaware of their immediate future, dodging flames, and the wrath of God.

As they passed the airport, Cindi woke up.

"Have you been reading my diary?" she asked.

"No," he lied. "But I can only imagine."

JACOB FISHMAN'S MARRIAGE: A NOVEL

9. Cindi's Diaries

"You promised that you were not going to ruin this for me, right?" Cindi asked as she and Jacob stood in Kenny's backyard, in front of her thirty-two-foot 2000 Fleetwood Terry Camper, pulling and then pushing the door, trying to get inside. "It needs some work, so don't, you know, be you."

"Be me? I promise. Even though you can't seem to get in."

"See? This is what I mean."

"Sorry, sorry."

"Where is Kenny, anyway?"

"Out with his mom."

"Hope she's buying him some new overalls."

"Don't count on it."

When Cindi finally got the door open, by turning the handle, using her shoulder, and shoving, Jacob saw a broken window straight ahead of him, in a frame that was heavily damaged by water. To his immediate right was a Formica table with three legs, leaning against the wall. Some of the Formica had been ripped up, some had bubbled up, due, he assumed, to the heat, which left a small section of particle board that looked like Portugal. A plastic tumbler sat on top of an old *Reno Gazette-Journal,* a chewed Bic pen was in the cup, as was some liquid and a straw. There were three chairs, red vinyl, all in remarkably good shape, save for one that had a perfect triangle cored out of the seat. The floor was half linoleum, half concrete, and the walls were covered in blond paneling. There was a spot for a refrigerator and stove, but there were no appliances. The sink wasn't chipped, save for a brown line that bifurcated the right side from the left. There was no faucet.

The whole place was dusty and smelled of mold.

"Can I just say—" Jacob started to ask, moving to the kitchen table and tracing his finger down the Atlantic and the "Portuguese" coast.

"You promised."

"I know, I know. And I'm sorry, but the place, Cin, is uninhabitable. How did you get it here, because I'm assuming it doesn't run . . . drive. It can't drive, right?"

"Of course not. You hook it up to a truck."

"Which you don't have."

"Which I don't have . . . yet. You're not going to ruin this for me, no matter how much you try."

"Can I ask how much?"

"Four."

"Thousand?"

"Yeah, why?"

It was five thousand.

"Nothing."

"You think too much?" she asked.

"Look, it's yours, you wanted it, but . . . I don't know. Sure seems like it will be a lot of money to get it fixed up so someone could live in it." He knew that his reaction to the trailer was important to Cindi—not that he like it, she wasn't expecting that, knew that was impossible—but that he not ridicule it, because by doing so he would be ridiculing her. He was trying.

"I know, but I wanted it, and then, when I get my piece of land, I'm going to move it there."

So much for Jacob's strategic use of "someone could live in it" instead of "you could live in it."

Cindi looked at him. The place was a dump, he was right, and she had had second thoughts about it; still, she hoped, because she always did, he might see her unhappiness in life without getting defensive, without trying to mitigate its effect on her, without showing her how he was more mature, more logical. Jacob saw her looking, knew that's what she wanted from him.

"You don't like it?" she asked. "It's okay if you don't."

Jacob could see his wife was about to cry. He wanted to make her feel loved, even if this trailer, motor home, camper—he didn't even know the distinction—was her way of saying she was no longer in love with him.

"I'm trying, but of course I don't like it. Why would I like it?"

"You're just not seeing the potential."

"I'm not talking about the cleanup and the paint job and the new door handle and the table and the appliances and the windows—"

"I get it."

"No, you don't get it. I'm not talking about that. I'm talking about the trailer and what it represents."

There, he said it, though he promised himself—and had promised her—he would not because the chasms between them no longer needed to be acknowledged, highlighted, italicized. And because it was so obvious what the trailer, motor home, camper represented.

"What do you mean?"

"Never mind."

But it was too late.

"What do you think the trailer represents?"

"Remember the sewer line we had to replace?"

"Yeah, so?"

"Twenty-five hundred, right?"

"You don't have to remind me."

"Just enjoy your trailer. Don't worry about it. I am happy for you."

"Tell me."

"I promised myself I wouldn't bring this up, but remember how you bitched and screamed about how the house on Codel, our house, was an albatross, a black hole, and how you couldn't afford to live there and didn't want to spend all your money and work just to pay for it? Remember?"

"Yeah."

"But that's our life, our home. That's us," he said, trying not to speak in the italics in which he was speaking. "But this trailer cost you more than that, and I know I have no right to say anything because it's your money, but it will be at least that much more fixing it up to where it's livable."

"What are you getting at?"

"C'mon, Cin, you know. You're going to spend all this money for this"—Jacob swept his arm—"for you, but our house, us . . . that's an albatross."

"I'm just trying to find something in my life. You won't give me a baby, so let me have this."

"Why does everything in our life come back to the nonexistent baby? We also have a life, you and I."

Silence.

Cindi shook her head.

"I'm sorry, Cin."

"Why don't we go?"

"Hold it, hold it," he said, putting his arm through hers, then embracing her. "Fix it up. You should have this."

"I don't hate you, Jake."

"I didn't . . . Wait—I know you don't."

"You hate the trailer?"

"I'm really the wrong person to ask. I see a trailer, even a nice one, and I think—" Jacob had no idea what he thought. "I don't know—uh, field mice, lopsided floors, and mobile-home parks with overweight people in T-shirts wrestling on the front lawn."

"Do you even know what a field mouse is?" Cindi asked, laughing.

"Not a clue. I'm thinking the obvious—a mouse in a field."

Leaving the trailer interior, Cindi had to close the door with such force, she lost her balance and fell backward. Jacob, behind her, tried catching her, but they fell—him on his ass, her in his lap.

"Wanna make out?" he said.

"No. Will you come visit me?"

"No."

"You're such a prick."

"Then kiss me."

And lying on the ground in front of a trailer that represented all and nothing and everything in between to the Fishmans, she did.

THE MESSIAH

"We shall have the Messiah," Cindi said, coming into the bedroom the next morning, naked, after showering, her head wrapped in a yellow towel.

"Huh?" Jacob asked, still lying in bed.

"You listening to me?" Cindi asked. "The Messiah. Our baby will be the Messiah!"

How can I not put this in the book? Jacob thought, still reasonably happy with the chapter about field mice.

"You're putting that in the book, aren't you?"

"No, of course I'm not putting it in the book."

How would the fictional Jacob respond to this, he thought, reminding himself not to think about that. He had promised Cindi, the real Cindi, his wife, on the drive back from seeing Sage at Gar Woods, he was not going to live his life as if there was a studio audience following him around. This was his life, he had just made love to his wife, and he had just made love with her because things were better—he was trying, she was trying. The fictional Fishmans were even getting along better. They made out on the ground outside a trailer.

Stay in the moment. Stay in the moment.

"That's aiming a little high, isn't it," he said, "naming our child the Messiah?"

"We're not going to name him the Messiah, but he will be—or she will be."

He saw where Cindi had cracked the mirror when she threw . . . he couldn't remember whether it was a shoe or a curling iron. The skillet was in the kitchen.

"I'd actually be happy if my sperm could create an accountant."

"No, someone has to have the Messiah. Why not us?"

"I have no answer for that," he said. "I don't know. We're Jewish. And you can't just decide this with a towel on your head."

"So were Joseph and Mary."

"They had towels on their heads? Did they even fuck? Does the Bible talk about that at all? Did anyone ever ask Joseph what he thought about his wife's celestial infidelity?"

"I don't think so."

"Wait. Sam Kinison did."

"Who?"

"Never mind."

"Anyway, are you done?"

"Yeah."

"Don't you want the Messiah?"

"Don't I want the Messiah? No. Yes. How do you answer that question? How do you pose one like that? And I know better than to ask if you're serious. Sure, if you want the Messiah, I want the Messiah. What would our little Messiah—or, for that matter, the actual one—think of us as role models?"

It made Jacob nervous when Cindi would joke about having a baby, almost more than when she wasn't joking, when she'd throw skillets or things at the mirror in the bedroom. He didn't know if by humoring her, by laughing along with her, if that's what she was doing, he was making matters worse. The joking was one thing, but he didn't want to mock her, either, for her desire was real—he was hurting her by not giving her a baby, he knew that. And if he had the balls, he would have told her years ago that he wasn't going to give her a baby. But he was not going to sully this moment with the real pathology between them.

"The Messiah," Cindi said, "rises above the parenting of the two who sired him."

"You're hilarious."

"I'm ovulating. That's why it's good we did it last night."

"Did it? That's just lovely."

"No, no, it was great. I came, like, four times."

"You're in a good mood when you come that often."

"What do we learn from this?"

"Give the girl a Messiah, clearly. I'm still amazed you can feel the egg drop."

"Don't mock me."

"I'm not. I'm really not. I have known, not a lot, but a lot of women, and nobody could ever feel the egg drop."

"Fuck you."

"Cindi," he said, grabbing her and pulling her toward the bed. "I'm not making fun. I'm not. You are actually the only woman I've ever known, ever heard about, who can actually feel the egg drop."

"Can I get up now?"

"What just happened?"

"Women have been having periods for five thousand years, okay? And I think they know their bodies better than you."

"I'm not saying I do or they don't," Jacob said, thinking it was probably best he not ask where she got the five-thousand-year figure from.

"I told you, I'm fucking ovulating. My body wants a baby. I want a baby! Can't you understand that? All I have is the dog."

And a trailer, which was on Ethan's property. The fictional Cindi wasn't the only one who had one on a friend's property. Jacob had changed Ethan's name to Kenny because Jacob promised he wouldn't write about Ethan, knowing, as he did, how such a transparent, cheap move would infuriate his wife—or, to be fair, another in the series of transparent, cheap moves.

"Yes. No, of course I can't understand that . . . about the ovulation. I didn't mean to suggest I could. I'm really trying not to argue with you."

"I could kill Ampara. Why would you get a vasectomy, anyway? How could you let her talk you into it?"

Charlize-Louise, a name for the dog on which they agreed, ran in and jumped on the bed. Jacob took a moment to remind himself that both this dog and Cindi's fictional dog were both very much alive and he had only tried to kill the fictional one.

Forget the drive back from Tahoe after meeting with Sage. This was never going to go away.

"I didn't know I was going to meet you, for starters, and, damn, that's quite a jump. I already had a daughter. I didn't want any more kids. I'm sorry."

"Then why did you talk me into marrying you and why didn't you let me break up with you when I wanted? Why?"

Jacob had had so much practice at this argument he knew how to win it. But winning wasn't the point. He promised his wife he wouldn't do that anymore.

"I don't want to change the subject, deflect it, but we just had a good night. Can't we bathe in that for a while?"

"I don't want to bathe in anything. I have to get out of here. I'm going to kill somebody."

"Cin, we can't keep having this discussion, although I guess we can. I know you want to have a baby, I know. But I can't . . . don't know . . . what to tell you."

"Jacob, I want a baby. I love you. And I want a baby. So don't constantly remind me of what I don't have. Why won't you let me have one? If not with you, then someone else."

"Not about that again. You can have one, okay, but we're not going to stay married."

"Why do you say that?"

"You're not talking about the other thing again, are you? Dave?"

"Forget Dave. But why not?"

"For the love of fuck, listen to me. I am not raising another man's child—Dave's or anybody else's."

"Forget about Dave!"

"You brought him up, remember? Look, I know this is tough for you, I am trying to understand the ten . . . five thousand years of, whatever it is, of collective eggs dropping inside you, but you have to stop bringing it up . . . bringing that up. Again, what would you throw out the window, what would be lying in the front yard if I came home and said, 'I'm going to fuck a girl, get her pregnant, and then we're going to raise the child she's carrying?'"

"You have Lisa! Why would you say that?"

"Would you want to raise another woman's baby?"

"But I did."

"You did not. We got married when Lisa was almost an adult."

"That doesn't make me any less than her stepmother. I've been there for her!"

Say "Yeah, you called her a skanky whore" and the marriage is over and you'll never finish the book.

"That's completely different. When Lisa's mom and I fucked, I didn't know you." But Jacob knew what Cindi meant. The dog, the real one, named just Charlize-Louise (he had given those other monikers to the fictional one), was now sitting on the chaise, staring at Jacob, and gnawing on a bone half her size.

The bedroom, which a few hours earlier was a refuge from all that ailed the Fishmans, was now its usual space of anger, sadness, exhaustion, and recrimination.

"What?" she said.

"Nothing."

"What are you thinking?"

"I'm not thinking anything. I didn't say anything."

The sound of Charlize-Louise tearing rawhide off the bone was getting increasingly louder.

"What are you thinking?" she repeated.

"I'm not fucking thinking anything."

"About your book, right? You're going to put this in the book?"

"No."

It's never going to get better.

"I wrote in my diary once, 'Underneath all this bile and resentment, I still love him,'" Cindi said.

Jacob knew that, for he had read it in her diary. He had given it to the fictional Cindi, and now she had written it in her diary, and the fictional Jacob had read that diary, too. How many Cindis was he prepared to give this line to? How many ways could he defile his marriage?

"So what did you say about me in the book?" she asked.

"Nothing. Forget about the book."

"I want to read it."

"No. I don't care how angry you get, no, you're not reading it until it's finished."

"Why?"

"Because, for one thing, I can't finish it if I know you hate or love it, and I doubt you're going to love. I can't write it worrying about your review."

"You're making me out to be a bitch, aren't you?"

"No, I'm not. And it's not you. You're more successful than she is."

"Why can't you just get a job like a normal person?"

"Tell me something. Why did you fuck me last night?"

"I wanted to."

"You know you couldn't get pregnant."

"I fucking know that. I wanted to fuck you. Christ! You know, you rip my heart out every fucking time I have a period. Do you plan it that way? Did you plan to not have any more children before we got married, before you suckered me into this marriage?"

"Suckered you into this marriage? What?"

"You know."

Jacob knew she was right, not about suckering her into marriage, but about the baby. He had lied. When she asked a few months before their wedding, "Now, you will think about a reversal, right?" he knew what she meant was "Don't marry me if you won't." He knew, too, that her desire for a baby was nothing he could talk his way through, out of, or around, and that eventually they would divorce over it, and knew, eventually, how ugly it would all get. But if her unhappiness in the marriage made her vitriolic, his resignation about it numbed him. Neither Fishman marriage was going to make it, he knew that now, but he was not going to be the one who walked out—not because she fucked another guy, not because he was unhappy. He envisioned that too, her cheating. And why wouldn't it be Mitch? There was something about the way she spoke of him—it reminded him of how she spoke once about him. Mitch was smart, not as much of a prick as he was, Mitch and Cindi had things in common, and Mitch probably wasn't sterile. Jacob imagined walking in on them. She would be rubbing his back, or she would be on her back, topless, with her pants loose. Jacob would stop at the door, say something quietly, and then tell them both to get out of the house. He'd let Mitch put his shirt on. He'd let Cindi get her wallet. Jacob envisioned them standing in the front yard. He hoped it would be chilly.

They wouldn't be standing there. Mitch would drive her to his place or the university.

Details. But he wouldn't leave. He would stay in the house. He felt good knowing he had a plan. He felt sick knowing he had a plan. He had been wrong about every other woman in his life, for he thought it was their anger that motivated them, propelled them out of their relationships with him, but it was their sadness that did it—and his wife was sad. And he couldn't stay angry at her, wouldn't stay angry at her, because she was sad. He and Mitch, he projected, would be friends someday.

"I hate this fucking marriage sometimes, this house. I think I should just leave, take Charlize-Louise, and just live in the camper. I'm drying up."

Charlize-Louise barked.

"I'm getting dressed," she said. Jacob watched her, naked, pick up Charlize-Louise, and bring her into the walk-in closet.

"You want to go to breakfast?"

"No."

"Can I make you something here?"

"No."

Jacob couldn't form another question, couldn't find another word to say. He just stared at the closet door and closed his eyes to the point where he could see just a sliver of light. He purposefully slowed down his breathing.

"Cin?"

"What?"

"Why are we doing this?"

"What?"

"This marriage?"

Cindi Fishman came out of the closet. Jacob opened his eyes wide. He motioned her to come sit beside him.

"Why do you want me to sit next to you?"

"Because I don't know what else to do."

Cindi, topless and in jeans, with Charlize-Louise in her arms, walked out of the bedroom.

Jacob Fishman's Marriage: A Novel

10. Field Mice

2:15 a.m.

The phone rang.

"I'm not getting up," said Cindi.

"You know, if we had a phone in the bedroom," replied her husband, "neither one of us would have to get up."

The phone continued ringing.

"No, it's not healthy," she said. "The electromagnetic waves—"

"That's only for cellphones, which, for reasons that defy understanding, you have but refuse to use. Anyway, it doesn't pertain to home phones."

The phone continued ringing.

"Jake, the electromagnetic ray, the rays, are not good shooting through your head. Science has proven it."

"You're not good shooting through my head. Nobody calls me anyway. It has to be for you."

The phone continued ringing.

"I don't wish to be disturbed."

"'I don't wish to be disturbed'? Who talks like that?"

"Like what?"

The phone continued ringing.

"Like this: 'I don't wish to be disturbed.'"

The phone stopped ringing. The call presumably went to the answering machine.

"Oh, good going, Cin. Now you missed the call."

"It's four o'clock in the fucking morning."

"It's not four o'clock. It's quarter after two, which is bad enough and which would have already made your point. Why exaggerate to four?"

"And my voice shoots through your head?" Cindi said, getting up. "You're insufferable, you know that?"

"So why are you getting up now? I thought you didn't care."

"To see if it's my lover."

"Nice. Ask him why he's calling so late. Inconsiderate prick. Tell him he has to pick you up this time. I'm not driving you again."

"Blow me."

"My wife, ladies and gentlemen, just asked me to blow her."

Cindi went into the kitchen, where the Fishmans had one of their two phones—the other in Jacob's office—and hit the "play" button on the answering machine.

She could barely make out the voice. Kenny.

"Call me," Cindi heard, but that's all she could decipher.

She called back. He picked up.

"Jacob, get up, please," she said, coming into the bedroom and into her walk-in closet to find clothes.

"What is it? Sure. Where we going?"

"Kenny's."

"Shit. Okay." Jacob picked up the pair of pants from the edge of the bed.

"He said he's going to kill himself."

Jacob was about to say "Again?" but didn't.

On the drive to Sparks, Cindi said she didn't want to find him dead, didn't want to see the blood.

"I've never seen anyone dead. Oh, Jake, shit!"

"Do you want his mother to find him like that? You're his friend. Unfortunately, that's your job, to find him dead if he is."

"You think we'll find him dead?"

"I don't think he would have called if he were dead," Jacob said, not trying to be funny.

"I'm still loopy from the three Tylenol PM. Thank you for coming with me."

"Where else do you think I'd want to be? You took three?"

"I love you," she said, patting his stomach as they pulled into Kenny's driveway. "I do, you know," she added as they got out of the car.

"Wouldn't that be something? Three?"

"Yes, I do, and yes, I did. Jesus! Ruin the fucking moment, why don't you?"

Kenny's door was open, and when Cindi pushed it, she found two unopened cans of Coke on the floor and Kenny tying the sash of his robe, his balls and cock visible as he walked toward them.

"Jesus, Kenny, what are those, cantaloupes?" Jacob asked, trying to divert his eyes.

Kenny took his cock in his hand and waved it around.

"Okay, honey," Jacob said, "he's fine. We can go."

The television was tuned to a car dealership's infomercial about financing for those with bad debt. On top of the set was an uncapped bottle of Fiji water. On the coffee table in front of the sofa were Kenny's shoes, carpet samples, cigarette butts, a beer coolie, and a lighter. The house smelled of Lysol and cat urine, even as the air conditioning blasted. Josh, Kenny's dog, was between the living room and the kitchen, barking rhythmically.

"Jesus, Kenny, that's your problem," said Jacob, motioning to the kitchen. "Shoot Cujo and you'll feel better."

Josh kept yelping.

"Please!" said Jacob, glimpsing Kenny's scrotum as he sat on the sofa. "Guys find that attractive?" he asked, pointing.

Kenny laughed, grabbed himself, and blew Jacob a kiss.

"I think *I* want to kill myself," said Jacob.

Cindi shot him a look. She sat next to Kenny on the sofa.

"What is it? You're just having a bad night. You were fine the other day."

"A bad year is more like it."

"Kenny, you just came out of rehab. Look what you've done out here. The chickens, the farming. It's nice."

"Yeah, well, Josh just killed, like, most of the chickens. Just ate 'em. And I beat him."

"I'm sure he didn't know why," Cindi said.

"He knows. I'm done. I'm going to get some drugs and I'm fucking going to do this. I hate everything. I cry all the time. I sit in the shower. Literally, I sit down in the shower, sometimes because I can't move, sometimes because I don't want to. I don't see the point in moving. That's not depression, that's paralysis. So, you take care of the chickens that are left when I'm gone, because you're the only one."

"What do you mean?"

"Cindi, I used to matter. I was never happy, but I mattered. Now, I am a complete fuckup with a lazy eye and huge balls."

Cindi took a deep breath. "Your eye is not lazy, it's . . . it's fine. Jacob, say something."

"Huh?" he said, his focus on the television and how a new VW Beetle could be leased for $149/month with nothing down.

"Say something!"

"Kenny, you know, you only kill yourself if you're a fuckup. And you're just fucked up. Difference between being a noun and acting like a verb. So, what, you want to kill yourself because you can't hold a job, your balls hang out, and this crazy fucking dog of yours killed your chickens—which, why do you have anyway? Okay, that's another story. Besides, like Cindi says, you came out of rehab, you tried to kill yourself twice already. You're obviously not good at it."

Kenny didn't say anything and started rubbing his cock under his robe.

"Would you stop that, please?" Cindi asked. "Tell you what, let's all go sit out back."

Jacob was immediately attacked by gnats and mosquitoes.

"Let's go to the coop," Kenny said, "and I'll show you."

"Look at what you've done!" said Cindi. "Jacob, look at the rooster."

Jacob had no interest in the rooster, or which one was the rooster, and was getting nauseous from the chicken shit and fertilizer, the heat, and the confinement.

"Jacob, come look," Cindi insisted.

Jacob stepped forward. "Wow," he said, but didn't see what he was supposed to see, unless what he was supposed to see was six to eight dead chickens—he didn't stop to count—lying on the ground, some peacefully (chickens can give themselves heart attacks running from an angry dog, Jacob remembered reading once) and some still bleeding, almost purplish, from what looked like bites.

"Do you see him? The rooster?" asked Cindi.

"Yeah," he said. But he didn't know which one was the rooster. He assumed the biggest one. "Wow!"

"I think Jacob wants to go in now," Cindi said to Kenny, who stood in the coop with his bathrobe open. "We'll be right in, Jake."

Even with the stench of the house, the air conditioner felt good, as Jacob retook his seat next to the big-screen television. He noticed the car dealership's fine print on yet another "incredible" deal—96-month loans.

That's how they do it.

"Kenny, why are you watching this?" Jacob asked as Cindi and Kenny returned and resumed their places on the sofa. "You're going to buy a car, kill yourself, and stick them with the payments? Pretty shrewd."

"I'm a hundred and fifty thousand dollars in debt, to the hospital alone," Kenny said.

"Send them fifty bucks a month. What do you care?"

"I'm not paying them shit."

"You know why you don't want to kill yourself?" asked Jacob.

"Why?"

"I'm going to get a Coke first." Jacob went to the kitchen. "Because you called us," he said, opening a can and returning to the living room.

"You would have done it otherwise. Something in your fucked-up-edness, in that mind behind that one good and one droopy eye knows that this is going to get better—or at least not much worse."

"That's all you got?" Kenny asked. "Gimme back my Coke. That insight is childish."

Cindi laughed. At this moment, she loved them both, but especially her husband, because, while crude, he was right.

Jacob continued. "Hold on, it gets better. And it's three o'clock in the morning, so fuck you if I don't sound like Solomon. I can't tell you that you're not a mess because you clearly are, but for whatever reason, you can't kill yourself. And maybe it's because you don't want to. You keep making these miraculous recoveries. You should be a vegetable right now, with people wiping your nose and ass—yet you're fine. I mean, you don't blink, which is a little fucking freaky, and that drooping eye is right out of *Sweeney Todd,* and your balls, God knows what's happening there, but you're here—"

Kenny made his eyes bulge out even more.

Cindi screamed in mock horror.

"—you can walk without a cane," Jacob said, laughing, making his eyes bug out in return, "you have most of your faculties, such as they are. It's too trite, what I'm about to say, but, Christ, somebody—like my wife, who God knows where she finds the reservoir sometimes for what she loves—thinks you're worth it. Maybe you should stop fighting it and, you know, put on some pants and cover up your balls."

And with that, Kenny's arm swept the ashtray, issues of *Gay Times* and *The Advocate,* a plastic cup, a glass, matches, and the TV remote off the table.

"Maybe I should clean first."

"You could do that, too."

"I'm going to throw up," Cindi said suddenly. "Between the Tylenol and not eating all day, I'm sick. I know this isn't about me, but, oh, Kenny, we're going to have to go. I'm all of a sudden not feeling well. Don't kill yourself, okay? In fact, stay out of the bathtub."

Kenny said nothing.

"Kenny?"

"Go!"

"Kenny, please, promise me," she said again.

"Okay. I won't."

"Oh, I'm going to be sick. Can I use your bathroom?"

"You don't want to."

She vomited twice in the bathroom. She came back holding her stomach.

"You okay?" Jacob asked.

"I have to go home. Kenny, you going to be okay?"

Nothing.

"Kenny!"

"Jesus, yes. Stop yelling!"

Jacob left first.

He picked up two syringes that were lying on a table by the door. He buried them in the bushes before Cindi, holding Kenny's hand, walked outside.

They all hugged. Cindi and Jacob got in the car and watched Kenny walk back into the house.

"Let's make sure he gets in before we leave," she said.

The lights went out inside.

"What do you think?" she asked, as they started the drive home.

"If Kenny wants to die, he's going to find a way to die."

They talked little on the way home. The reflections of light coming from McDonald's and Sonic and banks and car washes and casinos shone on Cindi's face as she leaned against the window.

"How are you feeling?" Jacob asked, though he knew she was sleeping. This is a beautiful girl, he thought, and for the moment, he wanted to lean over to touch her face and, later, when he got home, wanted to make love to this beautiful girl, who was also his wife, and wondered if, for the night, they could forget about trailers and babies and vasectomies and all the moments of disappointments that now defined them.

Maybe.

"What are you thinking about?" Cindi asked, suddenly awake, for the second time tonight.

"You feel better?"

"Yeah, I don't know what happened."

"So why do you think he called?"

"I don't know."

Minutes later, Cindi was asleep again, only this time she leaned against her husband's chest, his arm wrapped around her, which is how the Fishmans drove the rest of the way home that night.

Dave's 23-Year-Old

"We were about to set up camp one night in Ethiopia when we were approached by soldiers from Benishangul-Gumuzo, a region inside Ethiopia that isn't happy with the government. That night, we set up perimeter guards. Two on guard, one for each raft. After going to bed, I heard yelling across the camp. I came out and saw that the militia commander was sitting in my chair, telling us to come with him. I told them we're not leaving the camp, we're not leaving the equipment, the camps, the rafts, and we're not going anywhere."

Then Scaturro saw dozens of armed men and thought, "Ahh, shit!"

The story, another one for the geology magazine, was about Pasquale V. Scaturro, a geophysicist, who in 2004 was the first European to travel the Nile from Ethiopia to Alexandria and then to the Mediterranean. Scaturro was also the guy who led a blind climber up Mount Everest. Jacob had already written about Scaturro, and they were more or less friends, ever since Jacob asked what all those months away on expeditions did to his marriage.

"Oh, please, don't ask," Scaturro told him.

Jacob saw these geology stories as puzzles. He would email scientists like Scaturro a list of questions and, unless they'd insist on a phone interview, would receive their answers in an email, at which point Jacob would simply cut and paste their answers into a narrative, word for word, after some bland transitionary pablum like "Scaturro didn't always receive the warmest of welcomes." There was no fuss, no muss, Jacob said to himself, which is an expression he almost never used. Jacob crafted *Jacob's Fishman's Marriage* the same way, for he also cut parts of his life and pasted them into another narrative.

"Don't bring up any of the specifics of Sage's life to Dave, okay?" Cindi said on the way to Sage's ex-husband's house for dinner.

"You mean, like his soon-to-be-ex-wife's gasping, pre-orgasmic wonder at the approaching strange cock?"

"Pretty much exactly that." Cindi paused. "Did you already write about it in your book?"

"No."

"Jake!"

"I didn't. I wanted to, but I didn't," he lied. "Tell me again what the kids' names are."

"Eros, Eritrea, Elegance, Edina, Ephedra, and Eddie. Don't forget," said Cindi, as she and Jacob got out of the car.

"Eddie is the one that kills me. I guess at some point you decide to stop making going through life impossible for your kids. And Ephedra? Is that a Greek goddess or a banned substance?"

"I'm not laughing," Cindi said, stifling a laugh. "Look, I don't know how many of the kids will be home, but Dave and Sage swear they were told by God to have the six children."

"God told them this?"

"Yes, Sage and I were upstairs, painting each other, smoking dope—"

"Painting each other?"

"Watercolors. We might have been topless."

"What could go wrong there?"

"She has great boobies."

"Oh, boy."

"What?"

"Boobies?"

"Tits! Better?"

"Yes. Much."

"Anyway, we were painting each other in watercolors when she said she was told to have six children and to name them Edina, Ephedra, and Eddie."

"And the other three?"

"She just said she liked the names."

"God just had to have Eddie, but gave her free will on the other three names?"

"Why are you still talking?" she said, laughing.

Dave and Sage both joined the Mormon Church after marrying, but over time, Sage told Cindi, they found the religion too liberal, so they joined Potters House Christian Fellowship Church, a charismatic denomination, where they heard about the demons who come in through the television.

As Jacob and Cindi walked into Dave's house, they noticed the living room was empty, save for a hardwood table with three additional table leaves. It ran the length of one side of the room. Dave told them he made the table himself, highlighting the three new leaves, after seeing them in a dream.

"The table means 'welcome' in some cultures. A larger table signifies a bounty of welcome. Here, sit," he said, patting the wood of the table and pulling out a chair.

He went into the kitchen and returned with a salad bowl, made from the same wood.

"It's quinoa. Hope you like."

"We do," said Cindi, kicking Jacob under the table, squeezing his thigh. "It's a beautiful table and a beautiful meal."

"Made the table from a tree out back."

"It's beautiful, really," Jacob said.

"I have to tell you," Dave said, "even though my church isn't a big fan of such things, I went to a psychic who confirmed I should build the table. By the way, you guys want something to drink?"

"I'll get it," said Cindi, getting up.

"Anyway, this psychic told me that the table represented not only 'welcome' but 'strength,' and that when I was building the leaves for the table, I was actually building my own strength back up. Since Sage left, I kind of like that."

"Tough deal what happened—" he started to say, but seeing Cindi, he halted.

"What do you mean?" asked Dave.

"I meant the dream. That's not what it means—the strength part of it."

"Believe it or not, Dave, Jacob interprets dreams," Cindi said, sitting down after bringing two herbal teas and a Fresca.

"He does?" asked Dave, who, while liking Jacob, always thought of him as dark and impure.

"This one's easy," said Jacob. "The leaves represent your children."

"Really? Actually, I can see that," said Dave.

"Yeah. It's the connection between you and Sage—you made them stronger. Plus, it's the old world of the table and the new ones, the leaves, after your divorce. What the dream is telling you is that your worlds will co-exist. Your kids, your new world, the remnants of your old life. It will all fit, if you do the work. And you did it."

Cindi loved her husband at times like this, and Jacob could sense it. She winked at him and let him see her sweetly exhale.

"See," she said to Dave, "told you he was good."

"Wow. That psychic cost me a hundred and fifty dollars."

"I would have done it for half that—maybe a little more than half. Seriously, though, you okay with it all? Sage leaving?"

"It's better now."

"That she's gone?"

"No, no, since she's been gone."

"Do we know where she is now?" Cindi asked, interrupting because she was afraid where this was headed. It had been about six weeks since she and Jacob and Sage had been at Gar Woods. "Because I haven't heard from her since—"

"Yeah, we saw her in Tahoe," Jacob said.

"She's with her mom," Cindi added.

"I thought she moved in with the drummer," Dave put in.

"You know about Demko?" Jacob asked.

"Jake!" Cindi said.

"No, it's okay, Cindi. She told me about Demko."

"And she told us she told you," Jacob said. "Remember, Cindi? She told us about the band."

Cindi glared at her husband and mouthed "Don't" when Dave wasn't looking.

"What is with you two?" asked Dave, seeing the moment between Cindi and Jacob.

"Nothing," said Jacob, "but Sage asked us that a lot, too."

Jacob tried to eat his salad, but, with the exception of the two small cucumber slices, there was literally nothing—from the chickpeas to the red pepper to the endive to the black olives—he liked.

"She is going to Washington . . . soon."

"Are you really going to go?" Jacob asked, surprised to find an avocado, which he ate without chewing. "Sage said you were thinking about it."

"I mean, well, I was, but that's kind of crazy. It's not over yet. The divorce, I mean. There's still the house and the money and stuff."

"I'm sorry," said Cindi.

"Let me ask you two something," Dave asked, filling Cindi's plate with salad, "and you don't have to answer. It's probably too personal, but . . . what would you do if one of you did that? Cheated . . . left?"

Cindi stopped eating.

"Is it just me," Jacob said, "or do we get asked this question a lot?"

"I don't know," Cindi said. "Let's talk about something else."

"Great idea. Let's talk about something else."

"C'mon, you guys," said Dave. "I'm spilling my guts out here. Give me something."

"I don't know," said Jacob, wondering why Cindi all of a sudden didn't want to talk about it, "but for me, try not to whine. I guess, like you, I'd try to understand, because I'd have to, though I don't think I could be as understanding with Cindi if she did to me what Sage did to you."

"Hold the fuck on," said Cindi. "If I did to you? What if you did to me? What if you fucked Ciara?"

"Ciara? Who?"

"Who? You know who."

"Much less chance of that than you fucking Mitch."

"Why are you talking about this again? You promised."

"What are you talking about?"

"I'm not fucking Mitch—for the four millionth fucking time."

"And I'm not fucking Ciara."

"Who are these people?" asked Dave.

"Ciara is nobody, a waitress. Cindi works with Mitch."

"Oh, and so because I work with Mitch, I'm more likely fucking him."

"I didn't say that. I just mean I don't even know why you're bringing Ciara up now."

"Hold it, hold it," said Dave. "All I wanted to know, and I shouldn't have asked, is has either one of you ever thought about either one cheating? Not . . . this!"

Jacob looked at Cindi, who returned the look, her mouth now full.

"You first, babe," Jacob said.

"No, no, you first," Cindi replied.

"Chickenshit. Okay, yeah, I have thought about it."

"You have?"

"Oh, you have, too."

"So, I don't need to talk? And what makes you know for certain I've thought about it?"

"You thought about fucking Dave, for Chrissakes!"

"What?" said Dave, just as Cindi slammed down her fork, which hit her plate and landed in Jacob's quinoa.

"You motherfucker!" Cindi screamed.

"What do you mean?" Dave asked.

"Don't listen to him," Cindi said.

"I have to now."

Cindi pushed herself away from the table but stayed seated.

"Dave, look, Cindi wants to have a baby, and since I won't give her one, she told me once that she would fuck you and have your baby, even though she would just do it for . . . sperm. We would raise it, and she thought you'd be okay with that."

"I'm sorry, Dave," Cindi said, leaning forward and slamming the table again. "This is what happened. Jacob and I were talking, and I told this fucking asshole over here that I just wanted to have a baby and, yeah, your name came up."

"And?" Dave asked.

"And I never thought about it again. Fuck you, Jake. I mean it. Fuck. You."

"I don't know what to say," said Dave.

"I'm sorry," said Jacob. "I shouldn't have brought that up. It was stupid."

"And you didn't go to Mario's that night I was in Vegas and try to fuck Ciara?" Cindi asked.

"What? No, I didn't even go out."

He had gone out. He'd told her he had gone out. She'd know he was lying about something because he had already told her the truth about going out. He'd fingered Ciara outside. That part he didn't tell her about, obviously.

"Yeah, you sat home?" Cindi asked.

"And how many times did you call to check on me?" Jacob asked.

"I called."

"The fuck you did."

"Well, I tried."

"You tried? Was there a cellphone outage?"

"I don't know. It didn't go through. It was all static-y."

"What, are you making this up as you go along? I had surgery. You should have been concerned about me. I was the one recovering. I didn't have to call you."

"You had a fucking colonoscopy, not a heart bypass. And I did try calling you."

"Not enough. Guess you were too busy with Mitch."

"What is your fucking problem with Mitch?"

"Nothing, except when you went to Vegas and stayed the extra night."

"What are you talking about?"

"When I had the colonoscopy, and you went to Vegas anyway?"

"You said I could go."

"And you stayed an extra night."

"So I stayed an extra night."

"That's a great answer."

"What do you want me to say?"

"I'm just saying you went."

"You fucking told me I could go."

"I know. And then you didn't call. I'm not saying you fucked Mitch, I'm just saying—"

"That I fucked Mitch."

"No. Just that it was possible."

"Not any more possible—less, probably—than you fucking Ciara, who you want to fuck, clearly."

"No."

"Sorry, Dave," said Cindi. "This night was supposed to be about you."

"I feel like I shouldn't even be here," Dave said, "but it's my house, so I really can't go anywhere." Cindi and Jacob both laughed. "But to change the subject, sort of, I will tell you, I had sex last Thursday."

"You did?" Cindi and Jacob said in unison, both thankful there was something else to talk about.

"Yeah, the kids were at my mom's. And it was the best ever. And I didn't feel like I was cheating."

"Why would you think you were cheating? Sage has fucked half of northern Nevada."

Cindi dropped her head.

"No, I was cheating. In Galatians five, nineteen through twenty-one, '*Now the works of the flesh are evident: sexual immorality, impurity, sensuality, idolatry, sorcery, enmity, strife, jealousy, fits of anger, rivalries, dissensions, divisions, envy, drunkenness, orgies, and things like these. I warn you, as I warned you before, that those who do such things will not inherit the kingdom of God.*'"

"But that's only if your wife isn't fucking like a banshee. And what a tough deal. You fuck once outside the marriage, you lose the kingdom. That's some bullshit! And how do you remember all that?"

"Jake, please. For the love of fuck!"

"Sorry. Dave, sorry. Cindi's right. I'm an asshole sometimes. This is so not going well."

"It's all right. But here's the thing. No matter what she did, she's still part of me. It kind of sucks, but God must have laid this on her heart, and, you know, we're still one."

"Even if you're not," Jacob asked.

"Even if."

"But the sex was good, right?"

"Good? Great! I feel lighter."

"So there's that," said Jacob. "You look better than I've ever seen you. You're alive, awake. You always had that strange sort of glazed pastiness of born-again Christians."

"Jacob has a tough time expressing himself like a grown-up," said Cindi. "Tell us about the girl."

"Oh, she's twenty-three."

"Really?" said Jacob. "What's that like?"

"You going to throw this in my face?" Cindi asked.

"What?"

"Youth. Healthy eggs."

"What are you talking about?"

"You're such a cocksucker."

That night in bed, Cindi and Jacob Fishman lay on their backs, in identical poses, hands behind their heads, staring at their respective parts of the ceiling.

"Are we ever going to talk again?" asked Jacob.

"No."

"Can I just apologize again?"

"Doesn't matter."

"It does. Everything you asked me not to do, I did."

"Forget it. You're not even here now. You're thinking about the book right now, aren't you?"

"Oh, God, I don't know. No."

"I knew it. Let me ask you something about Jacob and Cindi in the book—what's going on with them? Same thing that's going on with us?"

"Yes and no. I mean, Jacob's an asshole, if that's what you're getting at."

"I don't care if he's an asshole—that's not what I'm asking. I assume he's an asshole. You're an asshole. I'm just wondering if I'm an asshole. If Cindi is—Jesus, I sound like you now. Anyway, if they do this any better, if you let them do this any better than we do it."

"I try," Jacob said with a laugh, "but, no, they don't do it any better."

"Why don't you make them do it better?"

Under the Bed Again

12 February 2012

I thought we were getting better. We had this nice drive, a nice moment back from Tahoe, and I don't know, something was different. We were in the car and, it was weird, and J was talking about a new us, which he never talks about. It takes him awhile to get to the point :) But of course being J, he couldn't leave it at that. Kept asking about Mitch, which was crazy. I think he thinks I want to fuck him, or have . . . I don't know. Mitch is fucking brilliant and if he were single, I guess, but, no, God . . . having to put up with his orbit. Jesus, I think J's is tough enough. And Mitch has some Russian girlfriend with a tight ass and an exotic name and what would he want with me anyway? I think J gets me talking about anything but the baby, which he's not giving me, so we waste all this energy on other things—like Mitch. Anyway, on the trip back, he told me he wanted to be different, which was sweet and not believable, but sweet and I love my husband. But I'm getting worse about the baby. I think he thinks it will go away. Men and their fucking sperm control everything and yet—YET—women are still expected to be nice, to buy presents. I told you about the "grandpa" shoes, right? I don't know what he wants from me sometimes. I don't know what I want from him. I have to get my own *thing going on. Finally, he's gone . . . to the university to walk. His presence is all over this house. Maybe he's having an affair, too, I don't know, but he sure walks a lot. I shouldn't be worried, but there's this chick at the restaurant he likes. He so wants to fuck her. She'd fuck him, too. I know it. I don't know if J knows it. Maybe they have. Probably. Between you and me, I couldn't blame him. But I'd be furious.*

I should fuck Mitch. J should fuck this chick—Ciara. What a fucking name, huh?

So, a few nights ago, we're at Dave's and that motherfucker, my husband, tells Dave that I wanted to fuck him because a few months ago, or maybe last year, I said that Dave could father my baby and J and I could raise it. I WAS FUCKING JOKING. Dave got embarrassed and I was furious and he brought up Mitch again. What is it with him and Mitch? Yeah, I want to fuck Mitch and Dave. How about together? I want to have a baby and sometimes I get crazy thinking about how, but I wouldn't, even though a lot of women get pregnant and aren't married, which I know isn't the same thing, but what if I had a child—J had one— and he raised it with me. Is it really THAT different? I mean, of course it is—the fucking part—but not the raising. I did it with Lisa, J's daughter. I spend exactly no time thinking about how J fucked Lisa's mom. Anyway, I'm not going to do it. I like Mitch, sometimes more than J, but I wouldn't fuck him—and I think when I was in Vegas, the time J didn't call me, I could have. BUT I DIDN'T. It sucks because a man can think about fucking women all the time, but a woman can't think about a man that way. Mitch was really, really, REALLY brilliant at this conference thingy.

And what would it matter anyway? I'm not going to, but what is the point of fucking J anyway. It's not all that good, but maybe it's me, and he's not going to give me a baby. He can't because that fucking Ampara made him get a vasectomy.

He should just fuck Ciara, I should fuck Mitch, and we'll be even.

Did I say that already?

AWFUL AWFUL

A week after they went to Dave's, the Fishmans—the real ones —looked like the Fishmans again. Cindi was on the floor, cross-legged, taking a flat iron to her hair and applying a little bit of makeup under her eyes, and doing both badly, and Jacob was sitting up in the bed, watching her.

Cindi watched him watching.

"Can't you go somewhere?"

"I live here. Where do you want me to go?"

"You don't really want me to answer that, do you?"

"Seriously? This moment is bothering you? I'm just lying here."

"All you do is watch me," she said, trying, and still failing, to master her flat iron. "Fuck," she said, looking at her hair, which was still not doing what she wanted it to do. "I am working my ass off and you're just sitting around, doing your little writing." Cindi, once again, made that big sweeping move with her hand, mimicking a kid drawing on a large canvas.

"How many times already on that? I got it. What I do—"

"Oh, stop being a baby. By the way, have I killed anybody in the book of yours, which, by the way, I hate?"

"No. But I may have you killed off."

"Good. I don't want to be in it. Who's going to kill me?"

"Your husband."

"Lovely."

"So why can't I go tonight?"

She looked at him in the mirror. "What's the big deal? The dinner is on behalf of Brooks, a guy I hate, I told you about him, and he's retiring at the end of the semester. You're going to hate it. I mean, do you want to come?"

"Am I invited?"

"I can't stop you. Come if you want."

"There's an engraved invitation."

"It's a faculty goodbye dinner for a guy I don't even like."

"Not Mitch, then?"

"Again with Mitch? Jesus! No, but Ciara will be there."

"What do you mean?"

"Believe it or not, we have a table at Portofini."

"Fin-o."

"Whatever, but your little girlfriend will probably be there."

"Forget Ciara."

"Then forget Mitch. Why do you keep talking about him, anyway? I like Mitch. You like Mitch. I might as well just fuck Mitch because you already think I am."

"And you think I'm fucking Ciara."

"I think you fucked her. I don't think you are fucking her."

"Interesting distinction. But, no, I have not fucked her."

"Well, I have not fucked Mitch," she replied, mimicking his emphasis. "I don't even know why we're talking about this."

"Fine."

"Fine."

"So, can I come?"

"Okay, for Chrissakes, you can come. I want you to come," she said, stopping her flat ironing mid-stroke.

"You want me to come?"

"I just said I did. Now, could you leave me alone while I get dressed? Christ, look at me," she exclaimed, moving closer to the cracked mirror.

"I've aged forty-five years since this marriage . . . since this conversation started."

"Forty-five?"

Jacob quickly got dressed.

On the drive to Mario's Portofino, Cindi jerked the Scion with every shift between gears. She had insisted on getting a standard because, she told Jacob at the time, "Americans are too fat and soft."

"Something wrong, my beloved?"

"Just . . . forget it."

"What?"

"Don't embarrass me tonight, okay? I don't know why you have to come."

"You asked me to come."

"Yeah, I asked you."

"You didn't ask me?"

"You told me you wanted me to come."

"And then you asked me to come."

"I'm getting a migraine. Just don't turn it into 'The Jacob Fishman Show.'" Cindi slammed on the brakes at the intersection of North Center Street and Sixth when she realized she had missed her turn. The car stalled. She restarted it, but not before the driver in back of her hit the horn. Cindi rolled down the window.

"Fuck me, you asshole!" she yelled before she took off again.

"What are you talking about? Look, if you don't want me to come, tell me, but you asked. You really did ask."

"Fine, I asked."

"Cin, look, I don't have to go. In fact, just drop me off at the Legacy. Really, I'm fine. You go. I'll see you at home tonight."

Cindi didn't say anything, but she drove to the valet at the Silver Legacy, between Fourth and Fifth, and waved to the attendant that she was just dropping someone off.

"You can come," Cindi said, as Jacob opened the door.

"You go. I'm fine."

"Is this where you want me to leave you?"

"Doesn't matter."

Jacob got out of the car and walked into the downstairs lobby. He didn't turn around.

Cindi pulled out but then circled around, hoping Jacob was still there. He was gone.

"Christ, I fucked that up," she said to herself. She pounded the steering wheel with her ring-less hand. "I am the worst wife."

Jacob had gone to the restroom, but decided, instead of going upstairs to the casino, to go back to the valet, hoping Cindi would come back. He just missed her.

"Christ, I fucked that up," he said to himself.

Convinced she wasn't coming, he walked outside and headed for no particular reason to the National Bowling Stadium on North Center. He leaned against the silver bowling ball.

The phone rang. It was Cindi. He let it go to voicemail.

He checked the message. "Hi, sorry. You could have come. Call me if you want me to come back and get you."

He smiled, for she wanted him. She didn't want him to go to the dinner, he knew that, and probably not because she didn't want to appear not interested in Mitch around him, who knows, but she still wanted him. It wasn't much. It wasn't enough. But it was something. He wanted to go and show her he could behave, show her he could be nice to Mitch, show her he was capable of not embarrassing her, show her, mostly, he was proud of her. But Jacob Fishman, remembering the drive back from Tahoe, decided to not trouble his wife any more than he already had. He texted her.

I'm sorry, too. Nah, I'll just hang out in town. See you later.

She texted back.

Love U :)

He smiled. Would it have killed her to spell out "you"?

He walked back to the Silver Legacy and to the bar outside the Catch a Rising Star Comedy Club, where he hoped his friend Matt would be working. He was.

"Diet Coke with an orange?"

"You remember? I'm flattered."

"What's the orange for again?"

"It kills the taste."

"Why don't you drink something else?"

"Because then I wouldn't have conversations like this."

"How's married life?"

"Blow me."

"How's Cindi?"

"Blow me."

"You don't start being nice to me, I'm charging you for these," he said, pointing to the orange he was cutting up. "You want to talk about it or just sit here and annoy me?"

"Annoy you. But it is good to see you."

"You too."

"Jacob?" a high-pitched voice called out.

"Yes," he said, turning around.

A blonde girl in a short black skirt with a white top was standing next to a fat man in a yellow sailor's hat, Bermuda shorts, and a shirt that appeared to have squid on it. The couple looked like a circus duo.

"Is that you?" the girl asked again.

"I think it's me. This is my friend Matt," Jacob said, pointing, hoping she'd introduce herself because he would need to know her name pretty soon.

"I'm Aurora," she said to Matt, "and this," she said to both of them, "is Bob," patting the side of the man's head.

"Bob?" Jacob asked.

"Hi," said Bob.

"Bob—Matt."

Jacob's phone rang. He checked. It was Cindi. He ignored the call. Matt waved.

"You know this guy?" Matt asked Aurora, referring to Jacob.

"He's been trying to get in my pants for years."

"Have I?" Jacob asked, searching for Bob's reaction. "I need to behave, Aurora. I'm married. For a long time. You know that."

"You're not married. Where's your ring?"

He felt for it.

"Oh, right—it's in a drawer, under some socks and shoelaces."

"What?"

"Nothing. So, you and Bob . . . together?"

"No, no, we're just friends. He helps out."

"And she helps me out," said Bob, winking.

"Whatever works, huh?" said Jacob, the only thing he could think to say.

"You're really married?" she asked Jacob.

"Why don't you believe me? Yes."

"He's really married," Matt said.

"You look like shit," she said, smiling, tussling his hair. "Let's go, Bob."

"This," Jacob said to Matt, pointing to Bob's left hand sliding inside the back of Aurora's pants, "is the kind of day it's been."

"It's going to get worse. And don't turn around."

Destiny, one of the cigarette girls who worked at the Legacy, was standing behind Jacob. Her breast implants, at least one size too big, were lined with angry varicose veins, as if her breasts, now filled with silicone, gel, and saline, were in pain and furious.

"Hey, babe," she said to Matt.

"Hi, sweetie. You remember Jacob?"

"Sure."

Jacob and Destiny shook hands.

"Good to see you again."

"You don't remember me," Destiny said, her words slow.

"I do. A little. We probably met here, right here on these two bar stools."

She slapped his arm.

The last time Jacob had seen her, she was wearing flashing earrings, a button promoting an upcoming Michael Bolton concert, sparkles on her cleavage, and gold stars on her face, and she was carrying a tray of snacks, playing cards, pins, and cigars. She was just over five feet tall and was cute in the way women who work in casinos serving drinks and selling glow-in-the-dark yo-yos are cute.

"Hi again, honey. Whether you know me or not, remember me or not, it's okay, because it's all okay," she said. "It's all good." She collapsed onto the bar. "God, I'm drunk."

"Now that's how you make an entrance, Matt," Jacob said.

Matt smiled. "What's the matter, Desty?" he asked.

"My boyfriend is an asshole," she said, lifting her head.

"Jesus!" Jacob said. "Can nobody do a relationship?"

"The hell are you talking about?"

"Nothing. Been a long day."

Matt was called over to the other end of the bar.

"Bye, honey," she said.

"Bye, honey," Jacob echoed. "Lots of honeys tonight. I think it's the word for the day."

"You're funny."

"Thanks."

"So why are you here?"

"I don't know. I like Matt, I like this bar."

"Don't you like me?"

Jacob laughed. "I do."

"How much?"

"How much? Ah, this much," Jacob said, extending his arms. Destiny looked confused.

"I want a hambur," she said.

"Hambur?"

"Hambur."

"Hambur . . . ger?"

"Yeah, a hambur."

"Okay."

"Would you buy me a hambur?"

"I will buy you a hambur. Here?"

"No. Awful Awful."

"Oh, sure. I know that place."

They got up to leave.

Matt mouthed, "What are you doing?"

"I don't know," Jacob mouthed back.

Awful Awful Hamburgers was a dive of a restaurant inside the Nugget Diner, behind the Little Nugget Casino, a short walk, which they decided to take, from the Silver Legacy on Virginia Street. Destiny kept falling off her heels and decided to walk barefoot.

"Wanna hold my shoes?"

Jacob did. As he held them in one hand, he heard his phone ring.

Cindi. Again, he ignored it.

"What do you usually get here?" Jacob asked, as they stood waiting to order.

She ordered a hamburger with mayonnaise, hot sauce, and pickles.

They found a table. She unwrapped the burger and ate with abandon, as mayonnaise oozed from the corners of her mouth.

"I'm so fucking . . . hung-ery," she said.

"Hung-ery," Jacob repeated.

Pickles stuck to her cheeks. She picked them off with aplomb and put them back in her mouth. There was picante sauce on her lower chin as well, which she kept retrieving with her tongue.

"You are hung-ery?" he said, wincing at the carnage on her face, and promised himself to not say "hung-ery" again like that.

"I haven't eaten today," she replied with an open, full mouth. "Or yesterday, either."

Jacob picked fries off her plate.

She pushed the plate aside. "I'm better. Oh, so good. I was so hung-ery," she said again. "You want to come home with me?"

"I don't know. Do I?"

"You like cats?"

"Yes." He didn't.

"C'mon, then."

"Let's walk back to the Legacy and get a cab there," Jacob said, handing her the shoes. She put them on as he held her arm.

"Why?"

He had hoped by the time he got to the Legacy, he'd have talked himself out of this, for he didn't want to fuck Destiny. He wanted her to want him to fuck her. He was thinking of sex and condoms and cats and probably an unmade single bed and perhaps a stoned roommate with tattoos, as she misjudged the curb and fell to the sidewalk, her wrist covering her face.

"Oh, fuck," he said, crouching to get her.

"You pushed me."

"I didn't push me."

"You."

"You?"

"You said, 'I didn't push me.'"

"Who pushed me?"

"Nobody pushed me."

"Then why are you saying someone did?"

"I didn't. You—oh, forget it. Where are we going?"

"I'm taking you home."

"Do you want me to pee in your mouth?"

"Huh?"

"Do you want me to pee in your mouth and then you can pee in mine?"

Destiny had somehow lost her shoe and appeared to be readying to vomit. She smelled of alcohol and makeup.

"You should probably go home," he said.

"You want to pee—"

"Not tonight."

A cab was stopped by a red light.

Jacob took Destiny by the hand. The passenger window was open. "You taking rides?"

"Yep," came the reply.

Jacob opened the back door and gently put Destiny inside.

"I have no idea where she lives but take her home. She'll tell you."

"Hey," Destiny said. "What? Why?" she said. "C'mon, come with me. I have a cat—"

"Night," he said and closed the door.

Jacob walked over the Virginia Street bridge, over Interstate 80, and past a black man in a suit who was picking up empty cans of beer and putting them in a multicolored knapsack. A few yards north of the bridge, a woman in red shorts, under a streetlamp and drinking an RC Cola, was sorting her laundry on a concrete barrier, separating colors from whites. He passed Jimboy's Mexican Fiesta, Silver Dollar Motor Lodge, Sundance Motor Lodge, Recycle Records, Capri Motel, and the Breakaway Restaurant and Bar to Eleventh Street. He had walked by these places for years, and while he always saw the seediness, he now saw the sadness. Jacob thought about giving the evening to Jacob, but not this scene. He would have the fictional Jacob go to the dinner. He would be that Jacob. Jacob would give Cindi the dinner scene with Brooks.

When he got home, he walked through the kitchen and realized that Cindi, in all her nonfiction glory, was home and on the chaise with Princess Charlize-Louise, both asleep.

He was happy to see both of them.

"Where you been?" asked Cindi, suddenly awake. "I tried calling you."

"I know."

"You were ignoring my calls?"

"Not really. Just figured it would be better this way. The night got off to a bad start—all me—and then we had a nice moment outside the bowling alley, so I thought, 'Let her have her world. Play hard to get, don't be too desperate and panicked, and try again another time.'"

"You're always desperate and panicked."

"Sweet, babe, thanks."

"You know what I mean."

"I'm afraid I do."

"I'm really trying to control this thing about me. I love you. Listen to me. I love you. I do. Everyone at the dinner missed you, asked about you. Mitch asked about you."

"Mitch asked about me," Jacob said, laughing.

"What do you mean? Why wouldn't he ask about you? What is it with you and Mitch? Every time I bring him up, you seem confused, angry. Are you okay?"

"Yeah, fine. It's nothing. I like Mitch and I know you like him."

"Yeah, I . . ." Cindi said, shaking her head. "Whatever. So what did you do tonight?"

"You don't want to know."

"Tell me."

"You want to know?"

"I'm asking."

"I walked and then I walked some more, went to the casino, and then walked to Awful Awful, had a hamburger, and then walked home. There are parts of Reno that remind me of Nathanael West's *The Day of the Locust*."

"Another reference I—"

"Just a weird night, Cin."

"How so?"

"At the Legacy, there was a guy who fingered the ass of his not-quite girlfriend in front of everyone outside the Keno pit—a girl who knew me and didn't believe I was married because . . . I don't know why. And there was a girl with pickles and mayonnaise on her face who wanted to pee in my mouth."

"Oh, dear."

"Why are you smiling?" he asked, smiling.

"Is there some reason she wanted to pee in your mouth?"

"I don't know if there's a good answer for that."

"At least I wasn't the worst part of your night."

"Oh, no—you were."

JACOB FISHMAN'S MARRIAGE: A NOVEL

11. Ethan's Call

"And, of course, she's right here," said Cindi, spotting Ciara behind the hostess stand as she and Jacob walked in the front door of Mario's Portofino. "Amazing. First thing I see."

"First thing?"

"Don't start with me."

"Be nice, darling wife."

"I didn't know you were coming to this dinner," Ciara said, acknowledging them both. "Oh, sure, of course. You're with the big table from UNR. I should have known. Cindi teaches there, right?"

"Someone in this family has to work," Cindi said. "Maybe you can get Jacob a job here, busing tables or something."

"You'll have to excuse my wife," said Jacob. "The charm school she attended went out of business. Do we have you tonight?"

"Oh, fuck," Cindi muttered, rolling her eyes. Then she imitated Jacob, "Do we have you tonight?"

"Quiet down," Jacob said, quietly. "People can hear you."

"No, I'm hostessing—just seating people," said Ciara.

"You look good, Ciara," said Jacob.

"You two do, too."

As Ciara walked in front of the Fishmans on the way to the UNR table, which was along the rear wall of the restaurant, Cindi said, "Why don't you just fuck her right here?"

"Oh, stop! I'm just being nice."

"Nice? You nearly came back there. She does have a nice ass, I'll give you that. I'd fuck her."

"You're so delicate sometimes. Besides, how do you know she'd fuck you?"

"God, you make me laugh sometimes, even when I want to clock you."

"'Clock me'? In what vault do you keep these expressions?"

Cindi snorted as they arrived at the table, which was already full.

"Sorry we're late," Cindi said, "and for that noise I just made. And, while I'm apologizing, for my hair. I still can't figure out my flat iron."

Nobody said a word.

"God," Cindi said, biting her lip, to the table, "could there be any worse way to make an entrance?"

"Your hair looks fine," said Rouslana, Mitch's girlfriend, standing to hug her. "I love it."

"Hi, Rouslana. You know Jacob, right?" Cindi said, happy for the lifeline.

"Of course. Hi, again," she said, giving him a little wave.

"I'm her husband, in case you didn't know," Jacob said, shaking her hand. "She sometimes leaves that part out."

"Only because I don't want to ruin your stellar opening, babe, and I know how much you like reminding people we're attached at the hip."

"I know you're her husband," said Rouslana. "Mitch tells me she talks about you all the time."

"I'm sure she does. Hey, Mitch," said Jacob, shaking his hand, as Mitch stood. Mitch hugged Cindi, kissing her on the cheek, a kiss she returned, playfully wiping it off after she did. Cindi put her hand on Rouslana's shoulder.

"Oh, good, sitting with you two," Cindi said, taking a seat on one side of Mitch, who was next to Rouslana, as Jacob sat on the other side of Cindi. Around the table was Hal Howland and his wife, whose name Cindi didn't know; Jack Brooks and his wife, whose name Cindi didn't know; Monica, Howland's executive secretary, and her boyfriend, whose name Cindi didn't know; and Virginia Ralph, another professor, and her wife, Kaylynn, the only spouse other than Rouslana whom Cindi knew by name; and Tamara Price, last year's hire, who was brought on to anchor the department's newly formed epistemology tract, and her husband, whose name Cindi didn't know. Cindi smiled at Tamara, who smiled back. "This is Roger," Tamara said, pointing to the man next to her, who looked up from his phone and nodded. Cindi and Tamara both shook their heads.

"Roger," Cindi said to herself, in an effort to seer his name into her memory bank.

"I see what you mean," she said, smiling, which made Tamara cackle.

"What's so funny?" Roger asked.

"Nothing, honey. Go back to your phone."

"I wasn't on my phone. I was just checking something."

A few months back, Tamara, after three Chardonnays at Doc Holli-days inside Harrah's, told Cindi that she should be happy for eternity that she was married to Jacob, for she, Tamara, was married to a remorseless liar, and so "sleeping with a man who's always in his own head is not, all things considered, such a terrible thing."

There were handshakes across the table, more waves.

"Everything okay?" Ciara said, suddenly appearing.

"Yeah, we're good. Thanks for checking," said Jacob.

"She's like a rash. She always shows up. Has she nothing else to do tonight?" asked Cindi, laughing.

"She's just being a good host," said Jacob.

"You know her?" asked Mitch.

"No, not really," said Jacob, leaning back. "She's a waitress here and Cindi keeps torturing me about her."

Mitch smiled. "You know, at Portofino, the women are more dangerous than shotguns."

"What?" asked Cindi.

"My name is Michael Corleone," said Jacob. "Now, there's people who would pay a lot of money for that information, but then your daughter would lose a father, instead of gaining a husband."

"Cindi, they're doing *Godfathers*," said Rouslana. "I think they're in Part One."

"Not *Godfathers*—*Godfather*! Singular," emphasized Mitch.

"Sometimes I think I shoulda married a woman like you did—like Rouslana," said Jacob. "Kids—have a family. For once in my life, be more like Pop."

"It's not easy to be his son—it's not easy."

"You two are insane, you know that?" said Cindi.

"We're not married, and we don't have kids," said Rouslana.

"You're missing the point," said Mitch. "All our people, Rouslana, are philosophy people. Their loyalties are based on that."

Mitch and Jacob high-fived over Cindi.

"You two want to be alone?" asked Cindi.

"Maybe," said Jacob.

Food started arriving—Howland had planned the evening, down to the menu. Ciara brought garlic bread and put it next to Jacob. Cindi noticed, or thought she noticed, Ciara placing a hand on Jacob's shoulder.

"What the hell is this?" Mitch asked, as a waitress put a dish next to him.

"Gnocchi," said Jacob. "It's a potato dish."

"Here, I'll eat it," said Cindi. She took her fork and stabbed two pieces off his plate.

Jacob turned to the front door and saw Ciara's ass. When he turned back, Cindi was looking at him.

He smiled. "Hey," he said.

"Hey. Thank you," she said.

"For what?"

"You know—this," she said. "What are you looking at?" she asked, watching him look toward the door.

"Nothing."

Cindi looked to the front, where Jacob was looking, but Ciara wasn't there. He was relieved.

"There comes a time in every man's career—" said Howland, rising,

later in the evening, and tapping a knife against his glass, about to introduce Brooks.

"When a man comes to this point in his life," said Mitch, doing a
Hyman Roth speech from *Godfather Part II,* which Howland, Mitch
was convinced, had no idea he was instigating, "he wants to turn over
the things that he's been blessed with—turn them over to friends. As a
reward for the friends he's had—and to make sure everything goes well
after he's gone."

"I hope my age is correct," added Jacob, from the same speech. "I'm
always accurate about my age. Make sure that everyone sees the cake
before we cut it. I'm very pleased you were all able to come from such
distances to be with me today."

"Would you two shut up?" said Cindi.

"Mitch!" said Rouslana over Howland's introduction. "Stop!"

" . . . my good friend and colleague Jack Brooks," Howland said,
starting the applause before sitting down.

Brooks stood.

"Thank you, Hal," Brooks said, acknowledging everyone. "I'm not
very comfortable speaking to small gatherings, so I'll keep this merci-
fully short, unlike Mitch, who might as well wear a cape when he walks
into class."

Rouslana cackled. "He wears one around the house, too."

"Not all the time," said Mitch. "Just on special occasions."

"I've seen the cape," said Cindi.

"You have?" asked Mitch.

"No, I'm joking."

"But I do want to say to everyone here," Brooks continued. "Mitch
and Hal and Virginia and Tamara, who I just got to know, and what a
welcome addition she will be to the department, and everyone else,
including Melanie and the support staff and all the interns and graduate
assistants, thank you from the bottom of my heart—oh, yeah, yes, yes,
my wife, too, Arlene, who's been with me since the beginning of this
ride." He pointed to her. "This moment wouldn't mean anything
without her . . . without all of you here. There are so many people who
got me to this point. I will miss you all. Thank you, thank you so
much."

He sat down amid applause, as Howland raised his glass to him.

"Congratulations, Brooksie."

Jacob recognized it immediately. The fuck didn't mention her name. Everyone in the goddamn department but Cindi!

Jacob squeezed Cindi's thigh and whispered, "Sorry." She put her hand on top of his and patted it twice.

"I'm okay," she whispered. "Thank you." She grabbed his fingers and squeezed tight. Jack could feel her trembling.

"What a *coglione*," said Mitch.

"Is that from *The Godfather*?" Cindi asked.

"No. It's from me."

Jacob felt two hands on his shoulders. He turned his head. Cindi did too.

Ciara.

"How's everything going?"

JACOB FISHMAN'S MARRIAGE: A NOVEL

12. The Streak in Her Hair

With Charlize-Louise and a copy of *Mind* magazine on her lap, Cindi, having just finished an article titled "Spinoza and the Metaphysics of Scepticism," while half-watching the New Mexico Bowl between UNR and the University of New Mexico, had fallen asleep. She was dreaming that she and her daughter, in matching hats, were in a park, sitting on the grass. Charlize-Louise, whose paws were furiously moving in front of her, was dreaming about rabbits.

The ring abruptly woke both of them.

"Hello," Cindi said, finding her phone and sitting up. The motion knocked Charlize-Louise to the floor. The dog barked.

"It's Kenny," said a woman's voice.

"Olivia!"

It was Kenny's mom.

Charlize-Louise barked again.

"Huh . . . what? Kenny?" Cindi asked, dizzy. "Is he dead?"

"Worse," said Olivia.

Worse?

"Cindi, you okay?"

"Huh? Yeah."

"Were you sleeping?"

"No."

"Did you hear me?"

"I don't . . . I don't understand," Cindi said, her heart pounding. She put her hand to her chest to feel it.

"This time it's worse," Olivia said. "He's not coming back."

Cindi thought that an odd way to put it, as if Kenny had gone to Ixtapa, fallen in love, and decided to stay. He once did go to Ixtapa, where, he wrote Cindi in a postcard, "I got my gay on. His name is Juan. (Of course his name is Juan)." He was not now in Ixtapa.

"Cindi? Cindi!"

"Olivia, yes, I'm sorry. I'm here. Juan? That was so funny."

"What?"

"Nothing. I'm sorry. Where . . . what happened? I'm sorry."

"I know," said the woman whose auburn hair had developed a one-inch swath of gray in the front after her son's second suicide attempt. "This is my mark," she once told Cindi, "of the beast."

"How, Olivia?"

"The same, but more, I think. I don't know. Methadone, heroin, Oxycodone, Ritalin, three or four others. Does it matter? What's Ketamine? "

"It's a horse tranquilizer."

"What?"

"Jesus, Olivia. I'm sorry, so, so sorry."

"He left you a note."

"Me?"

"Yeah. You want me to bring it to you?"

"No, I'll come. You at the house?"

"It's in the kitchen. I'll leave it for you. I may not be here. I tried calling earlier, but—"

"I know. The phone. Jacob and I don't always—"

"Do you want me to stick around?"

"No, you go home. I'll call you later. I have a key."

Two days earlier, on the morning of December 21st, Kenny was out back, shooting squirrels from a lawn chair and watching *The View* on a small television he had hooked up and placed on a lopsided picnic table, its antenna covered in tin foil. First, he took the Oxycodone, then the methadone, the bars, the Ketamine, and the heroin, which he shot into his arm via two small holes above his wrist. Then he went and took a bath. It's where the ambulance crew found him, out back, head down in the tub, the shotgun, syringe, and an empty two-liter plastic bottle of Smirnoff in his lap. He hadn't shot himself.

When Cindi got to his house, the outside looked as it always did: cinderblocks stacked near the front door, an overgrown lawn, and rusted lawn furniture on the curb, but once inside, she could see that Olivia, who had gone home, had tried to clean up. Why did she try to clean up? As Cindi entered the living room and saw the big-screen TV, she was reminded of how good Jacob was that night, yet she was glad he hadn't come with her and wasn't home when Olivia called. He would have offered his perspective, his insights into death or friendship, his . . . God knows what.

"Josh," she called. "Josh!"

Where was the dog?

Josh was not in the house, eating whatever food Kenny had dropped or spilled, so Cindi went out back.

"Josh," she called again.

Gone.

Cindi went into the chicken coop. All the chickens were dead, the smell of shit not awful in the cold. She walked toward her trailer, her trailer, which was illuminated by a falling sun, making it look . . . if not habitable, at least poetic. She didn't go in. Back in the house, the place, too, she now realized, smelled of shit. In Kenny's bedroom, she found some remnants of marijuana in an ashtray and some gay porn on the ripped leather chair next to the bed. She was surprised Olivia hadn't removed the porn. In the kitchen, Cindi found the note—she had almost forgotten about it—that Olivia told her about. It was on the table. Olivia had put it under a two-liter Coke.

Cindi,

Take care of Josh, if you can find him, and the chickens, if there are any left.

This sucks,
Kenny

"Motherfucker," she said to herself. "Mother, mother, motherfucker." She crumbled up the note, then smoothed it, before tearing it up into pieces and putting the pieces in her pocket.

But he was not dead. The ambulance—and someone must have called for it— had taken Kenny to Renown Regional Medical Center and then, after he was stabilized, to Rosewood Rehabilitation Center, where he was given a single room. His Glasgow Coma Scale was at five, meaning that while his eyes might open from time to time, he couldn't and wouldn't feel any movement in his limbs, nor would he respond to pain or emit any sound.

This was what Olivia meant. He wasn't coming back.

Jacob insisted he go with her that first day Kenny was in Rosewood. Cindi didn't have the strength to tell him she didn't want him. And the first thing she said to Kenny at his bedside was, "You stupid fuck."

"He still couldn't kill himself," Jacob said, as they drove to Kenny's house to pick up some clothes for him. "I mean, this is worse than death." His voice was like a small knife in her temple. "Where did he keep getting the drugs, do you know?"

"Doesn't matter. Nobody killed him."

"Yeah, but—"

"I don't want to talk, Jacob. Please."

"It's just . . . I know it shouldn't matter," Jacob said. "I know I shouldn't be like this, but there's a difference between this and other diseases. It's all sad, but this was preventable. I know he's sick, but I can't, I don't understand how you can do this to yourself, how you can do this to people who love you. How fucking selfish."

"Not fucking now, Jake, okay?"

When they returned to the house the day after visiting Kenny in Rosewood, the shit smell was gone and replaced by lavender—Olivia had thoroughly cleaned the place in the interim. Cindi couldn't remember it ever being this clean. Olivia had bought flowers and set them on the coffee table in the living room. It looked and felt like an open house. There was no residue. Kenny was gone.

"I'm going outside," Cindi said.

"Can I come?" Jacob asked.

"Do what you want."

Jacob accompanied her, but only as far as the back porch, while Cindi went to her trailer. This time, she pried open the door with her fingers and was met by stagnant hot air, the cold of northern Nevada doing nothing to deaden the potency, but it was her hot air, her spider-webs, her mold and mildew, she told herself. This would be home. Maybe Jacob was right, maybe this was all about getting away from him, but as she looked around inside, she could see living in it, alone with Charlize-Louise. When the time was right, she was going to call Olivia and ask, providing they kept the house, providing it wasn't really an open house, whether she could keep the trailer there. She walked around inside, heard the creaking of the floor, and saw that all the cabinets needed replacing, as did the windows and pieces of the floor. But the more she saw the need for repairs, the more she wanted to make them. She pulled the door closed, came to the porch, and sat in Kenny's chair, next to Jacob. The blue cooler was still there. She opened it and saw about an inch of standing water, a six-pack ring, and a bottle cap. She felt Jacob's hand on her shoulders.

"You know, we say a lot of shitty things to each other," he said.

"Yes, we do, but I don't want to talk about us."

"But I have to tell you: You were a terrific friend, really. He couldn't have done any better."

"Thanks," she said curtly.

"What? I mean it."

"I know."

Just go away. Go far away from me.

"Honey, I'm proud of you. You brought Kenny some joy that nobody else could or did bring. That's wonderful. It's a mitzvah."

She hated when he used that word, like he was the arbiter of magna-nimity. Her husband knew at best a half dozen Yiddish words, and when he spoke them, he purposefully lowered his voice—she called it his rabbi voice.

Fuck you, you sanctimonious ass, what do you know about loss? You have a daughter, you have a life.

"Whatever," she said.

"Did I say something?" he asked, looking at the trailer this wife would soon be living in.

"No." She rolled her shoulders forward to let him know she wanted him to stop touching her. "Can I just be alone for a while?"

"Sure."

Jacob went inside, got her a Coke, and brought it to her, knowing he'd said something, done something, if not more than one thing, wrong.

"Honey, I'm sorry," he said, offering the Coke, which she refused.

Why are you back?

"I meant that, even though Kenny's in a coma, you did everything a friend should do. I wish I was that lucky. I wish I had a friend as caring as you. I know you blame yourself. Don't. You were terrific. I know you hate the mitzvah thing, but it's true."

I'm not blaming myself, you fuckwad! And stop reminding me what a lousy wife I am. Goddamn it!

"I love you," said Jacob.

"Give me a minute, please!" she demanded.

"No matter what's happening in our lives, you can always find time to shut me out, can't you?"

This time she didn't think it—she said it.

"Go fuck yourself. You and your whole goddamn life."

"I'll be in the car."

Jacob was in the house and didn't hear her "I'm sorry."

Cindi closed the cooler and put her feet up on its lid.

Jacob Fishman's Marriage: A Novel

13. Back of Ciara's Sofa

Jacob sat at the bar at Mario's Portofino, looking at Ciara's perfect ass against black polyester leggings. She and it were trashy and transcendent. Slightly bent over a table, Ciara was fanning the white tablecloth before smoothing it down. She put plates and silverware down with equal parts aplomb and boredom. She looked back at Jacob and smiled.

She knew he was looking.

He put his hand up and barely waved. He wanted to surprise her, his coming in, but she seemed to know, wagging her finger at him when she saw him as he arrived. She leaned on one foot and extended her body across the table, so he put his lower palms over his eyes and pushed, wanting to put his hands through his head. His anxiety and libido were raging. When he lowered his hands, Ciara was standing there. She placed one hand on his shoulder, one hand on his thigh.

"Can you drive me home?" she asked.

"Sure."

This can't be happening. She needs a ride home . . . tonight?

"No car?" he asked.

"A friend brought me. I was going to take an Uber."

"No, no, no," he said, too excitedly. "I'll drive you."

"Thanks. Let me finish up," she said, digging her nails into his thigh.

"You keep that up, you'll get me in bed."

"We're not going to make it to the bed."

The chase was over. He could have left now. He wanted to fuck her, yes, but he wanted her to want him to fuck her. He wanted that maybe more. He had won. The moment was his.

He fingered her over her leggings on the drive to her apartment. He could feel her wetness, her engorged clitoris. She put her hand inside her pants. Jacob fingered the fingers that were fingering her.

He was turned on.

He wasn't needed.

Ciara opened the apartment door. He stood by the doorway and looked in. It was cleaner than he thought it would be.

It smelled of pine and ash.

"Coming?" she asked, smiling.

He grabbed her hand, took a step in, closed the door. He pushed her up against the door, putting both her hands over her head. He held her there with his left hand.

He kissed her.

She bit his tongue.

"'We're not going to make it to the bed,' someone said."

"The bed isn't made."

"Not a deal-breaker."

She took a deep breath, arched her back, and strained against his hand. He ran his right hand over her breasts and then down between her legs and into her pants. He reached around to her ass.

"Pull my pants down. But leave them on at my ankles."

She had her own script about this, her own choreography.

He did as he was told.

As he yanked her pants down, her purple panties caught in her pants. He left them, as he was told, around her ankles. He thought of that word: panties. So infantile. He was fifty, she was twenty-six. Underwear—not panties. He wanted to look, wanted to see, wanted to take time to relish her ass and the rose tattoo on her lower back, vines of some kind or maybe a snake in red and green and black that started on her right cheek, then worked its way up her back.

He went to his knees and went down on her from behind.

"Give me your hand," he said.

She did, and he made her put her hand between her legs and masturbate, bent over the sofa, while he licked her fingers and pussy and ass.

But she was the one masturbating. She was getting herself off.

"I want you to come like this," he said.

"I have a better idea."

She stood up straight, so he backed up, hitting his head against the windowsill.

"You okay, baby?" she asked.

"Yeah. Fuck!" He rubbed the back of his head. "If I start convulsing, just throw me outside."

He watched her make her way to the television. He noticed her underwear was still on one leg. He watched her walk away from him, wondering how long it would stay tethered to her ankle. She picked up the remote sitting on the set, hit the power, and made her way to the sofa.

"Come here," she said.

He heard squeals.

Asian girls sat in robes, in a dungeon of some kind—some strapped to tables, some kneeling against the wall, and some holding candles. Big Sumo wrestlers watched an Asian girl being fucked from behind by another Asian girl with a strap-on.

"Eat me out," Ciara said, "while I watch this."

The tape was already cued up.

Jacob, between Ciara's legs, could hear the Sumo wrestlers mumbling in what he assumed was Chinese.

"You like lesbian Asian porn?" Ciara asked.

Jacob took his mouth off her clitoris.

"As a subset to regular porn, what's not to like?"

Who says "subset" at a time like this, he thought.

He resumed eating her out. He could feel Ciara come. She was looking past him, at the television. She threw her head back and closed her eyes. "Fuck . . . fuck . . . fuck!" Ciara said, as Jacob heard wrestlers grunting and Asian girls shrieking.

Ciara slid down the sofa. "Wow. That was good."

"I've never been with a girl who likes Asian lesbian prison porn," Jacob said, laughing.

"I'm not like every girl, I guess. By the way, Jacob Fishman. You eat pussy like a lesbian."

"Thank you . . . I think. You bi?"

"Pan."

"What?"

"Pansexual."

"Oh."

"You know what that is?"

"Yeah." He didn't.

"You do?"

"Yeah—hey, let's switch now," Jacob said, getting up. "Let me watch."

"No. I want you to fuck me."

"Do you have a condom?"

"Move."

Jacob backed up, as Ciara went to the coffee table, opened a drawer, and pulled out a condom. A thirty-six-count box of Trojan Ultra-Thin Latest Condoms spilled out on the floor. Ciara pulled a condom out of its package.

"Suck my cock first."

"Like this, baby?" Ciara asked, holding the condom in her hand. Jacob could feel it on his thigh.

"I want to come in your mouth."

"No. Inside me."

He felt himself get harder inside her mouth.

"Slow, slow," he said. "Put the condom on me."

She put the condom in her mouth and pushed and maneuvered her tongue to unroll the latex over his cock. He was about to come.

"Get on top of me."

He felt her slide over it.

"*Ohhhh,*" she moaned.

It was over.

"Did you come already?"

"I think so."

"Wow."

"Yeah, sorry."

"It happens."

"Sorry."

"No, don't be."

She got up.

Jacob could see an Asian girl sitting on the face of another girl.

"I'll be right back," Jacob said, getting up. "Your bathroom is . . ."

Ciara pointed.

When Jacob got there, he took off the condom, flushed it down the toilet, and washed his hands. He saw himself in the mirror on the medicine cabinet. He had done it. He fucked Ciara. He felt like opening the cabinet door and smashing the glass against his head, not because of guilt, but because he had fucked her so badly. He wondered if he looked like someone who was a lousy fuck. He wondered how disappointed she really was. He wondered if she would tell anyone, if he'd be the butt of a joke.

When he returned from the bathroom, Ciara was already dressed, in the kitchen and sitting on one of the stools by the counter. He heard the microwave.

"What's that?"

"Hot Pockets," she said.

"You always eat Hot Pockets after Asian lesbian prison sex?"

"Doesn't everyone?"

"I think they should."

"Tell me about Cindi."

"No."

"C'mon! Do you have an open relationship?"

Jacob laughed.

"No."

"I should feel guilty."

"*I* should feel guilty."

This was not the conversation he wanted to have. He went around to her side of the counter and started kissing the back of her neck. "Let's go back to the living room. I want to see how the movie ends."

"Stop," she said, gently pushing him away.

"Was that awful for you?"

"No, no—not at all. It was fine. It was really okay."

GUILT

Can I really kill her dog, fuck a waitress, and make her best friend a vegetable?

He hadn't fucked Ciara, and Ethan/Kenny was not sitting in a nursing home with a Gleason score of five, and the dog was alive.

"Go fuck yourself. You and your whole goddamn life."

There was no demarcation anymore. The fictional was now personal, too.

Jacob Fishman would have fucked Ciara just like that, it would have gone like that—he would have come too soon—so why didn't he, Jacob Fishman, make Jacob Fishman fuck her better? It was his novel, his characters, his erection. He could have made himself better in bed—who doesn't want to be better in bed?—but he concluded this was the fair thing to do. The verisimilitude was already unrecognizable—lesbian Asian prison porn?—but on this matter, Jacob's sexual performance, he wanted authenticity. The choreography of the evening, getting the two of them to Ciara's apartment, seemed off. The porn, any porn, was unnecessary and fantastical and, as much as he thought "erotic," inarguably not erotic. And Ciara's moment of guilt at the chapter's conclusion was out of character—this girl would not be bothered by infidelity and racked with guilt. Still, one of the Jacobs, Jacob concluded, had to fuck her. But it was more than that. He could fuck her without fucking her—it was masturbatory theater. He wrote this chapter as if he had a diary of actual events a half-body away. The only thing that separated the two Jacobs was font—even the erection was disappointingly similar. He had cheated on his wife by biting Ciara's nipple back at the restaurant. The fictional Jacob had the bigger balls, fictional though they may be, by actually having intercourse.

Before writing this chapter, Jacob had written one called "Contemporary Social Issues," a class that the girl with the beautiful teeth and the yellow highlighter cut so that she and Jacob could fuck in her dorm room. In the scene, she—he called her Kelsey—fucked him while wearing her iPod earbuds, but Jacob jettisoned the scene from *Jacob Fishman's Marriage* because it was simply implausible that a girl named Kelsey with perfect teeth and wearing iPod earbuds would cut her sociology class to fuck a fifty-something whom she just had met, especially after he had a "heart attack."

If the fictional Cindi fucked the fictional Mitch—and she probably would, he had decided, to balance the fictional Jacob's infidelity—she would be better in bed than the real Cindi. Readers, he hoped, would appreciate his literary largesse in this matter, if not altogether repulsed by it . . . and him.

He wondered why life wasn't enough.

He looked up what it meant to be pansexual.

The Asian porn was probably too much.

Why did every woman Jacob fucked—Ciara with the porn and Kelsey with the music on her earbuds—need a distraction to orgasm?

Both Jacobs had now cheated on both Cindis. Both Cindis had carte blanche to do the same, but he controlled only one of them. He couldn't blame either one, though, for cheating on either Jacob.

As for Ethan/Kenny, Ethan did have a drug problem, an Oxycodone problem, which did cost him his restaurant in Reno, which did land him in Passages in Malibu where he wrote Cindi, "The Pacific has so much promise; the Atlantic, I'm afraid, is dying. I'd like to come back here after I get better," where he discovered he was gay, but he was very much alive, if not particularly well. But he was not living in a nursing home. In *Jacob Fishman's Marriage,* Jacob had killed Charlize-Louise, and he had almost killed Ethan/Kenny.

His own monstrosity didn't bother him as much as he wanted it to.

Jacob heard Cindi bound up the stairs. From the sound of her steps, he could tell she was in a good mood. Jacob quickly saved his notes and closed *Jacob Fishman's Marriage* and put it back in a folder marked "GEOLOGY."

His password on the folder: Verisimilitude*

"Quick, quick," she said, reaching his office, "get rid of the porn."

"Walk slower, it's really great porn."

"What kind?"

"Asian."

"Nice."

Cindi appeared at the door. She was smiling. "You ready for a story?" she asked.

"Always."

Cindi moved the papers, CDs, big jar of pretzels, and envelopes from the chair that faced Jacob and sat down.

"Sage is pregnant."

"You're kidding?"

"Nope."

"Does she know who the father is?"

"Nope."

"Course not."

"It's one of two guys."

"I knew the sex was unprotected! Remember I said so?"

"You're so clairvoyant."

"Oh, come on! Give me this. Besides, you'd think that a woman who's still technically married with six children might want to consider asking the strange men she's fucking to wear condoms, because the idea of having seven kids, while unmarried, unmoored, is pretty fucking stupid. But you know how I hate to judge."

While Jacob was saying this, he hoped that even mentioning children wouldn't be like combining the wrong kinds of medication.

"In any event," Cindi said, "she's definitely going to have it. Unmoored? Jesus, you're weird."

Jacob didn't answer, still worried that his talk of children would unhinge his wife.

"But the thing is, she needs help and she doesn't know what to do, because, of the two guys who could be the father, the first is a married Catholic who already has, like, five kids with his wife, and the second guy, who's about ten years younger than she, doesn't have any and really wants one. He cried when she told him it might be his."

"So she told the one guy it might be his?"

"It's all about honesty."

"Wait! There's now a married Catholic guy? Wow! Did she say she'd get back to him when she was certain?"

"I don't know, but the honesty, Jake, think about it."

"I am. And it's selfish."

"I don't know what I'd do," Cindi said, watching Jacob for a reaction.

"That would depend if you were pregnant with my child or someone else's, right? I mean, I'd like to think so. Telling me that it might not be mine would have to be a tough conversation. Please tell me it would be a tough conversation."

Cindi opened the jar of pretzels and took one, bit down hard, loudly, and with a full mouth said, "It would be, but I would tell you in either case."

"Thanks. I think."

She took another pretzel.

"She didn't feel the need to tell Dave, did she?"

"No, she did tell."

"I'm so trying not to be judgmental."

"And I'm so very proud of you."

"What did Dave say?"

"He was cool with it."

"Cool? There's so much I don't understand about life."

"I know you don't, I really do. And she did say you lied to me."

"Huh? How did I get in this conversation?"

Jacob was looking at Cindi when she said that but managed to sneak a look at the computer and noticed the GEOLOGY folder was still open.

"What the fuck?" he said, looking at his computer. "I am going to have to turn the thing off." He reached around on the Mac and found the power button.

"What was it?" Cindi asked, getting up, coming around to the desk. "It was that fucking book of yours—or just porn?"

"Is there a difference?" he joked. "Just sit down."

"How do you know I haven't already read it?"

"How? How do you mean?"

"How do you know I haven't read some of it?"

"The same way you don't know I've been reading your diary."

"That's different. That's a violation."

"How is that a violation and you sneaking in here to read my book is not?"

"Because I've been writing the diary for years—and I'm not writing it to hurt you or get back at you. And my diary is not going to be public."

"I'm not doing that."

"Sure you're not."

"I'm not. Anyway, so Sage said I was lying to you. How? What did I do? Or did she read my novel too?"

"She said one time she was over and your phone rang, and when you got off you said it was your dad." Cindi returned to her seat and got another pretzel.

"So?"

"She said she heard a woman's voice."

"I have no idea."

"It's no big deal," Cindi said. "I am curious why she brought it up, though. You having an affair on me?"

"You having one on me?"

"Don't turn it around."

"*I* am not having an affair on you."

"What's with the I?"

"What are you talking about?"

"Do you think I'm having an affair on you?"

"You said 'I,' so it was weird how you said it. I'll give you this much about the book: No, I'm not."

"You fucking tease. What? C'mon, what? Give me something."

"I thought you've been reading it."

"Maybe. And maybe I just haven't gotten that far."

"Someone is fucking someone in the book."

"I'm going to so hate this."

"You're not going to hate it, because I'm not going to let you read it."

"I'm your wife. You have to let me read it, if, you know, I haven't already read it."

"What kind of reasoning is that?"

"I'm your fucking wife."

"Don't try to sweet talk me. You're not going to read it."

"You little shit!"

"Watch your fucking language. Hey, how's Ethan, by the way?" Jacob asked.

"Ethan? Fine. Haven't heard from him. Why?"

"Was just thinking about him. I don't know."

"Just wanted to tell you about Sage."

"Thanks. Never a dull, faithful moment."

Cindi, inexplicably, blew him a kiss and walked downstairs.

As Jacob was turning the computer on, though, Cindi was back in the office.

"Oh, Sage told me that if you want, you can use the story about her getting pregnant in the book. She likes the idea of being thought of in the third person."

"Really? You think I just take stories from my life, or her life, and put them in the book because I have nothing else to do, like I have no imagination?"

"I think that's exactly what you do. I think you're probably doing it right now, right here, with this conversation, so let me ask you something, seriously. I've been thinking about this. What if I asked you to not write the book?"

"It's almost finished."

"I know, but—"

"Are you asking me?"

"I don't know if I am."

"Let me ask you something. Would it change things if I did? Would you be happier?"

"I don't know. I just feel so violated sometimes. How badly do I come across?"

"Not terribly. I try to write your unhappiness and, where you have them, joys. But I make up a lot of stuff, so a lot of it isn't about you, even though, I guess, it is about you."

Cindi handed her husband a pretzel.

"Thanks."

"I hate being fodder, the cheap joke."

"You're not."

"I think I am. Okay." Cindi exhaled. "I'm going for reals." Walking out of the office, Cindi turned back, waved at her husband. "You're my life, you know," she said, before throwing him another kiss.

"So many kisses," he said, returning this one.

It was enough to make him want to move the whole book into the trash icon.

But he didn't.

JACOB FISHMAN'S MARRIAGE: A NOVEL

14. The Mail Under Cindi's Ass

Cramping, her PMS raging, Cindi stayed home from school this first day of the seventh week of the spring semester and spent the morning with Charlize-Louise, trying to watch *Good Day Reno.* After sitting through a segment on ways to attack spring cleaning, she flipped through the one hundred eighty-five channels (she had given Jacob a second-tier cable package the previous Hanukkah; he had given her a silk blouse, a spa certificate, and scented dinosaur candles) and briefly stopped on a Ron Popeil infomercial for the Electric Food Dehydrator.

"How is this thing still a thing?" she asked Charlize-Louise, trying to sound like Jerry Seinfeld and to get more of the references that every man in her life seemingly dropped, "and who eats that much beef jerky?"

In the weeks after Kenny's overdose (and doctors had upgraded his GCS to seven), Cindi found herself unable to concentrate on any one task, generally, and this morning, on any moment or program, specifically, so she kept her finger depressed on the UP and then DOWN buttons of the remote, trying to see how many moments on which she could focus as the images flew by. She remembered a scene from a movie where such flashings of light and sound caused an epileptic seizure in the person watching, and Cindi, though she didn't have epilepsy, was nonetheless wondering if she could induce it. Her eyes danced, her face illuminated in staccato code, watching the television cycle through its offerings at different speeds. Networks flew by, shows flew by: CNN, *Law & Order* reruns, Jewish televangelists, catheter ads, lawyers advertising for large settlements involving Round-up and bladder slings, football from Spain and England. Epilepsy would not be coming, but a headache over her left eye was. Ever since Kenny's overdose, she felt like she was walking through yogurt, three-quarter speed.

Charlize-Louise farted.

"Oh, Princess. Pee-yew!"

For the spring semester, Cindi had once again received survey courses, but this time she listened to Mitch, and told Howland she understood his position and that she would help any way she could.

"I always knew you had it in you to be a team player," Howland told her, a statement she found puzzling and insulting, thinking a simple "thank you" was all that was needed and all she wanted.

"Least you could do," she said, turning around at the door, muttering to herself, "is get me a uniform, you know, if we're going to be on the same team."

"What?" he asked.

"Nothing. Just, you know, joking about the uniform."

"The what?"

"No, no, nothing. Hal, I was just . . . Sorry. Sure, thanks."

How did I ruin that moment?

Charlize-Louise, post-flatulence, started barking. The postman, Randy, was here. He had a ponytail, which he futzed with constantly, tattoos on both arms, and broad thighs. There were days she wondered about fucking him on her sofa and what his blue shorts, which he wore regardless of the weather, would look like on the floor.

"Good girl," she said. "A little late, but good girl."

She didn't usually get the mail, leaving the task to Jacob, who, like many men once they reached fifty, was territorial about such things.

Still, she decided to get up and drag herself off the chaise, Charlize-Louise in tow, to the mailbox.

She opened the door and waved to Randy, who was already at the next house, as Charlize-Louise ran out toward him.

"Go home, sweetie," Randy said.

Cindi put her hand in the box, scraping the back of her hand against the metal. "C'mon, girl," she said to the dog, as Charlize-Louise ran inside.

"Shit!" she said, putting her scraped finger in her mouth.

She came back into the house and threw all the mail on the chaise. She went to the kitchen and returned to her chaise with a half-drunk Arizona iced tea and a bag of Lays Wavy potato chips, and plopped herself down, inadvertently landing on the mail, hearing it squish beneath her. She pulled out an *Esquire,* a Bed, Bath, and Beyond coupon, something from UNR, information on an LGBT cruise for the gay couple who used to own the house on Codel Way whose mail the Fishmans inexplicably kept getting, and a Bank of America credit application.

UNR?

She knew. She just knew.

She thought back to her last conversation—before the one about her classes and her "uniform" joke—of the fall semester with Howland.

"Hal," she asked, as she turned in her final grades. "What's new with, you know, my future?"

"You have a bright future," he said, smiling.

What a prick! she thought then.

"Could you be more specific? Please."

"No, I can't, and you know I can't."

"I can't decide if you're being coy, know something you don't want to tell me, or are just trying to remain professional."

"Yes."

"C'mon, Hal, give me something."

"February, March, you'll know."

The decision on her tenure, her life, was under her ass.

She reached down, pulled it out, and there it was:

She stared at it, saw the UNR logo—OFFICE OF THE PRESIDENT
Cindy Fischmann
1243 Codel Lane
Reno, Nevada 89503
She felt the envelope. It was thin. Too fucking thin. She tried looking through it. She tore it open, ripping a top corner of the letter.

The University of Nevada, Reno
Office of the President

February 18, 2008
Cindy Fishmann
1243 Codel Lane
Reno, Nevada 89503

Dear Assistant Professor Fishmann,

I regret to inform you that the Board of Trustees, in its meeting today, voted to deny your promotion to associate professor with tenure. This action was taken after a thorough review of your record by your colleagues in the faculty and administration.

Your service to the University of Nevada, Reno will terminate at the end of your current contract.

I personally want to thank you for your past efforts and wish you the very best in the future.

Sincerely yours,
Milton D. Glick
President
cc: MC Garvey, Dean
John H. Frederick, Executive Vice President & Provost
Mary Dugan, General Counsel
Halen Howland, Department Chair

• • •

Charlize-Louise had grabbed the edge of the letter and started tearing into it.

"No, no, girl, not this one," Cindi said, pulling it back, ripping it some more.

She looked at it again. She felt sharp pains running down both arms. She checked her name again, on the envelope and the letter.

She bit her lip, and kept biting it, then flung herself back in her chair, hearing a *crack* from the wood frame of the chaise. She flung herself back again. And then again.

And again.

The cracking sound got louder.

Charlize-Louise jumped off the chaise as Cindi tried to pull the letter apart.

I'll fucking kill them, those fucking, fucking fuckheads!

She reached for the envelope. She stared at all of the misspellings, her first and last name. Fishman was a name she never wanted to take, preferring her maiden name, Levia, which means "to join" in Hebrew, but she took Fishman, had to be talked into taking Fishman by Jacob and her family, and that name had been misspelled. A name she didn't want.

Didn't like.

That fucking name.

And Cindy with a "y"!

She threw the letter on the chaise, pounded her feet on the chair, then reread the letter. It hadn't changed. Charlize-Louise was now under the chair. Her iced tea had been knocked over. It lay on its side, contents pouring onto the floor. Charlize-Louise came out from under the chaise and started drinking from the waterfall from the overturned bottle and the pool on the floor.

Cindi called Mitch, but he wasn't in. She called Howland, but his secretary, that cunt Monica, said he wasn't in either.

Jacob was walking.

Just when I need him.

Charlize-Louise was now licking her own vagina as she lay sprawled out. Cindi looked at her.

I wish I were a dog.

Her contract wasn't up until a year from this coming May, but she knew she couldn't stay. She would walk into Howland's office tomorrow and quit. She couldn't think of anyone in the department who hadn't received tenure. She was the only woman on the full-time faculty and, surely, there was a lawsuit possible, even though she doubted she would win because of the patriarchy.

This isn't Princeton, not NYU, not Rutgers. It's UN-fucking-R. They have an institute for the study of gaming at UNR! For Chrissakes! They teach fucking gambling, and I can't get tenure at this shithole place.

Cindi was now screaming at walls and furniture and appliances and running around an empty house.

She was furious at herself for allowing Howland to give her those bullshit courses and, worse, for not making a bigger stink about it, even though the stink she always made was one of the reasons she was running around her house, screaming at the mixer. The phone rang. It was Mitch.

"Mitch! Mitch, did you hear?"

"What?"

"I didn't get it."

Silence.

"Mitch?"

"Yeah, I heard you. Shit. I'm sorry."

"Did you know?"

"Of course not. No."

"Do you know anything? Please."

"I can't tell you this."

"What?"

"Cindi, I cannot tell you this!"

"Tell me. Mitch, you have to tell me."

"I heard something. I know the vote was close. I voted for you, Brooksie we can assume didn't, Tamara, I can't imagine she didn't, so—"

"Howland?"

"Well, if he voted 'no,' which would make it a tie, it's death. Unless he voted 'yes' and Tamara fucked you over. You two get along, right?"

"I think, but I don't know anything anymore. What do you think? Howland?"

"I really don't know. I think he supported you, but you know, there's support and there's support."

"Fuck. Mitch."

"I'm sorry."

"What do I do now?"

"Nothing. Do not call him. Do not go *wahnsinnig*. Don't make any decisions about anything. Don't quit. Don't do anything. Cindi? Cindi, you listening?"

"Yeah, yeah."

"I think you come tomorrow and make like everything's fine."

"Tomorrow? Oh, shit, right, tomorrow. No. Impossible."

Every semester, the University of Nevada, Reno Philosophy Department had a party for students and the faculty. This year, the party would be held at the new Joe Crowley Student Union.

"Do I have to?"

"Yeah."

"Why?"

"Cindi."

"Okay, but then I'll sue these fucking motherfuckers."

"You're not suing anybody, because if you do and you win, which you won't, you'll be a pariah around here. And if you lose, which you probably will, nobody will hire you. Look, you've got until next May, right?

"Yeah."

"That's almost a year and a half to figure out what to do. You do not have to decide now. And stop tearing up your house, which I'm sure you're doing," he added, just as Cindi was tossing a pillow at the dining room table, knocking a vase to the floor. "You want to come over? I'm in the office. I have pot."

JACOB FISHMAN'S MARRIAGE: A NOVEL

15. Consorts to the Gods

"Do you want me to go with you?" Jacob asked, lying on the bed watching her get dressed, as he usually did, and wishing, as he usually did, that she would want him to go wherever it is she was going.

"I'm not staying long and I'm in a bad mood, so thanks, hon, but no," she said to him through the reflection of the mirror, as she straightened her hair. "I'm just going to make an appearance and then leave."

"You sure?"

"I'm sure. No, I don't want you."

Through the mirror, she could see him wince. She almost reconsidered. Almost.

"You know, fuck UNR, it's their loss," he said, smiling to himself, trying to deflect the rejection. Instead he focused on her flat iron being rushed through her hair. It made him smile.

"Why you smiling?" she asked.

"Nothing. Was just thinking about how many times we do this. You there, me here in bed. Can I say something completely off the subject?"

"Go ahead."

"Your breasts are gorgeous."

Cindi had dropped her abaya to her shoulders and was rubbing lotion over her chest.

"You're not even a breast guy."

"I know, but existentially I love them."

"Do you even know what that means?"

"Sort of . . . yeah."

"I appreciate you trying," she said, pulling up the abaya, "but I can't breathe with you around sometimes."

"What? I thought we were talking about something else . . . having a nice conversation."

"What do you mean?"

"I mean—wait. What do *you* mean?"

"I get no privacy. Like now."

"What just happened? We were just talking about breasts."

She tugged on her abaya, though it was already covering her breasts.

"I get it, okay. I won't mention them again. Promise."

"We were not talking about fucking breasts! You know . . . no, not now—I can't do this now, talk, look at you."

"We live here. We're together. We're going to run into each other from time to time in this house and actual words may pass between us. And my point here, Jesus, but my point here is that I love you, I want to go with you tonight, and I think you're gorgeous, including your breasts, which, apparently, I'm never going to see again. How is it possible we can't even get this moment right?"

"I don't want to get things right. I am a fucking failure. Have you been listening to what just happened to me?"

Cindi looked at her husband through the mirror, saw him swallow, bob his head up and down, exhaled. He looked like he had just been punched.

"I just don't—" Cindi said, turning around, while still seated. "Look, I fucked up. I didn't play the game, maybe the thing with Casey, not being published. It's not his fault. I mean, it is, but it's not. I was so stupid with Howland. I hate myself. It's not about you."

"So why did you cover up your breasts?"

"Fuck, really? You're asking me that now? I hate my body. I hate myself. I don't want you gawking at me like I'm meat and you're a dog who's hungry."

"A dog who's . . . why are we married, again?"

"Not now, Jake. Please."

"Sorry. I don't even know where we are in this conversation."

"I fucked up completely. It's all me."

"Maybe you could have done better at school, but you tried—anyone could see that. But I don't see how you could have done that much better."

"Jacob, let me help you out here: full support. Here's the 'A' answer: 'No, Cin, the university is a male bastion of bullshit. And Howland could have done much better. He doesn't deserve you.' Don't be wise, don't be objective. I don't need both sides here. I need a husband."

"I think I was doing that, wasn't I? And you need a husband now—just one who doesn't look at or compliment your breasts."

"Oh, for the love of God—"

"And anyway, when I am one, that kind of husband, you don't want me to be and then you scream about the possessive 'my' and the patriarchal bullshit and the thousands of years of subjugation, and when I'm not that kind of husband, well, you want the patriarchal bullshit because it's comforting or acceptable or because the moment calls for it —and I'm supposed to know which is which and when is when."

"What the hell are you talking about?" Cindi asked, smile.

"I can assure you I have no idea," Jacob said, returning the smile, glad for the reprieve.

"I'll see you later," she said, getting up, putting on a head scarf. She came over to kiss him. "I'm sorry I'm taking this out on you."

"Maybe it's both of us."

"How do I look?" she asked, fixing her bandanna.

"Like a folk singer. All you need is a beat-up guitar."

"That's a shitty thing to say."

"I thought it was cute."

"It wasn't."

As Cindi left the bedroom, she could see Charlize-Louise, lying on both the chaise and a piece of her rejection letter.

"Mommy loves you. I'll be back very soon, precious!"

She thought about getting the letter, putting it in her purse, but to whom would she show it? It wasn't like a picture of her son or daughter —not that I have one, she thought—but more like a cancer or a mastectomy scar at which people might look and then feign some interest for a moment before looking away.

"If I had a baby, I wouldn't care about this," she said to herself, as she walked through the kitchen on her way to the back door.

"What?" asked Jacob, still on the bed, watching the spot where his wife used to be. "You say something?"

"No."

As she got in the Scion and during the short drive to campus, she reminded herself that she not only didn't have a child, she also quite suddenly didn't have a future, nor a husband she wanted to fuck, or even one she wanted looking at her naked—or even one she wanted. She had Charlize-Louise and a broken-down trailer. That's what she had.

She parked the car at the university, close to the event, finished smoking her Indonesian cigarette, and checked herself in the rearview mirror. Her mouth and lips, which she'd never liked, looked even smaller than usual. She hated her vanity as much as she hated her reflection. What she saw looking back at her was taunting her. She played with her hair, felt her neck, turned and looked at her profile. She reached between her legs. She was inexplicably wet.

"Hi, Cindi. I love your kerchief."

It was Emily, a graduate student, who met her at the door.

Those words, "I love your kerchief," made her laugh loudly.

"You don't?" Emily asked, touching it.

"I absolutely love my kerchief. More than life itself."

Emily smiled and walked away.

Mitch, who had been standing by a group of students, quickly came to her side.

"You could have said thank you," he said.

"Somehow I pissed off Emily."

"How'd you do that? She adores you."

"It's my secret power."

"It is a cool kerchief, you know."

"Flight attendants wear kerchiefs. This is a bandanna, you rube, though I wish to be a flight attendant. I have always wanted to be a flight attendant. I can now be the best flight attendant. I will fuck all the pilots and first-class passengers."

"I see you're in a good mood. You want a drink?"

"I want to shoot heroin through my vagina."

"Is that even possible?"

"Keith Richards, I heard, shoots it through his cock."

"You heard that?"

"Maybe it was a joke, I don't know."

"This is going to be a long night, isn't it?"

"You have no idea."

They headed to the bar, where Hal Howland was standing with a group of students.

"What could go wrong now?" Mitch whispered, seeing Howland. "Easy, girl."

Cindi hadn't seen Howland, had purposely avoided him, since receiving the letter, but there he was, smiling, holding court, none the worse for wear for ruining her life.

"I'm going to be fine."

"You're going to be fine, yes. It's Hal I'm worried about."

"You know his full name is Halen?" She said.

"Cindi, don't."

"I won't, promise. But fucking *Halen*?"

Howland saw Cindi, smiled, and pointed to another part of the room, indicating he was wanted, but mouthed the words "Let's talk" and "Sorry" before tilting his head and putting his hand over his heart, a hand that was holding a beer. Were she in the mood, she might have taken it for what it was, a nice gesture at an awkward time, but what she wanted to do was take the glasses that were perched on his head and stab him in the neck with them.

"You're smiling?" asked Mitch.

"Mitch, *The Godfather*, with the glasses?" Cindi whispered in Mitch's ear.

"Glasses? What are you talking about?"

"The scene where he stabs the guy in the neck."

"Stabs the guy in the— oh, right. Yes! *Part III*. Lucchesi. Well done, signora."

"You boys and gangsters and the need to romanticize these pigs," she remembered saying to Jacob, after she watched the entire trilogy with him. "You just love jerking each other off, don't you? Just spread your seed and impregnate the next nymph."

"What seed is spread?" asked Jacob. "There are no nymphs in *The Godfather*."

They didn't watch movies together after that.

The thought of glasses impaled in Howland's neck—imagining him, too, writhing in pain, trying to extricate the tortoiseshell glasses from his carotid artery, while blood gushed and his beer spilled on the floor of the new facility—stayed with her.

"Ms. Fishman, I love you."

"What? Who does?" Cindi said, looking around.

It was Lacey, the student from Mitch's class who saved her from heat stroke that afternoon in his class, wearing—and it made Cindi laugh even harder—glasses with big red frames.

Glasses.

"Hi, Lace."

"Hi, Professor Aloisio."

"He's not only a full professor, he has tenure, which is more important than love or sex or children or intelligence."

"Lace," interrupted Mitch, "Ms. Fishman is obviously having a moment here."

"Blow me," Cindi said to Mitch.

"You two should get married, you know that?" said Lacey. "You may have to kill your spouses, but I really think it will be worth it."

"You first," Cindi said to Mitch.

"You two have this thing, you know? It's fun. A little weird, but it's fun," continued Lacey. "Anyway, that wasn't my point. I just want you to know, Ms. Fishman—Dr. Fishman?"

"Cindi's fine, really."

"Ms. Fishman, I love you, I want to tell you that, and wouldn't be majoring in this black hole of a discipline if not for you. We had that one course—you remember?"

"Global Ethics and Justice."

"Yes!"

"Well, that was back when I was allowed to teach."

"I love, love, love Professor Aloisio, but you're kind of my role model."

"Thanks," Cindi said, suddenly on the verge of tears and not thinking about Howland bleeding to death with glasses sticking out of his neck. "I can't tell you what that means to me, especially today."

She felt Mitch grab her arm.

"I mean it," Lacey said. "You're the only reason I don't go back to advertising. Can I ask you something?"

"Sure."

"I'm going to mingle," said Mitch.

"Okay," Cindi and Lacey said simultaneously.

"That sign on your door," Lacey continued, "the thing about the gods and omnipotence. Do we really not know who said it?"

"Oh, that! You noticed? No, we don't know, but I'm sure, pretty sure, it was one of the Sophists. Why do you ask?"

"I just love the thought of all these gods wishing they were better gods. It's, like, unrealized omnipotence. They're almost like ballplayers in the minors or ballerinas who want to go to New York but still dance in, well, Reno."

"Unrealized omnipotence . . . I like that."

"I know it's not the time, but I always wanted to ask you about that."

"Believe me, considering my courses the last year, this is wonderful stuff, a wonderful discussion. Ask away."

"The Sophists didn't believe in God, right?"

"It's not that they didn't believe, they just tended to advocate the otherwise shocking view that the gods are a human invention."

"That must have pissed off the Greeks."

"It did, which was kind of their point, but the Sophists were pretty much pussies, afraid to proclaim the ruse. And you can't really blame them. They'd be beheaded if they said anything so overtly sacrilegious. The Greeks were not known for their sense of humor when it came to matters of the Deity. So, the Sophists couched their cynicism in obfuscation."

"How'd they do that?"

"Well, they said—and this is simplistic . . . you sure you want to do this now?"

"Please."

"Well, let me quote Epicurus here. 'Is God willing to prevent evil, but not able? Then he is not omnipotent. Is he able, but not willing? Then he is malevolent. Is he both able and willing? Then whence cometh evil? Is he neither able nor willing? Then why call him God?' Hey, you don't really want to talk about this, do you?"

"I do, I really do, except I'm . . . I'm kinda pregnant, which has nothing to do with this. I don't think it does."

"Good! I mean . . . good? Jason?"

"I'm embarrassed to tell you, but I'm not entirely sure. Probably Jason's—I mean, I'm almost positive, I'm sure of it. But it's, I guess, possible."

"You happy?"

"You know," said Lacey, "there's a great line in *The Two Jakes,* the sequel to *Chinatown,* when the guy asks Nicholson, 'Are you happy, Jake?' Do you know it?"

"No," says Cindi, "but someday I hope to understand why everyone talks to me in movie quotes."

"Anyway, the Nicholson character says to the Chinese guy, 'I can't complain,' and then the Chinese guy says, 'Does that mean you're happy?' What's great is Nicholson then says, 'Who can answer that kind of question?' which you think is the moment, right, the lesson here, but that's not it, because the Chinese guy says—and this kind of broke my heart—'Jake, a happy person can answer that question.'"

"That's really good," said Cindi. "I like that."

"So, yeah, I don't know," Lacey said. She started to cry. "I'm pregnant, I have a degree I can't use, a boyfriend who I know is going to soon bore me to death, and I'm working part time at a place that does cremations. Only cremations. Burials, you gotta go somewhere else."

"They have such places?"

"I answer the phone and tell people, when they ask, what we do to their loved ones. I mean, really? We fucking burn them! You have to ask. It really is stupid, four years studying the great minds and people asking if we have a viewing room to watch loved ones be put in the oven."

"Do you?"

"We do, yes."

They both laughed and hugged.

"And now," Lacey said, "I'm going to have a baby with a silly name and I'm still wondering about the meaning of life, while selling cremation packages and urns. Sorry, wow! That was way too much."

"Pregnant and working in a crematorium," said Cindi. "Wait. Go back. Silly name?"

"I've been vomiting for three days—and Jase wants to call it 'Flash.'"

"Flash?"

"Yeah, it will be interesting to see who matures faster—my baby or my boyfriend. But, no, I shouldn't bitch. I'm happy."

"Really?"

"Who can answer that kind of question?" Lacey asked.

"A happy person."

Lacey hugged Cindi again and let her touch her stomach.

Mitch returned. "How was that?"

"I can't begin to tell you, but I'm getting the hang of this movie business."

"Anyone ever tell you you're almost impossible to follow?"

"Oh, yeah."

They walked to another group of students.

"I have returned, my young friends," Mitch said, "with my muse and valet."

"He's just trying to get me in bed."

The students laughed.

"I'm a freshman, undeclared," said a student in sandals with a mop of black hair, three days' worth of stubble, and wearing a Cheech Marin T-shirt. "So tell me why anyone still cares about this discipline and why it matters what a bunch of Greek homosexuals thought about twenty-three hundred years ago."

"Maybe other homosexuals cared," said Mitch to laughs. "But right. Nobody cares today, not even the homosexuals. You asked a glib question, so I should probably give you a glib answer, but let's try this because, God knows, I never get asked this question. I should charge you tuition for what I teach you outside of class, but here goes. Philosophers study the thought process, the passion of the hopelessness and the struggles of it all, and it is, if history is any judge, hopeless. You'll see that as you get older and aren't so ready to dismiss other people's struggles. Yet, knowing that, we humans think we can do better, because if we understand it better, as if there's something to understand better, we live better, more connected, richer lives. That's not a bad way to spend the day. Philosophers spend time on those thoughts. It's a lot of hubris, let me say that before you do, but this does, philosophy does, bring you closer to something. For some, it's God, for others, genius, for others, insanity, for some, life, a moment of happiness . . . wisdom, for lack of a better word."

Cindi smiled. "Told you he was trying to get me in bed."

The students laughed. Mitch laughed.

"Okay, but how does that matter to us today?" asked the kid with the mop of black hair. "Seriously . . . modernity and all that?"

"How?" repeated Cindi, deciding to join in. To see if she could. "For instance, to the question of whether I should buy the free-range chicken or the packaged Tyson chicken, the question is: Should I worry about the differences in how chickens live and die? Their quality of life, so to speak. Should that affect me and my decision? And what of my empathy? Is the nature of pain for a chicken, as I understand it, the same as mine? And then what of the notion of pain itself? Who else can understand the beauty of such ratiocination? The geologist . . . the theater major . . . the mathematician? No. The philosopher does. That's the calling. It's all I got. But it's maybe everything."

When she stopped talking, there was silence. Cindi, at that moment, reminded herself she was good at this, loved this, every part of it.

"So what do you do?" asked one of them. "You know, about the chicken?"

"I buy the Tyson. It's cheaper," said Mitch.

Cindi laughed.

"The thing is," Cindi said, winking at Mitch, "philosophy will bring you closer to truth, but it won't get you there. Worse, it brings you absolutely no closer to a job when you graduate—or," she added with a laugh, "keeping it once you have one."

Mitch smiled and touched her arm.

"I'm going to take a walk," she said, touching his lower back. "Listen to this man, but don't let him convince you that Lewis, Santayana, or Sartre are has-beens."

Walking outside, she was hit by a beautiful cold wind. It was March in Reno, and while the previous few days had been balmy, she reminded herself, as someone once told her, "Sixty-five-degree days in Reno in March don't mean shit," and, anyway, the chill was back. She made her way to a picnic table in front of the Getchell Library. She knew before even putting her feet up on the table that she wasn't going to quit teaching before her contract was up. There was too much goodness back in that room, too much possibility. She was going to go back inside, eventually, and smile and mingle, even be nice to Howland, but first she wanted to sit, look at the stars, generally, and the Pleiades Cluster, the Seven Sisters, made consorts to the gods by Zeus, particularly. She remembered a Tennyson poem and said it softly to herself.

Many a night I saw the Pleiades, rising thro' the mellow shade,
Glitter like a swarm of fireflies tangled in a silver braid.

"Consorts, huh?" Cindi said to the stars. "Zeus feels bad for you, so he makes you doves and puts you in the heavens? Those were days when gods knew how to treat women."

There was also a rather absurd tale that she remembered hearing about the Pleiades, from, as it was told to her, the Western Mono Indians. They saw in the Pleiades a group of wives who were excessively fond of eating onions and then, unfortunately, being thrown out of their homes by their angry husbands. The husbands felt guilty—apparently the onions weren't such a big deal after all—and wanted them back. By the time the men had come to their senses, however, the wives had wandered off, becoming the Pleiades.

Onions!

Peaches.

Mitch.

"I want a baby," she said to one of the sisters in the sky, one of the daughters of Atlas and Pleione, the one who feels shame for marrying a mortal, the one who's hiding.

"I see you, Merope," she said to what she thought was that star. "I want a baby." She laid her head down on a cold cement picnic table and fell asleep. She didn't wear a watch, had left her cell in the car, so she had no idea what time it was or how long she had been out there. She knew she was freezing. By the time she returned to the party, it was over. Howland was gone, as were the students—there was only Myrna, the San Salvadoran who cleaned the Cain Building, with a bus tub of empty glasses.

"*Como estas?*" Myrna asked.

"*Mas o menas,*" Cindi said, smiling. "*Donde Mitch?*"

"*Ido.*"

She went to Cain, hoping he might be in his office. She entered on the lower level, closest to the philosophy offices. Mitch's office light was on. The door was closed, not shut. She put her hand on Sacha Baron Cohen's face and pushed open the door.

"Hi."

"Where you been?"

"I fell asleep outside."

"It's cold as hell out there."

"I know. Why are you still here?"

"I thought you might come back. I was going to give you another thirty minutes."

"That's what students have to give full professors before they leave a classroom, right?"

"I don't know."

"You were brilliant tonight."

"Huh?"

"With the kids, with me."

"I wanted to wait, figuring you wouldn't leave without saying good-bye. You okay? Really, what were you doing out there?"

"Just sitting outside, talking to the Pleiades Cluster."

"Zeus steals them from Orion, keeps them for himself? What a prince! Any other age, he's a pimp. And, then, what, Merope is so ashamed at marrying a mortal, she hides?"

"I saw her!" Cindi said, excited.

"Merope?"

"How 'bout that?"

"Who told her to marry a mortal?"

Cindi walked to the desk, to the spot where her co-worker, her friend, her tenured friend was sitting. He looked up, smiled, and pushed back in his chair, tossing the pen on the table. He smiled again and put his hands behind his head. Cindi put her hands on the armrest, then grabbed his face, leaned forward, and kissed him. She pushed his head back and put her fingers in his mouth, pulled them out, licked her fingers, then his lips. She forced her tongue between his lips.

"Open your mouth," she said.

He did as he was told.

She straddled him.

"Cin—"

"I want to fuck you. I am going to fuck you, but then I am going to go home and sleep by my husband and you're going to go home to . . . whatever her name is."

Cindi wasn't wearing underwear, she never did. He pushed up to meet her, running his hands down her back until they made their way to her ass. He lifted her skirt.

Her breathing increased. Again she pushed him back in the chair and said, "Let me."

"I—" he started to say.

"Don't say anything. Just let me do this." She dropped to her knees, undid his pants, and freed his cock, which was already hard. She put him in her mouth. Mitch watched her, stroked her hair. He leaned back, closed his eyes.

"Keep your eyes open. Look at me," she said, as she slipped his cock into her mouth again. "Look at me," she said again, quietly.

He did.

She pulled herself up, straddled him again, and grabbed his cock and guided it inside her.

Cindi Fishman was Atlas's eighth nymph daughter. "I want you to come inside me."

"I want you to come," Mitch said, putting his hands under her hair.

"I just did. I'm embarrassed."

"I'm flattered."

What to do now?

DESPISING THE
FISHMANS

The sex that the fictional Cindi had with the fictional Mitch was better than the sex the fictional Jacob was having with the fictional Ciara—better than the sex the real Fishmans were having. It was, Jacob told himself, his way of apologizing to his wife for defiling their marriage. Cindi, one of them, at least, would easily orgasm. Such was his thought process that he thought this passed for an apology. The real Cindi would find the sex between the fictional Jacob and the fictional Ciara laughable, especially the Asian-porn business, not only because it was fatuous but because Cindi had actually found some Asian porn in Jacob's office (which was how Jacob got the idea for the scene). She made him throw it out. The fictional Jacob, she would conclude, would have his porn. As for Consorts to the gods, she would also hate the fictional Cindi's starved sexuality, the palliative effects of intercourse on her overall malaise, as if all she needed was a good fuck. ("And what," Jacob could hear her ask, if his wife ever read the book, which she surely would, "is that 'keep your eyes open' and 'look at me' bullshit in the chapter?") She would hate the whole proxy of intersectional novel sex but not, Jacob imagined, if she were honest, fucking a fertile man, which he was going to make sure Mitch was. Cindi, too, would notice that the fictional Jacob wore a condom, but the fictional Cindi didn't insist that Mitch do.

Of course she didn't.

Unhappiness, repressed desire, fantasies within reach, pettiness, sure, but no gnashing of teeth awash in guilt and despair. The Fishmans' infidelity, mostly fictional, was dispositive. They felt like they deserved their affairs, and for that, Jacob was proud of himself for allowing them to have them.

Jacob was not only seeding the clouds on the horizon, he was placing the clouds in the sky.

He despised all the Fishmans. He sensed they felt the same about him.

Jacob Fishman's Marriage: A Novel

16. Clearblue® Pregnant

It didn't surprise Cindi, as she sat between the tub and the toilet, looking at the plastic stick of the Clearblue® Easy Digital Pregnancy Test and the italicized *PREGNANT,* but she nearly dropped the stick in the toilet when she saw the word. It was such a simple declaration, so delicate, so beautiful, such a nice font. She bought the Clearblue® because the others indicated pregnancy with just a line or a "YES," but Clearblue® indicated a positive result with the word *PREGNANT,* and Cindi wanted the word. She wanted to take the stick and put it in a scrapbook, a box, even if she had no idea what happened to the *PREGNANT* after days or weeks pressed against plastic pages, whether it would fade or not, whether urine would leak and make the scrapbook stink. But she vowed to get one, a fancy one, with the plastic sleeves, and she would put it under the bed next to her diaries.

She didn't need to be told she was pregnant, because she had been nauseous the past few weeks, hadn't felt her eggs drop, something she could always feel, and for the past two days her breasts and nipples were sore, a good sore, especially her left one, which felt twice as big as it normally did. She was peeing constantly as well, and she was late. Symptoms so common and pedestrian, she resented her body being so obedient to the call of nature and protocol and commonality. She could feel the estrogen coursing through her body, and it made her body feel new, no longer hers, as if it had been borrowed from someone else. She was breathing differently—deeper, more hopeful.

There was no mystery, either, as to whose baby it was. The sex she had with Mitch was angry, hard, marathon events with little conversation and even less difficulty. Even fucking Mitch that first night after the faculty party, she felt an abandon she hadn't had since Bilal. She was the aggressor, the choreographer, the stalker, even if she came faster than a teenage boy.

One night at Cal-Neva, on the North Shore of Tahoe, after making love in a room on the California side of the hotel, she told Mitch, "If I get pregnant, I don't want anything from you. I swear."

"Why are you bringing this up now?"

"You never wear a condom."

"You never ask me to."

"I'm just bringing it up. You okay with it?"

"Are you pregnant?" Mitch asked.

"I don't know."

But it was not at Cal-Neva where she got pregnant, but at Harvey's, on the South Shore of the Lake—they used alternate sides of the lake—when it happened. This, too, she knew. The sex at Harvey's Lake Tahoe was particularly torrid that afternoon in a room overlooking the lake.

"I think I just got pregnant," she told Mitch, lying on her side with his arm around her and his cock still inside her. She noticed a plate of strawberries on the windowsill.

"Me, too," said Mitch.

"I'm serious."

"Okay."

"Why are there strawberries on the windowsill? Did we order strawberries?"

"No. Previous occupants, I guess."

"Housekeeping left the strawberries? Oddly serendipitous. They look kind of fresh."

"But kind of disgusting," Mitch said. After a pause, cupping her breast, he asked, "So, pregnant?"

"Yeah, I think."

"Okay."

"Okay."

March eighteenth. It was important to remember the date—the moment of conception, to her, was more important than the birth date. It's something Thich Nhat Hanh taught her—or should have, if he hadn't. She looked at the clock radio. 1:11.

Go through the Gateway, go through the Gateway, she remembered hearing somewhere.

She wanted to call Sage, but she had no way of getting in touch. With Mitch now lying on his side, she got up and walked to the window to a stark blue sky over the lake. She didn't want silence but didn't want Mitch to say anything either.

"You okay?" he called to her.

"I'm pregnant."

"I know. You told me. Should we celebrate with strawberries?"

"Jacob—uh, Mitch! Shit, sorry. God, I'm sorry," she said, coming back to the bed and running her hand over his chest.

"It's okay, really," he said.

"I'm sorry."

"It's okay."

She didn't want to get pregnant at a Harvey's on the South Shore of Lake Tahoe, but it would have to do. She'd hoped it would be in the South of France or on the Greek island of Lesbos. When she and Jacob talked about babies, the few times Jacob actually would talk to her about them, he once—to shut her up, she was sure of it—brought up in vitro fertilization, which Cindi rejected. She believed it would lead to a baby without a soul, if not malformed altogether (and they couldn't afford the procedure anyway) because the proximity of sperm to egg was without human touch. If she had to choose between a test tube in a lab or a junior suite at Harvey's, she'd take the suite with someone else's strawberries on the windowsill.

This baby, this girl, would have a soul.

"You seriously okay if I'm pregnant or get pregnant?" she asked

Mitch again, as she got up again and went to the window ledge and watched a catamaran go by below. She picked up the plate of strawberries.

"I'm okay. You can stop asking me."

"What about Rouslana?"

"Thanks for getting her name right, but you're the one who's married. You told Jake you were at a two-day retreat and now you have to say, 'Yeah, retreat was great. Oh, nearly forgot to tell you, I'm pregnant.'"

"My marriage is over, you know that."

"I'm sure it is now, if it wasn't before."

"I've wanted a baby forever. So, why are you okay with this?" she asked, bringing him a strawberry.

"Why do you keep asking?" Mitch asked, finding the freshest-looking strawberry on the plate and biting into it. "How old can this be?"

It was still juicy.

"You know, it's not bad, actually."

"You're avoiding the subject. But it's okay."

"Hey," he said, sitting up. "I love you."

"I don't know what to say. I'm a terrible wife, you should know that."

"I don't want to marry you. I just said I love you."

"This is a bad TV script, Mitch."

"But we have strawberries, so there's that."

They fucked once more that afternoon, which Cindi thought important to do. Irrationally, she wanted the sperm and the egg to be pushed even farther back into the cervix, so there would be no chance her baby would dribble out of her and land, ignominiously, on hotel sheets, a bathroom floor, or the inside of her jeans.

As they left the hotel, she with her fertilized egg, now almost three hours old, she worried about the uneven ride causing a miscarriage. She looked at Mitch and wished he mattered more.

It's not his, it's mine.

"You really think you're pregnant, don't you?" asked Mitch.

"I know it's crazy. Hey, drive north. Let's go get a Wet Woody."

"You want to go to Gar Woods?"

"Yeah."

"Why?"

"Oh, a friend of mine once . . . it's a dumb story. You mind?"

"No."

They sat outside.

"What do you think Jacob will say?"

"He once said he'd throw me out of the house."

"When?"

"We were talking about me getting pregnant this way."

"You did? This way? What does that mean—this way? And who talks like that?"

"We do. Did."

"Think he will?"

"Don't know. I wouldn't blame him, though."

"You need a place?" Mitch asked.

"What about Natasha?"

"You just can't help yourself, can you?"

"I got it right once."

"We broke up the night of the party—nothing to do with you—but she's still there. She's living in another part of the house."

Cindi smiled.

"Another part of the house? How big is your fucking house?"

"She's on the sofa, downstairs, until she finds something. Why you smiling?"

"I love cock."

"What?" Mitch asked, laughing and inadvertently spitting out his drink.

"This kind of reminds me of something, someone."

And now she was sitting on her bathroom floor, leaning against the tub, her feet up on the commode, opening and closing the toilet seat. Charlize-Louise came in yelping.

"Yeah, puppy dog, you're going to have a baby sister."

So this, she thought, is the moment she will share with her daughter: how she was with a dog when she found out about her. And it was a girl. She was sure of that. She thought of curly hair, curly blond hair, and a big smile and chubby cheeks and calves. Merope. She would call her daughter one of the seven sisters. Cindi would enroll Merope in modern dance, ballet, swimming, and guitar lessons. She'd teach her drums, too, mostly because she loved the title of Lynn Redmond's book *When the Drummers Were Women.* There was no question she was going to have Merope. The baby would be born in December. Her contract at UNR would be up the following May. She had decided not to appeal the tenure decision, so maybe the university would look favorably on a leave of absence . . . maybe even extend her contract another year. But there were more immediate concerns. First, she'd have to find a place to live, for even if Jacob didn't throw her out, she couldn't live in the house on Codel, a haunted house, getting fat and bloated with another man's baby. She couldn't go live with Mitch, even if Rouslana was now on the sofa—not that he'd really offered. It would have to be the trailer, which she would now have to fix up and make livable. She kept looking at *PREGNANT.* It wasn't changing, wasn't disappearing like Dith Pran's passport did in *The Killing Fields,* another film reference she suddenly, bafflingly remembered. She touched her stomach. She convinced herself she could already feel the change in her body, so she got up, looked in the mirror, and checked to see if pregnant women had, in fact, a glow about them. There was no glow. Surely, though, it would come. She sat back down on the floor, holding the stick.

"Charlize-Louise, see this?" Cindi asked, putting the stick in front of her dog's eyes. The dog tried to bite it.

"No bite."

She would tell Mitch when she was sure his reaction wouldn't matter to her. She'd let him have Merope on alternate weekends, if he wanted, but if he didn't, that was fine, too, because it was her baby.

It's not his fucking body!

Then she stopped herself.

What am I doing? Why am I angry? Why am I always angry?

She was sitting on the bathroom floor with a dog that had been saved from panthers and a stick soaked in urine and wonder.

RESEARCH

As Jacob stood over the toilet, one hand on his cock, the other on the Clearblue® Easy Digital Pregnancy Test stick, he wondered if all novelists went to such lengths.

He had decided that his fictional wife would get pregnant within weeks and that she would not be told by a doctor or nurse, she would find out in her own bathroom—she'd insist on finding out in her bathroom, as she didn't like or trust doctors, and in the house she hated—with the resurrected Princess Charlize-Louise de Secondat, Baron de La Brede Cougar Mellencamp Freckle Butt nearby (though she didn't know that he, the real Jacob, had almost killed her and sprinkled Comet over her). So, after Cindi, his real wife, left for the philosophy department's spring-semester party—the same event to which he was not invited and where he had already decided to have Cindi fuck Mitch—he went to CVS and bought a pregnancy kit.

He would pee on a stick so he would know what his fictional wife was thinking after she cheated on him.

"Big decision night, huh?" asked Crystal, a large African American woman in a smock at the register, putting the package in a bag.

"We're pretty sure we're not pregnant, but my wife asked me to come get this just in case," he said on behalf of the fictional Cindi. "She's pretty nervous."

"I can see the hope in your eyes," Crystal said. "She sounds like a special lady. And she's lucky to have you."

Jacob got home, walked into the bathroom, took off his pants, and stood, naked, save for a shirt, over the toilet, reading the directions. The box advertised "Over 99% Accurate," which made him laugh, for there would be a letter to customer service if this one was wrong.

He did as the package suggested: He removed the test stick from the foil, took off the cap, and held the stick by the thumb grip with the absorbent tip facing downward and the results window away from his body. The picture had the stick close to a woman's urethra, so he had to improvise. The woman in the picture was sitting, but he thought that unmanly for his purposes, so he stood. He peed on the floor, the bowl, everywhere; fortunately, he also managed to soak the applicator with enough urine to turn it pink, which was required, to achieve an accurate result.

He replaced the cap and put it down on the sink with the result window facing up.

And he waited.

Nobody could say he didn't do research. He, like thousands of women with thousands of blogs, would be writing about this moment.

"You don't know the first thing about smoking herb," Cindi told him once after he mentioned he was writing a scene where the fictional Cindi and Mitch smoked pot in his office, "so how are you going to write about my character getting high?"

"What's to know?" he asked. "I remember my last time. I was in high school, we ate Oreo cookies, said 'wow' a lot, and giggled. Have things changed much?"

"I'm telling you this for your own good. It's not about incense and drum solos and marveling at how roaches run across the kitchen floor. If you write it that way in your book, you'll look like an idiot. That's not how it goes, how it is, but if I try to explain it to you, you'll just roll your eyes and make me feel like one."

"Can I just hang out with you and Mitch and watch what you guys do?"

"What am I, a zoo animal? No. Besides, I have few pure moments of happiness left in life without you ruining them with a running commentary."

Three minutes he had to wait, so he took a washcloth, dropped to his knees, and wiped up his urine from the floor and the toilet seat. What else should a male novelist do while he's waiting to find out if he's pregnant?

He had denied his fictional Cindi tenure, he had almost killed her dog, he made her friend Ethan/Kenny a vegetable. But he was now giving her a baby.

I should be fucking thanked.

He wanted absolution, wanted to give Cindi something after taking away so much from her—by extension, taking away so much from his real wife—though he knew she wouldn't see it that way.

He wondered what the fictional Cindi would think of him if they ever met.

He checked the stick. Still nothing.

Which Cindi was pregnant? Which Jacob had bitten Ciara's tit? Which one came too soon? Which Mitch did he do dueling *Godfathers* with at Brooks' retirement dinner? Who had been denied tenure? What if he had so fucked around with the space-time continuum he had caused it to breach?

And now he was sitting on a toilet, a married man, an author, the embodiment of pathos and self-aggrandizement and cruelty and voyeurism, waiting for results of "his" pregnancy test so he could write about the pregnancy results of his fictional wife who cheated on him— and all so he could have this moment. Why wasn't someone chronicling his chronicling? He thought, as he finished cleaning up all the urine, it would make a great novel.

His paralysis was complete.

He picked up the stick.

NOT PREGNANT

Jacob Fishman's Marriage: A Novel

17. Sexy Knees

Cindi got up from the bathroom floor, picked up Charlize-Louise, and grabbed her keys from the kitchen counter. She called Mitch as she was backing out of the driveway, just barely missing the tree in the front yard.

"Oh, fuck! C'mon, please, pick up."

It went to voicemail.

"Oh, shit! I nearly hit a tree. Hi. Hi. Mitch, it's me—it's I. I don't know why I'm worried about subject pronouns right now. Okay, anyway, call me. Mitch, call *meeeeee!* Wow. I have . . . Tell you what. Just call me. Bye."

She knew he wasn't at school, so she drove by his house, where she had been just once, thinking he might miraculously be sitting out front, reading, even though there was no reason to think he ever did that. He'd wave to her as she drove by, motion her to stop. He'd stand up. He'd smile. She'd tell him in the driveway, his driveway, that she was pregnant with his child. Rouslana, or whatever her name was, would be away—or she would have moved out entirely. Cindi would be calm. She wouldn't be disappointed if he wasn't happy, but of course he'd be happy.

She rehearsed in the car.

"Hey, guess what?'

No, that sucked, she told herself.

"You got a bun cooking in the oven, Hoss."

That was worse. *Hoss?*

Of course he wasn't out front reading, but Rouslana was in the yard, in cutoff jeans and a tank top, dark glasses, a UNR cap, wearing AirPods, and cutting the grass. Rouslana was tall, Russian tall, and looked gorgeous, hot and sweaty, slightly bent over as she pushed the mower. The last time they saw each other was at Brooks' retirement dinner, but Rouslana wouldn't recognize her car. Cindi drove slowly, but not too slowly, pretending to be looking for a house, an address. If Rouslana was aware of her, Cindi couldn't tell.

Mitch is never going to leave her for me.

"What do you think?" she asked Charlize-Louise, now sitting in her lap, as they drove on. "Her knees are sexier than anything on my body. I'd rather fuck her than me."

She was not going to call Mitch again, not today, anyway. The man she cheated on was going to be furious. The man she cheated with would be, too, she concluded. She was pregnant and had a dog. She couldn't breathe. Cindi had nowhere to go and no one else to tell but Mitch, not even Sage, so she drove around Reno, Truckee, the university campus, and then, eventually, headed home, which seemed the worst, and yet the best, place to go. It was the only place left to go. She had been gone about forty-five minutes, and, as she approached Codel, she began to worry she had forgotten to do, or undo, something.

She saw Jacob's car in the driveway and checked the rearview mirror to see if she looked pregnant.

She was not glowing.

She turned off her car and sat in the driveway.

Don't look too happy. Don't look too sad. Don't pick a fight. Be normal.

She smiled, because to act normal meant she had to act pissy.

Back door open.

"Jake?"

Nothing.

"Jake?"

"In here," he said. His voice came from the bedroom.

When she entered the room, Jake was on his back, hands behind his neck. He was waiting for her.

"Hey," he said.

"Hey. What's up?"

Cindi looked over at her side of the bed, and there it was: what she had forgotten. Her Clearblue® Easy Digital Pregnancy Test stick was lying on a sheet of Puff's Ultra Soft & Strong tissue paper on her pillow.

She had left it on top of the sink.

"Shit! I didn't—"

"Don't. Don't."

Jacob noticed but would not tell her how gorgeous she looked, or how he liked her hair longer, the way she was now wearing it. He thought it a strange time to realize she was pregnant with another man's baby after all, that he would never see this woman, his wife, naked again. Would never see that small circular birthmark on her ass. He liked getting glimpses of her naked, of fingering her in bed when she would turn to face him. He could make her come like that. She would crush his hand between her legs, and then, for a moment or two, she'd fall asleep facing him.

He wanted to be angry.

"You going to talk to me?" she asked.

"It's not mine?"

Cindi didn't say anything.

"Just having to ask the question like that," he said, "is the indictment, don't you think? You're supposed to assume when your wife is pregnant that you fucked her, you made her that way."

Cindi was silent, wanting to call him out on how rehearsed that all sounded, but she knew even if his presentation was pure Jacob Fishman, pure self-conscious and choreographed bullshit, his hurt was real.

"I wish I could disappear, Jake."

"I don't know. I always imagined that if the marriage, when our marriage, ended, there would be a fight or anger. That you'd throw shit, break shit—you're good at that—or, I don't know, maybe just disappear."

Cindi couldn't help but laugh.

"It's what I . . . always wanted. Just to . . . poof. Go away. I'm really sorry you found out like this."

"That I found out like this?"

"I mean that I did it . . . this way."

"Is there a better way you wish you had done this and that I found out? That's what you regret right now? I guess it never crossed your mind that not fucking whoever it is you fucked, Mitch, I imagine, may not be the best way to go about this—get out of the marriage, to, I'll say it, break my heart."

"Sorry!" Cindi screamed. "I should have checked with you before undertaking how I would break your fucking heart! I didn't mean to break your fucking heart!"

"I thought I'd have more time, because in our marriage, I only have a certain amount of time here to feel anything, because it's important to not get you upset. Cindi must not be bothered with anyone else's emotions when she has so many unresolved. See, she has this rage, and it comes from the stress of not having a baby and having to embody the degradation that women have experienced at the hands of masturbatory men for the past ten thousand years—"

Cindi exhaled.

"And I am out of time already."

"My uterus was breaking—"

"What? No. Hold it. Let me wrap up here before we hear the rest of that. If only, only, Cindi could rid herself of the weight of the centuries of subjugation and suffocating patriarchy. If only someone would fuck her without a condom, if only someone would give her a baby, set her eggs free, and then her inner angel could come roaring out. You, of course, have the only angel that actually roars and, voila, it did. Now you can frolic with the angels—no, no, not the angels. What are they called? Plee . . . something?"

"Pleiades."

"That's right, the sisters. How many are there again?"

"Seven."

"Seven. So many muses, so close to earth, even if they have to pay the extra gratuity."

"I'm sorry you found out that way."

"You said that already. How would it have been a better way to find out? Ask me into the bathroom to await the test results with you? Or wait until I noticed your jeans stop fitting and your constant fondling of your baby bump?"

"That's not what I meant. I'm sorry I hurt you. It's not the way I wanted this to happen, which I know you won't—"

"Right, because now, for a while anyway, you can't be a victim anymore. I mean, you could if you weren't happy about the pregnancy, but you're beaming. You're gorgeous."

"That's not it." She felt bile in her throat. It was jabbing her. She needed to vomit. "I didn't leave it there on purpose."

"You didn't?"

"No. Okay, maybe I did. I don't remember thinking, 'Let Jacob find it,' but I don't know. I don't. It's not like someone's filming or writing about the Fishman marriage and we owe them the denouement. It's just you and me. No Greek chorus, no author following us around, no nothing, really. Fact is, we don't even have that good of a story. What? A woman, unhappy, tries for years to engage her obtuse, self-conscious husband, who doesn't listen, so she's forced into another man's fertile cock. Who'd pay money to see that movie, read that book? Who would write that fucking book? And, really, the lone pregnancy applicator, still soaked in urine, left inadvertently on the bathroom sink, it's too obviously Freudian, if not a downright cliche. 'I bet she wanted to get caught. Ooh.' Fade to red line on applicator."

"Of course not," Jacob said. "Freud bores you social scientists. So how would your discipline explain such careless cruelty? Surely one of the Enlightenment guys could tell us why. Montesquieu got anything on pregnancy test results the husband is choreographed to find?"

"Fuck you. You choreograph life. I don't."

"How do I choreograph life?"

"I didn't leave it there to humiliate you, even if I left it there."

"Well, okay, then, let's forget the whole thing—"

"Mitch,—"

"I'm Jacob."

Silence.

"I'm an absolute cunt."

She had called Mitch "Jacob" and now she had called Jacob "Mitch."

"You know, when I told you, a long time ago, that I understood you wanting a baby, even understood you getting pregnant—"

"You going to throw me out?"

"You late for something? You need to go? Actually, I wasn't thinking about that, throwing you out—you own the house. There's no throwing you out. But if it'll help the story you tell people, sure, I can throw you out."

"That's not what I meant. I don't want the story. And I don't want to hurt you anymore."

"So what happens now?" he asked. "You move in with Mitch, and then you two, along with the dog and the baby . . . what? You all move into the trailer and hope the field mice don't get into the pot he surreptitiously grows in flowerpots on the kitchen shelf? Rouslana, that's her name, right, is okay with this? You know, Sage will love it. Maybe she can move in, too, with her eleven kids and all the guys she's fucking. Think of all the throbbing cock you both can worship and have set you free."

"This was never about other men. This was never about cock. I was a cunt about this, but you never wanted a fucking baby and would never admit it."

"A pregnant woman bound for a trailer with a broken door and calling her ownself a cunt. Nice touch. Many points for your brutal take on yourself. Keep that up and I may even start feeling bad for you."

She got up, walked into her closet, mostly to hyperventilate, but she grabbed some clothes.

Jacob, lying on the bed, watched his wife leave the bedroom. He heard her call for Charlize-Louise.

Back door open.

Jacob Fishman's Marriage: A Novel

18. Ethan Responds

Cindi pushed open the door to one of the private suites at Advanced Health Care.

"You awake?" she asked, tapping lightly on the door, though she was already inside.

Kenny was on a ventilator, its whoosh and hum both frightening and reassuring to her, as she walked in. The oxygen hose in her friend's mouth jerked every time he swallowed, and his breathing, if that's what it was, was a muffled snore.

A gurgle.

"Hey, beautiful," she said. "Hope you're okay."

No response.

"Guess what?" She grabbed his hand, sat on a chair, and moved it as close to the bed as she could. She leaned forward, stroked his hair. "I can't wait to tell you."

Nothing.

"I had a baby boy. "

She waited for a response.

"Remember I told you that I was pregnant, showed you my stomach? Well, he's a month old today. Sorry I haven't been here the last few weeks, but that's why."

Cindi started rubbing his legs, which were bony and splotchy. She could see holes, small ones, and scabs in the skin. They had been bleeding, as if they had been rubbed by concrete.

"How does that feel?" she continued, feeling the scabs and dryness between her fingers. "Yes, a boy. I knew I was going to have a girl, told everyone, could feel it, but I didn't."

She stopped rubbing and covered up his feet.

"Maybe the seven sisters—remember I told you about that—had something to do with it. Anyway, he's beautiful. He really is. I want to tell you all about it, all about his smile, the motor home, your house—your mom comes by, we talk, she misses you—all about the last few months. Everything. I want to bring him up here to see you, but I'm afraid he'll be scared—not of you, but of this. Babies get scared, you know. He's only a month, like I said, but we already have quite the relationship. You would love him. He's got this mop of dark hair and he's already smiling. And I want to tell you something else: what I named him."

She grabbed his hand with both of hers.

She leaned on the mattress, still holding one hand, and moved up to his face. She whispered it in his ear.

This time she wasn't imagining it. She felt his hand close.

"You can hear me? I knew it! I knew it!"

Her voice was soft, but she repeated the name over and over in his ear. She buried her head in his chest. She felt him pulling her toward him. He moaned. And moaned again. He was now grunting, flailing, moving his head back and forth.

"Kenny. Kenny . . . Don't you love it?"

THE MESS

C indi had not thrown the twenty-seven-inch iMac through the window, as she had once promised to do if the book was as bad as she feared, but she had backhanded it off the desk, and it was now suspended, a few feet above the floor, tethered to a yellow surge protector that still sat on the windowsill. The laser printer was in three pieces near the window that looked out on Codel Way, crushed by the new pair of Frye boots she was wearing. Bits of plastic and glass were on the desk and floor. The laptop—as well as the home phone, keyboard, fax machine, calculator, external hard drive, router, modem, wireless mouse, fifty-five-inch Sony television and its remote, eyeglass case, reading glasses, envelopes, calculator, stapler, two USB hubs, *Associated Press Stylebook and Libel Manual,* desk calendar, an early printed draft of *Jacob Fishman's Marriage* (which Jacob had hidden under a pair of Avid speakers in the closet), seven embossed Jacob notepads, gooseneck lamp, and Philip Roth's *Zuckerman Unbound*—had been swept off the desk and now lay in a mound on the floor, doused by the contents of a day-old Diet Pepsi that Jacob had left on the desk. The pile, which resembled a pyre before conflagration, was under a pair of size-thirteen beige SAS Time-Outs, which Cindi had retrieved from the closet and which she had in fact given Jacob for his birthday the previous year and, unlike the fictionalized account in *Jacob Fishman's Marriage,* were in fact the right size. As Jacob stood at the door, seeing the sadness and the carnage, the residue of his conceit and disloyalty and cruelty, he thought he should take note of it all and then add it to *Jacob Fishman's Marriage,* before he reminded himself that fictional Jacob was not writing a book about Jacob and Cindi Fishman—*he* was—and that this was his story and Cindi was his wife and this was the mess in his office. Jacob replaced the computer on the desk and turned it on to see if it would reboot (it did) but did little else in the way of cleanup except to pick up the Roth novel and put it on a shelf. He went downstairs, grabbed a Diet Pepsi, went out to the front porch, sat, and rehearsed the last argument he would have in his second marriage. Forty-five minutes he sat, changing and practicing positions—legs crossed, legs up against the brick column, flat on the ground, over the bench—when he saw his wife drive up, quickly, too fast up the driveway. He knew she had seen him sitting there.

He waited. He counted back from one hundred by sevens to calm himself.

Ninety-three . . . eighty-six . . . seventy-nine . . .

He heard *Back door open,* heard it slam shut, and then heard the boots that broke his laser printer make their way across the hardwood floor of the living room.

Seventy-two . . . sixty-five . . . fifty-eight . . .

He heard Charlize-Louise being set down in the living room. The dog barked.

"Stay," he heard his wife say.

Fifty-one . . . forty-four . . . thirty-seven . . .

The screen door pushed open. Cindi stood there in a bandanna, tight blue jeans, and white button-down shirt and vest. Jacob was immediately reminded how good the women in his life looked when they were about to leave him.

"I told you, it's fiction," Jacob said first. "And was it necessary to destroy the office?"

"I'm leaving."

"You're always leaving."

"Fuck you. I mean, listen to me: Fuck . . . you!"

She swung a fist through the air, nearly losing her balance. "You killed Charlize-Louise! I knew you tried to poison her. And then you fucked Ciara. And you put Ethan in a coma and nearly killed him. And you made Sage out to be a whore. Aside from being an inconsiderate, duplicitous fucking parasite, a ghoul, what is wrong with you? You wanted me to fuck Randy?"

"Who's Randy?"

"The fucking postman. You don't even remember who you have me fucking."

"You didn't fuck him."

"You have me fuck a guy to have a baby? You did that to finish a book? You used me, your wife, your real fucking wife, to finish that piece of shit. You proud of yourself? You humiliated me!"

"First of all, I never tried to poison Charlize-Lou. The traps were there from before. As for the book, I didn't kill your dog. You didn't read the latest version. Next time you trash my office, wait until the final edit."

"You pissed all over this marriage. You start making jokes now, I will fucking kill you." She lunged at him, knocking his Diet Pepsi off the arm of the Adirondack chair. She fell on top of him, nearly hitting her head on the arm of the chair, which toppled over. She knocked over the table between the two chairs. She landed on the plastic cup, the diet soda, Jacob, and the ice cubes. Her breasts were on his face.

"Fuck! Ow, fuck!" she yelled, grabbing her shoulder. Her bandanna was tangled in her hair. She tore it off and threw it into the yard.

Jacob tried to move her breasts away from his face. "What are you, crazy?" he said, rolling off and away from her.

She kicked at him, her heel glancing off his inner thigh. He rolled farther, nearly off the porch and to the front yard.

"Let's go inside before the neighbors call the cops," Jacob said, standing up.

"I'm not spending any more time in there. The house is polluted."

"For the love of Christ. Really? Polluted? How long have you been working on that word?"

"Don't start with me. You rehearse life. Wait, you fuckhead, you already gave me, the fictional Cindi, that line. I so fucking hate you."

"I told you not to read it, that it wasn't ready. But, okay, here we are, so in no particular order: I did not fuck Ciara, the Jacob in the book did. You already know you didn't fuck Mitch. The fiction Cindi did. Charlize-Lou's alive—okay? Alive. It's fiction, anyway. The book is fiction! None of it happened. You—you—have tenure! Ciara was pure fantasy —not mine, his. That Jacob. And Cindi, that Cindi, the fictional one, fucked the fictional Mitch. You didn't. You know you didn't. And a fictional drug addict named Ethan did too many drugs, but not Ethan. He's Kenny. I changed—"

"Are you listening to yourself? It's not just a story. Jacob is you! And, worse, Cindi is me—the 'cunt,' remember? Every chapter was worse than the one before it. And you poured Comet on Charlize-Louise in a backyard grave? I don't know how anyone could be that sick."

"I did not kill your fucking dog, and even if I did, I didn't. It's inside now. Alive. The book is not for you, and nobody is going to know it's you, and I didn't write it for us in the first place. It's a novel. And, what, you're going to leave me because a character who has your name is called a cunt by a character who has mine in a book that fourteen people will read? I'm telling you I didn't fuck Ciara, that's the truth, if that's why you're leaving. And I told you not to read it."

"You're disgusting!"

"I'm a writer."

"You're a parasite, a scab, and you wrote you, that fucking Jacob, because you can't or won't do these things you want to do, so you fuck Ciara but you don't have the balls to actually fuck her. He fucks her. But that's not you, right? I'm not supposed to be upset by that . . . or that you, him, both of you call me and Cindi a cunt?"

"You think I'm too afraid to fuck Ciara, to call you a cunt?"

Cindi punched the air.

"You'd feel better if I called you a cunt?"

"We were getting along, remember? It was your idea. On the way back from Tahoe, you said—you fucking said—'Let's be better.'"

"These people are not us."

"I don't want to do this anymore—this argument about life and literature, as if you were any good at either. It's all you and it's all me!

And this book about our marriage was more important than your actual marriage. I am your wife—"

"'Am your wife'—you have said that more in this conversation than you have in our entire marriage."

"And the thought, you sick bastard, you demented fuck, that this conversation is going to wind up in the book too makes me want to put my fist through the wall or through your head."

Cindi walked by Jacob, picked up the matching Adirondack chair, turned it on its side, and hurled it off the porch. Charlize-Louise continued barking.

"You think anyone would believe you're not talking about me?" Cindi asked, turning back to him, throwing the table off the porch as well. "Do you really think I would fuck Mitch just to have a baby because you don't want to give me one? You make me out to be a pot-smoking, sex-obsessed...I-don't-know-what who loves her dog more than she loves her husband."

"Don't you?"

"Now? Yeah! You used me to get back at me."

"I've got nothing else to do with a book than get back at you? You think that's why I wrote it?"

"That's exactly why you wrote it. And why punish Ethan? What did he do besides be a friend to me?"

"How am I punishing him? He is a character of a friend who has a drug problem. And he's not Ethan. He is not your Ethan. Kenny in the book is what I'm afraid will happen to Ethan. It's a cautionary tale."

"He stopped doing drugs, you insensitive prick!"

"Haven't you ever worried about that phone call coming? Haven't you ever thought what you would do, how it would happen, what you would say? That he might start doing drugs again?"

"You send me to his fucking nursing home and then he cries when he finds out I named a child after him?"

"Yeah, I did."

"That's fucking terrible writing. It's clichéd. Jake, it's abysmal, even if I didn't hate it, which I do more than anything I have ever read."

"I don't think so. That Cindi would do that. Kenny would wish she didn't."

"What is wrong with you?"

"But the question: Don't you think of him dying . . . ever?"

"Of course I think about that, but I don't stage a scene where he's in a bathtub, naked and bleeding, after he slits his own wrists! No, I don't do things like that. Nobody does things like that. You do things like that."

"But it's not true, it's not going to happen. It didn't happen. It's fear, it's anger, it's frustration."

"Don't you believe in karma? How can you tempt fate like this?"

"Oh, come on! What I do, what I write has no effect on who lives and who dies."

"You defiled this marriage. Surely you're smart enough to understand that. I took off the ring. Some of it happened. And some of the good stuff I did, the sweet stuff you completely avoided—like the blueberries."

"What are you talking about?"

"I gave you blueberries for your birthday, remember, with the shoes? You never planted them. You never mentioned the fucking blueberries in your book."

"I'm sorry. I forgot. Why would you give me blueberries, anyway? I don't plant things."

"I gave them to you out of love, you fucknut! I should be thankful there was something in our lives you didn't put in the book. You don't remember that because that was sweet, nice, something a good wife would do and that wouldn't fit into this sewer of a marriage you wrote about. And the shoes fucking fit. I got you a thirteen wide. And that's your size. I remembered that. You lied about that just to make me look bad."

"That's not why."

"Why, then?"

"I don't know why, but not so I could suck the goodness out of the Cindi in the book."

"And you promised me you wouldn't hold me going to Vegas for that conference against me after your colonoscopy."

"I know. I shouldn't have done that."

"And since you were mad that I went, you wrote I masturbated in the bathroom thinking of Mitch."

"Yeah."

"I'm speechless at such cruelty."

"The Cindi in the book wanted a baby. She was desperate. Mitch was a good guy."

"I am the Cindi in the book. I was awful. I am awful. But that doesn't give you the right to tell the fucking world about how awful I am."

"I'm not telling the world that. I'm saying the marriage, their marriage, fell apart."

"And this is how you were going to fix ours? By fucking Ciara and that chick with the pen?"

"Chick with the pen? Wait, I didn't fuck her. I didn't fuck Ciara."

"The girl at the university, Ciara, you didn't fuck?"

"That Jacob fucked Ciara, not me. The girl at the university wasn't even someone the other Jacob fucked. Another girl entirely. Two different girls. And I didn't fuck either one of them. I'm sorry I didn't write about the blueberries."

"I don't care about the fucking blueberries!"

"But you didn't have Mitch's baby. You're not pregnant."

"And so why did you have the character, that Cindi, fuck him?"

"Wait. What are we talking about? The same reason the other characters fuck. And then don't fuck. I don't know. That's the point. As for Ciara, okay, yeah, Jacob the character did. Why? Because he wanted to, because he could, because that character would want to. People get laid in fiction a lot more than they do in real life. But I didn't. That's the point."

"No, that's not the point. You wrote he bends her over the sofa and she asks him to pull down her panties, and you're saying that didn't happen to you, that you didn't want her to say that to you before you fucked her?"

"No. I made that up."

"How fucking demented are you? You don't fuck her, but want to, so you have your character fuck her in a manner you'd like to fuck her and have her say things you want to hear but won't because you can't find a girl who will let you do those things? Did you want me to say it to you?"

"Stop."

"No. Fuck me! Pull down my panties! How'm I doing?" Cindi said, bending over one of the blue Adirondack chairs.

"Cin, please get up."

She did.

"Look, people doing things you won't do will do things I don't want you to do."

"Somebody named Jacob fucks somebody named Ciara over the back of a sofa, and somebody named Jacob kills a dog named Charlize-Louise and then pours household cleaner on her and tries to make it a poetic moment, and you don't think there's anything wrong with the person who writes that? And then somebody named Cindi fucks some guy she works with, but first blows him in a manner her husband would like to be blown. And since you created this, him, her—"

"He does, but I don't, didn't. And you don't. She does."

"Have you fantasized about fucking Ciara over the back of a sofa while she watches Asian porn? Have you fantasized about fucking wait-resses, women like that, over sofas while they watch porn?"

"No."

"You ever think it's the porn and not you that gets them off?"

"Yes."

"It's a rhetorical fucking question. When you wrote that, did it get you off? Did you jerk off to your own fantasy about jerking off? And you have me fucking Mitch in his office in a chair. Mitch? I wouldn't fuck Mitch. It's all about the cock in that scene, the glorious cock, isn't it? Am I that shallow? Friction is palliative, right, is that it? The girl needs a cock. All hail the cock! And now the glorious cock, the redemp-tive cock, the transcendent cock, the patriarchal cock saves the day because Cindi has a child. All thanks to the mighty cock. Cock, we salute you." Cindi got down on her knees and genuflected in front of Jacob's crotch. "Save me, oh cock, make me whole."

"Cindi, cut it out."

She stood up. "You fucking, fucking sick man."

"Why is that sick? A woman in a novel wants to have a baby."

"It's not a novel—for the millionth fucking time. It's me. Why are you so obtuse and dense? You won't give me a baby, so you have some guy I work with fuck me and that's how I get a baby? Could I be any more pathetic? On the bathroom floor with a dog in my lap? I'm sure you thought, 'Oooh, I'm creating great literature here. I am really a great guy because I'm giving her what she wants,' but, really, you know how gross this is? Do you even know anything about pregnancy tests? It's sickening."

"I make you sick? I ever tell you how bad you are in bed? I ever sit around talking about suicide on your birthday? I ever get so angry with you my face contorts like I'm possessed? I find a note that says, 'Sweet, sweet Mitch,' and my mind starts to wonder, because after all, my wife has no interest in me—and I think, 'Hey, if I'm writing a novel, maybe these two would have an affair,' and I think, 'Hey, wait, I am writing a novel. They will have an affair.' And, anyway, it's my fucking book."

"It was a Van Morrison CD. I bought him a Van Morrison CD. He bought me a Pez Pets Dispenser. That's what I was talking about. I told you that."

"So why are you upset? You didn't fuck Mitch. The other Cindi did. She got pregnant, not you. Look, I know it's too late for this, but I wanted to write something about people and marriages and expectations and disappointments. I didn't mean for the book to hurt you."

"You think this is just about the book?" she said, hitting herself in the head with an open palm. "You gave me away. You stole my fucking life! You didn't even give me tenure."

"You have tenure."

"You know what I mean. Every thought, every fear and emotion I've ever had now has quotation marks around them. You are now my ventriloquist. You might as well have both your hands up my ass and have me sit on your lap. Do you have any idea what that's like to read you're . . . subordinated . . . you're a punchline or a straw man just so some fictional prick can win an argument, or its author can blow himself at the notion of how good he writes? I don't even want my life anymore after you put your hands all over it. I need to be someone else. I'm a stain now—a two-dimensional joke. Were you at least going to change Mitch's name?"

"That's what's bothering you? Okay, I'll change it. Jesus! As long as Mitch is happy, because God knows, when I started writing, my intention was to make sure Mitch was happy and not embarrassed."

"Are you done? Forget Mitch. Tell me again: Which Jacob called which Cindi an atrocious cunt? You or . . . you?"

"Jesus! I told you. He, the other one, calls her that—character to character. And I don't even remember him calling her that."

"There's a distinction. My husband doesn't think I'm a cunt, but a character my husband creates, who just happens to have my husband's name, is married to a character, who just happens to have my name, and, well, she's the cunt. Anyway, that's what he thinks because he can't remember. Calling your wife a cunt is not a memorable enough occasion."

"You laughed when I told you the story."

"I am going to scream."

"Why can't you understand that these characters are not us?"

"They have our names."

"I'll change them."

"Oh, so my husband writing a story about a guy named, what, Eric who pulls down the panties of a girl named, I don't know, Annie, and fucking her over a sofa is going to make things better? No, no. Jacob's not talking about his wife. His wife works with Mitch Aloisio. In the novel the wife fucks Quentin. He won't get his wife pregnant. He can't. It's fiction. It's another Cindi blowing some guy in an office while talking about the Pleiades. What an artist Jacob Fishman is! Sure hope the Pulitzer people don't interrupt his breakfast when they call."

"I wrote a novel and people fuck and cheat in this novel and call each other names. Look, did I write some things when I was really pissed and thinking about something the two of us did or said? Yes. Do I think that other men, married to women who have behaved the way you sometimes do, would call their wives all sorts of names? Yes. Do I fantasize about other women? Yes. Sometimes, okay. But I imagine if we go into your room right now and find the journals that you've hidden, I might read one or two things about your sexual urges. As for wanting to fuck Ciara, whether I did or didn't, isn't the point. I didn't, okay? I didn't. Besides, and this may not be the best moment to bring this up, it's not like I've been doing a lot of fucking lately with you."

"So it's my fault you fucked a waitress?"

"I didn't fuck a waitress. And it's not your fault."

"I gave you the idea that she brings you to her apartment."

"What do you mean, you gave me the idea?"

"When you accused me of fucking Mitch that time after the Vegas trip."

"I don't remember that."

"Goddamn it, are you spineless. And who's this chick with the yellow pen?"

"What? Oh, her. She's an amalgam of every girl on that campus."

"Tell me, did you want to fuck her, too?"

"Why are you doing this? I want to fuck ninety percent of the women I meet." This was the second time in his life Jacob had said that to her.

"The author, so happy with his turn of a phrase, repeats himself."

"What do you mean?"

"Jesus! Nothing."

"But I don't fuck them. Jesus, what do you want from me? I can't just be unhappy, I have to make sure that my unhappiness doesn't make you angry because we cannot make Cindi unhappy because she ovulates, so, God forbid a waitress smiles at me."

"You killed me in this book. Don't you understand."

"I was freeing you."

"You can't free me."

"Cindi is free to have a baby. Why is that bad?"

"I'm leaving. But please, please, make yourself look good upon my leaving, make sure you're as kind as Jacob is. Will you cup my face so the reader, the audience, whoever you imagine is on the front lawn, or following you around, or whoever your studio audience is, will see what a good guy you are? Maybe a single, solitary tear rolling down your cheek. Scene. Fade to black. Maybe some music. The *Godfather* theme, that would be good."

"Right. I see myself inside out. I am the one outside the marriage looking in. Start the overture. The trailer you would gladly spend money to fix, but not your house, which was always mine when something went wrong. But the trailer, sitting in a field with a broken door and bad paneling and field mice . . . that's the oasis, the same place, Cindi's lair."

"Are you done with your monologue?"

"My monologue? Your monologue," Jacob said.

"No, yours."

"What are you, five? You hated this marriage. You hated the marriage I created."

"You don't get it."

"I gave you this novel."

"You gave it to me?"

"Yeah, I did. It's your baby. I gave Cindi, you, what you wanted."

She went inside.

"C'mon," he heard her say inside the house. Jacob heard the dog squeal. He heard the same boots, the same footsteps, though not as angry as before, walk over hardwood floors, area rugs, and the linoleum of the kitchen until he heard *Back door open.* He heard her car door, the ignition, then saw the car backing out of the driveway.

Her window came down. Jacob ran to the car, which Cindi stopped abruptly.

"How do you know I didn't fuck him?"

"What?"

She stared. "How do you know I didn't really fuck him?"

"What are you talking about?"

"Mitch, the real fucking Mitch. How do you know I—me, your real fucking wife—didn't really fuck the real one?"

"But you're . . . not—"

"You're not the only one with a book, buddy boy."

Jacob had to back up to avoid being caught by the window she was rolling up. He watched her back out of the driveway and then ran after her, to the street, calling after her, as the car picked up speed, "You're not Cindi and I'm not Jacob!"

ALMOST ROSES

The duck shit around Manzanita Lake was plentiful.

Jacob, having avoided most of it, stopped walking at the entrance of the university in front of Morris Alumni Center, south of the quad, and sat on a cement bench. He was surrounded by railroad ties and red flowers, almost roses, he told himself, though they might have been begonias or camelias or double tulips.

If I were putting this in a book, he told himself, it would be important to know the difference between them.

Jacob rocked his legs back and forth, scraping his skin against the concrete, listened to the new waterfall that had been constructed, and tried to read the names on the memorial to war veterans. At the gazebo nearby, a large Latina bride in a green dress was tousling her soon-to-be-husband's hair, as he stroked her face and traced a line from her cheek-bone to her mouth. The bride's mother—and it was clear to Jacob she was the mother, for she had the same shape to her breasts, same skin, same curl to her dark hair, and wore an inexplicable green dress—was fanning herself and smiling at the couple. A group of students, frater-nity types, were playing with a purple Frisbee behind him. Jacob had walked by this part of the university for the past four and a half years but had never stopped at this bench with its view of downtown and the memorial stone and now this new waterfall. He had stopped because he had developed a cramp in his calf, but also to get away from the duck shit and the blonde in the brown hair clip he had seen at the end of his first lap around Manzanita. She was about ten feet in front of him when he first noticed her, and as he made the turn to start his second lap, he sensed her pace picking up, as if she was frightened. There was no reason, Jacob told himself, that this girl should be afraid of him in his yellow Cannes Film Festival hat, black shorts, white T-shirt, and earbuds, but as she turned right, near Juniper Hall, the same direction Jacob was headed, she started jogging.

Don't worry. I'm not following you.

She cut between the buildings, the very path he took on his way to the quad, and then through the parking lot, just as he always did.

Please go right, please go right, Jacob thought, as he was planning to go left, his usual path.

Instead, she, too, went left, as well, north toward the Mines building.

He could have changed his route, but this was his route, damn it. In fact, this was the route both Jacobs took, but it was his first. This was just a walk. It was just life. Who was this interloper into this narrative?

The blonde in the brown hair clip had picked up her pace, but Jacob's pace kept her in his sight.

He thought about stopping, turning around, so as not to frighten her, but he wasn't doing anything wrong. He thought of running ahead, tapping her on the shoulder, telling her not to worry.

He decided that to do so would be insane.

She got to the end of the quad, and instead of turning right, as he was doing, she went straight, now in full sprint, toward the library.

It was about then his calf started screaming, so he found the bench, sat, flexing and massaging the calf. He removed his earbuds, placed them in his pocket, and turned off his iPhone. He then saw the blonde girl again, walking down the ramp in front of the university, heading down to Ninth Street. She was only a few feet in front of him. Jacob found himself raising his hand to wave.

Put down your fucking hand!

As she disappeared down the hill, Jacob noticed that a group of

Hondurans and Mexicans—he had given homelands to them all—in bandannas and university pullovers had started mowing the grass all around him. Jacob always smiled when he saw them work, because unlike American crews, the Central and South Americans, and this was always the case, would turn off the trimmers and edgers when someone would walk by.

"*Hola!*" Jacob said.

It was the only Spanish he knew.

Two of the workers smiled.

Jacob looked behind him, through the frat boys, down the quad, and saw two squirrels chase each other up a newly planted tree and thought how much like rats they were. Hearing the mowers all around him, he remembered how Cindi had once berated these workers. Early in their marriage, on one of those rare mornings after they made love, when the ring was still on her finger and she would drape her arm over his shoulder for no reason when they'd walk together, the Fishmans walked to and around the university together. It was a time when UNR officials had hired a beautification expert—that was the actual title—to spruce up the campus, and someone in administration had the bright idea that the trees that had been around campus for decades, centuries, were to be replaced by newer trees, the same type, for they would be easier to maintain and would ultimately stand straight and shed less. When the plan started, these old trees were being chopped down almost daily and lay in front of holes like fallen soldiers. It made Cindi apoplectic. In front of the Laxalt Mineral Energy Building, she saw a group of workers with a chainsaw about to attack a centuries-old oak.

"*Alto! Alto!* Why are you doing this?"

The workers smiled, pointed up, then to a nearby stump.

"*Trabajo, trabajo,*" they said, laughing, which infuriated Cindi, as one of them pulled the cord to start the chainsaw.

"*No trabajo, no trabajo!*" she screamed, running toward them. "Quit! *Deterner!*" The roar of the saw drowned her out.

"Honey, what do you want from them?" Jacob said, following her and then grabbing her around the waist, lifting her off the ground.

"Fucking America and those fucking fuckers who have nothing better to do than fuck with nature!" she said, pretending to use her fingers like a gun, as her legs moved furiously underneath her like a cartoon character.

"*Bastardos, bastardos!* Put me down, Chubs!" she said to Jacob before laughing at her own absurdity.

"Oh, yeah," she said, pointing to one of the workers. "*Gran bastardo!*"

"Great bastard," Jacob repeated. "Very bilingual of you."

On that day, on the walk home, Cindi said, "I'd be lost without you."

A few weeks before she found *Jacob Fishman's Marriage* on his computer, she and Charlize-Louise had gone out for a walk a few minutes before Jacob left for his. When he got to the end of Codel on his way to the university, he looked and saw his wife sitting on a curb at the end of a cul-de-sac. She held Charlize-Louise in her arms, as she would a baby, slowly rocking back and forth, stroking the dog's underside. He couldn't tell from where he was standing whether she was crying or laughing or thinking about anything or nothing, but she appeared to be saying something. He could have gone to find out, to be next to her, to ask what she was doing, but he didn't.

She looked like a stranger.

Old trees were still being replaced by new ones, and as Jacob sat, near the almost roses, with the bees flying around, many of whom were angry, not far from where the students were throwing the Frisbee, he felt like that dog at the end of *Vineland* or *Gravity's Rainbow* or *The Crying of Lot 49*, one of those Pynchon books he told everyone he'd read but could never get through. The dog was lying, spread-eagled, looking at and feeling the sun.

Cindi was still teaching—she, unlike fictional Cindi, after all, had tenure—and was living alone in the trailer with Charlize-Louise de Secondat Baron de la Brede, who had given birth to seven puppies, all girls. She named them Alcyone, Merope, Calaeno, Target, Maia, Electra, and Asterope. Ethan had opened another restaurant. Mitch, before taking a job at Boston College, had married Rouslana.

Jacob watched more guests arrive for the wedding and thought of ways he could incorporate those moments in *Jacob Fishman's Marriage*, but the book was done, the marriages were done.

Lara Izenberg, his agent, submitted the manuscript to Penguin Group, HarperCollins, Random House, and a few others in New York City, and to a small publishing house in Oklahoma City called Balkan Press, which seemed the most interested.

Cindi asked about it once on the phone.

"Is it coming out?"

"Too early to tell, but I think it will. One of the houses in New York told Lara it wanted a companion chapter."

"A companion—what do you mean?"

"They want—I can't believe I'm saying this—me to write about what I, me, was actually going through in my marriage, our marriage, while I was writing the novel."

"Your marriage?"

"Yeah."

"Wait. They want you to write about what you felt like while you were writing it? A book within a book kind of thing?"

"I guess."

"Un-fucking-believable!"

"I know. I don't believe it either, but the rep told Lara—and, again, this is what they said—that the meta, the genre—"

"I know what meta means. I teach philosophy, for Chrissakes—"

"—would be the conceit, the hook, if people could see me write the book of my life."

"I'm never going to escape Jacob Fishman's marriages, am I?"

"I don't know what to say."

"You going to do it?"

"I don't know."

"You're going to do it. It's perfect, actually. Tell me: Do you ever get tired of yourself, turning yourself inside out, upside down, just to be the center of it all?"

"More than you know."

"That's too smug. You have written yourself—forget me for a second—out of reality. You're now a thing, a device, a delivery system for Jacob Fishman. You're all the Jacob Fishman you need. But if you need more, Jake will give you more. You'll make up more you to define the you that you have fucking exhaustively deconstructed."

"Lara saved the dog for you."

"Thank her for me."

"I will."

"What bothered me most about it all—maybe not most, but close—I was worse in real life than I was in your fucking book."

"No, you weren't. I was."

"It was hard enough just being one Cindi."

"I'm sorry."

"I'm going to hang up now."

Jacob saw men in sombreros and polyester suits get out of a late-model van and, after getting their instruments from the back, head toward the gazebo and the couple, and stop to talk to the bride's mother. After they set up, the guy with the five-string guitar, the vihuela, began playing. The others joined him.

Jacob knew the song.

Lo siento mi vida
Yo sé que ya terminó
Corazones quebrados
Esperanza que se fué

Fuck, fuck, fuck, fuck, fuck, *fuuuuck,* he said to nobody, enjoying how the last *fuuuuck* sounded vibrating out of his mouth and through his lips. He threw his head back and shook it.

As the band, with their preposterous outfits, finished the song—a song he first heard Linda Ronstadt sing when she was young and desirable and healthy—Jacob could see Reno, the fact and fiction of it, splayed out before him. He shifted his position, crossed his legs, and draped his arm over the top of the empty bench. He ran his fingertips over his lips, up the bridge of his nose, and across his forehead. He calibrated every movement he was making. He wanted to look troubled, brilliant in thought, and longing for lost love. He exaggerated his exhale, opened his eyes wide. He slowed his movements. He hoped that someone from the wedding party, some university maintenance worker, some stranger . . . *anyone* would see him. He thought he might eventually wind up like this, miserable and insufferable, just as he imagined the real Cindi and the fake Cindi and Jacob might. He was envisioning and choreographing a tableau—the three of them, slightly out of focus, leering at and hovering over him as he sat in his office in front of his iMac. It would make a great photo for the cover of *Jacob Fishman's Marriage*. He found himself smiling.

He felt something at his feet. It was the Frisbee. He stood, bent down to get it, and then threw it back to the students, a perfect but weak spiral. He waved to them. In the parking lot beyond the gazebo, beyond the band and the bride and the groom, a man with a satchel over his shoulder was walking slowly toward a Subaru Impreza that had just pulled up. Jacob could see a woman in the driver's seat and two children in the back in car seats. The man got in on the passenger side, closed the door, looked over his shoulder, threw kisses to both of the kids, and then kissed his wife on the cheek.

ABOUT THE AUTHOR

Barry is also the author of *Funny You Should Mention It, Four Days and a Year Later,* and *The Joke Was on Me.* An essayist, reporter, and political columnist, his work has appeared in *Esquire,* the *Progressive Populist, Inside Media,* the *Las Vegas Review-Journal,* and *AAPG Explorer,* a magazine for petroleum geologists, which is all the more noteworthy, considering he knows little about petroleum geology and has hurt himself pumping his own gas. A native New Yorker, Barry is also a standup comedian who began his career in Tulsa. While it would have been clearly smarter to pursue such an endeavor in the clubs in Manhattan, the comedy venues in Oklahoma had more parking. This is his first novel.

He can be found at barrysfriedman.com and barrysfriedman.substack.com